CODE N[illegible]ME NANETTE

"The perfect combination of history, humor, and romance."

— Books and Beyond Fifty Shades

"A marvelous story, which had me hooked from beginning to end. Reading it kind of became a guilty pleasure.... The story-telling in this book is amazing and I definitely felt that I had been transported back to 1940's France. The characterization is also flawless...."

—Ingrid Hall, author of "The Tunnel Betwixt"

"This book by turns made me laugh (Nanette is quite the character), cry (heart wrenching stories), and made me hot (explicit love scenes). All of it combined to make a story that moved me...."

— Amy C. Haufschild

"I highly recommend CODE NAME NANETTE if you are a fan of historical fiction set during World War II and if you enjoy some romance mixed into the plot as well."

—Melissa Beck for FreshFiction.com

"Dawson's characters are drawn with such care they become living, breathing beings...."

—Carol A. Anderson

CODE NAME NANETTE

BEHIND ENEMY LINES

M. E. DAWSON

AQ Press
Palm City, Florida
AQPress@comcast.net

CODE NAME NANETTE

For information about the author or permission to reproduce selections from this book, write
AQ Press at AQPress@comcast.net or at
P.O. Box 1517, Palm City, FL 34991.

Library of Congress Control Number: 2014904118

ISBN-13: 978-0-9915184-4-9

Cover Credits
Photo: "Come sit by my fire" by Ceybeth Cordero
Cover Consultant: Sterling Stone

FOR THE AMAZON QUEENS

The thirty-nine women who volunteered to work undercover in occupied France during World War II gathering information for the British and helping organize the Resistance against the Nazis, especially the thirteen who never made it home again;

~

The local women in occupied countries who took up arms against the Nazis and fought alongside the men;

~

And all the other women before their time, who live the lives they choose rather than the lives society has picked out for them.

MAY ALL OF THEIR STORIES BE TOLD

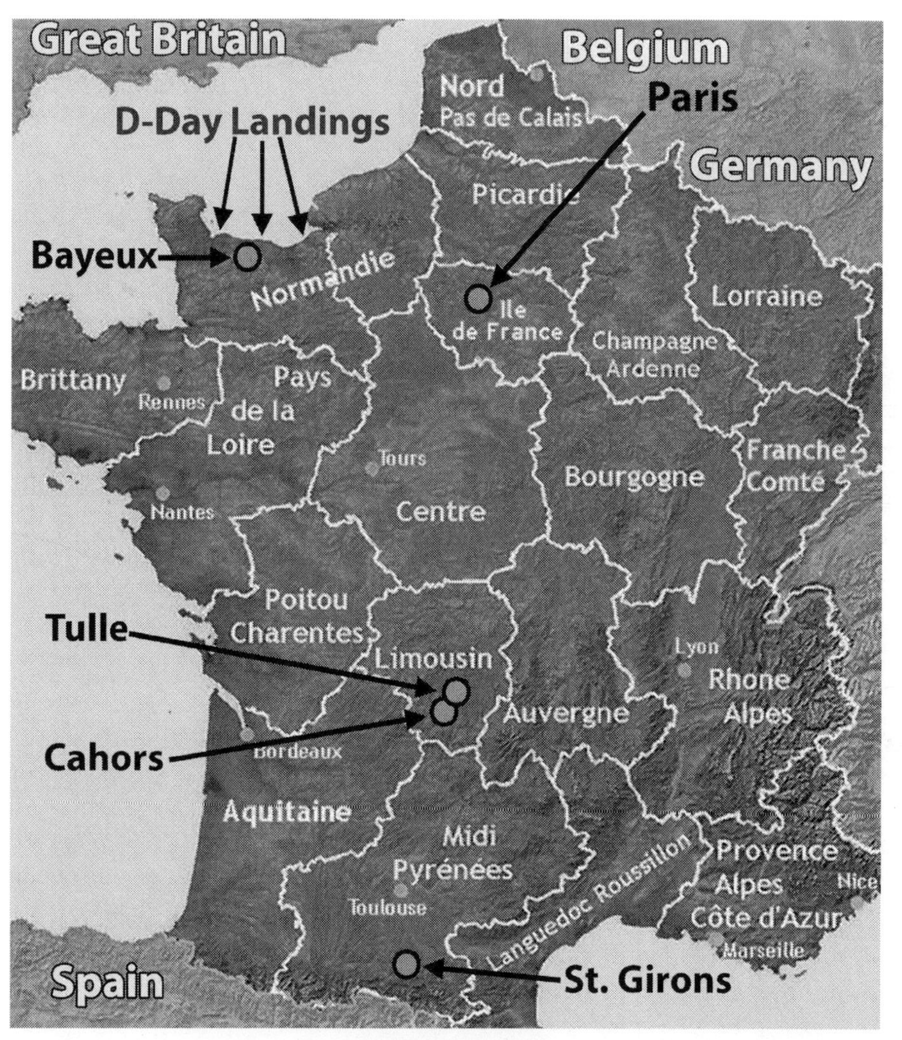

Nanette's France

Prologue

JOE – *On the Way Home, 1992*

"The Queen steps out into the night sky. I count to three, blow a kiss to the Royal Air Force bombardier who'll shove the arms and ammunition out behind me, then follow her through the cargo door into the windy darkness. The exhilaration of those first few seconds of free fall is always the best part. It's late. The moon's down. No ground fire to worry about. I just enjoy the ride…"

Joe replayed Nanette's words in his mind and marveled as he leaned his forehead against the airplane window and watched the lights of Montreal disappear below. He couldn't imagine what it must have felt like to take that first blind step over enemy territory fifty years earlier.

"Once I pull the ripcord, I float, swinging to and fro with the breeze, looking for the ground so that I can prepare for impact. I never see it. When my feet crash through tree branches, I cover my eyes with my forearm, cursing silently. Then the chute snags, and I'm no longer falling and hitting things. I'm dangling from my lines, arms, legs, toes, and hands all pretty much intact. Only, I can't tell where I am..."

He shook his head. One thing's for sure, he'd never look at women, young or old, the same way again.

One

JOE – *Montreal, Canada, the First Day, 1992*

Joe stood in front of the thick glass door, stretched up to his full six feet, and studied his reflection. Presentable. Black hair cropped close to his head, the warm brown of his sports coat complementing his café-au-lait complexion. After smoothing a couple of wrinkles from his jacket with the palm of his hand, he took in a deep breath and let it out slowly. This was it, the door to the future. He pulled the handle.

At the front desk, he smiled and announced to the matron who sat behind it, "I'm here to see Marguerite Jeandren."

The woman looked him over from head to foot then gave him a wry smile in return. "Who shall I tell her is calling?"

"My name is Joseph Parker. She's expecting me."

The edges of the woman's mouth twitched again as she picked up the phone with one hand and gestured toward a nearby waiting area with the other. "Why don't you have a seat over there, Mr. Parker."

She gave him a sideways glance as he settled into an overstuffed chair then turned away and spoke into the receiver.

Joe looked around. Nicely-decorated interior, well lit, with a few people walking around, some using walkers or canes. What you'd expect to see in an old-folks' home, he guessed. He checked his watch. He'd been afraid he might be late, but the taxi had made good time from the airport. He had fifteen minutes to spare.

Joe was excited to be in Montreal. At dawn that morning, he'd been sitting at his mother's kitchen table in Baltimore drinking coffee and waiting for Maya to pick him up and take him to the airport. When her horn blared out on the street, he grabbed his sports coat and the brown paper bag he'd packed the night before and bounded down the marble steps of the old Brownstone his great-great-grandfather had built almost a hundred years earlier.

Sliding into the Accord's front passenger seat, he leaned across the console to give the petite young woman behind the steering wheel a kiss on the cheek. Before she could pull out into traffic, however, he held up an index finger. "Hold on a sec. I've been practically paranoid all morning that I've forgotten something." He peered into the paper bag, inventorying its contents one last time.

Maya raised one eyebrow. "What's all that?"

"The old lady I'm flying up to see, she insisted that I bring a bunch of stuff."

"Insisted?" The young woman furrowed her brow and widened her ebony eyes, miming disbelief.

"Yeah." Joe laughed. "She went all cloak-and-dagger on me over the phone, like she was still a spy and it was still World War II or something. Refused to talk unless she could see the whites of my eyes and told me I had to bring all this with me when I came." He held the bag open so that Maya could see inside.

She let out a derisive puff of air and shook her head.

"I know. It's ridiculous," Joe agreed, closing the paper bag. "But she can answer questions no one else can answer."

He caught a short, quick breath. Questions he needed answered. When he got back that night, he and his mother would bury at least one of the ghosts that had haunted them all their lives, and he'd be holding the key to his dreams.

"So, I'm not taking any chances." He stretched his seatbelt over his chest then tapped the dashboard twice with his palm. "Okay, let's get this show on the road!"

Smiling at the memory, Joe smoothed the brown paper bag that rested against his thigh and started through his mental check list, nodding slowly as he went over the questions he intended to ask. They were pretty straightforward. He'd get the old spy talking. She'd tell him what he wanted to know, and he'd be on the late plane home that night.

At five minutes to one, the phone rang at the matron's desk. She listened and nodded then beckoned for Joe. "Mr. Parker, Mademoiselle Jeandren is ready for you, now." She smiled that enigmatic smile again and pointed at the linoleum in front of her desk. "Just follow the gold line on the floor. It will lead you to the Rec Room."

That golden thread wound its way through a maze of hallways and corners, leading him to another glass door. The word "Récréation" stood out in gilt letters just below his chin. He peered inside.

The room was empty except for one woman who sat framed between the doorway and a window. Brilliant afternoon sunlight poured in behind her, casting her features entirely into shadow.

She looked small, a lot smaller than he'd expected. She'd been a spy in the war after all. But as he imagined a spy might do, she had chosen a seat that did not expose her back to the door. A long table, the kind used to play games such as Bingo, stood between her and the rest of the room like a barricade. On it, two wine glasses sparkled in a ray of sunlight that hit the table to her right, also highlighting a corkscrew and an ashtray.

She beckoned him in with the hand holding her cigarette. It twitched intermittently, as did her head. Backlit, too, smoke from her cigarette rose in slow, sinister, dark loops until it escaped the bright frame of the window. Once free, the ceiling light transformed it into pale gossamer ribbons.

She reminded him of someone. Yes. Some actress he had seen in old black and white movies on television. He smiled as he approached the table.

"Miss Jeandren?"

The woman signaled him to sit in the only chair on his side of the table. That kept her directly between him and the window's glare. He still couldn't make out her face. Her features in shadow, smoke and tiny dust particles stirred up by his entrance danced around her like an aura.

"I.D.?" demanded the gravely, low-pitched voice and slight accent Joe remembered from the phone call that set up this meeting.

That was one of the ground rules she'd laid out. Before she would speak with him, he had to present two forms of identification followed by photographs of his grandmother between the ages of thirty-five and fifty.

It was a bunch of unnecessary rigmarole. After all, he'd met with one of her old friends, another former spy named Sigrid, in Colorado almost two weeks before. And Sigrid had even called Jeandren to set up this meeting. But Sigrid had also warned him that this woman could be volatile. If he upset her, she might refuse to talk altogether.

Joe reached into the bag and handed her his passport and Maryland driver's license.

She took her time reading them. "Photos?"

Fighting to keep his expression serious, he slid the black-and-white copies of old family pictures he'd brought from Baltimore across the table and chewed his lip.

She repeated the routine, scrutinizing each one thoughtfully, holding them up close to her nose. Their edges vibrated with the slight tremors of her hands. "Good." Her voice was cool, judging, in command. "Were you able to get the wine?"

"Yes, ma'am." Joe extricated the bottle of French Malbec she had stipulated from the bag and held it up for her to inspect.

"Open it and taste it." It sounded like an order.

Joe squinted into the shadow that hid her expression. Did she really want to know what he thought about the wine? Or was she putting him to a test, waiting to see if he'd drop dead of poisoning in some failed assassination attempt?

He stifled a smirk as he uncorked the bottle, swirled a small amount of wine in his glass, and sniffed it before taking a sip. Adding to the show, he worked the liquid over his teeth and tongue the way he'd seen wine tasters do then nodded and gave her one of his biggest smiles to emphasize the fact that he was both still alive and pleasantly surprised.

"This is very nice. You know your wines."

She tilted her head toward her glass.

Not being able to read her face frustrated him. After sliding her wine glass across the table, he stood to move his chair so that he could see her better.

"No. Stay where you are." That was definitely an order, more forceful than the first.

"But I can't see you from here. The light's too strong."

"I know."

Joe almost laughed out loud. Was this some kind of *Spy vs. Spy* game? Then he remembered the golden path that had led him to the Rec Room. *The Wizard of Oz* meets *Mad Magazine*? Was this a loony bin instead of an old-folks home? He covered his mouth with his hand and started to sit back down.

"Wait!" She barked.

He froze in mid crouch then eased upright as she lifted her glass to her lips, apparently intending to judge the wine for herself. After a moment, she let out a little, "Ahhh," followed by, "It is as good as I remembered." After another pause, she tilted her head and added, "There is nothing like the black wine of Cahors to start a relationship off on a strong foot."

"Cahors?" Joe had never heard the word before.

A few beats passed before she answered, "A place in France I visited during the war."

As she said it, she raised her glass. It glistened in the sun. The wine was so rich and dark the light almost couldn't pierce it. One dot of red, deeper than a ruby, pulsed in its center as her hand quivered. She studied it for a time, seeming to forget he was there.

Then her focus turned back to Joe. "Why don't you move your chair nearer to the bottle so that you may pour more easily."

Shaking his head, Joe slid his chair to the same place he'd tried to move it before. Finally he was going to get his first look at the woman he was counting on to unravel the mysteries of his past and, by doing so, throw open the door to his future.

Two

NANETTE – *Montreal, Canada, Ten Days Earlier, 1992*

"Allo?"

"Nanette?"

The silence on the phone line lasted a full three count before the first woman's terse reply came in Quebecois French, "Comment puis-je vous aider?"

"Tell me … what was that pitcher's name, again? The one Boston traded to the Yankees back in '19?"

"Sigrid! It's been too long. How are you?"

"I'm very well, thank you. And how are *you?"*

"Eh! As good as can be expected all things considered." The Canadian woman cleared her throat. "But enough civility. You used the code. What do you need?"

"Well…" Sigrid laughed softly. "I got a call last week … from our mutual friend." Her voice dropped as she spoke the last two words. "He asked a favor and suggested I contact you if I thought it was the thing to do."

"So, this is business rather than pleasure. It's been a while."

"Perhaps a bit of both, I think." Sigrid chuckled again.

"Don't keep me waiting, then. It's boring as hell up here, you know."

"You're not going to believe this." Sigrid paused then proceeded, "But the Queen's grandson just left my place. He asked to meet with you."

"The Queen's grandson? What does he want?"

"He just found out about the war."

"Just now? It's been fifty years."

Another soft laugh. "About our part in it, I mean. And don't forget, the Queen stayed in the game. She needed to keep secrets."

"Hunh!" The French-Canadian blew a small puff of air out through her nose. "What led him to us?"

"Her family found some old letters that opened up a Pandora's Box full of questions."

"Hmmm. What kind of questions?"

"Well, personal at first. It seems the Queen never told anyone who the father of the boy's mother was. That's what led the young man ... Joseph is his name ... to our mutual friend," she paused again. "And then I told him that the Queen had been in France working with you ... and Blue Eyes."

"Blue Eyes? What's Blue Eyes got to do with it?"

"That's who wrote the letters. The boy's trying to find out if Blue Eyes is his grandfather."

"Ha!" The Canadian woman laughed so hard she cackled. When she regained control, she asked, "And what if he is?"

"Well..." Sigrid lingered over the word as if she was unsure. "I get the feeling that would complicate matters."

"For whom?"

"For the boy, mostly." The American inhaled a deep breath before continuing, "You see, if I read him correctly, he's got a thing for Blue Eyes' great-granddaughter."

"You are joking, non?"

"No, sad to say, I'm not."

"This is *too* good ... better than your American television." The Canadian emitted a low chuckle. "But I am surprised this Joseph would reveal such a thing to you."

"Come on, Nanette. I was in the business too, you know. And he's easy to read because he's had no training. He let a few facts slip. I asked a few questions. It's likely he doesn't even realize I've figured it out," Sigrid explained. "Anyway, now he wants to talk with you. I told him you'd contact him if you're interested."

"How much should I tell him?"

"That's up to you. Tell him nothing if you want to. Or everything."

"*Everything*?" Nanette lowered her voice, drawing the word out slowly, making it sound naughty.

"All right. So maybe not everything." The American joined the chuckling. "I'm not even sure I'd want to know ... *everything*."

"But it could be *very* interesting ... and *so* much fun. And it's been so long..."

"Oh, Nanette."

Both women sighed nostalgically before Sigrid continued, "One other thing. Nothing's secret about the S.O.E. and O.S.S. anymore. It's all been declassified or should be soon."

"Puh." The Canadian blew a small puff of air through her lips. "What the agencies want is no longer of import to me. Just one thing ... is the boy good looking?"

"Yes. He's a nice-looking young man. Tall. Light-skinned. Hazel eyes."

"Like the Queen."

"Yep. And serious and smart like her too. I think you'll like him."

"Enough selling, Sigrid. You have piqued my interest. Give me his number. If he presents as well as you say..." She paused then continued in a lower voice, "I just may give him what he *needs*."

"I know that tone. You're planning something."

"Moi?"

"Yes, you!" The American laughed. "But seriously, he seems to be a nice boy, just a little lost ... in over his head, I think. So, don't be hard on him, okay?"

"Not just a little?" The Canadian exaggerated a tiny, pleading voice. "You would deny such a decrepit old woman even *that* small pleasure?"

Sigrid half sighed and half giggled. "You'll never change, will you, Nanette?"

"I hope not, Cheri. I hope not."

Three

JOE – *Montreal, Canada, the First Day, 1992*

Marie Jeandren was not what Joe expected.

The old woman was tiny. Her head thrust forward from hunched shoulders. Thin, gnarled hands extended at odd angles from spindly arms like misplaced bird claws. Her skin, with the exception of a rough spot on her right cheek, was almost as white as writing paper. Piercing blue eyes bored out from beneath bright red eyebrows that arched upward to meet a halo of hair dyed the same cross between crimson and orange, with dry curls pulled up and away from her face by combs but still unruly. Her pursed lips matched the scarlet of her nails. Enamel and gold earrings covered her ear lobes, a set with the heavy brooch pinned to her dark blue cardigan.

"So, tell me, Joseph," she continued in that softer tone she had used when talking about the wine. "Which do you prefer?"

"Which what?"

"Which me. The mysterious or the revealed?"

Heat flooded into his cheeks. She'd caught him gawking as if she were a freak in a sideshow.

"It's nothing to be embarrassed about," she cooed. "Sometimes it startles me too." The woman emitted one ironic half laugh and lifted a crooked finger to her chin. "To find this ugly old stranger staring back at me in my mirror." She sighed and lit another cigarette.

"I fear I shall never get used to it. Yet…" A hint of a smile and a small shrug of resignation. "C'est la vie, is it not?"

Joe relaxed a little, let off the hook.

"Ah, but enough about my burdens." Pausing to sip her wine, she sighed again and repeated, "So, which *do* you prefer, Joseph?" She waved the hand holding her cigarette in front of her face. "Knowing that *this* is who you came to see?" The smile grew broader. "Or speaking with the shadow spy?"

"Well," Joe equivocated. "I can read you better if I can see you."

"And what makes you think that?" Her tone and eyes suddenly cold as stone.

He almost slapped his forehead with his palm. He should have realized a former spy might take that as an insult. He decided to start over. "Look, I'm sorry Miss Jeandren—"

She dismissed his effort by waving her hand in front of her face again. "What you *see* here is a seventy-two-year-old woman who is prematurely confined to a retirement home because she suffers from osteoporosis, arthritis, and this..." She ran the tips of the fingers holding her cigarette over her cheek. "This disease that is attacking my skin. That makes you wonder, does it not? 'What can so old and wretched a woman possibly offer me?'"

Guilty again. Joe had known all along that the woman had to be at least that old, and he shouldn't have been surprised that she was suffering from some sort of medical problem. After all, she'd been a secret agent with his grandmother fifty years before, and she lived in a retirement home. But until that moment, he hadn't given any thought as to what that would mean. Or whether it made a difference.

"Whereas the shadow spy?" The old woman shrugged and drew in a lung full of smoke, then leaned forward as if whispering a secret.

"Perhaps the shadow spy could still be powerful. And meaningful. Right?" Smoke leaked out the sides of her mouth as she said it.

He waited, acknowledging by not defending.

"The flaw in your thinking, Joseph? Do you know what it is?" She leaned back again.

"No, ma'am."

"You're the one who changed when you moved your chair. Not me."

Joe narrowed his eyes and nodded. She was right, but—

"So. Now that you have created two versions of me, which one is real?"

This was all too theatrical. Joe chose what he thought was a safe answer. "Neither?"

"Very good." The old woman watched him through a long, slow stream of smoke she blew toward the ceiling. "But let us ask the question another way. Which *me* did you come here to speak with?"

That one wasn't hard. "The spy."

She set her cigarette carefully on the edge of the ashtray and extended her crooked right hand. "Marguerite Jeandren, code name Nanette, at your service."

Joe breathed out in relief, thanking God that was over. He carefully wrapped his large brown fingers around her boney white palm, afraid that he might hurt her if he applied too much pressure. "Joseph Parker. From Baltimore. But then you knew that."

She nodded. "And now, Mr. Parker, please tell me. What is so important that the other old spooks had to send you to me?"

"Like I told Sigrid..." Joe leaned forward, hands on his knees, eager to get down to business and hoping that the reference to the woman's old friend would lighten her mood. "We recently discovered some letters William McPherson … I believe you knew him by the code name Blue Eyes during the war … wrote to my grandmother."

The old spy cleared her throat and raised both eyebrows.

"So, I contacted McPherson's family down in Florida," he continued, "to let them know about the letters. They're full of family history and things like that."

"When were they written?"

"On and off over forty years. Starting in 1915, right after my grandmother's family moved back to Baltimore from Florida. Evidently she and McPherson had become friends while she lived down there. When they were kids."

Marguerite Jeandren's red head and bony shoulders bobbed up and down.

Amused? Or agreeing? Joe went on, "His family was every bit as surprised to find out about the letters as we were. William's son started looking into it. He contacted someone who had worked with his father in the C.I.A. That man put me in touch with Sigrid, and—"

She nodded and cut him off, "You are working together then? You and Blue Eyes' son?"

"Yes, well..." The answer to that was complicated. "Let's just say, we're looking for the same thing."

"And what would that be?"

How did she end up asking all the questions? "You see, my mother was born in 1937." Joe paused, hoping the old woman would respond to the date in some fashion. She didn't, just sat there watching him, those glistening eyes sharp, inquisitive. So he went on, "And my grandmother never told anyone in my family who the father was."

"And now you think it was Blue Eyes?" She dismissed the idea with a derisive snort and a wave of her cigarette hand. "Because of this stack of old letters?"

"No. At first I did, but not anymore."

"And yet you are here."

She had him there. No matter what he believed or how much he now wanted McPherson not to be the one, he still needed the proof. "You're right. So, all you have to tell me is—"

Bam!

The old woman had hit the table so hard with the palm of her hand that the corkscrew jumped and wine rippled in the wine glasses.

"I *have* ... to tell *you* ... nothing!" She spit the words out through clenched teeth.

But before Joe could react, she leaned back in her chair and went on in a calmer tone, "Still, you may yet convince me to tell you what I know. So..." She tapped a cigarette out of a box and waved it in a circular motion that indicated he should get on with it. "I'm assuming from your silence that these letters you found do not cast any light on the issue at hand."

Joe willed his voice to calm. "No, ma'am. They don't. But they led to more. For example, you knew that Blue Eyes was seriously injured in a car wreck back in the '50's?"

She nodded.

"And did you also know that as soon as my grandmother heard about the accident, she dropped whatever else she had been doing and moved to Florida to take care of him?" When the old woman didn't respond, he went on, "She took a job as his nurse. Stayed with him for ten years ... until he died."

She sucked in her cheeks, narrowed her eyes, and rocked ever so slightly in her seat, as if that was a new fact she was putting together with the others she already knew. But she didn't say anything. Instead, she raised her eyebrows at him again.

He took that as a sign he should continue. "And the whole time she was there, neither one of them told anyone in his family that they had known each other before. It was the same with my family. She led them to believe she was doing something else and never so much as mentioned his name … not to a soul."

Joe was surprised to find his palms up at shoulder height and his head shaking as if that story made no sense at all. He dropped his hands to his lap and waited for her to call him out on it.

"And this is suddenly important? Why? Are you writing a biography? Is there a medical emergency?" The interrogation came in rapid fire.

But it was not the line of questioning he had anticipated. He shook his head even harder in surprise. "Oh, no! Nothing like that. It's just that I'm curious—"

"Don't make me laugh," she hissed.

"I beg your pardon?"

She inhaled and released a cloud of smoke in his direction. "I may be old, Joseph. And I may be confined in this place. But that does not mean that I have grown stupid. No healthy twenty-eight-year-old man flies hither and yon across the continent at the drop of a hat just to satisfy some idle curiosity about his grandparents. You are seeking revenge?"

Joe blinked. Revenge? For what? For William McPherson breaking his grandmother's heart seventy years before? For his marrying a white woman instead? Joe didn't know enough of that story yet to tell if revenge was justified. After all, the letters weren't exactly love letters and his grandmother had gone back to care for the man all those years later.

"No, Ma'am."

"So, you're trying to claim your long-lost inheritance then."

His jaw muscles clinched. He was tired of having to explain that he hadn't known McPherson had money when he started this quest. He'd simply been trying to find out who his grandfather was, because, he now realized, he'd thought that would help him figure out who he was and what he wanted to do with his life.

And then he'd met Carrie, and suddenly he'd known exactly what he wanted. Her face flashed before him. So beautiful. At first she'd assumed he was after money, too. But now she knew she could trust him. He took a slow calming breath and started to explain.

But before he could get a word out, the old spy tisked, leaned forward, and added in a conspiratorial tone. "Sigrid is right, isn't she? You're here because you have the hots for a girl."

"What?" Joe jolted upright as if stung.

A smug, knowing half-smile crinkled the skin around her eyes. "But she's a McPherson…" She let the sentence die off, shook her head, tisked again, and reached for her wine glass.

Shit. How did Sigrid find out about Carrie? Joe slumped back in his chair, his arms crossed over his chest. He didn't want to talk about Carrie. Not now. Not to this pushy, crazy woman who made his feelings for her sound dirty.

The old woman took a sip of wine then cleared her throat, egging him on.

Ever since he walked through the door, she'd been doing just that, pulling his strings to see how fast she could make him dance. It was time he took control of this interview.

Joe leaned forward, placing both palms flat on the table. "Look, Miss Jeandren, I didn't come here to talk about me."

"Good bye, then." She set her glass down on the table with a clunk and waved him out of the room with the back of her hand. "And on your way out, will you please tell the orderly I'm ready to return to my apartment." Jerking the wheel on her chair, she swiveled away.

"Wait!" Joe stood up so fast his thighs struck the table almost toppling the wine and the glasses.

Amusement danced in the woman's eyes as she lifted her glass to safety while Joe fumbled about trying to right the careening bottle. She didn't even attempt to conceal the fact that she was laughing at him. Smoke slipped out of her mouth in little bursts.

Joe walked in a tight circle, rubbing his forehead with the fingers of his right hand. "I mean, I came all this way. Brought you everything you asked for." He stopped. "And you *said* you'd tell me what I want to know!"

She jerked the wheel again, swinging back to face him defiantly. "You remember incorrectly, Mr. Parker. Have you learned nothing about the spy business from your James Bond films? What you *want* to know is irrelevant. I said I would tell you what you *need* to know."

He stared at her hair.

Casting a stony glare back, she sucked in a long draft from a new cigarette and took her time exhaling the smoke through her nostrils before continuing in a lower voice, "How can I be sure what you need to know unless I understand who you are and why you are here?"

Joe looked down at his feet.

"And really. How could telling me the truth hurt you?"

The old spy was right. She already knew the worst of it, and now that he was there, she held all the cards. Maybe if he just gave her what she wanted…

He sat back down, took a deep breath, and capitulated. "Yeah. Her name is Carrie. She's a McPherson."

Four

JOE – *Montreal, Canada, the First Day, 1992*

The old woman narrowed her eyes.

"Are you in love with her?"

Joe opened his mouth to respond then paused. He couldn't get Carrie out of his mind. But did that mean he was in love with her? "I think so. That is I may be. I'm not sure," was the answer that finally came out of his mouth.

The old woman tilted her head to the side, demanding to know more by raising her eyebrows.

"You see, it's like my mother said—"

"Your mother?" She hooted. "You discuss such things with your mother. Yet you play coy with me?"

"No." How did she keep putting him on the defensive? "It's not like that. It's just that Carrie's been through some tough times lately, and my mother warned me."

The old spy waited.

"She warned me that a princess in distress can be very seductive."

"Hunh," the caricature of a woman sitting across from him snorted, her head bobbing up and down. "And you envision yourself as this woman's knight in shining armor?"

Joe sucked in another short surprised breath. That was it exactly. Ever since Carrie had turned to him for help, so soft and pale, tears glistening on her cheeks in the moonlight, all he could think about was holding her in his arms again, smoothing her hair, and whispering in her ear that everything was going to be all right now that he was there.

"Yes. That's it. I just want to take care of her." Relieved that the old lady understood, Joe leaned forward, eager to explain.

"It's not that you want to screw her, then?"

Screw her? Those crude words coming out of that old mouth startled Joe so badly that he was half-way out of his chair again before he got control of himself. Who did she think she—

Take a deep breath. The truth? All he'd wanted to do since that night in the moonlight was to screw Carrie. No. That wasn't it. He wanted to make love to her. There was a difference. Her blue eyes would smile up at him as he—

Shit!

He had to stop doing that. His cock had started rearranging itself in his pants.

Joe sat straighter, trying to find a more comfortable position in the chair, and gave in again. "Sure, I want to be with her." He faced the woman eye to eye, almost pleading for her to leave him alone. "She's beautiful. Who wouldn't?"

"And she wants to *be* with you?"

"Well, I'm sure she…"

Once again, he didn't know how to finish the sentence. The truth was he'd been the perfect gentleman, staying close by playing the role of friend, but keeping his feelings to himself. What was he actually sure of?

The old spy arched one eyebrow and sniffed so hard her head and shoulders shook. Then she signaled her impatience by tapping her fingernails on the table.

And Joe was suddenly back in the car that morning with Maya, her eyes on the road, her hands restless on the steering wheel, right before she said, "Carrie called. She's coming for a visit and she's going to be here for a while."

His heart had leaped.

Then she'd added, "And I didn't want to be the one to tell you this, but I think she's coming to see me … not you."

At the time, Joe had dismissed it as one of Maya's little jokes. But sitting here in Montreal across from this unpredictable, difficult woman, something he had overlooked before hit him so hard that his stomach muscles contracted. Carrie had called Maya instead of him.

What if he had misread everything?

"I don't know." His doubt found voice the instant it formed in his mind.

Having watched Joe's internal struggle through narrowed eyes, the old spy cleared her throat, demanding a fuller explanation.

Disoriented by his newfound insecurity, Joe ran his palm across his forehead and looked for the words to explain, "What I mean is right now she's with Maya and—"

"Maya?"

"My um, my ex … girlfriend."

"And what do you mean … *with*?"

The old woman's tone left no doubt what she was insinuating. Why had he used that word? He shook his head and hands in an effort to stop her from going any farther.

But before he could get a word out, the old spy cackled out loud and flailed her cigarette, then took a sip from her glass and scrutinized him with a wicked smile.

"Oh, Joseph, you poor boy." The woman shook her head slowly. "Sigrid forgot to mention *that* particular complication."

"That wasn't what I meant," he blustered, more defensive than ever. Then he gathered himself and started over. "It's just that Carrie's husband turned out to be a very bad man. When he died, she needed someone—another woman—who wasn't family she could talk to about it, and Maya was there when she needed her. So, they've gotten very close lately, and Maya told me..."

But then Maya's words of earlier that day tripped him up again. Her eyes still on the road, she had reached over, and grabbed his hand, stilling the tattoo his fingers had been beating on the paper bag.

"Try to understand, baby. It's not you personally. It's just ... men in general, you know?" She'd glanced over at him, fighting off a grin. "The bastards!"

Not taking that seriously either, Joe had wrinkled his nose and stuck his tongue out at her like he always did when she went all Women's-Libby on him with those kinds of remarks.

But how that the old witch had planted the seed, those Women's-Rights people Maya had been working on her Master's Thesis with had filled her head with all kinds of weird ideas. And Carrie's S.O.B. of a husband had given her plenty of reasons to want nothing to do with men. And she and Maya did seem awfully close.

No!

Joe slammed that door shut before he could go through it. Maya had been hassling him for the fun of it like she always did. And now this old woman was trying to mess with his head.

"They're just friends. I'm sure that's all it is," he concluded, leaning back in his chair and crossing his arms over his chest to show how confident he was.

"As sure as you are that Blue Eyes is not your grandfather?" The old biddy's body shook as she chuckled silently.

The way the woman kept twisting his words back on him made Joe want to pull out his hair. But he was done with that conversation.

When he didn't reply, she rubbed her jaw, nodded as if she had reached some kind of conclusion, and said, "But, now I am convinced. It is good that you came to see me."

Relieved that she was dropping the subject and was finally going to start talking about his grandmother, Joe watched as the little Canadian woman settled herself in her wheelchair, rearranged her ashtray and wine glass on the table, and smoothed wrinkles from her skirt with those misshapen hands.

When she looked up again, she greeted him with a bright grin that made her seem softer, almost grandmotherly, except for her eyes. She couldn't keep a devious sparkle from shining through. "And won't you please have another sip of this delicious Malbec. Did you know this is the wine Eleanor of Aquitaine served at her wedding to Henry the Second?"

"Eleanor of Aquitaine?" Was the name supposed to have some hidden meaning?

She shook her head slowly as if exasperated with his ignorance again. "A very unusual and powerful woman who lived in the Middle Ages. She insisted on accompanying her first husband to fight in the Crusades." She lifted her glass in a toast. "A woman before her time, you could say." The old spy smiled.

Joe relaxed. She was just reminiscing about France and the wine again. So he'd told her things he hadn't meant to tell her? She was finally going to talk, and she'd be out of his life in a few hours. He raised his glass and matched her salute.

Marguerite Jeandren held his eyes as she formalized the toast with one small sip and set her glass down. Then she drew in a deep breath, clasped her hands in her lap, and asked in a soft voice, "So, let us begin at the beginning. Tell me, Joseph, what did you call your grandmother?"

Not taking any chances, Joe gave the full answer. "Her name was Williamina Regina Hall. Back home, we called her Momma Willie. From what Sigrid told me, she went by the code name Regina in France during World War II."

"Regina, yes. That was her official name." The old woman's face took on that faraway look of someone remembering something she was fond of long, long ago. "But we called her the Queen."

Joe winced. McPherson had called her that, too. But what did it prove? Apparently everybody except Joe's family had called his grandmother the Queen at one time or another.

He reined in his thoughts. No more side tracks. Now that the old spy had finally started talking, he intended to keep her on point. "So, Sigrid told me you knew her and McPherson well?"

Marguerite Jeandren's expression came back into focus. She shook her head slowly and shrugged. "Sigrid is only partially correct, I'm afraid. I cannot tell you much more about Blue Eyes than what is in the dossier. He was a spy master for the American O.S.S., the Office of Strategic Services. You know. It became your C.I.A. after the war."

She paused, giving Joe time to digest that information then continued, "And I do regret having to tell you this, but I do not know whether he was your grandfather. *That* indiscretion your grandmother did not discuss with me either."

"What?"

Joe didn't even try to stay in his chair this time. He towered over the table. "But you promised—"

She stopped him by putting down her cigarette, folding her hands in her lap, and arching her brows.

He turned his back and took two steps away from those eyes, replaying their phone conversation in his head. Damn. She hadn't actually promised anything. She'd even refused to let him tell her what it was he wanted to know. She'd just said that the only way she'd talk about the time she spent with his grandmother in France was if he made this trip.

But wait. What was it she had said about Carrie? "She's a McPherson." The old spy had known all along what he wanted to know.

Joe whirled. "You put me through all this?" His arm swung around, encompassing the wine, the paper bag, the empty room. "For nothing?"

She leaned back in her chair, her elbow on the arm rest, her cigarette next to her chin. "I suppose that depends on how you define nothing."

He squinted down at her, tried to control his breathing.

"What do you know of the war, Joseph?"

He was in no mood. "The Allies won."

She closed her eyes as she took a long drag then looked up at him and tisked. "That is all? Your American schools should be ashamed."

"Momma Willie was some kind of courier for the Resistance in France. Somehow she got shot, but she didn't come home. She went back." It was his turn to spit out words.

"Do you know why?" Her tone was oddly sad and fierce, a challenge. When he didn't answer, she added softly, "I didn't think so." When he still didn't respond, she sighed. "And has it ever occurred to you that it might help if you did?"

Joe held her gaze as long as he could then let out a slow deep breath and gritted his teeth. No, damn it. She couldn't be right again. Ever since he got involved with Carrie, he'd been so fixated on proving McPherson was not his grandfather that he'd lost sight of the other mysteries he'd originally set out to solve.

Why had his grandmother kept so many secrets? What had she done during the war and where had she gone all those times after it was over when she'd vanish for weeks or months?

As much as he hated to admit, even if he'd never found the letters, he'd have gladly thrown anything this old woman demanded into a paper bag and jumped on the next plane to Montreal just for a chance to learn the answers to those questions.

Plus, why was he so surprised? He'd been following a trail of crumbs from the beginning. Some detail she told him might still turn out to be the key.

He sat back down, smoothed his slacks along his thighs, and blew air out through puffed cheeks. "I'm sorry Miss Jeandren. I got carried away. Please, tell me everything you can."

The old biddy's eyes narrowed, focused hard on him. "*Everything*?"

Joe let out a little snort. There she was again, the puppet mistress playing the game. Well, he could play, too. He flashed a challenging smile and answered, "Yes, everything. Who knows? Something you can tell me may turn out to be exactly what I *need* to know."

She studied him for a moment then looked inward, chewing on her lip. Then, apparently having made another decision, she smiled brightly. "It will, Joseph. I assure you … it will."

Her eyes never left his, but the gleam in them intensified as she blew smoke slowly out the side of her mouth. "And please, do call me Nanette."

The old redhead was planning something. So what? Joe leaned back in his chair, stretched his legs out ankles crossed, and raised his eyebrows, giving her a taste of her own medicine, daring her to hit him with her best shot.

She looked down at the table and began, "I worked with the Queen several times, once very closely. I was not with her when she was wounded, but she told me the *details*." She glanced up at him, as if making sure he'd heard what she said. "*All* of them." She paused again. "I think you *need* to hear the whole story."

Joe ran his teeth over his lower lip and glanced at his watch. He still had the rest of the afternoon to kill, and now that he was refocused on the larger picture, he actually wanted to hear the whole story. He nodded.

Nanette lowered her eyelids. "It all began back in the summer of 1941, when the Queen went to the Limousin region of central France to help organize the Resistance."

She opened one eye and scrutinized Joe with her mouth pursed to the side before continuing, "Relax, Joseph. Let your imagination take you there. You need to see it through *her* eyes … the way she told it to me."

Five

THE QUEEN – *South of the City of Tulle near the rural Community of Laguenne in the Limousin Region of France, July 1941*

There it is up ahead, the intersection with the road to Tulle. Honore was right. I made good time since leaving Saint-Priest-de-Gimel this morning. The narrow, back road he recommended followed a river valley through the rough hills of the Limousin. Good for bicycling, and I saw only a handful of people. This empty and heavily-forested region suits our purposes well.

I stop and take a few seconds to adjust the scarf over my hair and pull up my long white socks. There's no such thing as being too careful in this business. I'm dressed conservatively, like the country folk, dark cotton skirt dropping just below my knees and wood-soled leather shoes the locals call galoches tied up over my ankles.

The backs of my hands catch my eye, and I can't help smiling. France is so close to Africa that people of almost every color are common here. There's even a Negro from the French Colony of Martinique sitting on the Vichy council that governs what's left of the country these days. I fit in like I never could in America.

And my cover story's almost perfect. The documents I'm carrying say I'm Angelique LeClerc, a fifty-one-year-old nurse with a French father. My Martiniquan mother immigrated to Marseilles long before I was born. That accounts for my paper-bag complexion and curly more than kinky hair, as well as the Marseilles accent I've always had, thanks to my French professor all those years ago at Morgan College who had come straight to Baltimore from the South of France.

Although I was nervous at first about passing for a woman more than ten years older, that's turned out to be an advantage. With a little carefully applied make-up added to the sagging posture I've practiced for weeks, people hardly notice I'm there. Nobody seems to pay attention once a woman reaches a certain age.

My eyes flit to the crossroads again and there's a flutter beneath my ribs. Excitement or fear? It doesn't matter. I'm as ready as I'll ever be. One deep breath, then back on the bike.

According to my mental map, my target's not far. I stick to the plan and take a right turn toward Tulle. A couple of kilometers up the two-lane road, the fields on the east give way to forest, all the way down to the verge. Double check. Nobody's watching. I pull off and carry my bicycle up the hill into the trees. Honore's words guide me. Be careful to step on stones. Don't break any branches.

The bike's well hidden. No tracks betray the fact that I've been here. After unbuckling the wicker basket from the handlebars and my backpack from the rear rack, I sling them over my shoulder and move carefully uphill on foot.

Before long, I find the remnants of a little-used path that takes me in the right direction. That's good, because I'm in a hurry to reach the other side of the hill before noon so that I can spy on the doctor.

As I climb, I review what I know about the doctor. Genevieve Marie Duphresne. Unmarried. Mid-thirties. Not involved in the Resistance. To the contrary, her father is a high official in the French government, one of those who retained his position by joining the

Vichy French when they sided with the Germans after the invasion of the north.

Normally I'd stay as far away as I could from collaborators, but Honore assures me that the doctor's father has lived in Paris for years and that neither he nor any other member of the doctor's family has returned since leaving.

Honore has also heard that the good doctor is in need of a nurse. If things look right, I'm going to ask for the job. It'll give me a place in the community and provide an excuse for being out on the road if I'm ever stopped by the Vichy gendarmes or worse the Service d'Ordre Legionnaire, the corrupt militia locals call the S.O.L. The fact that the doctor's father is a well-placed collaborator will divert suspicion even more. It's the icing on the cake.

There. The doctor's farm. From this overlook, I'm close enough to see everything, to monitor it all afternoon if necessary. Get a good sense of the place and the woman before I take my chances knocking on her door.

The doctor's house sits up close to the Tulle road, one of those solid rectangular, two-story manors with steeply pitched slate roofs that dot the region. A high dust-colored wall made of the same hewn granite surrounds it and about two acres of land. It could easily have served as a small fortress during earlier times when this area was so wild and lawless that its residents had to build such sturdy walls to protect themselves from marauding bands of thieves or packs of wolves.

On the road side, the gate opens to a small graveled auto park and the main entrance to the house. Farthest from the road, another stone building comprises most of the back wall. Likely a barn or a stable.

In the center of the courtyard lying between the two buildings, a grape arbor shades a rectangular wooden table and two chairs. Vegetable, herb, and flower gardens bloom in orderly fashion around it, separated by patches of lush green grass. Chickens wander, pecking leisurely. Near the barn, two pigs grunt peacefully in a pen.

There's obviously a second gate in the back wall on the far side of the barn. I can't actually see it, but a well worn path leads from there to apple and cherry orchards and a small area dedicated to grapes that occupy the sloping hillside beyond the walls.

The manor house and grounds are simple and attractive. The doctor appears to be very conscientious and structured. When will she show her face?

As I wait, I continue to replay the information Honore gave me. When the Nazis first invaded northern France last year, the Limousin was overrun by refugees. Three families had been assigned to the doctor's house. However, as soon as the Vichy government took control, all three had been repatriated back to the North.

Since then, the doctor has lived and worked alone on this property. That's another reason she might be amenable to taking me on. It's likely she could use an extra set of hands to run the place.

The shaded back door of the manor house opens. The doctor steps out into the courtyard.

No? It's a man?

Honore's report didn't mention a man on the premises. I'm glad I trusted my instincts and checked this out before committing myself.

Wearing dark pants, a straw hat, and a long-sleeve white shirt that billows loosely, not having been tucked into his trousers, the man sets to work hoeing the rows of the vegetable garden that takes up almost a quarter of the courtyard. From a distance, he looks slightly taller than the average Frenchman of the region and a little on the thin side. But then, everyone looks a bit thinner since the Vichy started issuing rationing coupons.

Wielding the hoe efficiently, he makes short work of the weeds. Someone obviously does this regularly, because there are so few of them to deal with. Then, he cuts a cabbage off its stalk and carries it and a couple of green squash back to the house.

When he gets to the flagstone stoop, he steps out of the wooden work shoes he's worn in the mud of the garden and into what appear to be cloth slippers before entering the house with the garden's bounty. Judging from the late morning hour, he's probably gathered produce for lunch. I wonder whether he'll be back out before it's served.

He is. After only a few minutes inside, he replaces his cloth shoes with his wooden ones and strides across the courtyard into the barn. He's obviously doing the daily chores. That gives me time to pull half a baguette and some soft cheese out of my backpack and finish them off with a few sips of water I collected when I passed a creek near the top of this hill.

I'm licking the last crumbs off my lips when the man rolls a wheelbarrow out of the barn and up a broad wooden plank that's been laid on the slope of a compost heap. After he dumps his collection of dung and straw onto the heap, he pushes the wheelbarrow back into the barn.

The compost pile explains the lush richness of the gardens. The doctor's man has been mucking the stalls and isn't about to waste anything. Good thinking in these spare times.

But where is Dr. Duphresne? Honore assured me she would be here. On the other hand, he had been wrong about her being alone and needing help to run the farm, hadn't he? These oversights worry me.

I lean back against a tree to continue my surveillance. Having returned the wheelbarrow to the barn, the man moves directly to the house. This time, though, when he steps out of his wooden shoes he picks them up one at a time and rinses them off with water that flows from a spigot in a cistern on a high stand to the right of the back door. Then he places them upside down in the sun to dry.

After he finishes rinsing his shoes, he stands in the little trough that catches the run-off from the spigot and cleans his feet. That done, he fills a basin with water, withdraws a bar of soap from a crock on a shelf near the cistern, and sets it alongside the basin. Then he removes his hat, revealing an unruly shock of wavy dark brown hair that reaches halfway to his shoulders. And then he takes off his shirt.

I watch all this with idle curiosity. Generally, people's personal habits are of little interest to me, and what I've seen of this man is not attractive enough on a physical level to warrant my detailed attention out of any prurient interest. In fact, now that they are uncovered, his shoulders, although square, are a bit narrow and downright bony for someone who does physical labor.

When the man steps out of his pants revealing his pale backside, he does it as if entirely confident no one could possibly be watching. My eyes fly to the surrounding countryside to see if such confidence is warranted, not that men usually care about such things.

It seems to be. Not a house or structure in sight. The manor sits at the bottom of a slope. Any voyeur would have to be in the woods above the orchards, which I can see are deserted, or sitting up on this hill with me.

Back to the man. He scrubs first his hands all the way up to the elbows and then his face. This is all unlike any of the Frenchmen I've met out here in the countryside. They work hard from dawn to dusk. I can't imagine a man like Honore fully disrobing in the middle of the day to take a shower after a few hours labor. An every-now-and-then once-over with a rag could make do for days, if not weeks. If he did clean up, he'd probably make an event of it by demanding a hot steamy tub attended by his woman.

My mind is wandering. Meanwhile, the bathing man has opened the spigot all the way and is rinsing his hair under a steady stream of sun-warmed water. If he turns to rinse his back, I may as well evaluate the rest of his attributes. You never know when you might need the upper hand in an argument.

And the truth is it's been a long time. My sigh surprises me. You can never tell. He may yet give me something to think about.

As the man finally begins his turn, he lifts one arm to hold his hair aside so that the water can run down the back of his neck and gives me my second surprise of the day. A small round breast with a dark upright nipple pops into profile against the gray slate that lines the wall below the cistern. His continued turn reveals a matching breast and nipple on the other side of his chest.

To verify what I think I'm seeing, I drop my gaze to the triangle of pubic hair that lies centered below the two. It's the same color as the hair on his head, and no male appendage dangles out of it.

It's the doctor.

Suddenly, intruding on the woman's privacy this way feels like eavesdropping. I avert my eyes. When I force them back to the courtyard, she's turned the spigot off and replaced the soap and cloths where they belong. The trousers, shirt, and hat have disappeared along with her, presumably into the cool privacy of the manor house.

Putting my fingers to my lips, I suppress a giggle. I had come this close to having a sexual fantasy about the doctor's handyman taking his midday shower. Even worse, although I feel as if I intimately know the doctor's uniformly brown hair, slender build, and erect nipples that stand out in dark contrast against her pale skin, I wouldn't be able to pick her out of a crowd if she had on clothes. I'd totally forgotten to look at her face.

Some spy I'm turning out to be.

But I shouldn't have laughed. Mistaking Dr. Duphresne for her handyman was a serious lapse in judgment, the kind that could end my spy career before it even gets started. And there's no telling what else I may have missed today.

Such as the fact that I haven't seen any patients yet. Honore told me the doctor treats them out here, mostly farmers who live in the countryside around the tiny village of Laguenne, which lies about four kilometers to the south.

I wait and watch, wishing that the blueberries within arm's reach were ripe. Half way through the afternoon, a middle-aged couple who look to be a farmer and his wife pedal their bicycles into the doctor's car park from the south. They leave after about half an hour, smiling and bobbing their heads in the direction of the manor house's front door which is not visible from my vantage point.

Sometime later, a cart pulled by a donkey rumbles in, also from the south. The woman driving the cart uncovers a small child sleeping in the back and carries him to the doctor's door. After a while, she places a bundle in the cart and goes back inside. Moments later, when she reappears carrying the child, who is now crying, she too smiles and bobs her head toward the door.

No sooner has the donkey trotted south toward Laguenne, than a car appears on the roadway from the north. It's only the second car I've seen today. Automobile travel is greatly limited due to gasoline rationing. I'm surprised when it turns into the doctor's gate and crunches to a stop in front of the manor house. Two young women dressed like city dwellers get out and enter.

They must have come from Tulle, which lies about sixteen kilometers to the north. It's a much larger community, bordering on city size. I know that several different doctors practice there, because I considered seeking a position with one of them. Why have these women come all the way out here?

After about two hours, they return to the car. No nodding and smiling this time. The driver walks the other woman slowly to the passenger side, her arm around her waist, and helps lower her into the seat.

It turns out they're the doctor's last two visitors of the day. Of course by the time that becomes evident, it's too late for me to realistically knock on her door looking for work. Plus, there've been so many unexpected occurrences that I want to see what the night might bring before making my move. I came prepared for this eventuality with a canvas sheet and enough rope to fashion a serviceable tent. It won't be the first time I've slept in the woods.

Six

THE QUEEN – *The Limousin, France, July 1941*

I needn't have worried about night-time surprises. Nothing happens. As dark falls, lights come on inside the back of the house revealing parts of its interior. I see only one person moving around. It appears that the door from the courtyard opens into a wide hallway next to the kitchen, and the doctor is preparing her evening meal. Eventually, the light goes off and the courtyard behind the house is illuminated only by the moon. A lamp switches on upstairs in the part of the house nearest me. It's extinguished within the hour.

But stretched out in my tent, I toss and turn, can't get to sleep. It's not the makeshift accommodations or the thought of wolves keeping me awake. According to Honore, the locals rid these woods of all such dangerous creatures long ago. No, this time there's no denying it. It's nerves.

But why now? I was hardly ever nervous last year when I was helping my friend Jo smuggle military secrets for the Free French. The answer comes immediately. Last year I was not on my own, and Jo just happens to be Josephine Baker the most popular movie star in Europe.

Images float in and out of my mind. The weeks on the steamer as we cross the Atlantic after Jo leaves the Ziegfeld Follies. Her storming through her chateau in southern France when we hear that the Germans have invaded Poland and then again when Belgium falls. We help the Red Cross tend to the injured until the Nazis invade France, too, and the Free French make contact.

From there on is a blur of candle-lit dinners with high-officials, fine gowns, small talk, and dancing the evening away, exchanging information with whispers and subtle touches, and copying codes onto sheet music in invisible ink until dawn. Spying with Jo was like playing a role in an elaborate theatrical production.

The most dangerous part? I catch myself smiling. Crossing check points with blueprints pinned to your petticoat. No matter how you walk, they rustle. So we flirt and giggle to cover the sound. Touch your guard's arm. Tilt your head. Laugh. Engage him in conversation while Jo signs autographs. Even S.S. officers grin and slap each on the back, then escort us across the border.

But that all ends with Jo doubled over in pain. We almost don't get her to the doctor in time. I sigh. The Free French won't send her back into the field after she's released from the hospital. Now, Vichy-controlled southern France is almost as dangerous as the Nazi-occupied North, and she's too valuable a symbol for the cause. They'll keep her some place safer like Morocco, and she'll spend the rest of the war hosting diplomats and putting on shows for the troops.

But I've seen what Hitler's really up to, and I know that's not enough. My fists clench and unclench, and I'm back in the colored influenza wards in Baltimore after the first war. So many of our men survived the fighting only to come home and die of the flu.

But those who survived? As soon as they were strong enough to smile again, they had stories to tell and most of their stories were about France. How good it was here. How the French treated them the same as the Whites. You could see it in their eyes. For the first time in their lives, race hadn't mattered.

And that's exactly what Hitler's out to destroy. First, get rid of the Jews. Then the Gypsies. It won't be long before he starts on the Negroes. We're all in this together, and if we can't find a way to kick his Nazi butt back to Berlin, we'll all lose everything.

I take deep breaths trying to calm myself down. Tomorrow my new life begins. The Resistance has taken root in the Limousin, and I've volunteered to help it grow. I'll start out carrying messages from one band of fighters to another. It's a small role, but it's important and it's part of something that's getting bigger.

Rolling over onto my side, I adjust my backpack under my head and squeeze my eyes shut. This time it all depends on me. Nerves or no nerves, I need to get some sleep.

The doctor's evidently slept well. She's up feeding her animals, talking nonsense to the chickens and pigs, as the sun rises above the hillside behind the barn. Cute. It's so gray I can't get a good look, but there's no reason not to assume it's her. The voice is distinctly female and there's been no indication that anyone else is on the property. Other than her alter ego the handyman, that is.

Two hours later, an older man parks his bicycle in the manor's driveway and limps to the front door. That's all I need to see. The doctor lives alone and practices out of her home as advertized. I'm going to take my chances. I climb back up the hill to the creek I found yesterday to clean up. I must not look as if I've slept in the woods when I introduce myself.

By the time I hike down the hill and pedal my bicycle to the other side, the car park is empty. I smooth the wrinkles out of my blouse and pat my hair into place under my scarf before twisting the little brass handle in the middle of the heavy wooden door. It tinkles like a bicycle bell.

The doctor answers the ring almost immediately. I don't know what I expected, but up close she looks more like old-fashioned French nobility than a farm hand. She's tall, maybe five foot ten, and all fine long lines. Oval face. Long nose with the slightest aquiline bump to make it distinctive. Her clothes add to the old-fashioned effect. Blouse buttoned up under her chin and brown skirt brushing the tops of her sturdy shoes. She looks positively demure.

Physically, she appears to be the thirty-six years old Honore told me she is. But there's something about her eyes. Her irises are the color of amber, with deeper brown rings at the center and edges. Accented by dark eyebrows and lashes, they give her a timeless quality. The doctor is not beautiful in the classical sense, but she has presence.

"May I help you?" Her professional voice is low and calm. Her accent tells me she's from this region.

"Dr. Duphresne?" I ask.

She nods.

"My name is Angelique LeClerc. I'm a nurse. I heard through Dr. Thibault in Saint-Priest-de-Gimel that you may be in need of an assistant."

I've surprised her. Her eyes narrow and she asks, "Dr. Thibault? How is Auguste these days?"

Just in case it's a trap, I answer as truthfully as I can. "Oh. I did not mean to give you the impression that Dr. Thibault and I are on a first name basis. We've met only casually. I've been staying with a friend in his town. But I do have references from the hospital in Marseilles where I worked … before the war." I deliberately let my voice drop and fade off when saying this last.

Still cautious, she quizzes me. It's appropriate. After all, I appeared out of nowhere and rang her bell. But I'm not worried. We chose my current identity because I've had plenty of nursing experience in the flu wards and with the Red Cross. I pass the test.

Her final question, "And why does a nurse from Marseilles need a job out here in the middle of nowhere?" She's blunt and to the point.

"My husband." I pause to let the quiver in my voice take effect. "And child ... died in the bombing last year."

"I'm so sorry." The doctor's hand flies to my forearm. It's warm. Offers comfort and aid.

I press the small advantage that gives me. "I fled to his relatives in Lyon, but ... but it's just too hard being with them, you understand?" I meet her eyes and she squeezes my wrist. "An old friend invited me to stay with her in Saint-Priest-de-Gimel. But..." I pause and swallow for effect. "I can't just sit around and do nothing."

Still holding my arm, she nods her understanding.

"And I can't make myself go back and face what's left of my life in Marseilles..." I look down as I let the words drift off.

"Come in." The hand on my arm pulls me across the threshold into the broad foyer.

It's an old-style house, with high ceilings, open beams, and a formal parlor to the right of a wide entrance hall. The doctor has converted what was probably a dining room on the other side into an examining room.

"I'm out of coffee, what with the rationing and all," she apologizes. "But I do have some herbal tea."

Within minutes we're drinking tea in the kitchen and I'm showing her my forged recommendations. She's impressed but doesn't really need a full-time assistant. We chat until I get lucky right before lunch time. A mother brings in her young son who has cut his leg. Dealing with open wounds is one thing I got good at while volunteering with the Red Cross.

As we wave the two on their way, I smile wanly up at the doctor and say, "That felt good. Being … of use again."

She frowns in response and looks away.

Seeking another entrée, I press on. "This is a lovely property but so large. How do you take care of it all?" Hopefully that seed will grow.

The doctor hesitates then asks, "Would you like to join me for lunch?" She still looks concerned about my loss.

While we dine on last night's soup with bread and cheese at the kitchen table, I try another way to strike a deal. "Could you use a part-time assistant?"

"Yes." She nods. "Most of what I see out here are minor illnesses or injuries, like the boy. Sometimes no one needs my services for days on end. And no one has enough money to pay the full fee. Not these days."

I'm starting to wonder why she answered, "Yes."

"So you barter?" I guess to keep the conversation going.

Her smile lights up the room. "I've had to stop taking chickens and pigs. Now I make them pay in sausage and bread." She shakes her head and laughs as she says it, spooning a bite-sized chunk of sausage out of her cabbage soup to demonstrate.

It was a wise decision. The sausage is delicious.

Then she turns serious again. She puts down her spoon, and her eyes meet mine. "So, I have taken a few patients in Tulle. Now they come out here when they need me, but it would be better if I could go to them."

That's it. She needs someone to man the store, so to speak, while she's gone. But there's something I don't understand. "Tulle is not that far. Why is that a problem?"

Her eyes are hooded now and she looks me over as if she's evaluating. "It would be best, for business I mean." She looks away. "If I could stay at least two days at a time. That way I could fit everyone in and earn enough to sustain this place." Turning back to me, she adds, "And I don't have a car."

Ahhh. I have to suppress a smile. It's the chickens and pigs and whatever else lives in the barn. She has to be here every night. But she doesn't know that I know about them, so I say, "I don't understand."

She tilts her head at me and, seeing that I have gulped down my lunch like a castaway home at last, smiles and pats her lips with her napkin. "Come," she says, "let me show you the grounds."

The back door opens off the hallway next to the kitchen. She leads me through it, past the cistern and wooden shoes. Apparently she intends to stay on the pathways. Up close her gardens are lush. It's going to be a good harvest. Rich purple grapes dangle from the arbor. She picks one and bites into it, then shudders and spits it out making a face and laughing, "Still too early."

One by one, she introduces me to the chickens, starting with the rooster. "Madame LeClerc, this is Ferdinand, seigneur of this domain."

The barn is cool and dark. It's neat and orderly like everything else, but has an earthy smell. Hay and cow pies. It's empty except for one black and white cow that the doctor introduces as, "Matilde." A separate room holds the chicken feed, milk buckets, and miscellaneous tools it takes to maintain the place. We bypass the pigs. Perhaps she hasn't known them long enough to give them names.

Honore was right. I would be a perfect fit. "It's lovely," I let a touch of awe slip into my voice. "So, peaceful. You're lucky to live here."

"Thank you." She accepts the compliment the way she apparently does everything, economically but gracefully. I have a hard time reconciling this with the woman dressed in a man's clothes I saw yesterday.

"But..." She evaluates me again. Then makes her decision. "Sometimes it does get lonesome."

My heart jumps, but I give her a questioning look.

"Out here by myself."

"I know..." This time I pause as if deciding something, then continue looking her in the eye as if understanding, "Sometimes being alone can be almost unbearable."

The precursors of tears glisten in her eyes. "I'm so sorry." Her hand is on my arm again. I've made her feel guilty for complaining.

"No," I shake my head, looking away. "It's okay. I'll be going," I say to the ground and start slowly toward the kitchen.

When I turn to thank her for lunch, she's rooted to the spot, watching. If she doesn't bite now, I'll lose her. I give her a slight, tentative smile.

"Where are you staying?" She sounds tentative, too.

Whew.

"I don't know." I slump my shoulders. "I think I will ride to Tulle. I can get there before dark. I'm sure I can find some place to stay and..." If this doesn't do it, nothing will. "Someway to make myself useful. Thank you, again for the meal." I take a few more steps away.

"I can't pay much." Her voice is soft, unsure.

I stop.

"But I have a spare room."

I've done such a good job of assuming the personality of poor Angelique LeClerc that I'm actually moved by the offer. That and the haunting loneliness I now hear in the doctor's voice.

Dr. Duphresne beckons me to follow her into the foyer where she opens a door across from the kitchen. "It's small," she says in the way of an apology for not offering me more. "The great hall where the original seigneur of the manor entertained his guests used to take up this entire half of the first floor."

She pauses. "But my father..." She shrugs and her voice drifts off. "My father closed off this end to make an office when he started in politics. Now I have a parlor and this room."

It's not that small, and it's appointed like a bedroom rather than an office. In addition to a bed, there are an armoire, a desk with a small lamp, and a chair. Sunlight filters in through the lace curtains on the windows.

Seeing me eye the furniture, she explains, "When he started rising in the political ranks, he no longer had need of an office in the house. Anyway, my father always would have preferred ... a servant." Distaste has crept into her tone.

So all's not well between the good doctor and her father. Perhaps that's why he stays away. "It's beautiful!" I exclaim, running my fingers over the soft nubs of the white chenille bedspread and touching the lace curtains before lifting grateful eyes to hers.

Seven

THE QUEEN – *The Limousin, France, August 1941*

Dr. Duphresne and I listen to the BBC in the evenings. According to the radio, things are heating up in the war. The British and Russians have entered into some kind of mutual assistance agreement because the Germans are threatening Russia. Hitler clearly intends to control the entire world before he's through.

My country, the United States, has placed embargos on Germany and Japan. I know that the people of America wouldn't hesitate to come to Europe's aid directly if they could only see firsthand what's going on over here. As it is, though, they're still dragging their feet.

In the Limousin, Dr. Duphresne and I have settled into a pretty good routine. When we went to mass that first week, she introduced me to the priest and to most of Laguenne's residents and merchants. She's also shown me how to contact the hospital in Tulle should I need to while she's not here. Both the rectory and the small inn on the village's main street have telephones we are welcome to use.

We're averaging about two patients a day. So far, only minor complaints. The gardens are so well-established by now that they need little tending. The two of us can work our way through them in half an hour.

This has freed up the doctor to build her practice in Tulle. For the past three weeks, Celine, the driver of the car I saw that first day, has arrived on Monday morning to collect her. She brings the doctor back late the next afternoon.

When I ask her how it's going in Tulle, she answers, "Fine," and I leave it at that. We spend a lot of time together, but she's maintaining her distance. I get the feeling she doesn't quite trust me.

Our evenings are quiet. After dinner, we retire to the parlor. Sometimes we read, but often we listen to the radio. The BBC's good for news that's not slanted in favor of the Germans, but what the doctor looks forward to is music. Her favorite is a show on the Nazi-controlled Radio Paris that plays classical pieces rather than propaganda. Tonight, Debussy floats gracefully into the manor.

"The Germans are being smart here," she says. "Playing French music instead of their own." She leans back in her chair and closes her eyes. The slightest smile creases her lips.

"So you prefer French composers?"

"Anything but propaganda," she laughs.

I don't know that I've seen her so relaxed before.

"What music do you like?" she asks.

I have to be careful here not to give myself away. What to tell her? "My mother always played music from Martinique. Are you familiar with a singer named Jenny Alpha?"

She shakes her head.

"She's from Martinique, but she's lived in Paris a long time. I saw her perform with Josephine Baker."

I wish I hadn't said those words as soon as they leave my mouth. Everyone knows by now that Jo has sided with the Free French. But no one knows Jenny has or that I'm counting on details she provided to carry me through if anyone challenges my claim to be Martiniquan. I hold my breath, hoping the doctor doesn't make the connection between Jenny and Jo.

"So, you prefer Negro music?"

That connection I can deal with. I shrug as if I haven't escaped disaster by accident. "I hadn't thought of it that way. Where I grew up, jazz was a big favorite, but really anything with a lively beat, because we liked to dance." I laugh. "But I can't say I prefer that kind of music over any other kind, Dr. Duphresne, because I don't know enough about other kinds of music to make a comparison."

The doctor is out of her chair as the words leave my mouth. "Come see." She indicates that I should follow her across the room.

Kneeling in front of a fine wooden cabinet I have never opened, she flings the doors wide. It's packed tight with twelve-inch tall phonograph records standing on their edges in paper sleeves.

"I like everything!" The doctor's smile glows as she retrieves disc after disc to show me as if making promises. "Tchaikovsky ... Ravel ... Duke Ellington." She smiles at me as she holds up the last. Then she roots through some more as if looking for something specific and pulls another out. "But, this is my favorite ... Edith Piaf."

"I've heard of her but I don't know her music." It's only a partial lie.

That's the only invitation the doctor needs. She turns off the radio, lifts the top of the console revealing the turn table, and carefully slips the wide flat disc onto the silver spindle. She smiles over her shoulder at me before setting the needle down gently on the turning grooves and saying, "Listen."

Edith Piaf's world-weary voice fills the room, a tortured beautiful soul, weaving tales of love and loss, but also of never-ending hope. The voice of women since eternity began. Trying, believing, dreaming, no matter what. It's heartbreaking, but at the same time, there's something strong and powerful about it. And something else I hadn't realized before.

"She reminds me of Billie Holliday," slips out. It's not the style or the voice. But it's like they're sisters at the core.

The doctor who has been swaying with her eyes closed, lost in the Little Sparrow's paeans to longing, returns to the room. Her face tells me she doesn't have any idea who I'm talking about. That's a good thing, because mentioning Billie Holliday was another mistake. She's too American.

THE QUEEN – *The Limousin, France, September 1941*

According to the BBC, Hitler's still facing east. The Germans have attacked Leningrad and Kiev. They're rounding up the Jews everywhere in their path.

I've started listening to General De Gaulle's speeches on Radio London when Dr. Duphresne is in Tulle. De Gaulle is still the titular head of the Free French Forces, even though he fled to England last year when the Vichy inked their pact with the devil. Lately, he's been entreating Frenchmen to rise up against the Germans. And it's working. Young men are dribbling into the Limousin from all over the country. New bands of resisters are forming every day.

I've already carried two messages this month. One to a recently-formed band south of here. Another to my old friends to the northeast. They've been short trips. At this point the Resistance groups are so loosely organized they're going to need a lot more help coordinating.

Getting away has been easy. The doctor accepts my professed need to visit friends of my former family at face value. She covers for me when I'm not here the way I cover for her when she's in Tulle.

We're eating bread and cheese with thin slices of sausage, tomatoes, and onion for lunch in the kitchen when the bell on the front door rings and keeps ringing. It's frantic. Something's wrong.

We rush to the door and find little Marie Claire LaGuste, the eight-year-old daughter of the doctor's closest neighbor crying and wringing her hands.

"My father! Come quick!" she wails.

The doctor kneels in front of the girl, steadying her shoulders with both hands. "Slowly, Marie Claire," she soothes. "Tell me what's happened?"

"PaPa," the girl snivels. "He was in the old barn and the wall fell." Her eyes flit from the doctor to me. "He can't get out."

This could be bad. The old barn on her family's property is made of granite blocks and heavy timbers just like the doctor's. "I'll get our bags."

I race into the office, as the doctor tells the girl, "This is what I need you to do, Marie Claire. Hurry to Mr. Benoit's. Tell them we need as many men as he can bring." She holds the girl firmly and reads her round blue eyes. "Can you do that?"

The girl gulps and nods as I hand the doctor her bag. Within a minute, we're pedaling south as fast as we can while Marie Claire continues north.

A few minutes later, we drop our bicycles and race down the slope to the pile of rubble that used to be the LaGustes' old barn. Marie Claire's mother, Lucile, leaps up from where she's been flinging stones off the pile and calls to us, "Hurry! Oh my God, Robert's down here!" Her infant son wails from a basket in the shade a safe distance away.

Without stopping, the doctor tells her, "I sent Marie Claire to get Benoit. Help will be here soon."

On hands and knees now, I peer into the space Lucile has been clearing. "I see him!"

Marie Claire's father is a handsome young man, robust and strong. He's on his back. Blue eyes that match those of his daughter stare at me about six feet away. At least he's alive.

"Can't … breathe," he manages to rasp.

Now that my vision has adjusted to the dark, I can see that Robert's gotten lucky. A couple of beams are holding most of the structure off of him. There's enough space for me to shimmy toward him on my stomach.

But when I get close enough, I realize he's not that lucky after all. One of those beams is resting on his chest. His face is red. He's sweating. "Getting … heav …ier." He can barely squeeze the words out.

Looking under the beam, the rest of his body seems free. If it weren't for the beam... When I lift my head I see the doctor's face above his other shoulder.

"The rest of him's free," I report. At that moment, the pile of debris above us shifts. A rumble cuts me off, and dust and small stones rain down on our heads.

Air is audibly forced out of Robert's lungs. His eyes panic.

"Come on," I shout at the doctor and shimmy backwards toward the sunlight.

We stand at the same time. Lucile rushes to us, her hands raised to cover her mouth.

"I have an idea," I shout, my eyes scouting our surroundings for the things we need to implement it. Both women look at me, waiting. "There!" I point at a stout length of wood that Robert probably intended to use to shore up the structure. "Bring it here."

Lucille flies into action.

"You're right." The doctor understands. "We can pry it off him."

Her eyes light up when they settle on a thick log we can use as a fulcrum for our lever. She slides it next to the entrance to Robert's lonely cave. I, in the meantime, shove pieces of wood of different thicknesses into the space I previously occupied and stack as many as I can tightly under the beam to keep it from settling any farther. When I pull back out, the doctor and Lucile have almost got our lever arm in place.

"Here," the doctor says, beckoning for me to stand. "You help Lucile. It will take two of you," she orders.

"No." I shake my head.

She looks astounded.

"There's not much room in there." I indicate the dark hole I've just slid out of. "And you need to be out here." She's at least four inches taller and twenty pounds heavier than I am. Those extra pounds on the end of the lever arm might make all the difference.

I don't have to wait for an answer. The doctor's nothing if not quick and logical. I shimmy back under the pile, sliding more boards in front of me. When I'm in position, I call out, "Okay. We're ready."

Immediately, the two outside maneuver their long piece of timber into the hole behind me. When it's under the beam, I yell, "Now, lift!"

The lever arm strains up against the beam. It creaks. Nothing happens.

"Wait," the doctor calls out. My end of the timber drops to the ground. They push the fulcrum into the opening behind me. "Here we go." It's a warning.

This time when the women lean their weight onto the long board, the pile of rubble groans and shifts. Through the rain of dust and pebbles, I see the beam raise an inch and slide another board under it.

"Move the log again," I call out. They release the tension and my new board holds the beam higher than before.

They slide the fulcrum even closer. This time the beam rises almost two inches, but I still can't see daylight between it and Robert's chest. "Again!" I cry out. This is taking too long.

This time a fairly large stone hits me on the forehead. The structure is becoming unstable. But Robert's chest is free. "That's it!" I yell, sliding in another board and reaching to grab his arm. Only to see the doctor's face appear again on his other side.

"Here!" She hands me one end of a long, three-inch wide canvas strap, the kind farmers use for towing things. We loop it over his upper chest and under his armpits and throw the ends out to his wife. By the time we've scrambled out to help her, she's already moved Robert about a foot closer to freedom. With three of us pulling, he's completely out in a matter of seconds.

But he's not breathing.

Lucile crumples to her knees, her head on his stomach. The doctor kneels down beside him, placing her ear on his chest. I pull his wife away.

The doctor turns her face to me. For a moment I see immeasurable sadness in her eyes. But only for a moment. It is suddenly replaced by clarity. She straightens her body and takes a deep breath. Then she leans down toward Robert's face, opens his mouth with her fingers, and places her mouth on his. Pinching his nose closed, she blows her breath so forcefully into his lungs that both of their bodies shudder. Then she pulls away and does it again. And again. She's brilliant.

Lucile and I watch in silence, mesmerized, praying even if we are not aware that we're doing so. The doctor takes a fourth deep breath and leans forward again. But as she grows close, instead of putting her mouth on Robert's, she lets out the breath and places her ear to his chest, then slumps there for a moment.

When she raises her face to meet ours, there are tears in her eyes. My arms tighten around Lucile's shoulders as both our hearts break.

But the doctor doesn't give up. One more breath. And then another. One more and the doctor drops her ear down to Robert's chest again. But this time when she rises to face us, her tears have been replaced by a smile.

"He's breathing?" I'm astounded.

Lucile collapses to her knees, and Marie Claire runs into her so hard it almost knocks them both to the ground. I have no idea how long she and the other neighbors have been here. They're muttering behind me, "Never seen such a thing."

Neither have I. When I look down again, I'm thrilled to see Robert dazed but wincing in pain as the doctor conducts her examination. When she's done, she helps him sit up and tells Lucile, "He's very lucky. Doesn't seem to have any broken bones." As she packs her stethoscope away, she adds, "He'll be sore, though. Should get some rest. Keep an eye on him for a day or two. Send Marie Claire over to get me if he starts having trouble."

Then she ruffles the hair on the top of Marie Claire's head, kneels to her eye level, and says, "You did a good job, young lady."

The girl beams in reply.

As the neighbors move in to help transport Robert to his house, the doctor and I retrieve our bicycles and make our way home much more slowly than we came. We trudge past the front door straight through to the kitchen. The calm after all that excitement feels almost as weighty as that beam. I fill a glass with water and sink heavily into the chair I always use.

The doctor places her bag on the table and reaches across the table, taking my chin in her hand and tilting my face upward. It's strange she does that. She never touches me. Not since that first day. Then, she releases my chin, wets a cloth at the sink, and sits down next to me. "Lean this way," she says.

When I do, she takes hold of my chin again and dabs gently at my forehead with the cloth. It comes away pink. The stone. I had forgotten.

Before I have a chance to react, she says, "That was very brave of you, Madame LeClerc, going under to shore up the beam. The whole pile could have collapsed."

"But he would have died anyway except for you," I blurt. "I've never heard of such a thing. How did you know—"

She cuts me off with a shrug. "It works with newborns. His lungs needed air. It was the only thing I could think of."

"But, Dr. Duphresne..." I stop because I can't think of words to tell her how brilliant what she did was and how much it means to me that Robert is still here with his wife and children. I lost my father when I was young. It's a miracle.

"Please," she stops me by placing the tip of one finger on my lips. "I would like it if you called me Genevieve..." She pauses. "Or Gen, like my friends do."

"My friends call me Angelique." I smile.

"I'm surprised they don't call you Angel."

She looks at me seriously for a moment then makes a show of scrutinizing the wound on my forehead, laughs, and changes the topic. "Once you're all cleaned up, I think you'll survive, too."

Eight

The Queen – *The Limousin, France, December 1941*

It seems to me that the winters have gotten colder since the war started. By mid December, an inch of snow layers the ground, giving it a brown and white speckled look, and the low gray sky threatens more. The locals assure me that, while snow is not a rarity in this part of the Limousin, temperatures significantly below freezing are highly unusual. But then, why would anyone expect things to be usual?

It's been a slow week for both doctoring and resisting the Nazis with one very major exception. A few days ago, the BBC announced that America has joined the war. It's about time. I'm frustrated that Japan had to attack Pearl Harbor to bring us in, but I'm excited nonetheless. Now things will get better.

Celine picked up Gen this morning. She isn't scheduled back until tomorrow. With little else to think about, my mind drifts toward Christmas as I putter around the kitchen. This is such a lovely place.

Looking out through the rippled glass of the kitchen window I smile. The snow gods are following through on their threat. Big wet flakes float lazily down on a light breeze and start sticking to everything. I can't remember the last time I saw snow like this.

Something catches my eye out in the courtyard. A small figure scurries around the side of the barn making haste toward the house. I open the door just as little Paulie, the twelve-year-old son of Gen's neighbor, Benoit, lifts his fist to knock.

"Dr. Genevieve!" he blurts breathlessly. "We need the doctor now!" He turns as if to run back the way he had come, then stops as if realizing he hasn't given anyone enough time to follow him. I pull him inside and close the door.

"What's happened?" I wipe my hands and reach for my cape.

"A man..." The boy's wide eyes look from me to the empty silent house behind me.

"Who?"

The boy seems at a loss for words. "I don't know him. But, he's hurt. Very badly hurt."

A stranger? And Paulie had approached the house from the woods. My instincts tell me there is more to this.

"How did he get hurt?"

"I don't know, but he's bleeding." The boy indicates his upper chest area.

Glad that Gen isn't here to take this call, I throw my nursing kit and a few extra supplies into my knapsack, adjust my cloak and scarf, and follow the boy out the courtyard's back gate.

As we climb uphill through the orchard, the bare limbs of the trees stand dark gray against the lighter gray sky, offering little hope of shelter. Engulfed in that eerie quiet and the blue light that accompanies a late afternoon snowfall, the only sounds are our breathing, which manifests itself in little puffs of gray mist, and the crunch of our wooden soles smashing icy stems of grass.

Paulie leads me out the back of the orchard into the woods beyond. I've wandered these woods before, with Gen picking berries, gathering chestnuts, and searching for truffles and mushrooms. They're vast and dark, cloaking the top of this hill and the long beyond that runs for a least a hundred kilometers from southwest to northeast.

After a while, I know where we're headed. To the cledier, the round stone smoke house Gen's family used to dry chestnuts before they abandoned nut harvesting for the city life of Paris. It hasn't been used in years, other than by an occasional hunter. No one should be up here. Who is this mystery man? What is he doing in Gen's cledier, and how did he get hurt?

At this elevation, the cold settles in as the sun sets. I'm shivering by the time I make out the pointed silhouette of the cledier's roof. The smallest sliver of illumination shines under the door.

Paulie and I burst in on a hellish scene bathed in yellow light from a kerosene lantern. Two men hover over the prone figure of a third man who writhes and groans on a raised drying platform. One of the upright men is Paulie's father, Benoit. I've never seen the other man before.

"Oh, you must be the Mulatto," the new man says without moving from his position. "I was afraid we wouldn't find you."

The Mulatto. That tells me he's a resister. I wish they wouldn't call me that. Referring to my skin color gives away too much. "Regina," I want to correct him. That's my code name, but I don't yet know how much Paulie and Benoit have been told.

Then my eyes adjust and I can make out the details. The new man is pressing hard on the injured man's chest while Benoit holds a cloth up to the man's side. Both are covered in red.

"He's lost a lot of blood." The new man brings me up to date. "Damn S.O.L. thugs!"

So, the S.O.L. did this. That's not a surprise. That bunch of mobsters from Marseilles doesn't hesitate to shoot.

I step over and take Benoit's place. "You can go now," I tell him. He's a simple man with a family who isn't the kind who should be getting involved in this sort of thing, and he's already heard too much.

"Miss Angelique," he says picking up his hat and looking as lost and frightened as Paulie had, "I didn't know who else to call."

Ah. So it had been Benoit's idea rather than the mystery man's to send Paulie after me. "You did the right thing, Benoit." I gesture toward the door with my chin. "It's getting bad out there. You'd best get home."

In the meanwhile, Paulie has made a few trips in and out the door of the cledier depositing a pile of small branches and sticks on the floor. "In case you want a fire, Miss Angelique," he whispers like a conspirator. His wide brown eyes reveal more understanding of the situation than I wish they did. What else has the new man let slip?

"We'll build a pile by the door before we go." It's Benoit's turn to confirm the same silent secret.

So, everyone knows the bleeding man's a fugitive. And now they know, if they didn't before, that I'm here to help him. But, I'll have to worry about that later.

I've been evaluating the man's condition while we said our good-byes. It isn't good. It appears he was shot only once and that the bullet entered and exited the right side of his upper body from back to front. When Benoit removed his hand from the lower wound, blood bubbled out of the little hole with a hissing sound. The bullet probably pierced his lung. If I can get him stabilized, I'll have to move him to a hospital.

"English?" I ask the new man as soon as we're alone.

He nods in response. "A pilot."

"Rifle?"

The man looks angrily at the ceiling. "Long range. Never saw them. First shot hit Honore. We dove for cover. The second shot came almost immediately. Caught the Englishman as he hit the ground."

Honore? My contact to the north. My heart breaks. What a nice, strong man Honore is … was.

Seeing my look, the man continues, "Honore told me to bring the English to you if there was any trouble." The man lets out a deep breath as I wrap a compress around the smaller wound in the Englishman's side. "I don't think they followed us. It's possible they only saw Honore." Indicating the wounded man he explains, "We were behind a bush when the shooting started."

He'd been lucky to run across Benoit and Paulie coming back from a small hunting trip. They had helped him hide the pilot in the cledier.

I nod without looking at him as I work, "And you are?" I should have known better than to ask.

He shakes his head. "This is going to get worse. The less any of us knows about the other the better."

For all our sakes, I hope he remembers that rule in the future.

Then lifting his chin at the moaning airman, he asks. "It's not likely he'll make it?"

I shrug. I'm a nurse, not a surgeon. It's dark and cold and I don't have any sophisticated tools to work with. Who knows how much blood the man lost before I got here.

"I've never done this before," the stranger goes on, worry and fear deepening the creases of his face in the flickering lamp light.

"Got a family to take care of. Would have left him where he fell, but Honore told me this one had an urgent message that had to get through."

"Did he give you the message?" If I can't save the man's life, maybe I can take a small bit of revenge for his … and Honore's … death.

But no. The stranger shakes his head. And then he stands up. I can tell he wants to leave. And what good can he do here anyway? I've cleaned and compressed the exit wound he'd been in charge of.

Now I'm working my way through the Englishman's pockets one by one. He's clearly been in the underground for a while, because he's wearing French clothes and carrying valid-looking identity papers, but nothing I can decipher as a secret message. Then, drawing from my experience with Jo, I go through the linings and cuffs of his clothes, pinching them to feel or hear the telltale crackle of paper. Nothing.

The Englishman groans and flails about, then lets out one low-pitched whine and lies still. I fear he's died until I hear his raspy breath. Unconsciousness has spared him the pain, at least temporarily.

Looking up at the stranger, I say, "I must go back to the house for supplies. It's not necessary for you to stay until I return. He's as good as he can be for the moment." When the man just looks at me, uncertainty in his eyes, trying to figure out the right thing to do, I add, "Your family is probably worried about you."

He nods, and after I cover the Englishman with my cloak, we walk out the door together into the deepening dusk. After he's taken a few steps, he returns and hands me the lantern. "I can find my way without it," he says.

I hope he's right. But even if it's not easy, carrying a light through the woods at night when S.O.L. snipers are out hunting Englishmen is probably not a good idea. I don't take it either.

The wind and snow have picked up by the time I reach the courtyard. It looks like this could turn out to be one of those rare Limousin blizzards. Half frozen, I pack more medical supplies, food, and two down comforters into my knapsacks and throw on a jacket and my heavy cloak. By the time I make it back to the cledier, there is no doubt. Temperatures are plummeting. Snow, falling heavier now, has started to drift. The inside of the cledier is the same as the night outside, cold and black as pitch.

I hear the man before I see him. Still breathing short raspy breaths, he's moaning again, but he's still alive. Using the small flashlight I relied on to find the path back, I light the lantern and lift the cloak that's covering him. His bleeding seems to have stopped. Only a spot of blood has oozed through the bandage on his chest. He's beyond my medical knowledge. All I can do now is pray.

As I tuck my cloak around the Englishman again, I hear scuffing on the stones outside the heavy oak cledier door. I've already worked out my strategy. I'm the doctor's nurse after all. If it's the S.O.L., I will tell them a neighbor found this man in the woods and called me. I stand a better chance of surviving a lie than I do a fight.

"Come in." I hold my breath, and the door opens, sending light from the lantern streaming out onto the snow-covered stones.

"What in the hell do you think you're doing?" Gen stomps her boots on the stoop and beats her shoulders with gloved hands so as not to track snow into the cledier. Leaving the door open, she strides over to the rack where the injured Englishman lies and sets her medical bag down beside him.

"No!" she commands without looking at me when I start to close the door. "Clediers are built to hold smoke. Without fresh air, the fumes of a fire, even a lantern, can kill you in a place like this."

Embarrassed that I had not thought of that, I withdraw my hand from the door and move to stand beside her.

"Rifle?" she asks.

I nod.

"S.O.L.?"

Another nod.

She seems to get the gist even though she isn't looking at me. Her hands explore the Englishman's bandages and then pull her stethoscope out of her bag. After listening for a moment, she sighs and puts the stethoscope away shaking her head. Looking at me for the first time, she says, "You did a good job. There's a chance he'll make it till we can get him to a hospital."

Only when I relax do I realize I'm shivering. The wind roars. Snow billows through the threshold, and the door slams so hard it rattles the roof beams and makes the flame in the lantern waver.

"But we can't take him now. Hell..." She brushes her hair off of her forehead as she walks to open the door again. "The roads are closing. I hope Celine made it home."

Using one of the branches Paulie had left for a fire as a stop, she closes the door all but a crack and turns a worried face to me. "The way it's coming down now, the two of us might have trouble making it down to the house by ourselves. Trying to drag him with us would be almost impossible and likely reopen his wounds. Plus we wouldn't be able to get him to the hospital, anyway."

Shaking her head with her eyebrows raised, she looks helpless. The Englishman will have to stay in the cledier for the night, and we'll be staying with him. There's no better answer.

As soon as things calm down, I realize how seriously I've underestimated the drop in temperature. My teeth chatter even though the draft has been greatly reduced. Beckoning Gen to sit with me, I pull a comforter out of my bag and hand it to her. After draping the second blanket over my shoulders, I rummage through the knapsack and pull out the loaf of rough peasant bread and homemade cheese I had grabbed from the kitchen. Tearing off a piece of the bread, I hand it to her and ask, "I thought you would be in Tulle all night?"

Giving me a sideways glance, she ignores my question. "So, this is the kind of trouble you get into while I'm away?"

"No." I shake my head and look over at the man, who groans loudly. "This came up very suddenly."

"There was a rumor in Tulle..." She narrows her eyes at me. "That the S.O.L. had ambushed a dangerous English spy in the hills just north of here."

I don't meet her eyes as she says that.

"And that there are more spies in the woods." When I still don't comment, she capitulates, "With that and the snow, I felt the need to come home." After a moment of silence she adds, "Just in case you needed me."

How much has she figured out? How long has she known? I panic and turn to her, my eyes and mouth wide open, but with nothing to say.

"Dai...sy," the Englishman groans and thrashes as he says it. "Daisy!" He seems to be trying to get up. "I can't now. Need ... to tell them."

We rush to his side, as he continues to thrash. "What do you have to tell us?" I ask.

His eyes open, and he stares at me. "Who ... are you?"

I don't hesitate. I lie to him in French-accented English. "Agent Mary Jones. From Morocco." Indicating Gen, I continue the charade, "This is Doctor Elise Robard. You made it to Gibraltar, and we'll be moving you to Portugal soon. But first you have a message to deliver."

He starts to nod, but a look of suspicion creeps into his eyes stopping him. "How do I know—"

I don't let him finish the question. I drop my face so close to his I can smell the blood on his breath as he wheezes. "We're running out of time, Airman." Then I do something I did not want to do. I speak my code name in front of Gen. "After you were shot, Honore turned you over to Regina as scheduled. She moved you down the line. Now, Airman ... where is the information you are carrying?" I pronounce the last as an order.

"Honore?"

I hold my breath hoping he did not see the bullet strike Honore on the trail. Or at least that he doesn't remember.

His eyes flit right to left across my face and back again as he weighs his choices. "Regina?" He whispers. "Yes. That's who..." He lets out a breath that obviously causes him great pain and little pink bubbles pop on his lips as he starts reciting the secret they were all willing to die for.

Gen and I lean so close to hear his gasping words our heads touch. And thank goodness, she has the presence of mind to write everything he says down on paper she always carries to make medical notes. By the time he's finished, his breath is labored and he moans again.

But I can't afford to relent. "Let me make sure I have this right." I read the message back to him point by point. He nods slightly at all but one point and makes a correction. When he finishes, he seems to relax for a moment. Then, it's as if the will to complete his mission has been the only thing keeping the pain away. He coughs. His face contorts into a combination of wail and moan, and he flails from side to side.

"Hold him still!" Gen orders, and I do. "He'll reopen his wounds." She fumbles in her medical bag and comes out with a syringe and vial of clear liquid. "Morphine," she whispers as she injects the painkiller into his arm. Then she gives me a knowing look and adds, "I guess it's a good thing I didn't give it to him before."

When Gen and I lock eyes over the Englishman as he begins to relax on the platform, I know it's a choice we'd both make again. Even if he doesn't die, those few additional hours of his pain might save the lives of thousands.

But what to do next? By now it's the middle of the night. The light from the lantern that makes its way through the crack in the door reveals that the snow is falling even heavier than before. Drifts are piling high against everything that stands upright. Not able to see the path, much less follow it, I turn to Gen for suggestions.

She shrugs, tilting her head towards the Englishman's shallow breathing, and says, "There is still nothing we can do before morning." She looks at him long and hard and shrugs again, this time with a sigh.

Then she surveys the rest of the cledier, landing on the wood Paulie and his father had stacked and the knapsack I had jam packed with blankets. Turning back to me, she pats the platform and concludes, "In the morning if it has stopped snowing … and if he is still alive … we can find our way home and bring the sled back to get him."

I sit down next to Gen, and we assess the situation. We have two down blankets, three cloaks, and enough food for a light supper to see the three of us through until dawn, which according to my watch, is still seven hours away. This would have to happen on one of the longest nights of the year and with a freak storm dropping the temperatures twenty degrees lower than normal. Now that we're out of crisis mode, I notice that the vapor from my breathing extends almost arms-length in front of me.

Gen and I hear a strange clicking noise at the same time and turn to the Englishman. Lying there with only my cloak to cover him, his teeth are chattering. Gen grabs the thicker of the down blankets, and we wrap him in it like a cocoon, lifting him gently to pull the blanket underneath him, because the hard wooden slats of the drying platform offer no protection against the cold.

That done, Gen and I huddle side by side under our cloaks with the remaining down blanket across our shoulders and look at each other. Giving an ironic raise of her Gallic eyebrows, Gen digs around in her medical bag again. This time, her hand comes out holding a different medium-sized bottle of clear liquid. She tilts her forehead to me. "Regina, huh?"

My eyes widen. Where is she going with this?

Then, she gives me a wink as she unscrews the top of the bottle and raises it, saying in English, "Hail to the Queen." She takes one sip and hands the bottle to me.

It's not the first time I've heard that toast. After all, Regina is my middle name, and that means Queen in Latin. Acknowledging that fact with a tip of my head, I raise the bottle.

The liquid I swallow burns my tongue and everything else it touches on the way down to my stomach where it explodes, filling me with heat from the inside. I sputter and almost spit out my sip it's so strong. "Oh, my God!" comes out of my mouth as a croak.

Laughing, Gen beats me on the back and then squeezes my shoulders, pulling me close as she hands me a chunk of bread from my backpack and says, "One hundred proof. Sorry, that's all I carry. Medicinal purposes, you know. Makes a good cough syrup."

Releasing me, she claps her hands and giggles at my red face and watering eyes. Once I catch my breath, we finish off the bread and cheese, talking as we do.

We have a lot to talk about, most of which I can't or don't want to tell her. The less she knows the better. For everyone. Especially her. So, I stick with the story I came in with. I'm still Angelique LeClerc, still born in Marseilles, still widowed by the war, still fifty-one years old.

All I admit is that I have been working with the Resistance. My code name is Regina. Since I knocked on her door intruding on her life, I have done little for the cause, delivered only a few messages. This is the first fugitive who's been placed into my hands for safe keeping, and I am dreadfully sorry to have dragged her into it.

Gen simply watches me work my way through my litany of lies with an expression that says, "Okay, if that's the way you want to play your hand, that's the way you play it."

For her part, she also holds her cards close to the vest, not giving me anything I didn't already know. With one exception. "I hate them."

Her eyes have hardened. She does hate whoever *them* is.

"That's why I work in the brothel."

"Brothel?" This is the first I've heard of any brothel, although in retrospect, now that I think about Celine…

"Yeah. Some of the girls..." She can't hold my gaze. Looks away. "Well they..."

"You take care of them. When they catch some disease…"

The Nazis and Vichy have figured out that one way to keep their soldiers out of trouble with the locals is to provide them with sex partners. The girls who work in the brothels supposedly do so voluntarily, but there have been rumors, especially from the north in occupied France.

Her eyes are wide. She seems to be holding her breath.

And the broader truth hits me. "Or get pregnant."

"Many of them don't want to bring children into this world. Not here. Not now." She looks away again. "Especially not Nazi children."

"This is what you do in Tulle?" I'm amazed I haven't figured this out for myself.

"Part of what I do." She sounds almost apologetic. "Nobody else will." She pauses. "And it's the only way I knew how to fight back."

With that, she opens the bottle again and takes a much bigger sip than her first. I can't understand how she manages to swallow it, but not a hint of distress shows on her face. She closes her eyes as if relishing the heat flowing through her body and when she opens them again, they are softer, almost back to normal.

"Until today." She hands me the bottle.

My head's fuzzy already, but I take another sip and do a better job of swallowing it before screwing the cap back on and handing the bottle back. We sit there with nothing to say, until we realize we're shivering and the Englishman is too. All attention shifts back to him.

"What should we do?" I ask. "Will the shaking hurt him?"

"It could." She nods.

I remove my remaining cloak and fold it in a double layer over his body, tucking in the sides. Then I set about trying to find a way to defend myself against the deepening chill.

I insist on at least trying a small fire. Gen shakes her head and rolls her eyes but lets me find out for myself. Of course she was right. The cledier holds all the smoke in. Opening the door a little wider doesn't provide enough air and only lets more cold in. Before long, the Englishman's damaged lungs can't handle the fumes. He coughs up little pink bubbles. The fire will kill us all if I don't put it out.

Then we try closing the door completely. That means blowing out the lantern. As she prepares to do so, Gen comments, "We should get some sleep anyway. We have a busy day tomorrow no matter what happens."

Nine

THE QUEEN – *The Limousin, France, December 1941*

Gen's right. We should get some rest. We lay on the platform back to back, Gen in her cape and me in my jacket, and pull the remaining down comforter over us. But, I'm still so cold that I'm shivering violently, unable to hold my lower jaw still, and thinking this night is going to be memorable, if I survive it.

Hearing shuffling and the sound of cloth rubbing on cloth, I sit up and turn on the flashlight. Gen's taking off her cloak. Shaking my head, I start to tell her it's not necessary yet. He seems to be okay with just mine and the comforter. But she is spreading our down comforter on the platform and laying my backpacks side by side at one end.

"Come here," she says pointing to the down-filled coverlet. "We'll share the comforter and my cloak. Our combined body heat should keep us warm enough."

I almost laugh out loud. I had learned that survival trick back when I was a girl. The alcohol must have affected my brain.

Gen directs me to crawl onto the comforter on my hands and knees and lie with my head on the backpack nearest the wall. I do so. The blanket's long enough to cover my head and my feet. Once I'm properly situated, Gen throws her cloak over me and slides under it by my side. Then she pulls the other half of the down comforter over us, giving me one edge to tuck around myself. Still, I am shaking so wildly from the cold I'm afraid my elbows are bruising hers as we next lie to each other.

"This will help." She adjusts her position under the comforter. "Roll onto your side."

As I turn to face the wall, I am startled by the feel of her right hand sliding around my waist and pulling me so close to her body that her breasts press against my shoulder blades.

"Now bend."

Applying pressure to the back of my knees, she curls me halfway into a fetal position so that her body fits against mine from my heels to the back of my neck. "Now relax." She laughs. "And let me know if I need to remind you to breathe."

Her mouth is so close to the back of my head I feel little blasts of heat through my hair when she exhales, but she's right again. Before long, half of my body, the half that's tucked tight against hers, feels as if I were lying next to embers. That warmth slowly spreads all the way around to the front, permeating the air beneath the comforter. Only when my shakes subside and my muscles relax does she release her grip on my waist. By then, however, we are curled together as comfortably as lovers, and for the first time I believe I may be able to sleep.

Until I feel her lift her head to whisper in my ear, "You know I don't believe you."

What can I say to that? Why should she? I shrug.

"But, it is a good thing you are doing." She sighs. "And I promise I will do whatever you need me to do."

When I start to reply, her fingers fly to my lips to stop me.

"Shhh." Her mouth is so close to my ear, the sound and the heat of her breath send a shiver down my back. Then she whispers the words, "Because I love you."

It is that moment, lying there on the hard platform, wrapped safe and warm in her arms, that I realize how much I love her, too. The smartest, kindest, most gentle soul I have ever known, isolated out here in the middle of this God-forsaken war. More than the sister I never had or the mother I left behind long ago. A very, very good friend. How could I have not realized before how amazing she is?

"I love you, too." It comes out as a rasp. The realization of how much she means to me has deprived me of the ability to speak. So, I reach my right hand back over my shoulder to let her know what I mean by patting her hair.

But she turns her face so that my palm slides down her temple and cups her cheek. When I don't jerk away, she breathes in deeply and nuzzles into my fingers, moving slightly side to side as if trying to nestle there for a moment. Then she moves her face again until the center of my palm covers her lips, and she kisses it. Once. Softly. And, letting out another deep breath moves her face away and says, "I hope so."

My eyes wide in the darkness, I drop my hand slowly back under the cover and lay there confused and overwhelmed. This day. Too many things. What does any of it mean? My heart still aches so much it throbs. In the midst of all this turmoil, I realize the Englishman seems to be breathing better.

Only now, it's Gen's slow deep breathing that's keeping me awake. She has something she wants to say, and when she can't find the words, she follows my lead. She relies on touch to convey what words can't.

Her right hand, the hand that is holding me so close, keeping me warm, moves ever so slightly and I feel the soft caress of her fingers on the bare skin of my belly. They burn like fire, igniting all my senses. The small little gasp I suck in tightens my abdominal muscles. Her hand stops moving but does not pull away.

JOE – *Montreal, Canada, the First Day, 1992*

"Whoa!" Joe's chair scraped across the floor as he shied away from the table, his palms at chest height as if to ward Nanette off.

She observed his reaction with eyebrows arched in amusement and cackled, "A little too much information for you, son?"

He shut his eyes and shook his head. He knew exactly what the old bird was up to. "Momma Willie didn't tell you that," he insisted again. "You made it up because of that stupidity before … about Carrie being with Maya."

She studied him for a moment then shook her head calmly. "Non, Cheri." She paused again, no sign of a smirk on her face now. "But that *is* what convinced me you need to hear the truth."

Joe rolled his eyes and snorted to show that he didn't buy it.

She took a drag from her cigarette and let the smoke out in a thin stream without taking her eyes off him. "Tell me, Joseph, why does the thought of two women together make you so uncomfortable?"

"Oh, come on." He wasn't about to get sucked into that debate. "Nobody'd be comfortable hearing the intimate details of his grandmother's love life … even if it was normal."

"Normal?" The woman leaned back in her seat resting her elbow on an armrest and grinning an air of superiority at him. "Tell me then, what exactly *is* normal?" The combination of her casual shrug and her French accent made it sound more like a totally obvious statement of universal truth than a question.

She didn't wait for an answer. "Have you known fear?" She dismissed any positive answer he might try to give to that question by raising her eyebrows and pursing her lips. "Have you watched bombs fall from the sky? Killed a man at close range? Been pulled from the wreckage of an entire world by the only creature in existence you know cares for you?"

She took one last long deep drag on the butt of her cigarette. Smoke trailed out of her nostrils and slowly floated to the ceiling as she waited for Joe to answer. When he didn't, she concluded, "I thought not."

Stubbing out the cigarette in the ashtray, she smiled as if forgiving him and then shrugged. "So … you have lived less than half a life. How can you possibly know what's normal?"

Joe stared back at her. "Look. I didn't come here to listen to—"

"Ahhh, but you said you wanted to know *everything*."

He mentally kicked himself for challenging her with her own words. He should have known she wouldn't quit till she found a way to one-up him with them if he did. He played the only card he had left. "But I mean, really … even if it was true, how could I possibly *need* to hear it?"

She studied him for a moment, and when she replied her voice was calm, serious, softer in a way. "Patience, Joseph. You will see."

Joe leaned back, evaluating the woman through narrowed eyes and rethinking his position for the umpteenth time. If there was one thing he'd learned from all the business classes he'd taken in grad school, it was the importance of picking your battles carefully.

He knew the old spy well enough by now to realize that she had a point she wanted to make and wasn't going to get on with the rest of what she had to tell him until she made it. Why waste time fighting over something that probably wasn't even true?

And even if it was, he'd heard such stories before. The truth was he usually found them *very* interesting. He coughed into his hand to disguise the laugh that threatened to overtake him, shrugged, and leaned so far back in his chair that it rocked on two legs. He just wouldn't think about his grandmother as she told it.

She grinned. "Pour yourself some more wine, mon cher. You are likely to need it."

THE QUEEN – *The Limousin, France, December 1941*

Gen's smooth fingers, gentle as feathers, make small little circles right below my navel, and I see it all now. The last hours, the last weeks, even months, have been building to this moment. It's up to me to say or do something to stop what's going to happen next, but I don't. I know what it is, but I don't know what it really is or what it means, and the core of me doesn't want to stop it without finding out.

It's going to change everything. But she loves me. No matter what happens, it's going to change nothing. Unless it does change everything after all.

I can't breathe. I just lie there with her touch burning a hole in my skin and my mouth open in a silent gasp. She sighs. It is a small quiet sigh, but there is her breath hot again on my neck behind my ear, sending another chill down my spine. Her hand slides so slowly over my navel and up my body its movement is almost imperceptible.

The only way I can be sure time is passing is by counting the little rasps of her breath. And then, her palm and fingers slip like silk beneath my left breast, wrap themselves around it, and lift its entire weight. The shock of that touch is so intense I think I may die and gasp again, this time so loudly the sound of my own voice startles me in the darkness.

Then she brushes her thumb across my nipple and gently squeezes it against the inside of her palm, and I am lost. A blast of electricity and heat shoots from my breast through my abdomen all the way down between my legs, and my buttocks muscles clinch so suddenly and involuntarily they throw me forward and seem to shake the whole building.

It has been so long. And never before as hot and sweet and gentle as this. I can't even moan. It comes out as a squeak.

By now my senses are so acute I can count the stitches in my camisole and hear the snowflakes settling gently on the roof. I wait breathlessly for the next thing to happen. This time, she rolls my nipple between her thumb and forefinger, and I do moan. That small pain combined with the new flood of pleasure it releases is exquisite. Now, we are both breathing hard.

And she stops. Instead, there's a hitch in her breath. I feel its tremor wrack her body which is still wrapped around me, shielding me from the cold. Her open mouth presses helplessly against my hair so that every time she lets out a breath, the fire inside her burns me indelibly.

When her hand gently releases my breast and slips out of my blouse, I want to scream, "No!" But that word, like my feelings, is so ambiguous in this context. I don't say anything. I wait again, holding my breath again.

This time her hand, still so hot it must leave a mark, finds my face and cups my cheek, pressing her palm against it. Reminded of how she had nestled her cheek into mine, I move my lips to kiss it, but she arches it away so that they cannot touch. Instead, she brushes that remarkable thumb across my upper lip once as another breath scorches my skin and shakes both of us to the core. Then her arm returns to its place around my waist, and she is still.

Lying there, I'm in greater turmoil than before. It takes forever for my heartbeat to return to normal. A short time later when I think I feel lips brush my neck and hear whispered words that sound like, "What are we going to do?" I'm not sure if I'm imagining things. I could even have been dreaming the whole time, because the next thing I know Gen is shaking my shoulder and telling me it's morning and the Englishman has survived the night. We have so much to do.

And maybe nothing did happen, because that's the way Gen's acting today. We turn the Englishman in to the authorities. It's the fastest way to get him to the major hospital he so desperately needs to save his life.

Our cover story works well. We tell them we heard a noise at the front door in the middle of the night and found him when we looked outside. Whoever had been transporting him had probably realized he needed a doctor. Gen stopped his bleeding and I walked through the early morning snowdrifts to the LaGustes' to get their donkey and cart to carry him into Laguenne. The gendarmes are the only ones out the in the countryside who have cars and gasoline to run them.

This whole episode might work to our advantage in the future. Perhaps the authorities will ignore any forthcoming suggestions that the local doctor and her fifty-something nurse are harboring members of the Resistance, because we handed this one over to them.

From the airman's perspective, turning him in is a gamble. We've destroyed his false papers, but he's not in uniform. We can only hope he will be sent to a prisoner of war camp rather than a detention center once he is well enough to move. But, even if he is treated harshly, the surgeons tell Gen he would have died without an operation, probably later this day. At least this way, there's a chance he'll survive the war and eventually go home to do whatever he didn't have the time to do with Daisy before.

His life will go on. But what weighs most heavily on my mind as I return from dropping the cart back off at the neighbor's is whether ours will, now that the episode with the Englishman is over.

I guess I should start the conversation, but I don't know where it will lead. Not for Gen or for me. You see, now that the words have been spoken, I have to admit I really do love her. But I don't know in what way. Just that it's not any way I've felt about a woman before.

And I still don't know what made her cry. Perhaps she's as conflicted as I am. Maybe she stopped to save herself as much as me, and if I push the issue, she'll go crashing over some invisible brink and be lost to both of us forever.

So, I leave the ball in her court. When she does nothing, it's easier to breathe. Maybe this whole incident will pass over without doing any irreparable damage.

It seems to be the right decision. When I return from delivering the Englishman's message down the line, we start our daily lives again as if nothing has happened.

Initially, I watch things closely, but as the weeks lead to Spring, we have so much fun planting the garden, going on hikes, and curing the occasional minor ailments that plague this small farming community, I start to relax. There are only a few inconsequential messages to deliver during this time, and when I return, everything seems normal. Is it possible it was a dream after all? Was it all in my head?

Still, no matter what it was, it changed one thing. Now I see beauty in everything she does. The way she drops whatever she's working on when a neighbor's child has stepped on a nail, talks to the chickens, laughs out loud or whispers obscenities at the official Vichy announcers on Radio Paris. Sometimes, when rays of the late afternoon sun catch the planes of her face a certain way or when she tilts her head just so to concentrate on the music she loves so dearly, my heart swells and aches so deeply I must find something else to focus on.

And now that I'm watching her so closely, I also see how delicately the joy she finds in such small things seems to be poised against an otherwise overpowering pain of loss and longing. This balance is so precious and fragile I would die to protect it.

If I'm right, I have to be very careful, because I am now the biggest danger. For that reason, we have returned to the beginning. We never touch. Once, when our hands brush by accident in the kitchen, a spark leaps between them. Startled, we pull apart laughing, but it's a false laugh. She immediately leaves the room and when she comes back, the air between us is so thick it cannot enter my lungs.

Thus strung as tight as a wire, I am equally positioned on the point of a mystery.

Ten

JOE – *Montreal, Canada, the First Day, 1992*

A uniformed woman, Joe had not seen before entered the Rec Room. Seeing Nanette and the half empty bottle of wine, she gave an exaggerated frown, shook her head and tisked then said, "Mademoiselle Jeandren, you are incorrigible." Only she said it with a French accent so that it ended, "ahh-bluh."

Nanette beamed at her, responding with a comment in French that must have been saucy. Taking a sideways glance at Joe, the woman brushed the comment off with a wave of her hand and a giggle and left with a swing in her hips.

Joe wished he spoke French. Instead, he said in plain old English, "Okay, but something doesn't seem right. Why would Willie … er … the Queen tell you all those intimate details?"

Nodding emphatically, Nanette said, "At first I wondered about that too." She leaned forward as if preparing to share a confidence. "But then, I was twenty-two and intensely intrigued by all things erotic and sensual, especially those I had not yet experienced myself."

She giggled, "I must admit I encouraged her."

In response to the dismayed look that overtook Joe's face despite his best efforts, she reached into her bag which hung from her chair, saying, "But wait." Then she slid a five-by-seven black-and-white photograph across the table. "This will all make more sense if you don't think of us as I am now. Think of us this way."

In the picture, a child-sized young woman stood between two swarthy, rough-shaven men with dark berets on their heads and cigarettes hanging from their lips at casual angles. The men posed cockily with rifles, butts resting on their hips, barrels pointing to the sky.

The girl's curly bobbed hair, knee-length plaid skirt, short white ankle socks, and square-heeled shoes reminded Joe of women he'd seen in movies set in the forties, but her pose leaped off the page. All of her weight on one jutting hip. One hand holding a rifle almost as long as she was tall drooped nonchalantly across her thighs. Chin held high and to the left. Cigarette dangling from lips parted slightly in a smile that reminded Joe of the Mona Lisa if the Mona Lisa could bite. But it was her eyes that revealed the most. Alive, excited, and hard at the same time, they screamed directly through the lens, "Try me if you dare."

"You?" Joe looked over at Nanette for verification of the obvious.

She nodded, then blew smoke out of her nose with a shrug, "And two of my lovers, Georges and Pierre." With a small smile, she added, "Good men actually. Headed up an early band of Maquis."

"Maquis?"

"Yes, resisters. That's what they came to be called, after those scrubby thickets in the Limousin that made hiding from the Nazis so easy." She answered the question without letting it distract her and continued, "I was sorry when I had to leave them."

"Why did you?"

"I went back to England for a new assignment. Never saw them again." She sighed then brightened. "But what I learned from them?"

Her expression shifted from wistful to knowing. She raised one eyebrow, and said, "Ahhh ... at least I have memories."

"Wow," Joe looked at the picture again. "You sure were something, weren't you?"

"I was, Joseph." She paused, momentarily lost in her thoughts. "I was indeed."

Joe studied Georges, Pierre, and the young Nanette one more time before sliding the photo back to her.

Tapping her face in it with her forefinger, she said, "*That* woman was alive. *That* woman wanted to experience ... to do everything! All of it! *That* woman savored every detail of the Queen's story because she wanted to know what the Queen knew and feel what the Queen had felt."

For a moment that woman also sat across the table from Joe. Then the little old lady came back and explained in a softer tone, "And as her story went on, I realized she was telling me because she wanted to."

"Why did she want to?"

Nanette paused, muscles twitching and quivering all over her face as if it could not come up with a coherent expression. Once she had brought them under control, she answered, "I think she had learned something important, and she didn't want to be the only one in the world who knew it. She didn't want it to die with her."

"What was it?" All Joe could manage was a whisper.

"That, Joseph, is what you are here to find out." The tough old bird was back. "Shall I continue?"

Joe pushed back against his chair and sipped his wine. He nodded. How bad could it get?

THE QUEEN – *The Limousin, France, April 1942*

Gen and I maintain that delicate balance of loving friendship for months. Then Paulie brings us the pig.

He and Benoit also pretend the night of the Englishman never happened, but they don't let the fact that it did get in the way of our friendship. Benoit's wife still makes extra bread and sends it over. We repay her with some of the coffee Gen's sister has started secretly sending her from Paris. It has become clear over the months that the families of political collaborators are issued more generous rationing coupons, and it's not like Gen not to share.

Today, Paulie offers us a proposition which we accept. We will keep and feed this pig from our abundant leftover slop in return for half of the meat when it's butchered in the fall. It's a good deal. The pig weighs forty pounds now. By autumn he should weigh over two hundred, and all it's costing us is garbage, which would be going into the compost heap that we supplement with pig droppings. It's the circle of life. We stand side by side smiling at the boy when he turns and waves before closing the back gate behind him on his way home.

It is one of those glorious late-spring days when time seems to stand still. The light takes on a golden glow, and we revel in the aromas of early flowers and fresh-turned garden soil. After lunch we lay in the grass soaking up the warmth of the sun, exhibiting that lazy confidence that comes from knowing that winter has done its worst and we have survived. Bees and other spring insects drone invisibly as they fulfill their duty to the future. They create such a soothing mid-afternoon lullaby that I drift off.

I awake to find Gen's fingertips brushing lightly against my cheek. Our eyes lock, for only an instant, but long enough to tell me none of it was a dream. She is so beautiful and so vulnerable that my heart leaps into my throat and my breath catches. I want to scream because I finally realize for the first time there is nothing I can do to protect her from what is going on inside her, much less from the questions that burn inside me.

Still, like our hopes for the Englishman, perhaps until something irrevocable happens, there remains a chance for survival. I brush the place her fingers touched with my own and smile.

"A leaf." She laughs it off and stands so tall above me I can't see the features of her face for the shadow the sky casts. "I was trying not to wake you," she explains it away. "You looked like you were having pleasant dreams."

"I was," I say rising to stand next to her.

Because we succumbed to spring fever, it's past eight o'clock by the time we finish the list of tasks we have laid out for ourselves, and dusk is sneaking into the courtyard from the orchard. It's time to feed the animals and call an end to this wondrous day. As Gen puts away the garden tools, I approach the pigsty carrying buckets of slop made from cooking debris and other odd delicacies pigs seem to enjoy.

But pigs are territorial by nature. As I pour the slop, it becomes clear there's one thing we should have added to our list of things to do. Each of the two dominants has their own trough on different sides of the sty. Neither intends to share. If Paulie's pig is not able to gobble his food at the same time they devour theirs, he will lose rather than gain weight today. He needs a separate trough.

As I walk through the gate, however, the biggest hog decides to make a point about it. Grunting louder and whirling faster than I knew a hog that size could grunt and turn, it charges Paulie's interloper. The little one understands full well its position in this hierarchy by now. Rather than fight, it turns even faster than the aggressor and escapes squealing through the gate I have foolishly left open a crack. More than a little frightened by the violence of the assault myself, I flee behind him and manage to slam the gate shut before the larger pig can burst through after us.

I'm relieved at that. It's not that we might lose either of them, because all of our outside gates are closed. It's just that even one small pig can do a lot of damage running wild through flower and vegetable gardens. I'd hate to have to chase down two and clean up after them.

"Come here, you stupid pig!" I shout as I take off after the little one. "I'm just trying to feed you, you idiot!"

But the race is on. He's quick, and the courtyard's large with a lot of obstacles he can run behind. Out of the corner of my eye, I see that Gen has come out of the kitchen where she's been starting dinner. Wiping her hands on a towel, she's laughing at me. And why not? I'm flying around the courtyard, playing a game of tag with a little pink pig, and the pig is winning.

And knocking things over. And running directly toward the garden we worked so hard on all day. Seeing its intention, Gen drops her towel and spreads out her arms and legs trying to make herself look like a wall. I pull up, because it seems to be working. He slows down in front of her, but only for an instant. The minute she drops her hands to collect him, he recognizes the trap and leaps aside to safety.

The game is on again, and now Gen has joined the fray, flailing her arms and yelling, "Get out of my garden, cochon!"

Now I see what was so funny, and I also see that it'll be easier to catch the thing if we work as a team. As she follows behind him, I anticipate where he is going and try to head him off. The result is Gen and I end up running toward each other, and when the pig cuts toward freedom at the last second, we are left staring into each other's surprised and frustrated faces. Her eyes light up with amusement, and both of us giggle as we start after him, even though this impromptu little athletic event is making a shambles of the order we had worked so hard to create.

Deciding once again to divide in hopes of conquering, this time I take off after him and see an opportunity. Working from different sides, we herd him toward the only corner of the courtyard where there is nothing for him to hide behind.

When the pig realizes he's in a trap, he stops and turns to face us. For a moment, we three form a strange tableau. Two women in calf-length skirts standing in hunched positions six feet in front of a pig that comes up to our knees. All three of us are breathing so heavily our bodies heave. But the pig's eyes don't hold mine. He's surveying his situation, planning something.

A preemptive strike is what this needs. I crouch further down so that my hands can reach him if he tries to go by and move slowly in his direction. Seeing me shrink must confuse him, because he freezes. Now he looks from me to Gen, who hasn't moved. I slide another foot closer. His eyes shift back and forth between us faster now. I can tell he's about to panic. Another step and I'll be close enough.

He bolts, but it's in the direction I anticipated. I lunge at the right time, but my foot slips in mud left over from yesterday's rain. I'd forgotten to include the fact that this is the low part of the courtyard where water stands for days in my calculations. Thank goodness my knee hits the ground, giving me enough purchase to propel myself forward. My hands close around his belly before he can slip past.

But I don't have a good grip, and this pig is strong for his forty pounds. His little split hooves flail at the ground kicking up grass and mud as he wiggles and squirms. I feel him slipping through my hands toward the open expanses of the courtyard as I blink to clear my eyes and spit God knows what from my mouth.

That's when Gen tries to help, but when the pig sees her, he changes direction so suddenly I lose my grip as he propels himself back through my arms toward the wall. Already on my knees, I throw myself after him and manage to grab one back leg. Now flat on my face, I swear he's jerking me in little three-legged pig leaps through the mud.

Just as he's about to break free, he squeals and stops pulling. As I regain my hands and knees, I see that Gen has abandoned all propriety and has joined us in the mud bath we have churned up. For the moment, she's done better than I have. She has both arms around his belly, but he's double jointed or something, because he's finding a way to squeeze out.

Panting and still spitting small things I don't want to identify off the tip of my tongue, I crawl to them on all fours and grab the pig from behind. Wrapping both arms around his chest under his front legs, I sit back, lift him onto my lap, and hold him tight against my body. Now that his feet no longer touch the ground, he loses the will to fight and starts to calm down.

Only then do I get a good look at Gen next to me. That gives me a hint of what I must look like covered in mud, holding a pig in my lap, panting. And laughing. We are both laughing our fool heads off. For some reason sitting here in the corner in the muck with darkness settling in all around us seems like the perfect end to our perfect day.

As soon as we catch our breath we are faced with the reality that we have to do something next. Gen stands easily with that grace she

	(Volume 1)
Cond:	Good
User:	bs_list
Station:	ListingComputer
Date:	2021-05-26 14:08:35 (UTC)
Account:	Bay State Book Company LLC
Orig Loc:	J-6
mSKU:	BSM.54J
Seq#:	15
QuickPick	JSM
unit_id:	2057017
width:	0.83 in
rank:	4,022,842

delist unit# 2057017

XXXXX

always has, but I can't get my balance right with a forty-pound pig in my arms, and I don't want to chance letting go of him with one hand or setting his feet back on the ground.

Seeing me struggle, Gen has the gall to laugh again, this time so hard she has to hold herself up by grabbing her knees. When she's finally through making light of my situation, she bends down. It's about time she takes this pig from my arms.

But she doesn't. Instead, she kneels in front of me and the pig and raises her hand to my cheek, cupping it the way she had the night of the Englishman. Neither of us closes our eyes as she leans over the pig's big pink ears and kisses me full on the mouth, mud and all.

My lips part, but other than that, she does all the work. It's not a hungry kiss, all probing tongue and pressure. It's a sweet, gentle, lingering caress that constricts my chest. Thank God I've got both arms wrapped around the pig. It's the only thing that keeps me from falling over into the mire. When she slowly pulls away, she's smiling and her eyes look more relaxed and calm than I've ever known them.

Standing above me again, Gen claps her hands once and laughs as if nothing unusual has happened. "Come on, let's get you two up." Then she walks around behind me and, lifting me by my armpits, helps me struggle to my feet.

"You." She points at me. "Take him." She points at the pig. "And find a place to put him. I'll go get cleaned up and finish making supper." Then she turns and walks away leaving me alone in the corner.

I watch until Gen stops next to the spigot and starts to take off her blouse. That's my signal to get on about my assigned business. We have always made a point of respecting each other's privacy. The only time I've seen any part of her unclothed body was that first day, that day I've still never told her about. I turn my muddy back to her naked one and head to the barn wondering if the scales have tipped beyond control.

I'm wasting time. After finding the pig a place in the barn for the night and feeding him, I do a few more chores just to let myself cool down. I don't take time to clean up first. After all, I'm mucking a barn.

Eleven

THE QUEEN – *The Limousin, France, April 1942*

When I finally stand next to the door and remove my shoes, it's pitch dark because the moon is just starting to rise. The only light pours out the kitchen window a few feet to my left, but it's enough that I can find the spigot, the soap, a the small towel, and a full length fluffy white robe Gen has set out instead of my house dress.

Before I have time to process the anomaly of the robe, the door opens and she stands silhouetted against the back light, holding a basin from which I see steam rising. I am rooted to the spot, once again not sure whether I'm afraid or excited. But the distinction makes no difference. Either way, every cell in my body is vibrating, and nothing is ever going to be the same again.

She smiles. That's all. Then she unbuttons the top button of my blouse out there in the courtyard under God and the cool night sky. When she sees how rigid I am, she stops and looks at me as if pondering some dilemma. Then, having come up with an answer, she brushes something off my cheek and whispers, "I love you."

Seeing that wide eyes and shallow breathing are my only response, she continues jovially in a voice that would sound normal if it weren't for the words she had just spoken, "And you have earned a warm bath."

Still receiving no answer, she adds, back to a more serious voice, "And I will stop whenever you tell me."

My doom is sealed. Full of both excitement and fear, and both to the extreme, I will never tell her to stop. Eyes and mouth still wide open, still not breathing, I manage the slightest of nods. And I gasp audibly when the backs of her fingers accidently touch the skin over my collar bone as she undoes the second button.

The tension is excruciating. She undresses me in slow motion. We are standing face-to-face when the blouse eventually flaps free and she sees me for the first time. Her body jerks with a little intake of breath before she sighs, "I knew you would be this beautiful."

Then she laughs and adds, "But you really *do* need a good washing. You have mud all the way down to your navel."

I'm afraid to look. And I'm even more afraid she'll trace the mud's path with her fingernails.

The skirt is nothing. It falls to the flagstones when the button is undone, leaving only my cotton underwear. That's when panic starts to set in. I'm not sure I can go through with this.

She stops and looks at me again. When I gulp, she gives me a small smile, places both hands on my shoulders, and turns me around. Once again, the heat of her breath behind my ear sends chills down my spine. This time, I'm sure she can see the little bumps rise in the light from the doorway, because she does use her fingernail, running it lightly once up the middle of my back. My whole body shivers in response. When I lean into her as her cheek brushes my shoulder, she says softly, "You like it when I touch you."

I can't tell if it's a question or a statement, but I do. About to explode, I nod again, and her hands cup my breasts as she pulls me to her and buries her face in my neck. Just for an instant.

I'm no longer breathing, but I'm still nodding as her fingertips slide my underpants down over my hips to my lower legs. Her long fingers wrap gently around first one ankle and then the other as she helps me step out of them, and I stand revealed completely to her as the moon breaks free above the orchard.

Still behind me, she takes her time, starting with my head. Her strong fingers massage my scalp and lather soap into my hair so hard that it squeaks. It feels so good I push back against her hands shamelessly, like a puppy does when you scratch between its ears. I can't see her as she dips a soft rag into the steaming water, scrubs, and rinses my back, but each individual drop etches an indelible trail down my spine.

And I can hear her. At first she's humming. Then she's telling me how strong I look. How healthy my skin is. Not at all what she expected from a woman of such *advanced* age. Okay, so she knows that's a lie, but it's good she's willing to go along with it, at least for now.

Soon, her voice starts to sound almost clinical, as if she were a doctor inspecting a patient. And for some reason, I find that soothing. The distance it creates reduces the tension a little, making it easier for me to endure the agony of expectation. No one has ever done anything like this to me before.

She washes everywhere. My buttocks, she tells me, are the cleanest part of my body, the only part the mud didn't reach. When her foot presses against my ankle coaxing me to slide my feet apart, I resist automatically. But her foot insists, and I give in without a fight. She washes the inside of my thighs all the way up to my torso, and the tension is back in full force.

"Turn around." Her voice is husky as fingertips lightly direct my shoulders, and I slowly spin.

Although intellectually I know it's coming, seeing her standing there, rag in hand, as I complete the turn catches me by surprise. When she looks at me with those golden eyes and says, "You were made for moonlight, you know." I cannot deny that I am totally exposed. At her mercy.

And I also realize that up until now, I've kept my eyes squeezed tight perhaps to hide that fact from myself. I close them again quickly as the rag moves up to my face. I keep them shut as it works its way around my breasts to my belly, touching my nipples with only a few drops of water.

When her lips close around the first one, I jolt as if I've been hit. They linger, her tongue making a circle around the nipple that's now totally erect before leaving. I'm twitching in anticipation by the time she reaches the second one and cannot suppress a groan.

And suddenly the towel is patting me down and the fluffy robe settles over my shoulders. Even then I do not open my eyes. I wait instead for her to take my hand.

When too much time passes in total silence, I dare a glance, only to discover her so close I should have felt her breath, looking down into my eyes as if she's been waiting for the lids to rise. Her head lowers slowly, and believing I am going to be kissed again, I raise my face to meet her. But this time her lips brush only my cheek before she finally intertwines her fingers with mine and leads me to what I used to think of as the parlor.

Gen has transformed what's left of the old seigneur's public room into a sheik's abode, with flickering candles and a small fire casting quivering shadows onto the walls. One of the down comforters that had sheltered us from the cold in the cledier, folded into thirds, covers the floor in front of the fireplace. Vials of different colored liquids line the edge of the low table, next to two glasses of wine, a decanter, a square of yellow cheese, and two chunks of rough bread. Dinner will be light tonight.

Seating herself on the comforter, she leans back against the loveseat and pats the spot next to her. When I comply, she hands me one of the glasses and raises the other in a toast. After returning the gesture, I take a sip, and heat the identical color of the flames that surround us courses through my belly.

Eyes fixed on the fire, she starts talking again in a soft low voice. "You said you love me."

Again, unable to tell if it's a question or not, I nod. I do love her, but all I can think about is that sitting next to me in a light-weight blue shift, her hair falling loose to her shoulders, she is so exquisitely, beautifully, enigmatically French.

As if in slow motion, she turns slowly away from the flames and asks, "You've never done this before, have you?"

The way my eyes stay fixed on hers as I shake my head tells it all. I have not.

Continuing slowly, she gently places one hand on my right cheek and the other on my left. Holding my face still, she leans close and, looking straight in my eye says, "May I make love to you?"

Before I can answer, she tilts her head and her mouth is on mine. Then her tongue slides between my lips and toys with my teeth until I separate them so that my tongue can meet hers. Their tips touch, and she works a little circle around mine before she withdraws. Again the kiss is not aggressive. It's almost indolent, but tender, and I don't want it to stop.

But she pulls away. Continuing to hold my face, she tilts her head and raises her eyebrows, letting me know she wants my answer now.

"I'm afraid." My voice is deeper and softer than I remember.

"I'll never hurt you." Her expression says she means it.

"N… not of you." The thought of baring my soul makes me stutter. "I don't know how. I mean, I'm afraid I won't be … what you want."

"What I want?" Our noses are almost touching and her expression is so soft and loving I could fall into it. But then she releases my face and leans close to my ear.

Her hair tickles my cheek as she tells me in a low voice that's little more than a whisper. "What I *want* is to explore you. All of you. I want the tips of these fingers to touch every inch of your skin." As she says this, those fingers caress the back of the ear she's talking into before sliding down my arm to the back of my hand.

"What I *want*." The tip of her tongue works itself in and out of my ear, making me shiver. "Is to make you crave *my* touch so much that nothing else exists in that moment but *my* love."

Her hair pulls away, and her lips come back to where I can see them, but only for an instant. I have to close my eyes because she's kissing my eyelids, pausing after the first kiss to say in an even softer voice, "What I want is *one* chance to make you love me the way that I love you."

The reply that slips out of my mouth is the truest thing I've said to her since I knocked on her door. "I'll try."

That elicits a long, pure sigh, and I know it's not the right response. How can I not hurt this woman?

But still she doesn't pull away. Instead, she kisses me softly again and says, "Thank you."

That part of our bargain struck, Gen sighs and lays her head on my shoulder. We watch little tongues of flame lick at the logs as we sip our wine. But there's more I feel a need to know.

"What do you want me to do?"

"Nothing."

"Nothing?"

"Well," she draws the word out. "Not exactly nothing."

I think she's teasing me.

She grins. "I know this will be hard for you, my strong, always-has-to-be-in-control little one, but I want you to do only what I tell you to do."

She's given me a way through. I can abdicate all responsibility by making that one simple promise even though I'm not sure I can keep it. It's all on her now. Relief floods through me as I nod again.

Then without saying a word, her hand reaches over and unties the belt of my robe. I don't even realize how much I want her fingers to slip inside and brush across my nipple until I'm disappointed when they move away. Instead she collects our glasses and turns to place them on the table before pushing me away from the loveseat and helping me out of the robe. Once again I'm exposed. This time I actually feel the fingers of firelight that play across my skin, flickering and teasing.

After I am stretched on my stomach with my face turned toward the fire, I hear her stand and walk across the room. A small click precedes the music. Recognizing that she has chosen *The Rite of Spring,* I am amazed at its appropriateness. During our evenings in the parlor, I've come to know this record well. Stravinsky himself is conducting, and it builds to a conclusion that is the raw essence of conflict, need, and passion.

Footsteps cross the floor again, and the comforter shifts as she kneels beside me. Glass clinks against glass. By the time she lifts my hair off the back of my neck, I am so prepared for contact that I behave once again like a puppy. I initiate it by lifting my head to meet her hand.

"Don't be greedy, my love," are the first of many words she speaks. The next are, "Remember. You promised to do what I want you to do." The statement does not invite an answer. "And what I want is for you to lie there as still as you can. Don't say a word. Don't think. Just be here and feel ... my touch." Her voice drops down into her chest as she says the last words.

I startle when the first drop of warm oil lands on my back. Then her amazing hands begin working their magic. It shouldn't be sexual at all, but the way her fingers insinuate their way into the tissues of my neck and shoulders is so personal I must fight off the urge to leap up and run. And when I don't, those hands start moving down my spine. Occasionally they stop, and the heels of her palms press the fullness of her weight into my body as she leans over me, spreading my muscles and working the oil deep into my pores.

Done with my back, she moves to my left shoulder and squeezes and pulls her way down my arm. When I lift it to help her, she shushes me, telling me to relax and let her carry the weight. That's hard. If I can't raise my arms, how can I defend myself?

It's a strangely intimate sensation when her thumb digs into my palm as those fingers work the bones on the other side. Then, without letting go, she stretches my arm as far as she can and gives each individual finger its own attention. Because it's my hand, I get the full benefit of each firm stroke. I've had a few small massages in my life, but no one has ever done this before. It's so sensual, heat floods my face.

Finishing with my arms, Gen leaves them stretched their full length above my head and won't let me drop them back down to my side. As a result, I am more exposed than ever when her hand touches the base of my spine. But I'm getting better at following her orders. I don't squirm, which shouldn't come as a shock, because I'm no longer thinking. All that exists or matters is her weight on my buttocks, grinding my hips and pubic area through the comforter all the way to the hardness of the floor.

Before long my legs are as extended as my arms. She releases the little toe on my left foot and moves back to my upper body. Hearing the words, "Roll over," I'm almost so lost and dazed I don't know if I can accomplish what's expected of me without dropping my arms. But I manage with her help.

"Good," she laughs and brushes my parted lips with a quick kiss. After holding my glance for a moment, she clarifies our pact. "You may leave now if you choose," she continues. "And if you stay, you still can stop me at any time. But if you stay..."

The pause is painful. What is the caveat?

She wraps the fingers of my right hand, thumb down, around one leg of the Victorian chair I seldom sit in, then orders, "No matter what happens, what you want to do, you will not let go," and caresses the outsides of the fingers with which I now clench the other leg.

It's the one thing I think she doesn't have to worry about. My fingers hold my hands to that chair as firmly as chains.

Then she's above me, one hand on either side of my bare torso so that our faces are parallel, and she says, "Close your eyes."

That wasn't necessary. They've been shut for a lifetime.

I nod my head, following the rule, and it begins. Slowly at first, with her fingers rubbing my temples, starting their downward trek.

It's not like making love with a man driven by his own engorged need to finish the task. It's leisurely. Small caresses that only someone focused entirely on your pleasure would take the time to lavish on you. Every now and then her hair brushes my skin. It's everywhere when I feel lips and the flick of a warm tongue on my neck. I'm filling with electricity again and twitch at the silken touch of those thick, dark strands.

She's still working oil into my skin, and she switches to a slightly warmer vial before she lifts my left breast. I do what I've been told. I don't resist.

Still, I almost scream when her palm stops at the tip of my left nipple and she slowly closes her fingers together pulling the breast up and away from my body so that she can rub oil underneath. She's holding my breast stretched full length by the nipple. I can't tell if this is pain or pleasure. It's too intense to distinguish. When she cups the breast in both hands, still stretching it tight, I feel her lips close lightly on that same nipple. She takes it slowly into her mouth and sucks.

I lose track of myself. Can no longer deal in details. Just tongue and lips and hands, swinging wildly from soft to firm and back again, sensations I have never known flooding down through my body. My hands hold onto the chair legs for dear life.

She tortures me like this for countless hours until the heel of one of her hands slides down my stomach and comes to rest on my pubic hair. It is now so close to the center of my agony that I dare to gasp, only it's not a decision, it's a primal response. When she simultaneously rolls my nipple between her fingers and pushes down on my pubic bone, my buttocks tighten involuntarily, thrusting my body up to meet her weight.

It's the first movement I've made without permission that she doesn't chastise me for. And it wouldn't have mattered, because even if she had I couldn't have stopped myself from rising to meet her again with more force than before.

"Tisk, tisk, tisk. So greedy."

I don't care that she's laughing at me. She's taken me so far I can't turn back. I don't want to. And then, her lips find my other nipple and she draws it into her mouth as she pushes, and I'm moaning out loud, pleading wordlessly for release.

Suddenly she's not there. Just like that. Nothing. I'm alone on the comforter panting, about to explode, clenching the chair legs as if they were hand grenades someone had pulled the pins out of. If I let them go I will die. All I can hear is the crackle of the fire and my own breathing as I flail my head about listening desperately for a hint of where she's gone.

I don't even realize my mouth is open until her lips find it and her tongue slips inside. She's taken a sip of wine. For a moment, I'm still, startled at the taste and wetness and hot smoothness of her. Her lips and tongue, the only parts of her she deigns to let me have, I grab on to them with all my might, sucking, begging, trying to pull her down onto me, to feel the weight of her body.

Instead, her mouth abandons mine for my belly, and I stiffen. Her weight shifts next to me, and her hand slips down my thighs. I'm so ready for her that they part and quiver to let her bare knee glide between them, and I think I hear the word, "Soon."

Her open mouth slides further down, coming to rest on the same spot she has been pushing hard against, blowing hot air through my pubic hair, letting me feel the fire that burns inside her too. I shudder.

Then, her hand is there again, and her mouth is devouring my breast, sucking and biting. Without warning, stretching my nipple to the fullest, she throws her thigh and all of her weight onto her hand and this time her fingers slip between my legs and brush back and forth, caressing my lower lips. I stifle a cry at the suddenness of it and rise to meet her. Mercifully she doesn't pull away. We suck and thrust in tandem until I am on the brink.

And she stops again. This time I do scream and lie there mouth open, clutching the chair legs, my chest heaving until I feel her nipples brushing lightly over mine through the cool silk of her chemise, her hair on my face again, and her hot breath on my neck.

"Do you want me?" she asks in my ear.

I'm almost too tense and weak at the same time to beg, but she gets the message and starts again, only not with the near violence of the last few moments. Softly and gently, she kisses the bridge of my nose and then my neck and starts building me back up slowly, kneading my breasts, licking my nipples, and pushing my hips lightly into the comforter with the palm of her hand. All the while her fingers tease that spot between my legs.

Now the music's louder. We're near the end of *The Rite of Spring*, beyond the circle of maidens, summoning the ancients. I vibrate like dark dissonant chords over the volcano. I am the chosen one dancing to my death ... engorged, needy ... demanding ... building to my crescendo.

And even she cannot take it anymore. She groans, and one small whimper escapes my throat as I arch my whole body up to meet hers and those luscious long fingers spread the tight folds between my legs to violate the final rule.

The force of my eruption screeches the chair across the floor. I buck and twist, and she matches me thrust for thrust, moan for moan, never letting go. We're bound so tightly by legs and mouth and fingers that we'll never come apart again, and only my grip on the chair keeps us from being flung across the universe.

Twelve

JOE – *Montreal, Canada, the First Day, 1992*

"Whatcha got there, cowboy?"

Mortified, Joe opened his eyes to discover he had a massive hard on. In the middle of the afternoon in the recreation room of a Canadian old folks' home. Plus, sometime during Nanette's story, he had started visualizing the sensual, sexy little Resistance fighter from the photo in the leading role.

That avoided the embarrassment of being aroused by his grandmother's escapades, but humiliated him a different way. That sensual, sexy girl was sitting across the table disguised as a bent and broken old crone, who happened to be staring at him and looking very amused by what she saw.

Nanette leaned back in her chair with a smirk on her face and tendrils of smoke curling over her head. She didn't let up.

"Need me to call one of the *girls* from upstairs to take care of that for you? You'd be surprised how horny old bitches can get." A licentious grin spread across the shadows of her face. "Twenty-four seven some of them would take it if they could get it. Especially from a young hard one like you. You could probably even deduct it off your income taxes as a charitable contribution." She chuckled to herself, still holding his eye, "And some of them still know a few *tricks* ... if you know what I mean."

Shit. Now she was ridiculing him about it.

"Men." Nanette gave a derisive little chortle that twitched her shoulders and let him off the hook by chastising his gender rather than him personally. "You are so easy. Never could decide whether I liked fucking you or killing you the best."

The steely come hither dare from the photograph glared out at Joe through the eyes in that old face. The cigarette in her hand, the red dye in her hair, and the words she had just thrust at him all said one thing: "I am Nanette. I break *all* the rules. Fifty years ago, during the war, I was a spy for the British government and helped save the world. Maybe nobody today remembers that I even existed, but I'm still here. Deal with it."

Catching Joe staring at her again, this time with his mouth open, Nanette leaned toward him so that he could see her smile and shrugged. "Hey, it was war. You get to do a lot of things you would not ordinarily get to do in a war. That's the good part."

The good part? War has a good part? He decided to ignore her comments. "Come on, you made that up. All those details at least."

"I guess you *could* say I embellished the best parts … just a little," she admitted, as she held her thumb and forefinger up so close together they almost touched and grinned. Tossing her head stiffly, she chortled, "But it did make the story more … *uplifting*, don't you think?"

Then surveying the empty room slowly she added, "It's boring as hell around here. A little spice every now and then livens things up." She dragged out the word spice suggestively. "Gets the juices flowing, if you know what I mean."

Enough! Did the woman never stop? Joe didn't want to even think about juices. He was just happy his blood had started flowing back to his head again. He kept forgetting that this was a game, and that this old lady was more experienced at it than he was. Somewhat offended, he tried to regain a bit of ground.

"Okay, so you're telling me my grandmother liked other women?" Today was the first Joe had heard of that. And he still didn't understand why Nanette was feeding him this crap. "What's the news in that? Lots of women like other women. And the question still remains. Even if she did, how can that possibly be something I *need* to know?"

"Men." She shook her head in mock exasperation, clearly including him in that category this time. "Young men in particular. So easily seduced by the surface of things. And always in such a hurry to get to the end." She paused to make him wait. "When so much of the joy is in the anticipation … the foreplay, you might say."

At that, her tongue slipped out and caressed her upper lip suggestively, obviously trying to scandalize him with the air of blatant sexuality exuding from that frail old body. At a loss for words, Joe forced himself to watch, calling her bluff, as she followed this display by taking a long, sensuous drag on her cigarette and stretching her chin to the ceiling to release an equally slow column of smoke.

"Tell me, Joseph … do you want to *know* what happened or *understand* what happened?" It was a challenge rather than a question.

But it also made a point that brought Joe up short. He didn't know who his grandfather was because his grandmother had erased the man from their lives, leaving nothing but a gaping dark hole. But why had she done that and kept so many other secrets? That was still an even bigger dark pit of questions.

Chastened, he muttered, "Understand."

"Ahhh. Good, then." The old woman showed her teeth, good naturedly this time, rubbed her hands together under her chin, and leaned forward. "Because it's complicated."

"How much more complicated can it be?" Joe was starting to get exasperated.

She silenced him by tilting her head and raising her eyebrows. "How complicated can anything be?" She shrugged, making it clear that wasn't really a question, then handed her glass to him and said, "Now, pour us another round."

He did, then let out a breath, sat back and took a sip of his wine. How complicated can things be? Images flashed through his mind. His mother, Carrie, Maya, and Momma Willie, now becoming more the Queen to him than his grandmother. They mingled with the shadow memories of his father who had vanished on patrol in Vietnam when Joe was five and the sound of his mother crying in the night, torn between hoping the man she loved was alive in a prisoner-of-war camp and praying for his sake that his suffering had ended long ago.

And then there was his great-grandmother's voice, the way she would recite the last telegram her husband had sent all those years ago from memory. "Start packing." She always smiled when she began with those words. "I'm coming to get you and Willie." He had signed it, "Love." Sixty years later, in her nineties, the woman had still been waiting.

All the questions that had always lingered, never answered, dipped and danced in Joe's mind, rearranging themselves like leaves being played with by the wind. He couldn't make heads or tails of his life anymore. Sighing, he conceded, "Things can get pretty complicated."

Then he remembered who he was dealing with, and his guard was up again. "So, this next part you're getting ready to tell me, is it all going to be true? Or are you going to make up prurient details as you go along like you did the last time?"

The way she smiled at that told him she appreciated the defense he was mounting.

"Oh, everything I am telling you is *true*, mon cher. You can count on that. But then … truth is never so much in the details as in the story, is it?"

Those enigmatic words sounded wistful, even though the licentious grin came back. "But I will be honest with you, Joseph. Given *who* I am and *where* I am..." The hand holding her cigarette swept out around her. "I do not get to spend time with too many handsome young men anymore. And these are secrets I have kept for half a century." She shrugged, "So please. Indulge an old woman a few small pleasures. I do so enjoy my little fantasies."

Joe saw now that the old spy's flirting game was all harmless fun. Why not play along? He nodded his acquiescence, then flashing a half-sheepish-half-salacious grin of his own, joined the play in earnest. "Okay. Only this time, I'll try to listen with my head rather than my dick."

"Oh, no, Joseph," the old lady chortled. "That's your problem in the first place. Your head keeps interfering." She tapped her temple with two crooked fingers and switched to a dramatic low voice. "But your head will never take you where you need to go. You have to live it … to feel it … *here*." Her half-closed fist pressed into the hollow just below her small breasts. "To understand."

Then shrugging and winking at him, "Plus, you're a man. Don't try to fool yourself. You can't do anything without your dick getting in the way."

With that most recent insult, she picked up where she had left off, taking him back to the manor house that spring night in 1942.

Joe did want to understand. This time he'd try not to get caught up in the details. And this time he wouldn't pretend the heroine was that sultry little curly-haired girl in the photograph from so long ago. He'd try to feel what all this meant to the forty-one-year-old version of the grandmother he'd never heard of before that day.

Hell. What else did he have to lose?

THE QUEEN – *The Limousin, France, April 1942*

When my body finally stops shaking, panting, and sweating, Gen's leg between mine and her arm across my stomach, so limp that I finally bear the entire wondrous weight of her, she nuzzles my ear emitting soft little sounds that vibrate in her chest before they're audible. I'm still clutching the chair for dear life. It's the only thing left in my world that feels normal.

I finally catch my breath. I've never felt so physically spent and satiated, but I realize I'm crying. Why? Because I love her so much? Because she loves me? Because she's made me feel things I've never felt before. I don't know what any of this means, and I'm afraid.

Then she rolls off and stretches out beside me, no longer touching, just looking, the air cooling us by evaporating our mingled sweat. After a moment, she uncurls my fingers one-by-one from around the chair legs and settles in next to me again.

Without my anchors, I lose my way. Turning my back to her, I curl up into a ball on my side. Now my tears disappear into the comforter.

The stroke of her hand as she glides it over my shoulder is no longer electric. It's silk like her chemise. I feel her hair and cheek, cool now rather than hot, against my back for a moment before she thinks better of it and settles in next to me again with a sigh, no longer making contact.

Instead, she tells me her story. It is the tale of a beautiful, young, intelligent girl from a privileged family who knew from an early age she was different, different in many ways, but in one particular way that ended up offending everyone who was important in her life, just as she had always feared it would.

"My first lover's name was Monique," she says matter-of-factly. "Monique was three years ahead of me in boarding school. I was new, only fourteen. Later, you know, I figured out she knew exactly what she was doing. She recognized how *unlike* the other girls I was and stole a taste of the forbidden fruit. For me, though, her attentions were proof that I wasn't alone in the hell that seemed to be my life. Proof that someone could love me."

As she tells me this, sobs stop wracking my body. I settle into a slow, silent mourning, for whom or what I do not know.

Of course, Monique tired of her almost immediately. Devastated, Gen tried too hard to hold on, and Monique, afraid that her own secrets would be revealed, did what she thought she needed to do to save herself. She filed a complaint with the school mistress that Gen had attempted to seduce her.

"The irony of that almost killed me," Gen continues. "You see I might never have been sure myself if she had not seduced *me*." After a pause she goes on. "Of course, the school expelled me and explained why to my parents in no uncertain terms. My family didn't care what my side of the story was, because even if I was telling the truth, their worst fears were still confirmed. I *was* a deviant. Two schools and three doctors later, I stopped trying and so did they."

It's amazing how calmly she tells me this.

Gen continues, "We all knew then that I could never be the daughter they wanted, and they could not abide me being myself. My father and twin brother, Renee, shunned me, and my mother followed their orders. Only my sister had the courage to treat me as human behind their backs, and when they discovered she was consoling me, they took their anger with me out on her."

She says nothing more for a few heartbeats then emits a bitter ironic laugh. "And then, you could say, I got lucky. It was fifteen years ago. My father's political career started taking off, and having a deviant daughter on public display just would not do."

There's anger in her voice now, and it seems to make this easier. Perhaps she needs to say it as much as I need to hear it, need to know about her.

"What my father needed," she explains, "was a politically acceptable way to get me out of his life and out of the public eye. By then, of course, I knew I wanted to be a doctor. So we forged a compromise. He sent me to Switzerland for medical school in exchange for my promise to stay as far away from him as possible and to be discrete. I've kept my part of the bargain scrupulously."

An ironic snort punctuates this statement, and then she continues, "Not that it's been that difficult. I hate his politics, and since Monique, it's been hard to find someone I am attracted to and can trust."

And how can she trust me, turning my back to her because of my confusion and fear? Without facing her yet, I sit up, pull on my robe, and tie it in front. Then I slide my feet around until we're parallel again and lean back against my new favorite chair.

Now, I'm dominant, because she's stretched out, one forearm across her eyes, her raised elbow exposing the shape of her perfect breast through filmy blue silk. My breath catches. She's so beautiful and so vulnerable.

"Do you still love her?" I ask.

"Who? Monique?" A pause. "No. I don't think I ever loved her. But then it's so easy to get confused about that the first time…"

She stops abruptly and I suspect it's because she's realized what she was saying. How it applies to me.

"How many have you found?" It's the only thing I can think of to say. "Women you were attracted to, I mean, who you could trust."

"A few who attracted me."

I'm astounded she's being this honest and want to ask what it was about them.

"None I could really trust." Her head shakes under her forearm. "Every now and then, when I'm in Tulle, one of the girls in the brothel stays with me to get away from the men. But she's not..."

I wonder why she's stopped herself until she explains what she was trying to say, "Sometimes, you know, you just need to feel the touch of another human being to prove to yourself you're still alive."

"Why don't you move to a bigger town? Wouldn't it be easier to find more..." I can't finish the sentence. I can't find a word to use.

"It might be." She ignores my slight, pausing as if thinking it through in detail. "But, this is my home, and … and I don't want to let *what* I am define *who* I am."

That I have to think about. Ultimately I decide it's the purest sentence I've ever heard a person utter, and I ache with love. She's even more exquisite inside than out.

I run my fingers across her forehead, smooth back her hair to let her know I'm here. It's the first time I'm the one doing the touching. "So Monique … did she show you the way you showed me?"

It's a long time before Gen answers. "No." Then after a much shorter pause, a soft laugh that's both bitter and sweet, "It came more naturally to me than it does to you."

There it is. My conflict. Gen finally knows something true about me, and I wish it was a lie.

Wanting desperately to convince both of us she's read me incorrectly, I grab the wrist that's covering her eyes and pull her to sit in front of me, but facing away. When she complies, I stretch my legs around her, hook them over her thighs, and pull her hard against my body. With me wrapped around her, pinning her arms to her sides with mine, she's immobilized. Lifting her hair by rubbing my nose and chin against it, I bury my face in the nape of her neck and hold her like that until our breathing becomes synchronized and she relaxes.

Then I release her arms and massage her scalp the way she massaged mine. She groans and leans into my fingers exactly like I did, and we both laugh. And when she takes my hand and slides it inside her chemise so that my palm cups her breast, we both gasp. She is so smooth. Smaller than I am, but solid. There's weight there, and I've never felt anything so soft and warm. Out of curiosity, I slide my thumb down over her nipple. It's like velvet. Then it stiffens, grows, in response to my touch. Intrigued, I roll it between my thumb and forefinger.

Gen lets out a little sighing breath and melts back into me. From recent experience I recognize what it means when her buttocks tense against my thighs. It's me. I can flood her with need and pleasure. I start to tease the upright proof of my power.

And I panic. This is nothing I've ever dreamed I'd be doing. I have a child at home, for God's sake. And a family. And maybe this is just one more lie. Maybe I'm like the show girls back in New York Jo told me about. They lived a hard life dominated by hard men, and sometimes they turned to each other for comfort. But for most of them, it didn't mean anything. They used each other to feel loved for the moment and turned back to the men the next night. My hand jerks away as if it's been scalded and seeks the relative safety of her shoulder, where it stays.

After some time, I ask, "So, what are we going to do?" But I already know that neither of us has that answer.

As expected, Gen doesn't reply. So I do the only thing I know to do. I'll never be the lover she deserves, but I do the best I can. Holding her close until the real world comes flooding back into the parlor with the dawn, I promise myself over and over that I will keep her warm and safe forever, even though I know I'm lying to myself this time. Nothing in this world is forever.

The cold light of day is called cold for a reason. It reveals all the sharp edges and dark corners without mercy. There's no place for the unanswered questions to hide.

I wake up wondering where I am and what I'm doing here. Shame? Guilt? For what we'd done? For what I couldn't do?

As soon as our bodies separate, the distance between us starts to grow at an alarming rate. By the time we make breakfast, it's a shock once again when her hand accidently brushes mine. We start building walls to protect ourselves.

Eventually, though, we have to look each other in the eye and say something, something about *us*. I can't. So I talk about me.

"I fell in love when I was very young."

She sighs, and we both sip her sister's coffee savoring the illicit fruits of collaboration.

"With a boy."

She rocks slightly back and forth in her seat. That's obviously not much of a revelation.

"He was tall. Fair haired. The most beautiful blue eyes that let you see down into his soul. And he was also smart and funny." I turn and find myself grinning, sharing this happy memory with her. "Wouldn't give me an inch if I begged for it. You'd have liked him."

And Gen would have liked him. He'd have kept her on her toes, too, with that sharp way of seeing the world he had. Just the thought of those two sparring makes me smile until I remember she'd think they were competing. And maybe they would be. I hope my telling her this isn't hurting her too much. She has to understand.

"But I couldn't have him."

Gen's waiting for me to go on, but looking down at her coffee. I reach over and gently pull her chin toward me till we are face-to-face. That's when the dam breaks and the words begin to flow.

"I thought that was it. I'd never love again. That you only get one chance because there's space for only so much love in your heart, and if one person fills it up, there's no way to get them out again. So you're doomed. There'll never be room for anyone else."

Tears well in Gen's eyes. That's all wrong. This is the happy part. At least I think it is. Laying my hand over hers, I try to make her see it.

"But now I know that's not true. Now I have you in here, too." I pat my heart twice with my open hand to make sure she knows that's where she is. "And it makes me so happy I almost can't stand it."

That this is true is such a relief. "You see," I continue. "I blamed him for keeping me alone all these years. I was angry that the tiny part of him I was allowed to have barred the way for anyone else. But I was wrong. The door could have opened at any time. It's just that until now, no one else ever had the key. They weren't the right one."

Gen looks down at her coffee again, but this time I can tell she's thinking because her eyebrows are pinched together and she's biting her lip. Without raising her head, she asks a valid question in a small voice, "But how can I be the right one?"

I don't want to hear the pain in those words.

"How can you love me and..."

Her words trail off, but I know she's asking the question I still can't answer. How can I be so drawn to her, crave her warmth and tenderness so desperately, and not desire to touch her the way she touches me?

"I don't know." It's a plea rather than an explanation. But how can I expect her to understand when I don't understand myself?

I lift her hand and press it against my heart and give her the only answer I have, "All I know is that this is where you are."

She doesn't say anything.

"I need time … to sort the rest of it out."

Silence separates us. I stare at her, and she stares at her coffee.

"Okay, then." She sighs and turns to me, her face the picture of French resignation. "C'est ce que c'est." As the words begin their journey across the galaxy, she raises my hand to her lips, kisses the back of it, and sets it back on the table.

She's right. It is what it is. That's all it can ever be.

Gen is settling for the reality that I may never be who she wants me to be. That is so much less than I wish for her, but it hurts less than all the other options. There's nothing more to say, and our new life begins.

Thirteen

JOE – *Montreal, Canada, the First Day, 1992*

Nanette stopped there and looked at Joe. "Complicated?" she asks.

"So, the Queen wasn't a lesbian after all?"

Nanette's flame-red hair bobbed up and down as she chuckled and shrugged. "I never asked." After thinking a moment, she added seriously, "Are lesbians women who love other women?" She raised her eyebrows and shrugged even larger. "But then … there are so many kinds of love."

Lips pursed, one eye closed, she started listing them, keeping score on her fingers. "Spiritual love. Intellectual love. Aesthetic..."

Looking up as if to assure herself that Joe was following, she continued, "There are even at least two forms of physical love, a tender need to express affection and … and raw sexual desire." She tossed him a provocative glance. "You know, that pounding need that demands release."

He thought of Carrie. Oh, he understood pounding need. But he didn't want to let Nanette have her way too easily with him. "And you're an expert in all this because…"

"I have a lot of time to *think* about it." Her tone exuded bitterness, as if she had been deprived of some entitlement, rather than self pity.

Nanette's reaction to his sparring surprised Joe so much, the word, "Oh," almost slipped out of his mouth. He tried to strike a light tone that would deflect the tension his question had provoked. "Well, you do have a lot more experience in these kinds of things than I do." He grinned and shrugged, trying to indicate submission.

Pensive now, she answered, "I believe I do."

Joe couldn't keep up with her emotional shifts. He let her go.

After staring off into the distance for a beat, the old woman continued, only now as if speaking to herself. "It was a time of cold and violence."

Returning her focus to Joe, she continued, "Everything is bigger, brighter, bolder in times like that. You get wound so tight."

Before Joe could comment, Nanette tilted her head, saying, "Later she told me she'd been wrong."

"The Queen?"

"Yes, the Queen. She told me one thing could last forever." Anticipating his question, she continued, "Love. And her only regret was that either one of them had wasted a single moment doubting it. That is one truth of this story."

In the silence following that pronouncement, Nanette and Joe considered each other across the table, pondering the Queen's words. Both sipped their wine, and then the old woman squeezed her lips together again and raised her eyebrows.

It was such a wry French gesture, Joe almost laughed out loud. Her mood had switched again. She was up to something.

"Their next eight months were *very* interesting. Would you like to hear the details?" she asked, adding coyly, "There's another sexy part…"

Before Joe could respond, the door to the Rec Room burst open and the attendant from the front desk came bustling in, pointing at her watch. "So you are still here, mademoiselle. I thought this was where I would find you." She winked at Joe. "I'm sorry to interrupt, but dinner is being served in five minutes."

Joe looked down at his watch. It was already after five. He'd lost all sense of time.

Nanette raised her eyebrows at him, shrugged, and started to swivel her chair away from the table.

"Wait. You haven't told me—"

Nanette gestured for the attendant to leave. "You can go on, Marie. I will join the others shortly."

"You're not going to quit now?" Joe was adamant.

"Schedules must be kept, Joseph. Institutions such as this…" She made a circle with her hand to indicate the building they were sitting in. "They live and *die* on schedule here." That bitterness had returned.

"But you can't just stop in the middle."

"I can't?" She tilted her head at him and pursed her lips. "Things end in the middle all the time."

Joe wasn't about to let her take him off on another of her philosophical side tracks. He made a point of looking at his watch again. "Well, I've got a schedule, too, you know. And I've got to be out of here in two hours to catch the last plane home."

She dropped both hands to her lap and sighed, the picture of patience. "Look, Joseph. I am a sick old woman. My dinner is getting cold. But the real question is what is on your schedule that you are in such a hurry to get home to?"

She may as well have kicked him in the stomach. There was nothing on his schedule. Not that night and not the next day. The last thing Maya had told him was that she and Carrie would be unavailable. Someone had given them tickets for a special tour of the aquarium or some other place he should be the one showing to Carrie.

So, what *was* his hurry? He studied the little old woman sitting across from him more closely. Even though she was still putting up a good front, she did look more than a little frayed around the edges. She needed a break. He could tell it from her eyes.

In that moment, Joe was startled to realize that he no longer saw Nanette as a strange, inappropriate, shriveled-up old woman with her hair dyed bright red in the pretense that time had not passed her by after all. She was actually a very interesting and kind of cute little French lady. His frustration dissipated, its weight lifting from his shoulders. What was one more day? He kept a straight face and answered her as nonchalantly as he could, "There's nothing on my schedule. Are you free tomorrow?"

She pounced, alert and energized again. "One o'clock?"

"One o'clock." Nanette's irrepressible grin made Joe smile. The old spy had played him again. She'd had it all planned, how she'd drag the story out and keep him there. It was a shame she didn't get more visitors. Still, he needed to exercise a little more control. "But, I do have to get back to Baltimore after that."

"Don't worry, mon petit chou."

Her tone was so overly reassuring it put Joe on alert.

"I'll be gentler tomorrow." Her breathless delivery left nothing to innuendo. "And…" She laughed. "In deference to the fact that you are such a *very* young man, I'll speed things up a little."

He shook his head as he started to rise, but couldn't help grinning back, joining in her high spirits. And she was feisty, too. He wished he'd known her when she was young.

"But wait!" Her fingers closed on air as if she were trying to grasp him to keep him from leaving. "There's one more thing I have to tell you."

He stopped, but she paused, and when she finally started to speak, her voice caught, as if what she was about to say had some deep personal meaning, "There is another truth in this story."

Another long pause.

"Love, Joseph. Hold it tight when you find it. You may never get another chance."

The emotion with which this crazy little Canadian woman said those words reverberated across the table. Who had she let slip through her fingers? And, hold it tight when you find it? But how are you ever sure what you've found?

In danger of becoming totally lost in that internal conundrum, Joe was relieved when the mercurial Miss Jeandren pulled him back to the present by leaning forward in her chair and whispering, "But of course, as in all good quests, you must earn the rest of the story by completing another challenge."

Joe waited. What now?

"Tomorrow you must smuggle in some contraband."

"Contraband?"

She looked around as if to make sure no one else in the empty room was listening, leaned forward, and whispered, "Canadian whisky. It's hard to get the good stuff in here." She pulled back a little, her eyes widening. "If you liked the wine…"

Infected by her enthusiasm for the game, Joe stretched low across the table, his palms on its flat surface holding his weight. With their noses almost touching, he checked again for eavesdroppers then asked in a low voice, "Any particular brand?"

"No." Her sharp eyes darted from side to side, triple-checking the security of their surroundings. "Just bring the best you can get."

"Canadian whisky it is then," Joe whispered back, then concluded the bargain by offering her his hand.

She didn't let it go right away. Holding him there bent over the table, she added, "And do get a good night's rest, my dear. From what I saw earlier today..."

The old bawd tilted her head, looked at his crotch, and actually sniggered. "You probably ought to go out and get laid. But, if you can't, drink three glasses of that exceptional Malbec with dinner. It will help you sleep."

The gleam in her eye was shameless.

Fourteen

JOE – *Montreal, Canada, the Second Day, 1992*

When Joe walked back into the Rec Room the next afternoon, Nanette was already sitting in her chair by the window waiting for him, two whisky glasses on the table, cigarette smoke hovering like clouds around her. This time she wore a blue housedress that complemented her hair.

"Ah, you're right on time, Cheri," she gestured at the small gold watch that dangled from her bony wrist. When she noticed the brown paper bag he carried, she patted the table in front of her and said, "I can't wait to see what you've brought me."

Enjoying the moment immensely, Joe stood tall and straight before her and reached into the bag like a magician preparing to pull a rabbit out of a hat. "Ta dah!" He sang in a rich baritone as he lifted a purple velvet sack with gold trim in the air. Holding it high, he took a bow and then placed it in the spot she had patted.

Nanette's tiny bent hands snatched it up like a greedy child on Christmas. Then becoming a perfect child, she rubbed her cheek against the velvet, saying, "Oooo ... my favorite."

Becoming a mature adult again, she placed the bottle upright on the table almost reverently and loosened the drawstring that held the sack closed just enough that it could slip over the bottle's ornate rounded glass shoulders one at a time and fall to the table in slow motion.

Joe shook his head in amazement. That woman could make something as simple as opening a bottle of booze a sensual experience.

Then, a kid again, Nanette picked the bottle up, planted a big sloppy kiss on the Crown Royal logo before trying to untwist the gold cap. Joe leaned over and did it for her. Eyes closed, she held the bottle up to her nose, breathed in the first fumes that escaped, and threw her head back, sighing to the heavens.

"You pour," she said sliding the bottle across the table to Joe. "I'll have a double."

"Ice?" Joe asked, "Do you want me to go find ice?"

"Neat," was her answer. "I don't want anything to dilute the experience."

He slid the glass across the table. She raised it to him with a wink. As he nodded in return, she inhaled the aroma again, practically rubbing her nose on the rim of the glass, and took one small sip of the honey colored liquid. Before swallowing, she closed her eyes and savored the whiskey, worked it around her mouth, her tongue even passing between her teeth and upper lip. "Ahhh," she breathed almost salaciously. "That is *so* good."

Joe took his own small sip as he watched this production. It was only one in the afternoon and, like his grandmother apparently, he wasn't much of a drinker. Even that small amount of whisky warmed his chest from the inside, but after the first shock of undiluted intensity wore off, it actually tasted good.

He grinned. Six months ago he would have laughed at the suggestion he'd ever be drinking Canadian whisky in Montreal at one o'clock on a Saturday afternoon, much less doing it with a little old woman who used to be a spy and loved telling erotic stories.

"It is what it is," he mused, catching Nanette's eye in a silent toast. He took another small sip.

Smiling as if she understood what he had been thinking, Nanette took control again. "Now that we are fortified, Joseph, I shall try to behave myself."

Although he didn't believe a word of it, Joe grinned at the woman and settled back in his seat. Then, possibly because of the whisky, he said what he'd been thinking about the night before.

"I'd appreciate that, because, to be honest, all this she-did-this-to-her and she-did-that-to-her detail is a little much for me. After all, it's my grandmother we're talking about."

"You are wrong, Joseph." The steely stare of the young Resistance fighter in yesterday's photograph flared out at Joe across the table. "This story is not about *your* grandmother! It's about a woman you have obviously never met, and if that's the road you choose, a woman you may never get to know."

The anger in her voice seemed real. He hadn't meant to offend. "But what does all that have to do with her getting shot or anything else for that matter?"

With a sniff, she threw her hands in the air and shrugged "All right, I give up. You can have what you're asking for. It was a young French policeman."

"What was a young French policeman?" Her new detached tone caught Joe off guard.

"A young French policeman shot *your* grandmother with a thirty-two millimeter MAB Model D pistol that had been issued to him by the Vichy."

She'd said it the way she might have said, "By the way, it rained yesterday." Sensing her disdain, Joe searched for words but didn't find any.

Scrutinizing him from across the table, Nanette lit a cigarette and blew a billow of smoke directly toward his face. Luckily, for him, it rose quickly and floated harmlessly over his head.

"In the chest." The hand holding the cigarette tapped a spot just above her right breast. "They were in the courtyard when it happened."

Nanette's voice had suddenly turned so cold that Joe realized telling him this story meant more to her than he had guessed. She had so many stories to tell and so few people to tell them to. He regretted what he had said and decided it was best to keep holding his tongue. Just take his medicine. Let her work them through it.

Nanette sipped Crown Royal and stared him down for a full five count before saying, "There … you may go now. And thank you for the whiskey." She leaned back in her chair, turning her whole body away and dismissing him with a wave of her cigarette hand.

It was the second time she'd played that card. This time he didn't bite, but he was surprised again by the force of her personality, her intensity. And she'd made her point. She'd told him everything and nothing at the same time.

"I'm sorry," he gave in. "It's just hard to sit here and listen to some of the details, you know."

When Nanette turned to face him again, her expression made it clear she was amused. Played again. He rolled his eyes at her, letting her know he knew she hadn't really beaten him that time.

Nanette reached out and patted his hand where it lay on the table. "I know it's hard, Cheri, but you must trust me. There is a reason for everything I tell you. Without understanding this story, you will never begin to comprehend what made the Queen the Queen."

She paused to study him. "That is what you want to know, isn't it?"

What made the Queen the Queen? And who was the Queen anyway? Yeah. Nanette had convinced him that was the question it all boiled down to, at least this part of the story. He nodded and prepared himself for the worst.

But Nanette shifted direction again, her voice softer. "I was younger than the Queen. Only nineteen when the Nazis invaded Poland and Britain declared war … and bored to hell in Mont-Tremblant." When Joe gave her a quizzical look, she gestured over her shoulder with her cigarette. "It's not far from here. To the northwest. In the mountains."

After chuckling quietly at some private thought, she continued, "It was a small town, and going to London to help with the war effort gave me the perfect excuse to be off on my own. Of course, they wouldn't allow women in the fighting back then, but..."

She stopped, lingered over a sip of Crown Royal, then interjected, "I have very good French, you know. Not just Quebecoise, but Parisian, too, from my mother's side. Plus the arts of war came naturally to me. I grew up hunting with my father and brothers. So, I already knew how to handle guns and knives. Blood does not frighten me."

A hint of excitement slipped into her eyes and her chest heaved as she remembered. "I was the perfect candidate for the S.O.E."

"What's the S.O.E.?"

"Oh, I forgot." Irony in her voice, Nanette continued, "Nobody remembers these days, especially not Americans."

Her dismissive glance told Joe he'd reaffirmed the depth of American ignorance on one more issue.

"S.O.E. stands for the Special Operations Executive. The British created it to manage spies and saboteurs behind Nazi lines." She paused to make sure he was following this history lesson.

"The Queen joined the Resistance fighters in central France very early in the war, when they were out there on their own, officially working for the Free French, but with almost no support. No money, no weapons, no communications devices. There were too many face-to-face contacts to be safe. Too many people knew your name ... your route ... the color of your skin."

The ramifications of that were not wasted on Joe. Even though the Queen was clearly part white, her café-au-lait complexion would likely have been distinctive. Hell, they had even called her the Mulatto.

Nanette shook her head now at the frustration of those times, getting back into the story. "That's why the S.O.E. was such an improvement. We had resources. But..." Another headshake. "It took us a while to get up and running. The Queen's group was still on its own in November 1942 when the Nazis finally marched into the unoccupied zone and took control of southern France."

Almost as if she were personally apologizing for the delay, Nanette explained, "I spent some time doing office work before I could convince them to recruit me. They thought I was too small. Then, there was all the training and planning. I was in London almost two years before they dropped me into France."

"Dropped you?"

"Yes, by parachute." Nanette tilted her head at him with a cocky grin. "Ever jump out of an airplane?" Arching her eyebrows, she added, "In the middle of the night? Over enemy territory?"

Joe shook his head.

"Didn't think so," Nanette laughed. "Well you missed something. It really is so very exciting!"

Drifting through the cold night sky to land God knows where surrounded by Nazis? Exciting? Joe couldn't get his mind around the woman.

"It was my first mission. Talk about … how do they say it? Expect the unexpected." After glancing again to see if he was following, she continued, "I wasn't planning on crossing the Pyrenees so soon and certainly not in the dead of winter. But, the Queen needed to get to Spain. She'd been shot a few weeks earlier and was in no shape to make it alone."

"Spain? Why Spain?" Every new thing Joe learned pointed out something else he didn't know.

Nanette nodded as smoke released through her nose. "That was the only way out of France, and the Queen had a message to deliver."

"What kind of message?"

Holding up two fingers, she answered, "Two parts. The Vichy police and the Nazis had a secret plan to round up all the Jews in Marseilles in January, and, two, the Nazis would soon start retaliating against the Maquis for acts of sabotage by executing civilians selected at random from nearby villages … including women and children."

Joe chewed on his lower lip with one eye closed as he pondered this. "Sounds like you could have delivered those messages on your own. And the Queen was still hurt, right? That had to slow you down." Suddenly startled at another thought, he added, "And make it a lot more dangerous." Why had she done it?

Nanette narrowed her eyes and seemed to consider her response carefully, "Let's just say, I knew somebody would want to debrief her, and with her experience, the S.O.E. would probably want to recruit her. It was my way of bringing her into the fold."

Her choice of words gave Joe pause. She seemed to be leaving something out. But at least, it helped him start piecing the puzzle together. Sigrid had told him that McPherson had come to Gibraltar to interview the Queen and had taken her to London. Nanette was right. It was complicated, too complicated. He needed more information.

"Okay," he gave in completely and confessed, "I can't make sense of all these bits and pieces. I need to see the whole picture. Tell me what happened."

She teased her teeth with her tongue again, as the gleam returned to her eye. "Including the details?"

"Whatever." He threw up his hands, resigned to the inevitable.

"Take a sip," she said pushing his glass closer to his hand. "You're falling behind." Then winking. "And, why not just relax and try to enjoy it?"

Joe closed his eyes and bit his tongue.

Using her cigarette to buy time, Nanette took a few moments to compose her thoughts then began in an entirely unexpected place. "Fear, horror, anger. Those are very strange emotions. They're intoxicating, heighten your senses. Wind you up so tight that the smallest thing of beauty, a pebble, a sunset, just the smell of the forest after the rain, makes you tremble. It's an exquisite torture, so intense you can't stand it, yet you can't break away."

"Hunh." She let out a short little burst of breath through her nose and didn't seem to be talking to Joe any more. "And love? When you find even the tiniest bit of warmth and tenderness, you grasp it as if you will drown without it, and it keeps you … the you that feels … alive."

While he waited for Nanette to continue, Joe watched the internal conversation that was going on in her head play across her face.

"The problem is … feeling makes you weak. That's why you have to kill it to survive the ordeal in the first place." She stubbed her cigarette out in the ashtray.

With that, she came back into focus, raising one eyebrow and shrugging. "It's an untenable position."

She was talking in code and Joe didn't have the key. Her words made sense on the surface, but there was something behind them she wasn't telling him.

Before he could ask for an explanation, Nanette returned to the task at hand, slapping a palm down on the table lightly and saying, "So, you want to know what happened next?"

"Yes." Joe was surprised that his voice quaked.

"I intend to tell you what their life together was like."

"Okay, tell me. What was it like?"

"Short."

Fifteen

The Queen – *The Limousin, France, April 1942*

The relationship Gen and I have is what it is, but we don't know what that means. So, we start over, slowly this time with tentative touches during the day. Being close enough to her to smell her hair, her skin is intoxicating, and I yearn to be intoxicated. Every chance I get while we go through our prescribed routines, I lean into her warmth.

At first, she's stiff, unsure. Eventually, however, she treats me as if I'm the puppy I'm acting like. She giggles and shoves me away, then reaches out to scratch my head or pat my hand, enticing me back for more.

It's a cat and mouse game that breeds intimacy. At the end of that day, I join her upstairs in her bed for the first time. This is not a night of passion but of awkwardness. We're both tentative, distant, and neither my skin nor my soul has healed from the volcanic scalding of the night before. Ultimately, we cling to each other and try to convince ourselves I can make her happy.

Waking in her room for the first time, I notice the man's pants I have not seen since that first day. Holding them up next to her, I ask, "Why don't you wear these to work in the garden anymore?"

"Anymore?" She's nervous now, suspicious.

I've slipped up. I never told her that I eavesdropped before knocking on her door. Now I have to. "I watched you," I say, "for a day before I took the chance of coming here."

Her eyes narrow, as she backs half a step away. I have to pull her back, but must also tell her the truth. "I had to be sure it was safe."

"And you saw me—"

"Working in the garden in a man's shirt and trousers. And..." Seeing her vulnerable takes my breath away. I so want to make her smile. "I was surprised to discover that you were not a man."

"How did you disc..." Her eyes widen when she realizes the most probable answer.

"The spigot," I nod validating her embarrassment. "From where I was watching on the hill, you could have been a man, you know. You're tall enough. Strong enough, and at first I saw only your back, but then you turned half way and raised your arm to hold back your hair."

Emboldened by my need to set things straight, I take hold of her hand. When she does not resist, I lift it up to the spot it had rested that day. "Like this."

Her breast juts out as it did the first time. Now, through the delicate gown she slept in, I'm privy to details I'd been too far away to see that day and watch her nipple harden and reach out to me through the silk. My body responds. Perhaps there's hope.

"I knew you weren't a man the minute I saw this." Still holding her elbow high, I touch the nipple lightly with my finger. It extends even further.

My voice is hoarse when I say, "I love you." But, I'm still inadequate and walk away.

To my amusement and joy, Gen doesn't stride brusquely into the kitchen as she's been doing lately. Instead, she stands tentatively at the door, and I see the trousers. She's demure about them, asking almost shyly, "Do you mind if I wear these?"

This is a secret *she's* been keeping. I smile and tell her the truth, "I find them attractive. Why did you stop wearing them?"

"I didn't want you to know … to think…"

"That you wish you were a man?"

"Oh, God, no!" Her laugh is defensive, but it thaws the ice and she steps through the threshold. "Men are so … so hard, and driven, and … and ... I'd never want to *be* one. It just that I found these clothes after my family left and..." She stops as if she didn't want to make an excuse and finishes, "I feel free in them."

Now that the shoe is on the other foot, I do what she always does to me. I demand further explanation by arching my eyebrows and pursing my lips.

Hers is a nervous, chance-taking smile, "I feel more like who I am." Then she hastily clarifies, "But I only wear them here … in the courtyard."

"Why?"

Her shoulders drop as if having to explain this is exasperating. "This isn't Paris, you know. Not everyone accepts flamboyant..." She shakes her head, unable to force labels out of her mouth. "And, I promised to be discrete."

"Well, mademoiselle," I stand and take her hand and swivel my head to look around the room, pretending I'm checking to make sure no one is watching, "This is as discrete as it gets, and I must say you look very charming. Are you going to ask me to dance or not."

She matches my curtsey with a bow that would do justice to a gentleman courtier and leads me in waltz steps once around the kitchen before we break apart giggling. It's a wonderful morning.

From that moment on, whenever Gen's not seeing patients or tending to other business, she's in her trousers. And I love it. She's freer, more relaxed, and I have to admit, she looks good, really good sitting there comfortably like a man, with her feet apart and her elbows on her knees.

We work side by side. Feel a need to touch each other, bump shoulders, slide a hand down an arm or over a backside when we get the chance. And we laugh. For some reason, we can't stop. At the end of the day, at the kitchen table finishing our dinner and wine, we talk but mostly still make each other giggle at some stupidity.

And the really odd thing is the sense of déjà vu this brings. Gen's trousers remind me of one of my mother's friends, who used to show up at our house in Baltimore wearing slacks and men's hats. It made me jealous that she and my mother would laugh like Gen and I are doing now, because my mother was laughing with her the same way she used to laugh with my father. It seemed too close, too intimate. Now I'm just glad my mother had someone. It's really important when you finally find someone who makes you laugh.

A few nights later, I try to make love to her again, but there are still taboos I cannot force myself to break. And somehow I end up the one consoled. Gen tells me just holding her brings her pleasure and the fact that I try makes her love me more. Stroking my hair, she asks, "May I touch you?"

Seeing the doubt on my face, she adds, "It will make me happy," and how can I deny her? To my abject horror, my body responds instantly when her lips reach mine, and I want nothing more in the world than for her to make love to me. I'm out of control in what seems like an instant, screaming in agony and begging for more, and hate myself for being so selfish when it's over.

The next morning, while Gen's standing on the ramp dumping muck from the barn into the compost pile, she lifts her head to the sky, takes a long deep breath that swells her chest, and flashes a smile so wide it reflects the sun.

"Know what that smells like?" she asks.

It smells like shit to me, but I don't intrude on her moment.

"Smells like the future."

And I don't know how to take that. On one hand, the world is a pretty crappy place at this point in time and will likely get worse. I choose to go the other way though, because the look on her face is blissful. The manure we've folded so carefully into the earth is the reason everything we've planted is sprouting green and strong and reaching for the same sun she's stretching to touch now.

And that pretty much describes the strange schizophrenic nature of our current existence. Our courtyard is Eden, protected by some powerful magic bubble. There's only one thing out of place in it. Me.

The world that surrounds it is hell. The war is escalating.

THE QUEEN – *The Limousin, France, May 1942*

In May, the Vichy appoint one of France's most notorious anti-Semites to head the Office for Jewish Affairs, and they start cracking down on French Jews. The various Resistance groups in the Limousin grow in response to De Gaulle's increased calls for French citizens to fight back against the Germans. They commit two small acts of sabotage, which do more to raise the morale of their countrymen and attract new recruits than to hurt the Germans. I carry four messages.

In the courtyard, the sprouts grow a foot and develop leaves. The little pig gains ground on the big ones thanks to all the extra scraps I sneak him.

As Gen and I search for early berries and mushrooms in the woods, which also seem to be under the protection of our bubble, I lead her to a familiar spot.

"Here," I say, "this is where I was the first time."

As she turns, she asks, "The first time?"

"The first time I saw you."

She looks down, and her fingers fly to her mouth. "Oh."

The view surprises me, too. Now the manor house and courtyard look like a miniature, a doll's house. I can imagine how silly we looked chasing the pig. From up this high, as Gen and I go about our domestic chores, we must appear to be a set of traditional dolls, the comfortable old-married-couple set.

"You can see so much." Gen spins on her heels, surveying the woods, a hint of concern in her eyes.

It apparently hasn't hit home before how exposed she is. I make her feel better. "I keep a look out. Plus, there's no reason for anybody to come to this overlook. It's not on any trail."

Then I lead her further into the woods. Pointing at the spring that overflows to create the small creek, I tell her, "This is where I cleaned up so that I could make a good first impression on you."

"I used to play up here as a child," she says sighing. Then she sits down, takes off her shoes, and rolls up the pants she's had the courage to wear to this protected location outside the courtyard.

I bare my feet, too, slide them into the clear, icy water next to hers, and she puts her arm around me sighing, "I'd forgotten how beautiful it is up here."

She's right. I rest my head on her shoulder.

Sixteen

THE QUEEN – *The Limousin, France, July 1942*

In July, the Vichy police round up thirteen thousand French Jews in Paris, more than half of them women and children, and turn them over to the Gestapo. Thousands of the detainees avoid having to board the death trains to Auschwitz by dying from the heat while being held in a glass-roofed cycling stadium awaiting transport.

Gen's learned this during a bicycle trip to Laguenne. She almost doesn't make it home in one piece, because she's too upset to ride. "My brother! My fucking brother!" She strides around the parlor knocking things over and screaming till her voice breaks. "My brother did it! My fucking father got him a position with the police, and he did it! Him!"

She's wild-eyed. "I'd kill him. If I could only..." Her fingers clench and unclench in frustration that his throat is not beneath them.

I cannot imagine the agony of knowing someone that intimately and hating them that much. My arms can't console her that night or the next few days.

When we hear that her brother's police have started rounding up French Gypsies and homosexuals, too, I'm frightened for her. "I can get you out. We should leave now." I urge, standing to pack, not wanting to wait until it's too late.

"Uh," she dismisses my concern with a puff of breath and a wave of her fingers as she looks at the sky before explaining with disgust in her voice. "Lesbians are just about the only kind of *anti-social degenerate…*" She emphasizes the phrase by making quotation marks in the air then continues, "That the Nazis don't feel the need to exterminate. They have other *uses* for lesbians."

I've heard that, too, but I don't believe it. They didn't pick up the homosexuals at first, either. And anyway, I don't want to see her cooking and cleaning for some Nazi frau, or worse, being forced to bear Aryan sons for the glory of the Third Reich. That conjures up images of what she'd have to endure to produce such a child and the agony of having it grow up to be everything she hates.

"I think we should go anyway." I'm surprised to discover I'd give up my work here. But then, I can come back once she's safely in Morocco with Jo. It's an easy decision.

"Nothing's going to happen," she continues speaking logically now. "Nobody knows about me. And my brother's *position* will protect me."

"Your brother's position?"

"Oh, yes. There'll never be any proof, because I've been oh so *discrete,* remember? And him? Even if I walked down the streets of Paris in a tuxedo and top hat, he'd still deny it. I can assure you no one in the police is going to mess with me."

Her lips have curled into a snarl. The hatred for her brother has grown wings.

"Plus," she goes on, "the Resistance is growing now that the police's … that *his* … atrocities are out in the open. They need you here, and you can't be here without me."

I'm still uneasy, but she's made a valid argument. We stay, and it's my busiest month yet with the Resistance. She's right. I'm needed.

But nothing is wrong in the courtyard. A week's gone by. As we pick the first beans and squash of the season, I remind her, "It's been one year."

"One year?" She tilts her head to question me.

"Since I watched you under the spigot."

The squash she throws bounces off my shoulder, but before I retaliate, I see that she's tensed and prepared to run. One strand of that chestnut hair she's tied up with a ribbon to keep off her neck has broken free and lies wantonly across her eye until she pushes it back behind her ear.

For months, she's made do with our limited relationship. We've lived like those comfortable old-married-couple dolls I'd imagined up on the hillside, slow dancing in the parlor or lying in each other's arms, as the music she enjoys so much washes over us. There's a lot of intimacy, but almost no overt sexual contact.

This time, though, precariously poised on a tipping point, she's so absolutely adorable I realize I'd give anything to make her happy. That's when it hits me with total clarity. I can. Why have I wasted so much time questioning what I am or what I'm not? All that really matters in this life is who you love and how much of yourself you're willing to relinquish to give them what they need.

In this perfect moment it is so clear it almost hurts. I love this woman. No matter what I expected for my life, or what other people may think or say, it's that simple. I love her, and what she needs more than anything right now is to know how much. That and to escape from this putrid war, if only for a few moments, and now that I have nothing left to hold back, I know exactly how to do it.

I'm going to assume control and strip away all her defenses, force her to surrender everything … her thought, her body, her soul … to me. My taboos are suddenly trivial compared with this new selfish desire to see her abandon them all to pleasure and to feel her clinging to me, begging for the release she's waited for so long.

This unexpected change in myself makes me smile, and once that smile starts, it's uncontrollable, racing across my face, stretching it wide. I think it's the smile that gives me away, because she senses some kind of difference instantly and blushes, tipping her face into shadow.

I feel such a sweet, intense infusion that I must bite my lower lip and shake my head slowly. She's still waiting to see how I'm going to respond to the squash, poised to flee. Maintaining my hold on her eyes, I let that new smile fill the space between us and say in a voice she's never heard before, "I'll get *you* later."

We're far enough apart that I see rather than hear the sudden intake of breath before she turns half away to avoid my gaze, revealing an even deeper crimson flush on one cheek. This is new territory. Something I've done has made her timid and shy, and the feeling is delicious. Let her wait. Let it feed on itself for a while.

The rest of the afternoon is divine torture, a sinuous Tango in which the dancers are not allowed to touch. We go through all the motions of tending to the needs of the courtyard, as I pretend indifference, and she takes small surreptitious glances over her shoulder to catch me looking. It's a particular delight to feed the pig that evening. I know it's absurd, but it feels like I owe him something.

Dining outside in warm evening air is a good choice. As we cover the small table and set it, we don't laugh as much as usual. When we do, it's short nervous bursts with no breath behind them. Surrounded by silverware and candles, we strike formal poses at opposite ends of the table and fail to conduct a coherent conversation. Color rises and falls in her cheeks, and it pleases me.

By the time we're done with food and wine, the moon is rising. It's almost full in a cloudless sky. "I think we should sleep out here tonight," I say.

Uncharacteristically submissive, she nods, and as we spread the infamous comforters out on the grass, I react like Pavlov's dog by getting wet between my legs, which are quaking. I know she can tell. I think she's shaking, too.

Taking her hand, I kiss her lightly on the lips and say, "We'll leave off the lights. No one will be able to see us." She *is* shaking. Being in charge makes me feel powerful. "Sit. I'll be right back."

Once all of the lights in the house are extinguished, I return and take her hand again, leading her to the spigot. This time she's the one who shudders knowing and not knowing what's coming. I hope it doesn't disappoint her, but I know exactly what I'm going to do. I've been planning this since the moment she threw the squash.

She awaits my command, her arms by her sides, anticipating correctly that I'm about to even our accounts.

"I will undress you," I say and do, starting with the buttons of that loose man's shirt. I'm right. The moonlight is almost bright enough to read by. It illuminates her nipples as they stiffen when the night air hits them and the muscles that work at the back of her jaw when she tries to retain her composure.

Unbuttoning her trousers and unzipping the fly, I slide them down over her hips. The fact that the wanton wench is not wearing any underwear almost derails my good intentions, but I maintain control. Stepping back a step, I also disrobe. She offers to help, but I decline. She has to watch.

Face to face, the moonlight caresses our skin, hers cool and pale, glowing from within. An ethereal light. Mine warm and dark, absorbing energy from the earth's core.

"Here." Handing Gen a soft rag and a bar of soap, I slide over one of the buckets of water I set out to warm in the sun earlier that afternoon. "We're going to bathe each other."

We do so scrupulously, taking our time with each other's hair, fingers and toes, ears and necks. Lifting each other's breasts with one hand, while lathering the skin below, spreading each other's legs to rinse the soap from between our thighs. As I'm kneeling to rinse her ankle, my cheek brushes against her bare buttocks and I'm tempted to give it a little bite, but I restrain myself, keeping to the plan, keeping her waiting.

Tall and clean and dripping in moonlight, Gen is mythical. One drop of water in particular glitters like a diamond from her dark eyelashes before it falls in slow motion, landing in the puddle we've made with a sound that echoes back at us from the hillside.

After we scrub each other dry with rough white towels, I kiss the back of her hand before standing on tiptoes to reach her lips. She lowers hers to meet mine, and I lead her to the comforters.

"I'll be right back," I say turning toward the house.

Gen makes a face. It's the second time I've said that and disappeared. This time, however, when I return, the low sound of Ravel's *Bolero* follows me into the courtyard, and she smiles as I hand her a glass of wine. We both know the piece is hypnotic. It repeats itself over and over, getting bigger and bolder as it does. I also know it will start again when it reaches the end, because that's how I have set the record player. I have all the time in the world.

The music builds and begins to fill the night. I stand and leisurely place our glasses on the table, then kneel in front of her and push her back onto the comforter, spreading my legs so that hers can slide between them till she's prone. Straddling, I hold my weight off with my hands and knees and work my way up her body until our faces are level. This time, I kiss her eyes, slowly, lightly, first one then the other, lingering to run my tongue over her salty lashes. Her breath hitches, and I roll myself away, stretching out beside her, our shoulders, elbows, and hips all that is touching.

What I say is, "Look at the stars." We're facing away from the moon, which is still low enough that it does not dominate the western far horizon where the inky depth of the universe is still revealed. It's not empty. It's full of little sparks of light winking and calling to us.

Lifting my arm to point, I ask, "That's a constellation, isn't it? Do you know which one?"

She answers in a small voice, and it becomes a game. I keep her talking by asking questions. But now I'm not looking at the sky. I'm on my side. She knows I'm watching her in profile. Moonlight glitters in her eyes as they flit from star to star and highlights the little bump on her nose and the fullness of her lips. And from my low angle, makes her breast look like photo negative of a mountain, cool white snow on the bottom, rich dark earth at the peak.

"My own little Kilimanjaro," I giggle, reaching over and walking my fingers up her belly to the summit. Suddenly inspired beyond silliness, I pinch her nipple gently, proclaiming in a sonorous voice, "I stake my claim with a monument rather than a flag." Then I stroke and tweak and watch the testament to my dominion rise to stand upright on its own.

"The territory's … always been yours. All you had to do was take it." She's turned to face me, and it's a gasping whisper, her mouth half open, desire already in her eyes.

I roll onto my hands and knees again and finally claim what's mine. Not by force, but with a kiss. Long and slow, and deep, so deep it seems I'm lost inside her. Then, I begin to explore every inch of my new domain slowly with my fingers, lips, tongue, and teeth. Taking my time. After all, we're floating through eternity under the infinite sky.

I go places I've never dared go before. There's no part of her I don't feel and lick, nibble and linger over. I learn every texture, smell and taste, compare them, take notes, go back for seconds to make sure I've got it right, sharing each new revelation with her in intimate detail.

Why did I worry I wouldn't know how to give her what she needs? Her body betrays her. Reveals her secret desires. A clinch of her buttocks, a short intake of breath, a moan. They're a code I easily break, a code that guides me inexorably to the source of her longing.

But Gen is used to being in charge, does not cede control easily. Her hands reach out to touch me, trying to change the focus. Pausing, I grasp her wrists and pull her palms to my lips, kissing them. Then shaking my head, "No," I place them back at her side.

I begin again. She's mine tonight. There will be no mercy. She moans. Her hips rise to meet me.

Bolero's half-way through the second time when she realizes the danger she's in and cannot take it anymore.

It starts as a groan and grows to whimpered screams. On the brink, she tries to save herself, writhes and pushes against me, rakes my shoulders with her nails, tries to pull me up and away by my hair, but I'm too strong. I take her swollen clitoris gently between my teeth and pull, all the while delving deeper into her, and she simply falls apart.

No explosion this time. Her hands drop to her sides, clutch and unclutch the comforter. Then they're in my hair again, but now they're holding me fast. Mouth wide, she arches her back, her body directing me openly now, begging unashamedly for what it craves, crying out with the spasms that wrack it over and over. I respond to its every command, fulfill every order until there is nothing more to add to the feast.

Left to my own devices again, I rest my cheek on the soft, smooth skin of her belly and ride out the aftermath. She thrusts softly against me, echoing her release with small moans and shuddering aftershocks. I'm with her for every one as they slow to intermittent and diminish to occasional quivers of pleasure.

She lies there panting for a moment, and then I feel her fingers brush my hair off my forehead. When I look up, she grins and beckons me to her, eyes flashing in moonlight. Laughing, I scramble on hands and knees to claim a kiss as my reward for that smile. She grasps me in her arms and pulls me down. Body on body. Skin on skin. Wrapped around each other, we giggle—innocents in the Garden.

JOE – *Montreal, Canada, the Second Day, 1992*

"Oh, Nanette." Joe tisked and shook his head at the old red head. But she just grinned at him, incorrigible as ever.

So, he stood up, saying, "I'm on to your game. You're wasting your time. Look." He turned sideways and struck a pose so she could see him, or the lack of him, in profile.

The old woman almost spit out the sip of whiskey she'd taken, trying to hold back a guffaw. Waving her fingers in front of her face, she struggled to swallow and giggle at the same time, a delighted gleam in her eye.

When she regained control, she apologized, "Forgive me, Joseph. I know I got carried away again, but..." Her hand flew to her lips, and she couldn't finish the thought until her shoulders stopped bouncing up and down with laughter.

"It was so much fun." She sniggered, "And it really was much nicer than just telling you, 'The world was going to hell in a hand basket all around them, but the most important thing that happened in July was that the Queen finally got her girlfriend to come,' wasn't it?"

The harshness of putting it that way set Joe back, but he still resisted. "And I still ask you, that's important somehow?"

"More than you can imagine ... if you take the long view, that is."

Nanette thought for a moment then puffed her cheeks in exasperation, blew the air out with an audible, "Hunh," and explained, "After she was shot, your grandmother, or should I say the secret agent who went by the code name Regina, became one of the most effective operatives we had during ... and after ... the war. Why? Because she was highly motivated. You must have figured that much out. You didn't think she stuck it out for so long because of some intellectual commitment to the democratic form of government, did you?"

Of course she'd caught him again. He had no idea how long his grandmother had stuck it out. Hell. Until yesterday he didn't even have a clue what she'd done, much less why she did it. Yet, something didn't add up.

"But you said she first joined the Resistance with Josephine Baker. That was long before she ever met your Dr. Duphresne," he argued.

"Before she met Gen, she was well-meaning but ill-prepared, an amateur who had never killed a man." The small young spy from the fifty-year-old photo glared out at him, challenging. "After Gen, she didn't bother to count."

"She killed people?" As soon as he said it, he realized how dumb it was to be surprised. It was war. His grandmother was a spy, stupid.

Nanette's eyes narrowed. Smoke swirled around them as she nodded. "Not people. Nazis."

Still... "How many?"

"Not as many as she would have liked, I'd say."

Joe and Nanette stared each other down, him horror-struck and her defiant, until she broke the deadlock, shrugged, and added, "That's what I'm trying to get you to understand."

He paced around the room several times. How could he reconcile the woman Nanette was introducing him to with the Momma Willie he had known, the old Willie that cooked in the kitchen with his mother, the young smiling Willie in the Harlem photos, the girl who'd sought adventure on the Florida frontier with her friends? Loving a woman named Gen and hating Nazis bad enough to relish killing them didn't fit. He couldn't bring all the different Willies together to make one coherent person.

After a few moments, he admitted defeat. Sitting back down, he said, "You have to understand. This is all so new to me."

"I can tell," was her only response. She seemed willing to wait for him to say something more.

After what seemed to be an eternity of silence, the tension was so high Joe felt a need to break it. He tried diverting her by giving in, but with self-effacing humor. It had always seemed to work before.

"Okay, so tell me what I need to know. But..." He raised his hand as if to stop her and gave her what he hoped was a wry grin. "Like I said, I'm new to this. There's only so much I can take. Show some pity ... please."

It didn't work. "Pity is not within my ability." The icy-cold spy made it clear she could have slit his throat as easily as she slid her glass across the table for a refill.

Her voice was so stark, so empty. What had created this woman? He poured and slid her glass back, never taking his eyes off of hers.

Nanette didn't look down to locate her glass and didn't blink as she took a sip and lingered over it. Then she lit a new cigarette, drawing in the first deep drag and savoring that, too. As she exhaled slowly, she closed one eye and tilted her head as if trying to see him even better.

What was she going to do next?

After a pause, Nanette nodded to herself, "I do have to work on that story, though. It should have gotten more of a *rise* out of you."

Seventeen

THE QUEEN – *The Limousin, France, August 1942*

In August, Gen and I can no longer take a moment to pretend we are not involved in the war. Not one moment. The Vichy police round up another seven thousand Jews, only this time in the unoccupied southern zone. They send them to a camp just north of Marseille where they're waiting to be deported.

The Resistance is growing by leaps and bounds. But, it's each to his own. The Communists, the Socialists, and the French Nationalists insist on running separate operations. With the different egos and philosophies involved, it's hard getting them to trust each other, much less to work together in a coordinated manner.

Still, I am buoyed by the news that the United States Army Air Force has bombed the railroad yard at Rouen, northwest of Paris. And Charles De Gaulle is finally in full command of the Free French forces. He and the S.O.E. have started sending spies with radios to support and unify the bands of resisters and to plan strategic acts of sabotage. I'm doing all I can to help. It gets hectic.

Gen continues to provide medical services to the surrounding villages and cover for my operations. Now, it's clear that my status as a resister is more of a danger to her than her sexual preference ever was, and I have a growing fear in my gut that I should have taken her out of here when I had the chance. But she won't go without me, and I have work to do.

At breakfast one morning when I'm about to head out to meet with the Communists, Gen's pensive. That's been happening a lot lately. This time, though, she reaches both hands behind her neck, unclasps the gold chain she's wearing, and without saying a word, walks behind me and places her Saint Christopher medal around my neck, moving my hair out of the way to fasten it.

"No." I reach back trying to stop her. "I can't take this."

Gen's sister had sent it to her secretly right after their parents took her away. Gen had showed me the note she enclosed. It said, "Fear not this difficult journey. Saint Christopher will protect us." Gen's initials, "GMD" are engraved on the back. She wears it everywhere she goes.

But Gen fends off my hands and closes the clasp, saying, "I don't know what I'd do if you didn't make it home safely."

Then she leans down, wrapping both arms around my neck, and pulls my shoulders against her breasts. When I set out an hour later, it feels good to be protected. I'm back in three days.

In the courtyard, I'm no longer an interloper. We pick the first tomatoes and eggplant, and once dinner's cooked we immediately take it out the back gate to the cledier, where I have hidden a S.O.E. agent. She's young, early twenties. That's way too young to be dropping out of the sky in the night. Far too young to be hiding here because informers have infiltrated the ranks of the Resistance to the north. Tomorrow I'll get her and the information she's gathered started south, but tonight we eat and chat like schoolgirls. I feel maternal.

That evening I give the pig extra scraps. I do that every chance I get, and it shows. He's so big now the other two don't mess with him.

Gen is talkative in bed. "I don't know how to feel about the bombing," she admits as if there were guilt attached to her ambivalence. "I know it's good the Americans are finally doing something, but … but, it's *us* they're bombing. France, I mean. And that girl... She's so, so…"

She's talking about the S.O.E. agent asleep in the woods. "Young? Naive? New?" I offer.

"Yes." Her eyes tear up. "It's not fair. It's not right."

Normally I would commiserate and try to make her feel better, but tonight it's wearing on me, too. "We're all naïve and new at this," I say, "and countless other children will have to risk everything, or nothing will ever be fair and right again."

We spend more nights consoling each other than making love these days.

THE QUEEN–*The Limousin, September-October 1942*

September and October bring more young girls like the S.O.E. agent into the ranks of the Resistance. It turns out that they make the best spies. Men wandering the countryside raise the suspicion of the Vichy police, but women, especially pretty young ones, garner only favorable attention. Plus, they're always bicycling somewhere, from the butcher shop to the bakery or tending to other domestic duties.

The Nazi philosophy that women are suited only for cooking, cleaning, and bearing sons works against the Nazis in this, leaving our new female patriots invisible even as they carry out their missions in full view. When the police stop them, the girls smile and bite their lower lips playing coy. Some things never change. Blood abandons the officers' brains. They lose all rationality and offer to carry the girls' parcels.

Recently, however, Hitler issued an order that spies are to be killed on sight. All the brave, clever girls are operating under a death sentence.

In the courtyard, the apple trees are over-loaded with the famous golden fruit of the Limousin because the weather's been good, but there are few hands to pick them and no gasoline to carry them to market. Gen invites neighbors who are less fortunate to pick at will, and as a result, wears her skirt all season.

Yet, tonight when I come in for dinner after mucking the barn, she's in her trousers. It's cool enough for a fire, and we sit before it after eating, staring into the embers.

"The BBC says that Stalingrad is still holding out and that the Americans and British are gaining ground in Africa," she says sipping her wine and staring straight ahead for some time before getting up to turn on the phonograph.

The slowest and saddest music she owns fills the parlor, and she asks for my hand by holding hers down to me. "Please dance with me," she says.

With my arms around her neck, hers around my waist, my nose nestled in the spot just under her collar bone, and her cheek in my hair, we hardly move, just sway to the music. Somehow this brings her enough relief to take slow deep breaths that rise and fall beneath my chin.

"Maybe this will all end soon," she says over the top of my ear, and I hear in her voice that hope has frightened her. "Maybe one day..." My hair collects her tears. They never reach the floor.

THE QUEEN – *The Limousin, France, November 1942*

November is traditionally the season for slaughter. This year is no exception. People are dying everywhere.

Russians stalemate the Nazis at Stalingrad. British and American troops attack Vichy Morocco and Algeria. The Americans finally wrest control of Guadalcanal from the Japanese, and the British bomb Berlin and Hamburg. In response, the Nazis start deporting Polish Jews to extermination camps and break their armistice with the Vichy government. They take control of unoccupied southern France and flood into the Limousin intent to crack down on the Maquis.

Death even comes to the courtyard. Its form is a donkey-hauled livestock wagon that looks like a miniature railway cattle car, with gaps between the slats on the side to let the air in and the smell out. To avoid being shipped off to work in German factories, the young men have fled to the woods. So, Benoit and Paulie have consolidated the annual hog slaughter to help out the women in the area who have no one in their houses to do the heavy lifting.

Although I knew all along this day was coming, somehow I've kept it out of my mind. Now that it's here, I'm so disconsolate over the fate of our pig that I make a fool of myself, essentially begging these country folk who need meat to feed their families to spare its life for sentimental reasons.

Benoit laughs out loud when I suggest our pig is so wondrous that he should be kept to sire generation after generation of others in his image. Stifling his mirth, the kind man reminds me what a runt the pig was when he got here. Then, unable to control himself, he points out that our pig has no balls. They castrate non-breeders at an early age to avoid fights and competition.

Gen is little solace in this. She doesn't believe in omens and such things, and she was raised on this farm. Back when men folk lived in the house, her family slaughtered their own pigs in the courtyard, hanging them up alive by their back feet and slitting their throats over a kettle to catch their blood.

"Makes the best black pudding," she says and then goes on to explain that some of her fondest memories with her mother are about the times they worked together in the fall, boiling a pig's head and seasonings into a gelatinous mess to make head cheese.

So, my anxiety is shared only by the pig. He's crammed into the small wagon with our other two and two more belonging to the widow who lives down the road. He can't possibly comprehend where he's headed. Yet, his snout presses against the slats, his eyes wide. Risking more ridicule for being a silly girl, I come to him and touch his ear through the slats, willing him not to be afraid. It will be over quickly. As they leave, I want to run beside the wagon screaming for him to hold on, I'll come and save him.

But I don't, because I finally realize there's nothing to be done about it. It's the way of the world. He's a pig. He has to die.

Eighteen

THE QUEEN – *The Limousin, France, December 1942*

It's December, only a week away from the darkest day of the year. In the rest of the world, the war seesaws in favor of the Allied Forces. They bomb Italy and the Netherlands for the first time. In the Limousin, the Nazi crack-down escalates.

In the courtyard, it's early evening, and I've returned from a courier run the day before. I'm rolling the muck from the barn up onto the compost heap, when Paulie comes flying through the orchard gate looking backwards over his shoulder as he runs.

"Miss Angelique," he gasps, "you have to get out. They're coming for you."

I don't have to ask, "Who?" But start to ask, "What happened?" Then I catch myself and ask the more relevant, "How long do I have?"

"I don't know. My mother overheard someone at the butcher shop saying they had heard that the Gestapo was after the Mulatto bitch..." He stops when he hears the word come out of his mouth and looks back at the orchard again, embarrassment on his face.

They've heard the name Mulatto. Shit. "Do you know who—" I stop myself. The answer doesn't matter.

He's nervous, shakes his head not needing me to finish the question.

The boy shouldn't be here. Saying, "Thank you," I twist his shoulders so that his back is to me and push him toward the gate. "Go home. Be careful." I'm thankful he doesn't hesitate.

Then I also spin and race in the opposite direction. I need a coat and whatever provisions I can grab on the fly. And I need to tell Gen I'll be back.

Calling her name, I burst through the door and don't have to say a word. It's written all over the speed with which I'm moving and the look on my face. I fly through the kitchen into my room and she follows behind me.

"I'm coming, too," she calls after me and starts to help me pack as I grab my coat.

But before we can do anything, a fist hits the front door. "Let me in, Genevieve!"

Genevieve? That doesn't sound like a Gestapo command.

"It's Erich Roehm," Gen whispers unnecessarily, because we both know the voice.

Since the Nazis arrived, when they aren't commandeering houses and chasing the Maquis, their officers have been hosting small dinner parties and attending social events with Vichy collaborators. As the daughter and sister of high Vichy officials, Gen has been on almost every list of invitees.

She hates these events, not only because she detests the Nazis so much she can hardly force herself to remain civil, but because she's constantly having to fend off their advances. Yet, she goes every now and then to keep up the front.

I don't like sending her out alone, but I'm not invited. All I can do is wait for her to come home. When she does, she stands under the spigot to wash the taint of their touch off her body, and I do the washing. When she did it the first time, she scrubbed so hard she drew blood.

Roehm, who is banging on our door, is a detective sergeant in the Gestapo and the most persistent Nazi pursuing the tall, politically-connected, lady doctor of the Limousin. It's the feel of his hands that I've been washing off of Gen lately.

He bangs three more times, each bang more insistent than the one before. "I know you're there. I'm coming in."

Gen gestures that I'm to leave through the window while she goes out to divert him. Before I can protest, she's through the bedroom door, closing it behind her. And she's just in time, because he's stopped banging and is turning the unlocked knob.

Perhaps I should have done as she said, but I don't and I'll never know if that makes all the difference. Instead, I stand with my ear to the door and listen, intending to take some kind of action if something goes horribly wrong.

"Detective Sergeant," Gen does a wonderful job of forcing the fear out of her voice as she greets him, "What brings you here?"

"I need to talk to you." It's a harsh tone, but to me it doesn't sound like the kind of thing a senior Gestapo official would say when coming to make an arrest.

"About what, may I ask?" She's trying to keep it light and social. We may have a chance. Maybe there's not a squad of goons lined up behind him.

"Where's the Mulatto?"

"The Mulatto?" She sounds confused, but then she's never heard me called that before. "Are you referring to my nurse?"

He must have nodded, because she continues, "I don't know, exactly. She went to Tulle a few days ago and hasn't returned yet. Why are you looking for her?"

I'm so proud of the way Gen is handling this. Her voice lilts as if she's almost sashaying around the room.

And it seems to be working because he clears his throat before answering her question. "We've … uh … I've received a report that she's involved in the Resistance and—"

"That's ridiculous," Gen laughs in a way that tells me she's stolen a page from those brave young girls. Flirting to distract. "Angelique is middle-aged, barely gets around well enough to help with the patients. And her family's from Martinique. They're Vichy. What would she be doing in the Resistance?"

"So, no one else is here?" He ignores her argument, and there's a shift in his tone.

"No, who would be?"

His footsteps move slowly down the foyer towards my room. Hers step away quickly, as she adds, "Here, this is her room. Look for yourself."

The knob of the bedroom door turns.

She's only offered to let him search because she thinks I'm long gone through the window. I've put her in danger by staying. Holding my breath, I force myself flat against the wall, as the door opens and covers me from sight.

"See," she says in that light-hearted voice again.

I thank God I'm holding my overcoat in my arms. It would have been a dead giveaway that I was not away on a trip this cold December day, had he seen it. He leaves the door standing open, and they walk away. Soon, their voices echo from the kitchen and then back up the entry hall into the parlor, as she explains that she has converted the dining room across the foyer into an examining room.

Now that it's safe to breathe again, I don't like the shifting timbre of his voice. He's here alone, and now he believes she's here alone.

When I'm sure they're out of sight in the examining room, I slip from my hiding place into the parlor and, grasping the poker, I stand against the wall next to the fireplace. I'm right. There, in that more private setting, he gets to the true point of this visit.

"Get away from me," Gen commands, as that dance of slow and fast footsteps starts up again.

"Why? Don't you find me attractive?" His voice is husky, now. After a pause during which I can hear his slow deep breaths, he continues, "I find *you* attractive. Very attractive."

"There was no report, was there?" Gen accuses.

"Heh." He lets out an arrogant little puff of breath, dismissing any threat Gen thinks her accusation might present. "There've been rumors of a half-breed."

Shit. He's put it together by accident.

"But then..." He continues, "I don't need a report. I just got back from Paris, and I'll be in charge here soon. All I have to do is give the order and the police will pick her up."

Gen cannot suppress a tiny gasp that betrays fear.

"You don't want that, *do* you?" His voice drops off and the pause is meaningful, but I can't see what he's doing. "I could even have *you* picked up." His feet move again. "Unless, of course—"

"Don't touch me."

It's what I feared. At least now I know I was right to stay.

Gen continues, unable to keep the disdain out of her voice. "Touch me again, and my brother—"

"Your brother?" Roehm laughs. "Your brother?"

His tone frightens me. It's cold and emphatic.

After a pause, he continues, "I just returned from meeting with your *brother* in Paris. He did such a good job rounding up Jews there he's being put in charge of eradicating them down here now that we're in control. That's what I was doing with him. Planning a similar raid on Marseilles. He'll be here in a few weeks."

This bit of information decides everything. I have to leave immediately, to get a warning somehow to Marseilles. And this time Gen will come with me. She won't be able to abide living under the same roof as her mass-murderer brother.

Roehm picks up where he left off, bringing me back from my planning. "Your brother won't protect you."

I slide along the wall toward the door.

"Heh." Gen mimics his dismissive tone. "My brother always takes good care—"

"Your brother gave you to me."

"That's ridiculous. He would never—"

"I asked him, if you can believe this." Emotion raising his voice, Roehm continues, "I was stupid enough to tell him I wished to court his sister ... that I was letting him know out of common courtesy. To get his permission." Disgust and more than a little wounded pride drive his words. "And do you know what he did? Do you know?"

"No." At first I'm not sure if I actually hear her response. It's so low.

"He laughed in my face!"

I'm almost at the door. From the sound of footsteps, Gen is standing frozen to the spot and the Nazi is pacing back and forth in front of her.

"Laughed in my face! Then he said, 'Good luck with that. My sister doesn't like men. My sister is an abomination that Hitler should have included in the eradication programs. My sister lies with other women.'"

"He's always protected me." Her voice has shrunk. She can't believe this additional betrayal.

With another derisive laugh, Roehm pushes his advantage, "He doesn't need to anymore … doesn't want to. The only one who can protect you *now* … is me."

Gen can't handle this. This time her gasp is audible.

Roehm's shoes slide over the floor, and Gen doesn't move.

"But you have to make it worth my while." His voice is greasy. "Berliners, you see," he continues, "are not as *narrow* in their tastes as French provincials like your brother. I find Sapphists … shall we say … intriguing."

His words are slimy and threatening at the same time.

"All those mouths and tongues." He breathes in deeply.

When Gen doesn't reply, his voice drips oil. "Ah. You're blushing." Then as if it's a revelation, he asks, "You've never been with a man, have you?"

I know what the answer is even though she doesn't speak it.

Then, in a hoarse self-satisfied whisper, he continues, "Well, I will show you things … teach you..." He can't even get a whole sentence out he's breathing so hard now. "You'd like that. Wouldn't you?"

"Yes." The whimpered lie tears my heart.

His feet move again. The poker stirs in my hand as if from its own volition. I reach the door.

Roehm howls, "Fucking cunt!"

"Get away." It's her voice. "If you touch me again, I'll kill you!"

"Sick fucking cunt!"

I turn the corner as the back of his hand strikes her cheek and the scalpel she's cut him with bounces on the floor. It's the first time I see him that day. Taller than Gen, his chest heaves and he sways on his feet. He's still wearing a long, brownish-gray wool overcoat over his gray Gestapo uniform.

Holding her wrist with one hand, he hits her again with the other and rasps, "Cunt-sucking bitch! You like to suck so much? You want to suck now? To your knees! I'll give you something you'll remember sucking on!"

He's hunched over her. The hand she cut drips blood as it wrenches her wrist, forcing her down. His other hand fumbles to undo his fly. He's so intent on brutalizing her for what she is and what she's done, on taking what he came here to get in the first place, that he doesn't hear me behind him, and his head splits open like a melon.

I've never killed anyone before. But it feels good.

Nineteen

JOE – *Montreal Canada, the Second Day, 1992*

"Shit!" Joe didn't remember getting out of his chair. He paced the room, rubbing his hand over his head and looking alternately out the window and at Nanette for verification that he had heard what she said correctly.

The bent, old Canadian watched his reaction closely.

Joe stopped abruptly and wheeled to face her, a look of relief on his face. "You made that up too!" He accused. "She didn't really say that."

Nanette dashed his hopes by shrugging slightly, tilting her head, and making an apologetic face, closed-lipped half-smile, eyebrows raised, eye lids dropped.

"Her exact words."

Deflated, Joe sat back down heavily, squeezing his eyes shut and blowing out a big breath. It was hard enough to deal with the fact that his grandmother had killed a man so up close and personally, but he'd expected her to feel at least some degree of remorse.

"It didn't bother her at all?" He felt desperate.

"It might have, if things had gone differently."

THE QUEEN – *The Limousin, France, December 1942*

I don't have time to celebrate the extinction of Gestapo detective sergeant Erich Roehm. Gen has used the table to pull herself up from the floor and is standing there in an almost catatonic state. I have to figure out what to do next.

When I place my hands on her shoulders, she jerks away, pivoting and pulling out of my grasp, not letting me touch her. "Come on," I say taking hold of her arm instead. "We have to get out of here."

She jerks that away, too, her panicked eyes searching the room blindly. She turns to leave, but stops as if she's forgotten where she intended to go. Her head swings from side to side, scanning but obviously registering nothing. She's going to break down completely if I can't stop this now.

Praying she won't feel it's one more violation, I do the only thing I can think of. I throw my arms around her shoulders from behind and grasp my wrists across her chest, pulling her tight against my body, my cheek on her back. With her arms pinned to her side, it's oddly reminiscent of that first night when I held her till dawn. How can the same touch feel so different?

When Gen tries to jerk away, I croon as calmly as I can under the circumstances. "It's me, Gen. I'm here. Let me hold you." The tension has to leave soon. We don't have time. "Everything's going to be okay. I'll take care of you."

I ramble on and on, making it up as I go, trying to sooth the unsoothable, and trying to exude a confidence I don't feel. Her brother has betrayed her. Even if we make it out of here, I'm not sure anything will ever be okay.

In a few moments that feel like an eternity, however, her breathing starts to slow. It's another lifetime before her hand covers mine and she sighs.

"Gen?" I need to know if she's there.

"I'm sorry."

The familiarity of her small voice gives me hope. "We have to get out of here. Are you going to be able to do this?" I'm still feeling her out before letting her go.

She nods and quietly says, "Yes."

So, I loosen my grip on her, and she spins in my arms, grasps onto me as if I'm a life preserver and sobs into my hair. I vow that once we're out of this place I'll find a way to make sure she never has to cry into my hair again.

But she's always stronger than you'd expect. This part of her recovery doesn't last long before she backs away, stands upright, and shakes her head as if to clear it.

"Even if he made up the part about receiving a report, we have to leave," I start laying out the plan that's formed as all this was going on. "He'll be missed. Someone may have seen his car."

She nods. Her eyes are clear. Both are good signs.

"All we can do is buy time."

She nods again, more emphatically, and looks down at Roehm's body. I can see she's back. She's evaluating the situation.

"I think we should hide the body in the compost heap. It'll be the quickest way to get it out of sight in case someone comes looking," I continue. "And we should also hide the car. Somewhere in the woods."

She looks at me, trying to follow my logic.

"It'll confuse them … not knowing what happened to him or where. Give us a chance to get far enough away."

Now that I have time to really study the situation in the examining room, the plan sounds even more plausible. Roehm died so quickly he didn't make much of a mess, only a few spots of blood and other things I don't want to think about on one wall, and a small pool of blood where his upper body fell on the Persian carpet. It won't take long to erase the fact that he's ever been here.

Kneeling, I quickly rifle through the detective sergeant's pockets, shoving everything that might come in handy, money, papers, and things like that, into my knapsack. His revolver is silver with a black handle. It barely fits in my coat pocket and is so heavy it weighs me down on one side.

Working smoothly as a team now, Gen and I swing the rest of Roehm's body onto the carpet and roll him up in it. It's sad to waste such a beautiful Persian, but we have to do what we have to do.

As we rise, our eyes catch, and I reach over to place my palm gently on the angry red welts where his knuckles struck her cheek. She does that thing again, closes her eyes and leans her face into my hand, sighing for an instant, and I believe she's going to be all right if I can just get her out of here.

"I'll go get the wheelbarrow," I say standing. "You clean up the blood."

When I return from the barn, the only signs that anything is amiss are damp spots on the floor and wall and the extra-thick rolled-up carpet. He's big and heavy. It's a struggle, getting him onto the wheelbarrow. We can't push it with him stretched out lengthwise because his feet bump along the floor and obstruct the wheel. So we lay him at an angle. That makes it impossible to get him out the door without standing him up and walking him and the carpet through. If this wasn't a nightmare, it might be funny.

By the time we've made it to the arbor, I'm sweating so badly I take my coat off and lay it on the table. Don't need it now. Digging the hole in the compost heap will keep me warm.

Gen heads back to the house to pack. Once we leave in his car, we're not coming back. Before she's reached the kitchen door, however, I realize I didn't find Roehm's car keys when I searched him. I'm almost certain they're not in his pockets, but I will have to search him again if they're not in the car and don't want to cover him up with compost until I know for sure.

I call out after her, "I didn't find his keys. They're probably in the car. Let me know if you find them."

She waves her understanding, and I start digging.

The next thing I know, I hear voices through the door Gen has left wide open. Voices? Throwing down the shovel, I start back toward the house, keeping in the shadows as best I can.

"Francois, I hope you're not totally frozen." There's a forced lilt to Gen's tone. She's speaking loudly so I'll know they're coming.

She continues, "If the detective sergeant had told me you were in the car before, I'd have come out to get you sooner."

Roehm brought a driver? What kind of arrogant son of a bitch has an underling drive him to a rape?

"Where *is* the detective sergeant?" The man's tone is nowhere near as friendly as Gen's.

He's more than a little suspicious. And getting closer. Realizing that she's bringing him out to the courtyard. I crouch and run to the table.

"He's out at the barn checking the property. You know my brother's finally coming home? He'll be staying here. You do remember my brother don't you?"

Gen's babbling, trying to put him at ease and warn me at the same time. Apparently she's known whoever this is for quite a while.

"I'm told he'll be heading up the entire southern Special Security Group," she continues, reminding him who he's dealing with.

"Yes, Miss Duphresne."

Well, at least he's almost properly deferential. I grab my coat off the table, sliding my hand into the pocket to grasp Roehm's pistol.

"I'm looking forward to it. His plan is extreme, but it should shut down the Resistance once and for all." The man says this as Gen precedes him through the kitchen door into the courtyard.

Francois turns out to be short and thin, perhaps a few years younger than Gen. The brass buttons on his blue police uniform shine with reflected light as he follows her into the dusky courtyard.

When she hears what he said however, she turns and asks, "How will rounding up the Jews shut down the resisters?"

"Oh, not the Jew plan." Francois sounds a little smug that he knows something the sister of his new boss doesn't know. "He's going to turn the countryside against the Maquis."

He's so absorbed in asserting his superiority that he doesn't see me standing in the shadows behind Gen, my coat draped over my arm, my finger on the trigger of Roehm's gun in the pocket. The problem is Gen's between us, and I've only shot a pistol a couple of times. Couriers don't usually carry firearms, because weapons are hard to come by, and they'd be impossible to explain away if we were ever stopped. At this distance, I have no confidence I'll hit him even if I don't hit her.

Plus, the Maquis need to know the plan. I decide to wait.

"And how is he going to do that?" Gen asks the right question.

"Oh, it's simple really. Make them pay."

"The Maquis?"

I don't follow either. They've never even been able to find the Maquis.

"No. We will make the townspeople pay for hiding them. When there's an act of resistance, we will randomly select a few people from the closest town ... to *interrogate.*"

Interrogate? He means torture and God knows what else.

"It won't take long. They'll be begging us to take the Maquis." He actually smiles as he says this.

It's time to shoot him, but before I get the chance, he sees me.

"Who's there?" He pulls his gun and oddly levels it at Gen rather than at me.

"It's just me, sir, Angelique LeClerc, Dr. Duphresne's nurse." Hunched as if I'm even older than I've been pretending to be, I shuffle to the side so that he can see me. I get almost to Gen's side before he shifts his gun to me and tells me to stop.

His eyes narrow as they flit quickly over our shoulders. "I thought you said the detective sergeant was in the barn." The gun swings back to Gen as his face hardens. "There are no lights. Where is the detective sergeant?"

"He's dead. He tried to rape me, and I killed him."

I pull the trigger.

Nothing happens.

"So, now you don't have to take his orders anymore," Gen continues unaware of my attempt and its failure. "You can help us. Warn the people."

The policeman's face is incredulous, mouth open, brow wrinkled, as she says this.

I squeeze the trigger again and nothing happens again.

"You come from a good French family." Gen keeps assuming she can win him over.

Hell. The safety must be on. I've forgotten the safety. I keep my face impassive as my thumb searches frantically for the safety.

"You're not one of *them.*" She sounds so certain he thinks like she does. "Not a Nazi. They're evil. They'll destroy—"

"No. you're wrong," Francois finally responds. "The Nazis live by a code. And once this war is over and we've eliminated all the degenerates and anti-socials…" He pauses and stiffens. His eye twitches. "We'll restore the glory of our people." His voice has dropped half an octave.

The sudden shift in his demeanor worries me. Finally the safety … up near the top. I slide it down and pull the trigger again. Damn. I should have taken the time to inspect the gun before shoving it in my pocket. I shouldn't have assumed it was loaded and cocked.

"And what if they randomly select someone like Eugenie to interrogate?"

"Eugenie? My sister?"

Gen nods, obviously trying to win him over by personalizing her argument. She steps closer, giving me a bit of cover to cock the pistol.

"How do *you* know my sister?"

Oh, God. The tone of his voice. Apparently Gen's secret is not as well kept as she thought. Abandoning caution, I grab the slide on top of the pistol through the cloth of my coat with my bare hand and pull it back.

But, she misreads him here, too. She answers, "Oh, she's a lovely girl. So intelligent. We had a wonderful time together—"

The gun makes an audible click as it cocks, but the policeman isn't paying any attention to me. Instead, he's shouting at Gen, eyes so wide the whites are showing, "No! She's not like you! She's not—"

Our pistols fire so close together the blasts echo off the stone of the house as one. And before that sound dies, I witness the end of my world with slow motion clarity I had not thought possible.

Gen's back arches. The bullet exits where her heart should be and she takes one jerky step backward. Before she hits the ground, the golden light of her eyes fades to ebony, and I know she's gone from me to a place I'll never find her.

I don't even get to say good bye.

I stand there a moment, inspecting the smoky hole in my coat. Then, idly curious as to what damage, if any, my bullet has done to Francois the Vichy policeman, I survey my inept handiwork. At first, it appears I have killed him. Blood spreads on the white shirt underneath that blue jacket, as he leans against the wall below the spigot.

Then, I notice *his* eyes. They're still alive and they're angry. He's not ready to flee this realm with unfinished business. Instead, he thinks that if he holds me in his stare hard enough I won't notice his hand inching its way toward the pistol lying on the slate next to his thigh.

Taking care not to further damage my coat, I remove Roehm's gun from the pocket and extend my arm to point it at Francois. He doesn't back down, still inching his hand and staring up at me with hatred in his glare.

So much hatred from someone I've never even met. It's tiring. Oh, so tiring.

But his blood oozes now onto the slate, and I wonder if that hatred will sustain him long enough for his hand to reach the gun. Lowering my pistol, I watch. He masks his elation well when his fingers wrap around the grip and he discovers he has enough strength to lift its weight and point the barrel at me.

He rasps, "Half-blood, degenerate."

"Yes," I answer, my arm limp by my side.

And he pulls the trigger.

On my back in the garden, the barren rose bush that will bear blood-red buds if spring ever comes towers above me like a tree. Behind it in the distance, the posts and rails of the pig pen rise like Stonehenge above the courtyard grass, gray and eternal in the silvery winter moonlight.

"Thank you." I say and close my eyes.

Twenty

JOE – *Montreal, Canada, the Second Day, 1992*

Joe had been listening with his eyes closed, his elbows resting on his knees, his head supported by thumbs hooked under his cheekbones, and his fingers making a steeple over his eyebrows. When he opened his eyes, the gray linoleum floor between his feet greeted him. Taking in and letting out a slow deep breath, he lifted his head.

Saying, "That's so … harsh," he wondered how those kinds of scars don't show. Of course everybody always thought Momma Willie was a bit unusual, but nobody ever...

Then he remembered. He'd been told that his great-grandmother Momma Lou had always taken up for her daughter, explaining away her frequent absences. And there was the story about how those two had stood watch over the family store during the '68 race riots by dragging rocking chairs into a shattered display window and sitting there all night with shotguns across their laps. Maybe Willie had told her mother. He hoped she had.

Only then did he notice Nanette watching him from across the table as she absent-mindedly stubbed out her cigarette. "She wanted him to shoot her." Joe practically whispered as if answering some question Nanette had asked.

"Desperately."

Joe started to ask, "Why," but stopped himself with a jerk of his head. Loss? Guilt because she could have saved Gen if she hadn't made a mistake, had done better? What difference did it make? He sat up straight, coughed, and rubbed a cinder out of his eye in an effort to maintain his composure.

It was a while before either of them spoke again. Joe broke the silence, "So, how'd she get out of there?" Before Nanette could answer, however, it hit him. "Paulie? Paulie and Benoit. Right?"

Nanette nodded, "The boy had run home to get his father. They were in the orchard when the guns went off. Disposed of the car and the bodies."

"All of them? Gen?"

Nanette nodded again, "In the orchard." Seeing the uncomfortable look on Joe's face, she went on, "Look. Like the Queen said, she wasn't there anymore. They had to get out quickly and buy some time."

Joe nodded back. He had come to see what the Queen loved in Gen, and now it was hard for him to think coherently about such a strong, caring woman lying next to her murderers in an unmarked grave for all of eternity. Of course he had heard all his life that millions of innocent people had been lost to unmarked graves during World War II, but now, somehow, that abstract concept had a face. It was real, and it formed a knot in his chest.

He lifted the bottle of Crown Royal and inquired with his eyebrows whether Nanette was ready for more. In response to her nod, he leaned over the table and poured her two fingers. Then, he added the same to his own glass and they both took quiet, small sips.

"So, how bad was she hit?" Back to factual details. They were so much easier to deal with.

"Not as bad as it could have been. Through and through. No bones or major arteries. Like I told you, here." Nanette straightened in her chair so that she could point at the right side of her upper chest. "By the time I got there, she was up and around. Far from fully healed, but up and around."

"Did you know her before then?" He'd forgotten to ask that earlier.

"No." She shook her head. "I came across her a little more than a week after the shooting." Nanette's momentary lapse into sentimentality was over. A hint of hardness came back into her eyes. "In a Maquis safe house, southwest of Tulle ... in Cahors."

Cahors. So his grandmother had been there, too. Now even the wine took on a greater meaning. "How was she?"

"Physically?" The old woman thought before continuing, "Coming along. But that wasn't the problem." Another pause. "Emotionally, she was shattered. Today, you would say depressed. Pretty much out of it most of the time. Morose silences. Staring off into space. Georges and Pierre were afraid of her."

"Georges and Pierre?" The photo. Now he knew exactly what they all looked like when this took place. He even knew the countryside. He could actually see it happening, but... "Afraid *of* her?"

"Oh, yes," Nanette's earnest expression gave Joe pause. "She was a great danger to all of us. Unstable, incapable of taking care of herself. Even forgetting to eat. And she'd been in place so long, she knew far too much. Too many faces. Names. Safe houses. If the Nazis ever made her talk, it could have collapsed the Resistance in the Limousin. We took a vote. It was two to one to kill her."

"To kill her?" Joe set his glass down so suddenly the whiskey almost sloshed out. "After all that, the Maquis wanted to kill her?"

Nanette nodded slowly, nonplussed, rocking in her chair as she did so. "Georges and Pierre did not *want* to kill her, but with the S.O.L. combing the woods for the missing men, they felt that it could become necessary."

The men in the photo, cigarettes dangling jauntily, had voted to kill his grandmother. It was beyond Joe's comprehension.

"It was war." Once again, Nanette said it as if that explained everything.

"So, how did ... she get out of there, then?" Joe's eyes suddenly focused on the tiny woman sitting across from him as if seeing her for the first time. "You!"

Nanette had not simply taken the Queen over the Pyrenees. She'd saved her from the Maquis and personally escorted her all the way from the Limousin to Gibraltar. That was why she'd cut her first mission short ... said good-bye to her two lovers. "How did you... Why did you..."

Nanette sighed as if it pained her to admit she'd done something good and nice and amazing. "What can I say?" She shrugged. "The Queen was one of the earliest female Resistance fighters. She had personally killed two of the enemy." The soft look left Nanette's face. "It was my first assignment. She was who I aspired to be."

Looking sincerely across the table as if seeking understanding, she continued, "I couldn't just let them take her out back and shoot her like a dog, for God's sake. She was a woman who did things women weren't expected to do. She was not expendable!"

As if she'd revealed too much, Nanette withdrew again, hiding behind a curtain of cigarette smoke. Once she had her walls rebuilt, she continued, "Plus, she had warned the Maquis about Renee Duphresne's plans to round up Jews in Marseilles and to retaliate against innocents in the Limousin. I told Georges and Pierre..." Her voice lingered over the names with regret. "I told them I had to get back anyway and promised I'd kill her myself if we were about to get caught."

"You promised to kill her? Would you have?"

"Yes."

The word hung in the air like a levitating rock. Joe believed her.

"But, I didn't have to."

Joe could understand the pride in that statement. Nanette had safely herded an injured and incoherent female spy through hundreds of miles of enemy territory.

Then he understood. "That's when she told you the story."

The bent-over old woman nodded again and took another sip of whiskey. Blowing smoke out of her nose, she said, "Not at first. Not until we were in the Pyrenees."

An enigmatic half-smile, took over Nanette's lips. "Hunh," she let out a little ironic breath and said, "It was like a triggered memory or something." She caught Joe's eye.

"All the way to Saint Girons … that's a town on the Spanish border … she hardly said a word. Just stumbled along, going where I told her to go and doing what I told her to do. We picked up two passeurs, guides, one French and one Spanish, Louis and Gaston, and headed into the mountains. It's always cold up there, and it was the first week in January, snow everywhere, but thank goodness little wind and not snowing.

Nanette studied Joe before taking a sip and a drag and continuing, "We walked as late as we could that first night, and when she could go no further, we pitched the little tent which was the only shelter we had from the cold. I crawled in with her and told her we were going to sleep together so that we could double our blankets and conserve body heat."

Nanette's chuckle oozed irony. "You can probably imagine the look on her face when I said that." Nanette looked to Joe for verification.

For all the world, he couldn't imagine.

"She froze. Lay there on her side, her back to me, and didn't answer when I asked if she wanted the front or back position. So I stretched out behind her and you know..." Nanette filled this pause with a resigned grin. "The first thing you realize once you're stretched out behind someone like that is you don't know where to put your hands. Heh? I mean..."

Joe got it. He nodded his understanding.

She went on, "I mean, especially if you're not on intimate terms with them. And you know … the only way to keep from rolling onto your back and hogging the covers is to put your arm around them."

Fate was heartless.

"Anyway, as soon as I decided what the hell and slipped my arm over her waist, she stiffened, then grabbed my wrist in both hands, pinning me against her back, and started sobbing. Sobbed us both to sleep and sobbed us up the mountain the next day. The next night, however, when I laid my arm over her, she sighed and simply started talking.

"She told you that night?"

"Oh, no. It took a lot more than one night." Nanette shook her head and raised her glass to her lips, but did not take a sip. "Once she started, it was like she wanted me to know everything, every intimate detail, as if saying the words could change the outcome in some way."

Nanette sipped. She played with the Crown Royal and let out a long, slow breath after she swallowed. "And as I told you …with *my* particular tastes." The gleam came back to her eye. "I was *very* interested in the details."She winked. "Especially the *intimate* ones."

Joe rewarded that with the exaggerated eye-roll he knew she'd been trying to provoke.

"And then, you know what was even better?" Nanette slapped her knee, remembering. "The effect it had on Gaston and Louis." Her smile was broad. She was obviously enjoying the mental image. "I've never felt so well-protected as we were the rest of that trip. Once they figured out what she was going on about, they never wandered out of earshot."

"And..." Nanette's shoulders shook and she covered her mouth with her hand, in an unsuccessful effort to restrain the hilarity. "You should have seen it. They couldn't control the effect it had on them. Bulging out to here." The old vamp flexed her hips upward and cupped her cigarette hand six inches in front of her belly.

"And Louis..." She wiped a tear from the corner of one eye. "Louis couldn't think or walk straight for two whole days. All he could do was grunt in little short sentences, like 'Oui' or 'Non.'"

When Nanette's giggle fit finally wore itself out, there were tears in her eyes. After brushing them away with crooked fingers and taking one last smiling breath, she posed a toast lifting her glass, "To the good old days."

Joe tilted his head in wonder. A four-day trek through the Pyrenees Mountains in the dead of winter while hiding from the Nazis was the good old days?

"Hey." It was as if she had read his mind and decided to ignore him. "I heard later that Louis told people it was the *hardest* passage he'd ever made." The closed mouthed giggle escaped through her nose.

Okay. So she was incorrigible. But it *was* funny. Joe raised his glass and joined her game in spirit if not in fact, "To hard times."

It was a good thing Nanette hadn't taken another sip yet, because her guffaw could have splattered the table with whiskey if she had. Once she regained control, her glistening eyes held his as she raised her glass again. "To hard times."

Joe enjoyed the open smile that lit up her face. Who was this woman?

After relishing the taste and feel of the good Canadian whiskey, Nanette leaned back in her chair, let out one more audible breath, and her reflective mood returned. "You know, Cheri, it really was a beautiful story."

Joe rocked in his seat. "And she had to get it out?"

"Evidently."

"How'd you react to it? What I mean is … what did you do?"

Nanette's tone turned sharp again. "What do you think I did?"

But before Joe could respond, she answered his question, "I held her in my arms that last night and stroked her hair. I told her Gen was an amazing woman, I wished I had met her, and I thanked her for trusting me that much."

That was not the answer Joe had expected. "How'd she respond?"

"She said she was ready to go back to work."

"Just like that?" Joe didn't believe it. "Just telling you the story gave her the will to live again?" He put down his glass with a thud.

"Non, mon cher," Nanette shook her head solemnly and sadly, letting him know how wrong he'd gotten it. "It made her angry. That gave her a *reason* to live."

Twenty-One

JOE – *Montreal, Canada, the Second Day, 1992*

Once Nanette and the Queen had crossed the Pyrenees, the rest of their journey to Gibraltar seemed mundane. Noticing that they'd made it through more than a third of the bottle of Canadian whiskey, Joe looked at his watch. It was approaching four o'clock, and the combination of activity and whiskey was taking its toll on Nanette.

And she had told him what he'd stayed to hear. "I should probably be heading out soon," he suggested.

"Ah," Nanette sighed. "All good things must come to an end, mustn't they?"

He nodded and stood to go.

Nanette responded by arching her eyebrows, pursing her lips, and dropping her hands to her lap. "What a shame," she said then took in and let out a breath so deep and slow that it caused both her shoulders to rise and fall. "It has been a pleasure meeting you, Joseph. On your way out, would you please let Marie know I'm ready to go back up to my room whenever she has the time?" She looked up at him eyes wide, positively helpless and pathetic.

The whole gesture was so overwrought and melodramatic that Joe almost laughed out loud. And at that moment, he realized how much he actually liked this crazy old woman, how much he wished he'd known her when she was younger.

Grinning, he placed his palm on his belt buckle and bowed at the waist. "May I escort you to your suite, mademoiselle?"

"If you insist." She dismissed his gallantry by switching from pathetic to bored, raising one hand to her shoulder, and flopping the wrist.

"It is entirely my pleasure, Milady." Joe bowed slightly again before moving to her side of the table and taking hold of the handles of her wheelchair.

She directed him through the rabbit warren of wide halls lined by doorways just wide enough for wheel chairs, around corners, up an elevator, and then through smaller corridors.

Joe lost his sense of direction early on. He wasn't sure he'd be able to find his way back out again by the time she told him to stop in front of door number 342. The name "Marguerite Jeandren" was written in ink on a small cardboard placard fitted into a slot just below the peep hole she wasn't tall enough to look through.

Nanette leaned over to insert a key into the lock, and the door swung inward onto a foyer. "Welcome to my tower keep, Milord," she said wheeling herself over the threshold and spinning the chair around to face him.

It was a more agile maneuver than Joe had thought her capable of. His grin matched hers, as she showed off her royal chambers. They were just her size. Small. Small bath, small bedroom, small combined kitchen, dining, and living area with a window that overlooked the facility's courtyard. Tastefully, if not expensively furnished.

A charcoal sketch hung in the place of honor over a glass vase on a lowboy in the living area. It was an exquisite portrait of a young woman. Joe recognized Nanette immediately from the photograph of her with Georges and Pierre.

"You?" he stated the obvious, looking from it to her and back again. "It's really quite lovely."

"Yes." There was something strange about Nanette's voice at first, but it evened out as she continued, "I've always been very fond of it."

Joe leaned closer to read the name of the artist, which was scrawled across the bottom, "Fritz Huegel, May 1944."

"This Fritz Huegel is quite an artist," Joe's honest appreciation for the detail and spirit Huegel captured in the sketch came through.

When Nanette did not respond at first, Joe glanced over to check on her. She was watching him examine the drawing, an unexpected, soft look on her face, her protective shields temporarily down.

Without changing expression, she said, "Yes, he was." It was little more than a whisper.

Joe knew instantly. This Fritz was the one. The one Nanette hadn't held onto tight enough.

But before Joe could take the conversation in that direction, Nanette's ramparts resurrected themselves. She wheeled to the kitchen, took the bottle of Crown Royal off her lap, and set it down on the counter. Stretching to reach the glassware, she asked, "Can I pour you one?"

"No thanks." Joe had already had way more to drink that he usually did. "I have to be going soon."

"There are more drawings in the lowboy."

Joe scrutinized Nanette closely. The wily old woman was tempting him to stay. Having the time, he reached for a handle, asking, "Top drawer?"

He wasn't at all surprised when she said, "Yes." Where else would she keep her prized possessions? As he slid the drawer open, his eyes fell not only on a sketchbook, but on a stack of four-by-six-inch boxes covered in velvet.

"What are these?" Figuring she had wanted him to find the boxes when she sent him into the drawer, he held the top one up for her to see.

She shrugged as she poured another two fingers of whiskey into her glass. "They're nothing. Just a few baubles I picked up along the way."

"May I?"

Nanette nodded. Joe opened the box and removed the sheet of cotton batting that protected its contents revealing a round bronze medallion the size of a silver dollar attached to a red ribbon and a lapel pin. A Roman Legionnaire's head and the word "Freedom" were engraved on the front. He held it up and wrinkled his brow to ask the question.

"That one's from the American president," Nanette had wheeled herself next to his elbow as he studied the medal.

Joe picked up another box and it held a medal he'd heard of before, "The Croix de Guerre?" he asked, not believing what he was seeing.

"Oh," Nanette dismissed his awe with a wave of her hand, saying, "The French gave the Croix to all the girls." She laughed it off, cavalier as ever. The other two boxes held, she explained, also light-heartedly, "Small trinkets awarded by the British Empire and the Free French." They were called the George Cross and the Médaille de la Résistance.

Joe looked at Nanette mouth ajar as she made light of medals that four different governments had awarded her for her services during the war. "What do you mean little trinkets?" He asked, disbelieving again. "These are amazing honors! Does anybody around here know who you *are*?" He indicated he meant anybody in the home by swiveling his head around.

"And exactly who *am* I?" Nanette's tone was cool. Not hostile, but hard.

Joe started to answer that she was "a frigging national hero, somebody everyone should look up to," but she beat him to the punch.

"Everybody here *was* somebody at some time, Joseph. But today, all I *am* is one more old woman who's afraid she'll break her arm reaching into the cabinet and who needs help to open a bottle of booze. What difference will flaunting a bunch of forty-five-year-old brass medallions in front of equally decrepit old strangers make in the face of that? Eh?"

Joe's eyes were so wide they hurt. He was in physical pain because he didn't know how to counter her argument. She was a woman who had lived a life women didn't usually lead. And now she had no family, no old friends to reminisce with, no one who knew and understood who she had been and appreciated what she had accomplished.

Just like his grandmother? The thought stopped him cold. Was that why she went back to McPherson? Because he had been there? Because he understood?

Nanette reclaimed his attention by switching to her insouciant persona. "Anyway, imagine what my life would be like if all my sex-starved fellow inmates…" She indicated the residents of the facility with a sweep of her hand. "Ever found out I'm an amoral nymphomaniac with a license to kill."

She laughed, shaking her head. "There'd be no end of midnight rapping on my door. Requests for my services. Men *and* women, seeking both *kinds* of services, mind you. I'd never get any rest. That's why I retired in the first place."

Joe knew that wasn't true, but he didn't say anything. Instead, he watched her set her glass on top of the lowboy next to the vase and lean farther into the drawer, pulling out the old-fashioned artist's sketchbook.

"Here, you will probably enjoy these," she said handing it to Joe.

The first few pages were covered with sketches, large and small, some with a few notes in German on the sides. Joe recognized the same delicate sense of detail in the charcoal that made the portrait of Nanette so outstanding.

"Fritz?" he asked.

"Yes, he was very good wasn't he?" Nanette seemed less reticent now to discuss the man.

"Where is this," Joe asked pointing to an especially fine rendering of what appeared to be a gothic cathedral, complete with towering spires and gargoyles.

"Bayeux." Without warning, Nanette sounded tired, her voice husky.

"Bayeux? Where's that? France? The Limousin?"

"Non," she chuckled lightly as if saying, "You silly boy," and explained, "Bayeux is a lovely medieval town near the coast of Normandy. Do you see that tree?" She pointed at a large tree standing in the square outside the cathedral. "That's an Arbre de la Liberte." Smiling up at Joe, she answered the question on his face. "A Liberty Tree. They planted it in 1797 to celebrate the French Revolution." She sighed, handing the book back to Joe. "I wonder if it's still there."

As Nanette told him this, Joe's eye wandered down to the date on the sketch. "April 1944." The only things he knew about

Normandy were that it was in France and that the American army's landing there was the beginning of the end for Hitler and the Nazis. He couldn't remember exactly on what date though. It had been so long since he'd studied such things in school.

Squinting at Nanette, he meandered his way to a question, "Normandy? That's where the Americans landed, isn't it? When was that?"

"Tisk. Tisk. Tisk. You are such a chauvinist." Nanette shook her head and lowered her eyelashes at him. "Yes. That is where the American, the British, the Free French, and the *Canadian* forces landed in Operation Overlord. What you now call D-Day."

"And when—"

"Five weeks after this sketch was made … to the day."

"You were there? For the landing?"

Still looking up at him, Nanette leaned back in her chair and retrieved her glass from the lowboy. Then, showing him those arched eyebrows and pursed lips that were designed to play down what she was going to say next, she told him, "It was our last mission together." She paused, switching now to her Mona Lisa smile, the cat toying with the canary.

Joe knew what was coming. Nanette was casting a net to capture him and keep him there as long as she could. But he went along with it. "Yours and whose last mission?"

"Why, the Queen's, of course."

Of course. Of course *his* grandmother was at Normandy for D-Day. Of course, it was too late and Nanette was too tired to tell that story that day. He'd have to come back tomorrow. Of course, there was no other way this could have played out.

Biting his lower lip, Joe couldn't help smiling in homage to the cunning little thing's devious manipulation. She'd worked him again. He actually admired her for that almost as much as he marveled at all the other secrets she'd pretended to let him ferret out of her. What else could be hiding behind those changeable eyes?

Then, he almost slapped his forehead. Why hadn't he thought of it before? "Mademoiselle," he started, "it's getting late. I really must be going."

He could see that caught her totally by surprise. She deflated, only a little, but her shoulders visibly sagged, and the light in her eyes dimmed.

"So, I was wondering," he went on quickly, "if I could escort you out."

Her mouth dropped open for an instant, before she lifted her fingers to cover it like a coquette. He loved her spunk. "Tomorrow? At one? To the p

ark?"

"Why, yes, mon jeune homme." She extended her hand toward him, the backs of her fingers up, grinning openly now. "I believe my calendar is free."

He took the tips of her fingers between his forefinger and thumb and bent at the waist to brush his lips lightly above her deformed knuckles as her gesture demanded.

She beamed as he mentally started making plans to change his airline reservation one more time. Carrie would still be there when he got home, and he'd have so much to tell her.

Twenty-Two

JOE – *Montreal, Canada, the Last Day, 1992*

As soon as they crossed the threshold to the outside world, Nanette lifted her face to the brilliant sunshine and asked Joe to stop. She surveyed her surroundings like a monarch evaluating her realm as she breathed in long deep draughts of the warm afternoon air.

"Beautiful," she whispered. Then leaning her head and shoulders forward as if she could propel herself that way, she jiggled a finger over her shoulder, directing Joe to start pushing again.

After leaving Nanette the evening before, Joe had wandered the rather large city park across the street from the veterans' home, selecting a number of sites he thought she might enjoy that were also suitably private. He had grinned to himself when making that decision. By now he knew there was a realistic chance something Nanette might say would scorch the ears of mothers with young children.

He knew he'd chosen well by the way Nanette sighed as he pushed her chair over the grass to the shade of a tree near the lake. Brown-backed ducks with heads that looked like brightly-painted wood carvings left v-shaped wakes near the middle of the lake, while swans flirted with the shadows on one side. The echoes of children's voices bounced across the water which also cooled the light breeze.

Shading his eyes to look up at the crystalline blue sky, Joe asked, "Want to start out in the sun? Or shade?'

Nanette smiled up at him, her eyes the same clear blue as the sky. Maybe it was just a reflection, but it was a perfect match.

"Shade, I believe," she twinkled. "One has to be careful. The sun does age the skin so."

After setting her wheel brake beneath the spreading branches of a sycamore tree, Joe untied the folding chair he'd brought for himself from the back of her wheelchair and set it to her left, almost touching hers. They'd spend this day looking out at the world rather than at each other.

When he retrieved a folding camp table from the backpack he had bought the night before and placed it at her right, Nanette clapped her hands and squealed, "You've thought of everything!" She immediately fumbled in the large bag she'd carried on her lap and pulled out her cigarettes, lighter, and an ashtray. As she put the ashtray down, she glanced over at him and asked, "What? You didn't expect me to leave my butts lying around in such a wonderful place, did you?"

He shook his head and sat down, his backpack at his feet. Bending over, he pulled out a bottle of Perrier and reached across her to place it on the table.

Nanette frowned.

"I had somebody translate the sign at the entrance. It says 'No alcohol in the park,'" he explained.

"But..." He leaned toward and opened his jacket, revealing the silver flask he had filled from a small bottle of Crown Royal in the lapel pocket. "I brought a little something extra, should an emergency arise."

Nanette feigned disapproval by leaning back and widening her eyes. Then she smiled. "This is so ... so... Thank you, Joseph. It's lovely here." She turned away, and they sat in silence for a while, listening to the leaves rustle in the trees and the distant sound of traffic on the street.

Without saying a word, Nanette reached into her bag again and pulled out the sketchbook. She looked over at Joe as she opened it and set it on her lap. "You didn't get a chance to see all of these, last night."

From the huskiness of her tone, Joe knew he'd made the right choice. He leaned in her direction to read over her shoulder, and she started where he had left off, with a drawing of a Nazi tank in front of a field with a stone fence.

"Fritz was an unteroffizier in the 716th Infantry Division of the German army. That's like a sergeant, a non-commissioned position. The military was *not* his career." Nanette glanced at Joe nervously, almost shyly, speaking in a timid voice as if seeking verification this was where he wanted her to go.

Or was she seeking approval of Fritz? He was German. But he wasn't a career soldier. She'd said it as if that was a redeeming virtue. Figuring she'd clarify the issue when she was ready, Joe decided not to pursue it. "Tell me about him," he coaxed her to do what he knew she wanted to do.

"I will." Nanette smiled. "But first I must tell you of Stanislaw."

"Stanislaw?" Joe shook his head, mouth open in surprise. "Who's that?"

"My young Polish boy." Nanette ran the tip of her tongue over her upper lip, giving Joe a sultry look.

"Ohhh." Joe arched his eyebrows and let out a sigh. "It's another one of *those* stories."

"Oh, yes!" She clapped her hands, eyes gleaming. "Perhaps the best of all."

"Why's that?"

"Because it has a happy ending."

NANETTE—*Normandy, France, April 1944*

The Queen steps out into the night sky. I count to three, blow a kiss to the Royal Air Force bombardier who'll shove the arms and ammunition out behind me, then follow her through the cargo door into the windy darkness. The exhilaration of those first few seconds of free fall is always the best part. It's late. The moon's down. No ground fire to worry about. I just enjoy the ride.

Once I pull the ripcord, I float, swinging to and fro with the breeze, looking for the ground so that I can prepare for impact. I never see it. When my feet crash through tree branches, I cover my eyes with my forearm, cursing silently. Then I'm no longer falling and hitting things. I'm dangling from my lines, arms, legs, toes, and hands all pretty much intact. Only, I can't tell where I am or how high up.

A light flashes on, blinding me. Then a voice I'm so glad to hear is French says, "Mon Dieu! What beautiful fruit the trees of this region bear!"

"Cut the French crap, JuJu," I hiss. "And turn off that damned light. You trying to get us all killed?"

I've worked with JuJu, as I like to call him, before. Been lovers, actually, whenever the opportunity arose. He's headed up a band of Maquis for eight months. Knows what he's doing and has flicked his light on only long enough to make sure I'm okay and to let me know I'm about four feet off the ground.

Because he's here so fast, I also know we landed in the designated drop zone and can visualize exactly where we are on the map I've memorized. We're in the countryside about sixteen kilometers east-south-east of Caen near the Normandy coast.

I open my pocket knife and cut my lines, dropping the final distance. After we've gathered in the chute so as not to leave evidence of my arrival, JuJu throws his arm around my shoulders, saying, "This way, my little spitfire," and I run beside him to help the other resisters collect the parcels that are falling in slow winding arcs and hitting the ground with soft thuds.

Within minutes, the Queen finds me. She and her two suit cases made it through the jump intact. Her cases conceal a wireless telegraph, clothes, and makeup. This is her third drop into France since joining the S.O.E. Just months ago, she cut her most recent mission short, because a collaborator infiltrated the cell she was working with in Orleans and the Nazis had broadcast her description to all the police and Gestapo.

The S.O.E. would never have asked her to come back after that, but she and I both sense something's up. We don't want to be left out of whatever is going to happen. They couldn't turn us down when we volunteered. They need every experienced agent they can get on the ground in times like these.

It's amazing how the Queen's dealt with her problem. She's changed the way she looks, and it's very effective. The Nazis are searching for a mixed-race woman ten years older than her forty-four years. While she was in England, she lost twenty pounds in training and bleached her dark tresses to a coppery brown. Now, with the help of lighter makeup, she can pass for an olive-complexioned white woman in her mid thirties, a rather attractive one. The thing most likely to give her away, though, is still that chocolate-milk skin. The makeup does a pretty good job, but it's a chance we all know she's taking.

As for me, I've done a bit of redesigning, too. My naturally flaming hair is just too attention-getting for spy work. Several missions back, I dyed it closer to auburn. This time I've also died my pubic hair. Matching pubic hair is important given the job I'm undertaking tonight, the role I like to think of as the Patriotic Prostitute. It may just be the part I was born to play.

"It's good to have you back," JuJu whispers in my ear as we load the last canister into the car. His hand feels solid on the small of my back. Then he pinches my butt. It is good to be back.

Later, as we sip wine in a farmer's kitchen, I let him know our timeframe by asking, "JuJu, can you supply us with bicycles by dawn?"

He furrows his brow and pouts his lips to let me know he's disappointed, reaches up to stroke my chin between his thumb and forefinger, and asks, "But, do you have to go so soon, mon amour?"

"It's not *that* soon," I reply, and JuJu and I tell the others we're going to find the bicycles. Eyes roll all around, but who cares. I'm back in France and on a mission. May as well get into character.

The Queen and I'll be heading out in different directions tomorrow morning. Although we'll be working as a team, we'll see very little of each other. Our task is to traverse the Normandy coast from Caen to Cherbourg collecting the details about Nazi fortifications and troop deployment. It's a little over a hundred kilometers, and the deadline we've been given is to get the information we gather back to England "A.S.A.P." As fast as we can.

I'll be traveling the main roads, working in plain sight, one of the camp followers and ordinary prostitutes who make life in western France bearable for those poor Nazi boys so far from home. My job is to wheedle whatever information I can out of them and to see as much as I can see firsthand.

The Queen will convert the useful tidbits we collect into code and transmit it across the channel to the British high command. She'll be lugging her transmitter down the back roads, traveling alone and mostly at night, sleeping in barns and stables if she has to. Hers is the more dangerous and more complicated mission. The Nazis are always monitoring the airwaves. So, she can only transmit for short periods and has to keep moving. Plus, she's had to memorize all the codes. But she's good at that. So, it's a natural division of labor between us.

As the Queen and I say our farewells a little after dawn, we look like two ordinary French women, faux kissing each other's cheeks. "We've come a long way from Baltimore and Montreal," I whisper as we lean close.

For an instant, she pulls back and gives me an appraising look. Then she says, "Oh, the hell with it," and squeezes me in a bear hug. That's unusual coming from her. Since the Queen finished telling me her story that last day in the Pyrenees, she's rebuilt her walls. No personal attachments. She's totally focused on defeating the Nazis.

"That's how my momma would have sent you off," she explains pushing me away again.

"Thank you," I grin up at her and pump my fist in the air. "Now, let's go fuck some Nazis!"

The good news is her bicycle doesn't fall all the way to the ground when she laughs. We'd have a hard time reestablishing our professional credentials if we had to scuttle the mission because one lewd comment broke the transmitter. But it is curious how the oddest things seem downright funny in a war.

As we turn our backs to each other and start pedaling, our plan is to meet for a very short period every other day. She won't be carrying her transmitter at those times. I'll tell her what I've learned, and when the time is right, she'll transmit my information along with anything else she's dug up. As little as possible will be in writing, so as not to attract attention by passing objects back and forth. The good news is we've trained in this, and the Queen's very smart. She remembers everything.

The first meeting will be in the late afternoon at a rural intersection. We set that one before we took off last night. But, after that, I won't know where she is or what she's doing. It's a safety precaution. She'll travel ahead of me to reconnoiter for meeting places and tell me the next location at each meeting.

It's chilly as I pedal north along the Orne River toward the English Channel. And it's not hard to find Nazis. They're everywhere. On foot. In troop carriers. Sometimes I have to pull over to get out of the way. Something is definitely afoot.

I smile at all of them, but it's too soon to start plying my trade. I intend to wait till I get closer to the shore. It takes two hours, but I'm glad I waited. There's even more activity here. Taking it all in, I start my journey west toward Cherbourg smiling and singing and waving at the troops as if I don't have a care in the world.

Some soldiers smile broadly and wave back. Others elbow the fellows next to them and point. More smiles. A few call out. It's still too early to stop. So, I wave and keep riding. This is going to be like shooting fish in a barrel.

By early afternoon, I've warmed up enough to shed my bulky coat and am getting an even better response when I see six young soldiers resting in the shade of a tree. They've obviously been working down on the beach. One in particular attracts me. He's large, well built, and mopping the sweat off his brow with his forearm. I brake to a halt.

"Good afternoon, young gentlemen," I could be speaking to all of them, but my eyes are only for my prey. Pointing at his canteen, I say in awful fractured German, "I see you have some water. Can you spare a drop? All this riding has heated me up. I'd give anything to be wet right now."

The other five hoot and slap their knees. They know and appreciate a proposition when they hear one. But, my target seems to be blushing. How can it get any better than this?

Within minutes, the pink one, as I'm thinking of him at this time, has given me his canteen, and I've patted my face with his water and sprinkled a few drops on my neck, arching my back to make my breasts jut out. He still hasn't said much, but by the time the whistle calls them back to work on the beach, it's settled. I'll be joining them for the evening at the chateau they've commandeered.

The rectangular two-story chateau is large for the area and almost stately. With its solid, native stone walls and high peaked, red-tiled roof, it dominates the slightly rolling farm landscape and is surrounded by utilitarian outbuildings similarly constructed of sturdy stuff. Despite having been overrun by conquerors for years, it's amazingly tidy.

I do not expect the matron of the chateau to greet me at the door. It's surprising that she's still here maintaining her household. But she is.

Madame Orly is a classical French widow who appears to be in her early fifties. Only a bit taller than I am and thin. Not skinny, but that small-boned never-was-rounded-off kind of thin many French women are. She's graying, gunmetal hair pulled back in a bun, below-the-knee black dress buttoned all the way up under her chin and down to her wrists. Black stockings and shoes. Even her eyes and eyebrows are such a dark brown they look black in this light. Both her mouth and eyebrows cut straight lines across her face.

Her demeanor is so severe, when she sees it is me, I'm afraid she won't let me in, and the first words out of her mouth are unnerving. "I know what you are."

I'm not sure which *what* she's talking about. "Madame?" I respond as innocently as I can.

Those sharp, dark eyes look me up and down. "Stanislaw. He's not a Nazi. He's a conscript. A good boy."

Aw. She's just protective of Pinky. "I can assure you, madam," I whisper with a gleam in my eye that I hope is both conspiratorial and suggestive, "I have no intention of *hurting* him."

She steps involuntarily back. Her eyes widen and her mouth drops. She's not sure how she feels about what I just said. Behind her, there's a raucous laugh and the sound of a chair being dragged across the floor.

The widow sighs. "It's like this every night now. This group is different."

Suddenly she sees me as a confidante? "How do you mean?" I ask.

"The ones before. They were professional soldiers who worked all day shoring up the fortifications. Not perfect, mind you, but more disciplined. These..." She tilts her head back toward the sounds emanating from her parlor. "These are hardly soldiers at all. They're all boys, and most of them are not even German."

"Not German?" I can't believe the amount of potentially useful information I'm collecting already.

"Czechs mostly. One from Alsace. Stanislaw's from Poland. Most joined the army after the Nazis took over their countries to please … or to protect their families."

"But not Stanislaw?"

"Non. The army took him. He's a farmer. He gets up early to help me milk the cows. Says it reminds him of home."

The image of this stately, proper French woman squatting on a three-legged stool milking her own cows with a Polish boy in a Nazi uniform gives me pause. War is so strange. And I'm starting to see why she's protective.

Louder voices call out from the interior of the house. She wrings her hands and turns, saying, "I must tend to this."

I stop her by touching her arm. "Would you please tell Stanislaw I'm here."

At first, that sets her back, too. Then she understands and softens ever so slightly. I can tell when she's announced my presence by the hoots and jeers from the parlor, and in a moment the big Polish boy with the bright pink face fills the door frame. When I beckon him to join me outside, he looks positively relieved and after donning his coat walks with me away from the sounds of the others.

I speak no Polish. He speaks no French, and his German is almost as bad as I pretend mine to be. Our conversation is halting, but he warms up when I start asking him questions.

Pointing at the long, deep, trench that cuts across the yard fifty meters in front of the chateau, he explains, "The first soldiers housed here were afraid the British would attack and dug it to hide in."

When I ask him to show me the rest of the farm, he brightens. His color is almost normal as he tells me, "Madame takes very good care of the animals. In return, we eat well."

"Show me." I demand, and he takes me to the barn where black and white milk cows are munching on hay. When he talks to them and pats them on the back, I ask, "You like it here, right?"

"Yes," he grins over the back of a cow at me. "Sometimes I even sleep out here up in the loft just to get away from all that." He points at the chateau house where the sounds of ribaldry can be heard through the closed windows.

"Would you like it if we slept here tonight rather than at the house with all the others?"

It's hard to maintain a demure expression because the poor boy's face is flaming again. He looks so scared I almost laugh out loud. My first night out and could I have hooked a virgin? A fucking virgin? It's almost too perfect.

He literally gulps. His Adam's apple bobs up and down, before he croaks, "Yes." Then, he can breathe again and, suddenly in a hurry as if he's afraid I'll change my mind, he starts blurting, "Stay here. I'll go get my blankets. And some food. I'll be right back. Have a seat. It doesn't get too cold out here. The cows keep it warm. I—"

He's so solicitous, I'm afraid he'll never stop talking. So I step close to him, pull his head down to mine by his ears, and shut him up with a kiss. I don't want to scare him off, so I'm not too aggressive. It's a soft, sudden brushing of lips that makes him gulp again before he's capable of running off to the back door of the chateau. This is going to be so much fun.

When he comes back, he's got everything we could possibly need. You'd think he was a caterer rather than a farmer. We dine and sip wine in the barn loft and talk as best we can. He just turned eighteen. His life story doesn't take long to tell, including everything he's heard and done since being conscripted into the Nazi army. In return, I feed him my cover story. He seems to buy it, but then I'm not sure he's thinking clearly.

When there's finally no other way he can avoid the issue at hand, I ask him if he would like to dance. He looks at me as if I'm crazy, but is incapable of denying me anything. He offers his hands in formal waltz position, but I take them in mine and place them low on my hips. Standing on tiptoe, I reach up and clasp my hands behind his neck. This makes our bodies rub together deliciously. He moans.

"And what if the British do try to land here, how will that go?" I ask as I lead him around the loft taking small little swaying steps.

"Badly, I'm afraid," he sighs and rubs his hands up and down my back, growing a little bolder, pulling me tighter so that I can feel him stiffen between us.

But it's not clear who it'll be bad for. "Why do you say that?"

He exhales an ironic burst of air that starts so deep in his abdomen it jams the bulge in his pants against me even harder. "We're only playing at being soldiers. Since they took me six months ago, we've had almost no training. There aren't enough bullets to teach us how to shoot. I've only held two grenades and can hardly remember how to throw them. We're running out of mines." The litany of deficiencies goes on and on.

I can't believe all the information this dear, sweet boy is handing over without a fight. "So what would *you* do if they attacked?"

"Me?"

He leans backward so that he can look in my face. But when he does so, I slide my arms around his waist to keep his lower body pressed against me, and his expression deepens. He's starting to feel it, really feel it.

"The truth?"

I nod, giving him a knowing look.

"If I get the chance, I intend to dive into that trench in the front yard and not come out until it's over," he confesses in answer to my question.

His choice of words makes me laugh. I want him to dive into my trench right now. I take his ears again and pull him down.

Stanislaw is ready and willing, but he doesn't have a clue. It's a quick in and out that doesn't last nearly long enough for my taste. I think he may have figured that out, because he's adorably shy and nervous about his performance as we lie in each other's arms talking about everything and nothing at the same time.

And then he falls asleep. Asleep? Sure, he worked all day doing construction down at the beach, but he certainly didn't waste any energy here with me. Am I really that much out of practice? Frustration keeps me awake. I stare up at the roof of the barn. But, he's right. It's so cozy in the hayloft that I eventually drift off, too.

Having never slept above cattle before, I'm surprised to learn they apparently sense the dawn long before it shows its shining face. That's why I'm lying awake again in the dark with nothing to do. And still frustrated. Virginal boys? Hah!

Eventually, I can't stand it anymore and seriously consider sneaking down to surprise one of the more experienced house guests by negotiating a pre-dawn solution to my situation. Might even pick up some additional information. Talk about killing two birds with one stone.

But on the other hand, Stanislaw's here and he did show some potential. Why not give him something to remember me by. If he survives the war, that is. I awaken him by tickling his belly with my fingertips. His body reacts instantly.

"Pretty, naïve boy." My voice sounds husky even to me. I lick his nipple, and he flinches involuntarily when my teeth close softly on it.

"There's so much more I can teach you," I whisper in his ear, as my hand slides down to free his stiffening cock to the air. When I bend down to slide back his foreskin with my lips, it dawns on me that this thin flap of skin is probably the reason he's here. Had he been circumcised, he'd probably have been placed in detainment rather than conscripted. In honor of his good fortune, I slide it back and flick the smooth head it's protecting with my tongue.

This time he lasts long enough for me to control my own destiny by riding on top. It's nothing to write home about, but then altruism wouldn't be altruism if it wasn't its own reward, right? So, in the spirit of continued giving, I also collect only a small flat rate for the night, telling him the pleasure was all mine.

I feel an almost maternal pride when Stanislaw and I join the others for a hurried breakfast. I know maternal is certainly an awkward term to use under these circumstances, but it's as close as I can get to describe what I'm experiencing.

As he confidently ushers me into the kitchen with his hand in the small of my back and pulls out my chair, I can tell from the looks that circle the table he's a changed man and not only in his own eyes. I have to lower my head to conceal a prideful smile in the steam that's rising from a blessed cup of tea the house girl Madame Orly still employs has placed in front of me.

Twenty-Three

NANETTE – *Normandy, France, April 1944*

After breakfast, the boys, as I have come to think of the newly minted members of the Wehrmacht staying at Madame Orly's chateau, take me with them to the beach and have the courtesy to point out the different fortifications they have been working on. I show my appreciation of their efforts by going "ooh" and "ahh" as they explain in great detail how each trap and device will thwart the Americans and British if they are foolish enough to try to land here. Then, the whistle calls them to work and I wave au revoir.

Standing on tiptoes, I plant a quick kiss on Stanislaw's lips and say, "Thank you for a wonderful evening and," with a coy smile, "morning." He looks surprised, but puffs up a little and heads down to the shore grinning.

I pedal west on the road that runs along the top of the cliffs that line this part of the English Channel, waving at everyone I see while counting bunkers and fortifications. It's cool and sunny again, lovely really, with good visibility. Every now and then I stop and pretend to gaze out at the Channel while actually verifying the hazards the Nazis are laying on the beach. Now that the boys have explained all the different kinds of fortifications they're constructing, I gather so much detailed information I'm afraid I won't be able to remember it all by the time I meet with the Queen.

In fact, there's so much to see I almost don't make it to our rendezvous about five kilometers inland at the appointed time. As she pulls to a stop in the intersection next to me, I blurt, almost panting with eagerness to tell her everything. "Is there a place we can talk? I have a lot to tell you." I've found out so much. If this keeps up we won't be able to keep to our plan of having only short meetings.

"There's a small church just up the road. On the right. With a graveyard. You go straight in. I'll meet you there." She heads off in the other direction, having spent not even thirty seconds with me on the open road.

It's a very small church, more like a chapel, constructed of field stones covered by buff-colored plaster. The cemetery in the back is old but well-kept. No one greets me when I enter and kneel in the pew, crossing myself and tilting my head downward with my eyes closed. Because I don't hear the Queen coming, I almost jump out of my skin when her hand touches my shoulder. We're really not supposed to meet like this.

"Come with me, poor dear," she says, guiding me off my knees and down the center aisle by my elbow with her right hand while she pats my back with her left. Picking up on the fact that I'm supposed to be grieving, I shake my shoulders intermittently as if I'm sobbing. Who knows who could be watching?

She leads me to a grave that's neither old nor new looking, but has a clear view in all directions. We kneel side by side our hands raised palms-together in front of our mouths and noses, and I tell her in a low voice, "The Nazis are expecting something."

"I get the same feeling," she pretends to be praying and doesn't look at me. "Did you find out what or when?"

"No specific time frame, but soon," I answer. "It's a sea landing. A German combat division recently arrived, but they're not battle ready. Heck, they're hardly even soldiers. They have few weapons and little training. They spend most of their time helping fortify the beaches." Then I add the details.

More quickly than I thought possible, the Queen distills the information I give her and announces the time and place of our next meeting. It's only a little farther west. "I'd like to take a look at the fortifications to the east," I tell her. "Just to verify whether they're in the same state of readiness."

"Okay." She nods pensively then asks, "Can you make it to that meeting spot in two days?" Evidently she's prepared to change the plan if necessary.

After reviewing my mental maps of the area, I answer, "Yes. If I stay at the chateau tonight and tomorrow night, I can get a good start the next morning."

As she's standing and crossing herself again, she adds, "Good. From there it won't be far to Bayeux. I heard some kind of command post has been set up there. You should probably check that out next."

I'm only a beat behind, standing and crossing myself, too. Then I turn to face her and place my hand on her forearm, saying aloud, "Thank you for praying with me," before turning and walking away. As I said, you never know who could be watching.

I pedal back to the beach as fast as I can and get there in time to be waiting for the boys under a tree when they climb off the sand to head home. Stanislaw is obviously surprised but happy to see me, and the others hoot and snigger and elbow each other when they do. One leans over to speak in Stanislaw's ear, and he shakes his head vigorously in response.

"What did he say?" I ask after pulling him down by his collar to kiss him lightly on the lips.

There's a bit of swagger in his voice and step when he answers, "He asked if you were available tonight."

"And what did you tell him?"

"No." He tosses me a salacious grin and adds, "I told him you and I have a lot more business to conduct." With this, he drapes his arm possessively over my shoulders and we swagger together back to the chateau.

Tonight's different. Several local girls are here, and Stanislaw and I partake of the party. We dance a little and drink so much I'm afraid he won't be able to perform. I know the wine won't faze me. I've always been able to hold my liquor. Can drink ten men under the table if necessary. It's one of my special talents.

But, I don't want to spend another night staring up at the rafters in misery. So, I take him by the arm before he gets too far gone. Still, as we climb the ladder to the loft, I tell myself that if he can't take care of business this time, I *will* seek out one of the others. I've already decided who. After all, I should be interrogating as many of them as possible, shouldn't I?

Big surprise. Stanislaw's no shrinking violet. The minute we're up there, he starts unbuttoning his shirt and soon stands proudly at attention before me. "What you did this morning with your mouth," he says, "that was good." It's almost a command rather than a compliment.

That's when I realize he might need taking down a notch or two, and I come up with just the plan to do it. Instead of complying, I cup his cheek in my palm, look him in the eye, and say, "What's good for the goose is good for the gander, dear boy."

Of course he doesn't get it. Perhaps our combined misbegotten German isn't up to conveying so subtle a metaphor. So I try again, starting, "I have a question to ask you Stanislaw. Is that okay?"

He nods both heads. Funny boy.

"I can just blow you now, and we can go to sleep."

Before I reach the second part, he adds an eager smile to his nod.

"Or," I continue, "tonight I can teach you secrets. Secrets that will make you such a good lover that women will beg to have you in their bed." This time there's no altruism involved. I've figured out how to get what I want from him.

His eyes narrow at the thought. He truly is a greedy little bastard at heart.

"You're paying. It's your call." If I've read him right, he'll be putty in my hands the rest of the night. But I add for insurance, "I think you'll be more than satisfied doing it my way, but if you're not, I'll do anything you want."

"Anything?"

"But first," I step closer, lay my hand on his shoulder, and say seriously, "You have to promise me you'll do exactly what I tell you when I tell you. Okay?"

I've learned from the Queen's tale that imposing this rule adds an element of suspense that heightens the anticipation. He gulps. I'm tempted to go so far as to blindfold him, but then I'd end up doing all the work again. This time I want him to be the one taking action.

Instead, I say in the sexiest tone I can muster, "I want you to make love to me. Will you let me teach you how?"

His eyes wide as plates, his breathing deepens and he succumbs to the spell. "Yes." He can hardly croak out the word. Tonight's going to be just fine.

"Good then. You may undress me."

His fingers fumble with the buttons of my blouse, but eventually my breasts are exposed to the night air. He sinks to his knees to help me step out of my skirt and panties, so that his head is nipple high.

Seeing the moment he realizes his proximity, I say, "Touch me."

"Where?" It's a whisper.

"Anywhere you like."

His hands are rough from years of farming and fortifying. The calluses leave itchy little tingles on my back and butt and thighs as he scrutinizes and explores in the lantern light. When he moves them up to my breasts, however, I tell him to sit on the blanket and position myself between his legs with my back toward him.

He automatically wraps his arms around me, and I place his hands over my breasts, leaning back into his chest, ask, "Do you like them."

"Yes." He's milked cows. He knows what to do with teats. He cradles them, plays with the nipples, squeezing and pulling. But when I writhe slightly with pleasure and sigh, he stops and says, "I'm sorry. I didn't mean to hurt you."

"Oh, no." I lean to the side so that I can turn my head and look up at him. "That is not the sound of pain. That means I like what you are doing." He grins, and I reach behind his head and pull him down to a kiss.

Picking up on his cue, Stanislaw does better than I hoped he would. Kissing me deeply, he kneads and pulls my teat, connecting my mouth, breast, and loins with one long hot stream of pleasure and longing. This is going to be just fine.

"There's something else you need to know about pleasing women," I squeeze the words out between shallow breaths, pulling his other hand around me, down to my belly and below. "Feel this?" I guide his finger over the swollen knob in the middle of my lower lips, "That's the most important—" I'm unable to finish the sentence, because he's experimenting.

"I've heard of this." His boyish pride is endearing. "Does *that* feel good?" He tries something new.

"Ohhh, yes." I'm starting to believe he's not the novice he made himself out to be the night before. "Feel this?" I've forced his finger further down between the creases."

"It's hot," he whispers into my ear, "and wet."

"That means we want you." But we have a problem. This is going so well that I can't sit still. My back and bottom move in response to his touch, agitating his engorged member to the point that he stops kissing and starts breathing open-mouthed against my neck and pushing back at me.

"Stop," I say.

"Why?" It comes out in a gasp.

"Women take longer than men. You have to learn to pace yourself."

"But, how can I do that?" He sounds chastised, contrite.

"Think of something else. Do whatever you have to do, but don't come until I tell you!" It's an order. I know he'll make the attempt, but the way things are going, I'm not sure he'll succeed. So I change my tactics. It was about time anyway.

I disengage and lie down on the blanket in front of him. Giving me a relieved look, he spreads my thighs and kneels between them. The poor boy thinks I'm going to end his misery now. As he starts to lean over me, I say, "No. Not yet."

The look on his face is so disappointed I almost laugh, but I don't relent.

"Now, you're going to do for me what I did for you this morning."

Disappointment shifts to surprise so quickly I have to cover my smile with my hand to avoid offending him. Then curiosity takes precedence.

"Don't try to tell me you haven't heard of this?"

His expression gives him away. "I've heard of it. It's just that I don't know what to do," he admits.

Pulling him down onto me, I whisper, "That's what I'm here for. To teach you. Start with my breasts."

Following directions, he works his lips and tongue down my belly to the sweet spot. He's a natural. Before long, I'm forced to resort mostly to non-verbal communication, because my rational mind is losing its grasp. When he comes up with the idea to use his teeth I almost bounce out of the loft and fall on the cows.

"You like that." It's not a question. It's a prideful statement of masculine truth made in a husky voice.

"Yes. Ohhh yes." I open my eyes to find him grinning at me like a kid at school waiting for approval. I grab his ears and pull him up again for a kiss before guiding him back down there where he belongs and ask, "Do you feel how wet it is now?"

He nods and looks at me without losing contact. He is all forehead and eyes.

"That means I'm ready for you." I take time to breathe and calm myself down.

When I push his finger deeper into the gap we've opened, he lets out a soft breath himself before observing, "It's so smooth and hot."

"So are you," I respond, stroking his engorged penis. "But can you wait a little longer?"

He nods again.

"Good. I want you to keep doing what you were doing." My directions must be explicit. I don't want to miss this opportunity.

"But when I say 'stop,' stop immediately and..." I give his cock a little squeeze. "And take me as hard and fast as you can. Understand?"

"Uh huh." He's breathing hard.

My plan works brilliantly. In an instant, he's experimenting with a combination of fingers and tongue that has me moaning and lifting my hips to meet him. I reward him by begging, "Yes. Yes. Yes," and he groans.

I know there's a danger I'll take it too far and lose him before I'm ready, but I'm not there yet. If I stop too soon, I might not come when he does. "Don't stop!"

As if it's too hard to wait, he inserts a second finger and pushes deeper. "I'm so close!" I hope he realizes that's code for "Please keep doing what you're doing and hang on for just a little longer!"

He responds by sucking hard on the knob of my clit.

"Stop!" Thank God he follows orders!

"Now?" He's wide eyed, looming above me.

"Yes, damn it! Now!"

He enters me with a jolt, ramming all the way to the hilt with the first thrust. We attack each other furiously, grunting and pumping, and I hold on to him for dear life until our screams of release startle the cows.

"Wow!" I say later as we lie on our backs panting.

"You mean it?" It's cute he's insecure.

"Yes," I answer truthfully. "Wow!" My boy Stanislaw is going to be a star.

Twenty-Four

NANETTE – *Normandy, France, April 1944*

Nothing much happens the next day. The others greet us at breakfast with knowing looks, but I'm getting used to it, and it's actually good for my cover. I don't escort them to the beach this time, and they go through the whole snigger and adjust their crotch routine when I tell Stanislaw I'll see him that evening.

I spend the day exploring the territory to the east I hadn't visited before, but finding little new to report. Germans milling about everywhere. A few drilling in formation. Most fortifying the shoreline. Returning to the chateau well before the boys are due back for dinner, I help Madame and the house girl with the chores until she beckons for me to join her in the kitchen.

Handing me a cup of hot Nazi coffee, she directs me to sit. Coffee's hard to come by. So, I figure we're about to have an important heart-to-heart talk of some kind. I thank her for the cup and wait.

"Nanette," she begins, "it's good that you're here."

I'm not sure how to take that. Was this about Stanislaw or something else? I give her a coy smile and coo, "I told you I wouldn't hurt the boy."

I'm surprised to see a twinkle in her eye and a slight upward curl at the edges of that stern French-matron mouth. There's a woman with a sense of humor in there somewhere.

"This is not about Stanislaw." Madame Orly leans forward to use a low voice. Evidently she doesn't know whether she can trust the house girl. "It's the Gestapo. They're looking for a spy."

"A spy?" I maintain what I hope is a properly confused but disinterested demeanor. "Why are you telling *me* this?"

"Someone recently started broadcasting near here. Right about the time you showed up. The Gestapo questioned three of the boys this morning. They weren't sure what to tell them about you, other than you've been here."

She seems genuinely worried.

"But..." She pats my arm as if to assure me everything's all right. "That could be a good thing, because if you are here with us when the spy is transmitting..."

"Then it can't be me." I finish her sentence with more confidence than I had only seconds before. If the Queen broadcast all the information I gave her on schedule last night, I have an iron-clad alibi. And I'll have time to warn her before she's due to send again.

Madame Orly nods, her hand still on my arm.

"But how do you know all this?" I ask.

"Stanislaw rushed home during his lunch break to warn you."

My smile is genuine. That was sweet. "I'm sure Stanislaw had nothing but *nice* things to tell the Gestapo about me."

Madame studies me before responding, "You like him."

Nodding, I answer, "Like you said. He's a good boy."

"He'll be a good man ... if he survives this war," Madame adds her approval.

"Oh, in some ways, he's a good *man* already," I'm pushing the envelope a little here, but I think that, like so many other proper, upstanding women I know, Madame Orly has a secret frisky side.

My risk-taking is rewarded by the twinkle that returns to her eye and the grin that reveals dimples on her cheeks. "Oh, my Henri was a *very* good man," she offers and then hides the blush her words bring to her cheeks behind her coffee cup, pretending to take a sip.

"How long has he been gone?"

"Two and a half years," she sighs lowering the cup again.

"You miss him." It's not a question.

"Very much." She sighs again, setting the cup down on the table. "He became ill not long after the Germans came here."

We spend the rest of the afternoon as if we were two old friends, chatting about this and that but mostly about life and love. Madame Orly turns out to be quite a woman. If she and Stanislaw both survive the war, the world will be a better place.

Our respite is broken by the house girl reclaiming the kitchen so that she can prepare dinner. I take the opportunity to clean the sweat and dust of the day off my body and change clothes. Before long Stanislaw and the others return for dinner.

When we gather around the table, Stanislaw surprises me with a toast. "To Nanette!"

I can't imagine he's toasting me for last night's performance. But if he is, so be it. I drop my head demurely, waiting.

"She's not the spy!"

"Hear! Hear!" The others voice their approval of his toast.

Not knowing whether Madame broke a confidence by warning me, I act surprised rather than relieved. "Why in the world would anyone think I was a spy?" I ask as innocently as I can.

Madame Orly has joined us for dinner this night. Her glass is raised, too. She nods her approval of how I've played it.

"There have been radio signals." Stanislaw fills in the details, "A local man who works occasionally with the Gestapo reported that he saw a strange woman in the area at the time the signals started." He stops to take a sip of wine as serious nods of affirmation circle the table.

"And," he grins as he continues, "everyone down at the beach knows about *you*." This time the nods are accompanied by smiles and low but enthusiastic hoots. Then Stanislaw concludes, "But whoever it is broadcast again last night. And we know exactly what you were doing at the time!" He flashes me a knowing smile. "Don't we?"

One of the Czechs sniggers then picks up the tale, "It's really lucky you were with us the last two nights." He goes on to repeat the story about the collaborator, ending, "They questioned us all separately."

I'm touched, but a little worried when the Czech adds, "The Gestapo didn't like it when we all vouched for you."

It's time to get out of here. Sliding my arm through Stanislaw's and leaning against his shoulder, I purr, "I guess I got lucky in more ways than one then." Inside I marvel at exactly how true that is.

Stanislaw beams as hoots erupt around the table. But he doesn't blush. I guess Pinky was a short-lived nickname. That's the end of the spy talk until we make our way back to the barn, where he tells me everything he knows, including the fact that the Gestapo are so serious about shutting down the radio signals that they've offered a reward. I promise I'll keep my eyes out and share anything I discover with him.

This morning I'm pretty smug. Stanislaw's third class went well, very well indeed. I believe he's the best pupil I've ever had, and I'm going to miss him. But my work here is done. It's time to move on. I'll tell him when I bring the boys lunch down at the beach. Hopefully they'll know more about the spy search by then.

We spread out in the shade, and I unpack a French picnic, fresh baguettes from the boulangerie, cheese, and ham. I've even brought a bottle of Madame's table claret. It is, after all, my going-away party.

The boys aren't happy I'm leaving. I think they hoped I'd take on more pupils now that Stanislaw has his degree. Before I watch them walk down to the beach for the last time, I kiss all of their cheeks goodbye and throw my arms around Stanislaw's neck one last time.

"Good luck in the trenches," I whisper into his ear. He squeezes me to his body and gives me such a long, hard, probing kiss that it's impossible to think of him as a boy anymore. I wave sadly as he turns to face me when he's caught up with the others at the bottom, then start the slow ride back to the chateau to collect my things.

A man is leaving the chateau. I see him from a distance and pull off the side of the road into the trees. He looks in my direction for a long while as if expecting someone, but apparently doesn't see me. Eventually he turns and heads the other way on his bicycle.

He wasn't close enough for me to get a good look at his face, but I've mastered his general description. Middle aged, in his forties maybe. Medium height, a little stocky. Dressed like a local, brown slacks, tan work shirt tucked in, a brown beret.

After he's disappeared down the road, I pedal the rest of the way to the chateau and knock to announce myself before entering. Madame comes from the kitchen to greet me.

"I saw a *man* leaving, Madame." In light of our discussion about good men last night, I've decided to use a teasing tone.

"Him? A man? Hardly." She's obviously not impressed by her visitor. "That was Fabrice Fragonard."

I stick out my lower lip, lower my eyebrows, shrug and say, "Never heard of him."

"No reason to," she responds. "He's got a small farm this side of town. Has been trying to get in with the Germans since they first got here." Turning back toward the kitchen, she continues, "He thinks this spy business is his ticket."

Following her to the back of the house, I push the subject, "What gives him that idea? And why did he come here?"

"He's says he's the one who saw the strange woman. He didn't believe Stanislaw and the others that you couldn't be the one sending coded messages and wanted to see you for himself. But after he told me what she looked like, I assured him it is not you."

"What does this strange woman look like?"

From the description Fragonard gave Madame Orly, he's obviously seen the Queen and put two and two together. This is not good. She's got to get out of the area.

"And he's a mean one," Madame continues. "Never could trust him. Even the Germans seem to sense that. He's angry they won't listen to him."

When I tell Madame Orly I'm leaving, she tries to get me to stay. I like the woman and would enjoy spending more time with her. Instead, however, I go out to the barn, pack my bags, and say goodbye to the cows.

Madame and I chat as I tie the bags behind the bicycle seat, and I find myself concerned for her safety. "What will you do if the Americans and British land here?" I ask.

"Hide in the trench," her answer is quick. She's thought this out. "If they come ashore here, the fighting down by the beach will be over quickly. If they succeed, this will be the first place liberated. If not..." She shrugs as if she's weighed the danger versus the rewards and found them balanced.

"See if you can get Stanislaw to join you there," I suggest. From the look she gives me in response I gather it's not a new idea and continue, "I think he's meant to be a lover rather than a fighter."

Madame's eyes crinkle above the hand she's raised to cover her giggle. "I'll see what I can do," she offers, and when I think she's about to kiss my cheeks in farewell, she hugs me instead. I pedal away from the chateau with a sense of loss and tell myself I'll come back after this is all over to see how they fared. Good luck, my friends.

Having plenty of time to reach the spot the Queen has chosen for our rendezvous and anticipating that she will agree we need to travel tonight, I stop in the nearby village for bread and cheese to see us through. As I return with the baguettes, that man Fragonard is tying my suitcases back to my bicycle. He's obviously gone through them. It's a good thing I'm not the one with the transmitter.

When he walks in my direction, I step out of the doorway and say, "Bonjour," as we pass on the street. That gives him a good look at me. He tips his head in return and keeps walking. I hope that means he's convinced I'm not the spy.

But I don't assume anything. That's foolish ... and dangerous. Instead, I pay close attention once I am back on the road. It doesn't take long before I'm sure he's following me. This presents a problem. If I lead him to the Queen, he'll recognize her. How can I get him to let me go on alone?

I pull over at a farm house and knock on the door. Thank goodness nobody answers. I take time to write a note about how sorry I was to miss them and push it half way under the door, smiling inwardly at the confusion it will cause when the residents of the house find it. Then, shaking my head, I start back the way I came and tip my head at Fragonard as we pass for the second time.

Damn. He's behind me again. He didn't waste as much time looking at the note as I'd hoped. That would have given me a chance to lose him.

I'm stuck between a rock and a hard place. I have to keep heading in the general direction of the rendezvous spot. If I'm not at the meeting place within the designated time frame, the Queen will go on without me. I'll lose contact with her. Our mission will fail, and even worse, she won't know that Fragonard has given the Germans her description. But I can't meet her with him following me.

So, I start working my way in the right direction on a narrow winding back road the Germans don't seem to use. It's sparsely populated, lined with fields and woods. Good places to hide. I choose a concealed spot in the woods at the side of the road and wait. If he doesn't show up, I'll just go on my way.

I've learned a lot from other people's mistakes since starting this job, and now the story the Queen told me when we were crossing the Pyrenees pays off again. While I wait, I double check the knife I wear strapped to my ankle and make sure the two-shot derringer I always wear in a thigh holster when I travel to our meetings is loaded and half-cocked with the safety on.

The Queen and I have worked out a system. We've sliced the bottom of the skirt pocket on our gun sides. That gives us direct, but hidden, access to our derringers.

I hear him before I see him. He's puffing in the heat of the slight uphill climb. Holding my breath I watch him pedal slowly by and disappear around the next bend. My plan is to lose him by sneaking back down the road the way we came. I wait till I think he's far enough away, but I don't get far.

"Ah hah!" He bellows behind me.

Damn. He must have noticed the lack of new tire tracks on the road. There's nothing to do but face my nemesis. I stop and turn around, asking, "Why are you following me, monsieur?"

"Don't play coy with me," he's still bellowing as he brakes to a halt and drops his bicycle. "You know why I'm here."

Up close, he's still average. Maybe a little older than I had guessed, medium height and weight, brown hair and eyes, the craggy face of a man who's worked the Normandy soil his whole life.

"No, monsieur, you are wrong. I have no idea why you are here. Please tell me." I hold my ground, keeping my bicycle between us.

Whack! The bastard slaps me! The imprints of the calluses on the tips of his short stubby fingers and palm will probably be visible for hours.

Staggering from the blow, I almost drop my bike. Then he grabs my left wrist and I realize I should have. I should have run as fast as I could. But it's too late now.

"So, you've heard I am a prostitute and you're looking to steal a free blow job, is that it?" I strike a saucy pose, tilting my head back and pointing my chin at him. It's not easy with him holding my wrist.

"I don't do free blow jobs." I stomp my foot. "But I could give you a discount, if you promise not to tell."

"Fuck your blow jobs!"

The sentence is laughable, but his tone of voice is dangerous. "So you want the whole package then?" I keep up the teasing.

That just makes him twist my arm to silence me. Pulling me toward him and leaning down so that his face is up against mine, he growls, "You and that old woman and her bunch of pansy conscripts think you can pull one over on me? Well, think again. I knew you were connected with the spy, and the way you've behaved today proves it. It's that other woman isn't it? You're working together. You collect. She transmits."

For such a nasty, ugly, average man he's done an exceptional job of putting the pieces together. I give him a blank look and keep playing the role. "What other woman are you talking about?"

"You're going to take me to her," he orders, twisting my arm harder.

I want to ask him if he's looking for a threesome, but he's strong enough to break my arm and I can't take that chance. Instead, I whimper and fall to my knees forcing him to pull me back up by the wrist. That gives me a chance to turn my right side away from him so that he can't see my hand slip into my pocket.

He drags me over the fallen bicycle by the wrist so that I'm standing right next to him. Without saying a word, I flip off the safety, put the muzzle of the derringer against his ribs, and pull the trigger.

He's so arrogant and sure of himself that he can't believe what's happened. Like a burlesque pantomime of getting shot, his eyes widen and he rocks backward onto his heels, throwing his hands up to his chest and releasing me. Then his eyes accuse me of betraying him, as if I had owed him better. It would be comical if shooting another human being could ever be considered funny.

But my idyll with sweet Stanislaw must have taken my edge off. It's a mistake to go pensive in the middle of a firefight. Although Fragonard is average, he's bulky, and derringers aren't the most powerful of weapons. While I'm standing there watching and thinking, he realizes he's not dead yet and can possibly survive this encounter.

Catching me by surprise, he grabs a handful of my hair and swats wildly for the gun with his other hand. But I duck the blow by crashing into his chest instead of pulling away. Sliding the derringer up under his chin, I fire the second round. If that doesn't finish him, I've got a fight on my hands.

He staggers backward, and this time I don't lollygag watching my handiwork. I'm five feet away before he falls on his back. I wouldn't have been able to read his expression even if I'd been closer. The bullet removed his upper lip and nose when it exited.

By the time he stops breathing, I've already dragged him off the road. My watch showing how little time I can afford to spend cleaning up this mess and still get to the rendezvous on time, I leave his body as deep in the woods as I can. After going back for his bicycle, I take all of his money out of his billfold and then drop it open on his chest. If they find him soon, hopefully they'll think this was a robbery. After covering him with whatever branches and twigs are handy and obliterating the signs of blood and struggle in the roadway I'm back on the road with a lot to tell the Queen.

Thinking it through as I complete these chores, I realize that Madame Orly was probably right. Fabrice Fragonard was a bad man. As a result I regret only two things: that I couldn't do a better job of hiding the body and didn't have the chance to find out if he had told his spy theory to anyone else.

Twenty-Five

JOE – *Montreal, Canada, the Last Day, 1992*

"Was Fragonard the first person you ever killed?" Joe asked.

Nanette considered him with slitted eyes before answering in a flat voice, "What do you think?" After holding his gaze a while longer, she added, "I'd already been in the spy business for two and a half years. That was my sixth drop behind the lines."

Okay. So it had been a silly question. Joe was also pretty sure Fragonard wasn't the last.

Then she changed the subject. "So what do you think of Nanette?"

Joe didn't answer right away. Was the wily old woman seeking some sort of validation at this late date? Giving her a taste of her own medicine, he appraised her seriously for some time while formulating a safe response.

"Well, I can honestly say," he started and then paused, narrowing his eyes to match hers. "That I've never met anyone quite like her before."

A closed lipped smile spread across Nanette's face and lit up her eyes making it clear how much she loved that kind of sparring. Adjusting her posture in her chair to sit up taller, which almost made her look prim, she asked, "You aren't scandalized, then?"

"Hardly," Joe matched her smile with an intentionally sly grin and one arched eyebrow. "More like intrigued."

"Good." She settled her hands demurely on her lap. "Then it's time you met Fritz."

NANETTE – *Normandy, April 1944*

The Queen's happy to hit the road. She's had a second sense that she was being targeted, but then that's normal when you're the radio operator. The Nazis know you're out there the minute you start broadcasting. The hunt is always on.

I give her half of the bread and cheese, and we're on our separate ways. My next stop is Bayeux. According to my mental map, Bayeux is about twenty-four kilometers away. I won't make it early enough tonight to find a place to stay. So I ride to a village near the half-way point and, finding no handsome young Nazis to seduce into providing my night's lodging, I spend Fragonard's money on a room at the tiny inn and chat with the mistress of the establishment until she's ready to close the dining room. When I tell her the story that I intend to stay with a cousin in Cherbourg, she shakes her head.

"What is it?" I ask.

"Personally? I wouldn't go anywhere near the coast," she answers. "There is a rumor the British will attack soon, and the Nazis are preparing for them." Shaking her head, she concludes, "I wouldn't take a chance getting caught up in that."

This concerns me. If even the civilians know an invasion is coming here, how will we ever succeed?

The next day, I'm in Bayeux before noon. It's a quaint old town with a gray stone cathedral that was built almost a thousand years ago. In the middle of the cathedral square, there's a Liberty Tree that was planted during the French Revolution. It's huge and looks a lot like the sycamores we have in Canada. I don't have to pretend to gawk like a tourist.

When I walk around the big tree, I see something that takes my breath away. A man. A big man. But not big like fat or even muscle. It's his bones that are big. His shoulders seem a meter wide, and the knobs of them are well defined.

He's sitting on a small folding stool hunched so far over I can count each individual vertebra of his back and neck through the gray German uniform he's wearing. Without even thinking, I walk up behind him and look over his shoulder to see what he's so intent upon. His hair is a warm light brown, cut a little longer than usual for Nazis. It must tickle his ears. And he has the biggest hands I have ever seen, thick wrists, long boney fingers with every knuckle well defined, palms six inches across.

But what makes my heart skip a beat is what those coarse-looking, brutish fingers are doing. They are gliding a piece of charcoal quickly, but smoothly and precisely, across a sketch pad that's resting on his knees. This giant Nazi is not just creating a delicate and intricate drawing of the square. He's capturing the soul of the place on paper.

As if mesmerized, I lose track of time standing behind him, listening to the little scratching noises the charcoal makes, and watching the square come to life in his sketchbook. I'm intensely aware of everything around me, birds chirping in the tree, insects buzzing, children's voices, red and yellow tulips in a window box across from the entrance to the cathedral. It is such an amazingly beautiful, rich, world we live in.

"That's lovely," slips out of my mouth in French, and that reverie fades away.

He straightens as he slowly pivots on his camp stool. Sitting upright, his eyes are level with mine, he's that tall. They're deep-set, almost clear, and seem to reflect the sky. The pale edges of his eyebrows tell me his hair will lighten in the summer sun as his skin tans to brown.

Cocking one golden brow, he scrutinizes me from the top of my head to my toes and then back up again, but not in that leering way men usually do. He's evaluating, measuring. He has artists' eyes, and I know he sees things no one else sees. What does he see in me?

"What did you say?" he asks. His lips are full, and his teeth aren't bad. But they're not perfect. That gives him character.

But, from his tone, it seems that I've either confused or offended him. I offer my brightest smile and try again in pidgin German. "I'm sorry to intrude. It's just that your work is so beautiful."

He smiles openly now. I'm on solid ground.

Then, he looks me up and down again and says in textbook Parisian French, "Ah, five-foot-one. Ninety-five pounds. Yellow scarf. Speaks gutter German."

My heart stops beating. He's repeating a description he's heard. They're looking for me. I try to appear calm while my mind races and my eyes search for escape routes.

He continues, "You can only be the fallen angel who worked such miracles for that poor Polish farm boy over near Caen."

What?

"Congratulations." He offers one of those giant hands.

I'm surprised, but of course I shouldn't be. Stanislaw earned his bragging rights, and the other boys have functioned as a cheering section from the beginning. Plus, it's actually good for my cover.

Still, it takes a conscious effort to close my mouth as my hand rises to meet the big man's. When those powerful fingers close around mine they are soft and smooth and warm. "I beg your pardon?" It's all I can think of to say.

"I said 'congratulations.' We had a lottery going on the poor boy, and you beat the odds makers."

My hand's still captive, and now for some ungodly reason my cheeks are getting warm. I look everywhere but at him and try to pull away.

"No, don't take it wrong." Still holding on he explains, "It's good that poor wretch got at least one taste of heaven before he died."

Somehow my fingers have escaped, because both of my hands are covering my mouth. "Stanislaw? What happened to Stanislaw?"

"No, no, no. Nothing happened to the boy." The big Nazi's chuckling now, "I was rather ineptly attempting to make a philosophical point. And the odds did seem pretty solid that he'd go home at the end of the war as inexperienced as he was when it started."

That's a relief. But, now I'm surprised and concerned about something else. News, evidently all kinds of news, travels a lot faster and a lot farther among the Nazis than I expected. I'll have to be very careful to keep my story straight.

I'm supposed to be a coquette. It's about time I started acting like one. Batting my eyelashes, I say, "I'm sorry, monsieur. You must have mistaken me for someone else," and turn to walk away.

"*Stanislaw*? What happened to *Stanislaw*?" The squeaky little voice he uses to mock me does just that.

I turn and face him intending to appear defiant.

Rising from his stool, he extends his hand again, saying, "My name is Fritz Huegel. I was down on the beach north of Caen yesterday. I go there regularly, because it is my job to coordinate the delivery of the supplies they need to fortify the coast."

Now I notice the epaulette on the shoulder straps of his tunic. He's a low ranking officer, the German equivalent of a sergeant. That means he's possibly not career military. And he said "they." It's possible he's not even a Nazi. I breathe more easily.

He continues, "And *Stanislaw* just went on and on about his *multiple* accomplishments."

His eyes bore into mine. Instead of accepting his hand this time, I walk past him with my nose in the air and sit on a bench in front of the bakery that faces the cathedral. With my back pressed against the cool, hard stone, I make a point of not looking at him.

But, he's just what I'm looking for. An officer whose job is to supply all of the fortifications on the coast. I'm formulating the opening lines of the new conversation I'm going to start with him when the bench sags as he sits beside me.

I begin, "So, are they talking about me all the way to Cherbourg?"

"Probably not all the way. Not yet anyway. But I can let you know when I get back in a few days. That should give the story time to get there."

He does have a nice voice.

"Are you proposing I meet you in a few days?" I've got the upper hand now.

"Actually, my housemates will never let me hear the end of it if I don't bring you home for dinner tonight."

"Home?" I try to sound only somewhat interested, as if I have other options to consider. "Housemates?"

"Yes," he obliges. "Eight of us are staying in a rather nice estate just outside of town. It's very comfortable. And you do need a place to stay, don't you?" His perfect French is ripe with innuendo.

"Eight?" I hem and haw. "Is *one* of them as cute as Stanislaw?" I ask intending to limit his expectations.

"Oh, I'm sure you'll find at least *one* of them to your liking," he plays along.

It's a fine semantic game now. "Well, *one* is all I need." I make my point clear.

"Then I'm sure we can find some *one* to accommodate you." He laughs and then tells me how to find the house. Saying his lunch time is over, he packs up his stool, charcoal, and sketch pad and strides under the Liberty Tree and out the far side of the square.

I watch him disappear, thinking I'm a very lucky spy. Very lucky indeed.

Twenty-Six

JOE – *Montreal, Canada, the Last Day, 1992*

Nanette didn't look like she felt lucky. She looked distressed.

Joe reached down and touched her arm. "You okay?" When she didn't respond right away, he watched her work herself through whatever was bothering her.

Controlling her emotions was something she was good at. It didn't take long before the gleam reappeared in her eye. Nanette puffed up her cheeks and blew air out while shaking her head. "Where'd you hide that flask?"

Taking this to mean she didn't want to explain what had just happened, Joe let it go. He slid his hand inside the lapel of his jacket like a gangster retrieving his pistol. After looking around furtively in a pantomime of someone making sure there were no witnesses, he withdrew the flask and held it just out of Nanette's reach. "Is this something you want? Or need?"

"You little son of a..." But she was smiling. "Occasionally, there are exceptions to the rule."

She swept her hand up to grab the flask. Joe didn't put up a fight, but when she tried to unscrew the cap, she stopped, made a face that said the effort was painful, and handed it back to him. "Shhh." Joe arched an eyebrow. He unscrewed the top, and then leaned over close to her as if trying to conceal the fact that he was placing the flask back in her hands from prying eyes.

Nanette lifted the small opening up to her nose and inhaled deeply, eyes closed. Then, she flashed him a bright smile and said, "That is better than a lover."

Joe widened his eyes and bobbed his head twice in her direction, telling her to go on.

Still smiling, she explained, "It's always what it seems to be and..."

He bobbed his head again.

"It always keeps its promise." She took a first small sip, and then a larger second one. Saying, "Ah, yes," she settled back in her chair.

After a few moments of silence, Joe intuited that it was safe to go back to the story and said, "So, Fritz was a *procurement* officer?" It was hard to keep his face straight.

Nanette responded with a stern look that turned into an impish grin. "Yes he was, mon cher." She took an even larger third swig from the flask before lighting a cigarette. "But when he brought me home, he had no idea what he was procuring."

NANETTE – *Bayeux, France, April 1944*

Bayeux is only about ten kilometers from the beaches, and the house Fritz lives in is near the halfway point. From the front, his description is accurate. It is a rather nice estate. The large two-story main building made of natural cut stone blocks sits up close to the sandy road. An archway through the middle of the first floor leads to a walled cobblestone courtyard with sides about a hundred feet long.

But I have been directed to approach through the back gate that enters through the garden, fields, and orchard. Having been there the longest and holding the highest rank, Fritz has commandeered private quarters, an out building on this far side of the courtyard. He opens the door when I knock.

Standing with my two suitcases full of clothes and other feminine needs, I pause, temporarily startled again by the sheer bulk of him blocking the portal. He looks down at my bags for an instant before saying, "So nice you could drop by." Taking them from me, he pivots on his heels, and I follow him in.

Fritz lives in one fairly large room. It could have been the estate's saddlery, back when there were no cars. Every wall that's not a window is covered by sketches and water colors. My jaw drops and stays slack as I move slowly from one to another, bending at the waist to get closer looks when necessary and standing on tiptoes to see others. He's made his part of the war beautiful. Tanks, personnel carriers, cannons, sturdy young German soldiers leaning into shovels, wiping their brows. Each captured in exquisite detail.

"They're wonderful!" I spin around taking one quick flying look at all of them and coming to a stop facing him. "Absolutely wonderful!" I catch myself gushing.

"Dinner's in half an hour," he says walking toward the door. "You may join us whenever you're ready. There's a basin in the corner in case you wish to clean up." And then he's gone.

It's not the greeting I'd expected, or to be more honest, hoped for. But, he does have a point. I'm a little rough around the edges to make a good first impression. Twenty minutes later, cleaned, combed, and dressed in a slightly better skirt and blouse I stroll casually across the courtyard and enter the kitchen.

Like Madame Orly in Caen, Monsieur and Madame Roget, the current master and mistress of this manor, have chosen to live with the Nazi occupiers rather than abandon their home altogether. For almost four years, they have banished themselves to one upstairs wing of the house. However, they have apparently worked out an amicable arrangement for sharing the kitchen and dining area, because I see their backs leaving as I enter.

"Ah, there she is as promised!" Fritz booms the announcement of my arrival, and eleven new faces turn to study me. I'm surprised at how relieved I am to see the four other girls.

Half an hour later, I've learned everyone's first name, and they've all laughed at my inept German. They don't even realize they're telling me everything I want to know.

After a while, Fritz disappears into the kitchen, and of course I follow. He's not only an artist on paper, he's also apparently a culinary maestro as well, because dinner smells divine, and he's the only one tending the pots.

"You are the perfect man," I tell him, stepping over to help.

"Far from perfect," his back replies.

I ignore his unnecessarily dour response. Within minutes we are presenting his beef bourguignon to the table, and the party begins in earnest. So this is how these occupying Nazis spend the war. Good food from the estate's grounds, good wine from the estate's wine cellar. The Rogets' phonograph playing. Pretty-enough girls giggling and flirting as they take turns swirling around the parlor with each young soldier in turn.

The only problem is that Fritz seems adequately friendly whenever I approach him, but ignores me the rest of the time. He doesn't even seem to care when one of the others, a dark-haired, dark-eyed, lower-ranking soldier about my age named Johann, waltzes me across the floor one dance after another and refills my wine glass when it doesn't need refilling. Fritz hardly even seems to be watching.

As two of the other girls wander off with their lucky choices for the evening, I approach my puzzling giant and raise my hands to waltz position. "May I have this dance?"

He studies me and sighs before sweeping me around the room in his arms three times in a fast polka step I had not expected. It's so much fun. My feet hardly touch the floor. However, when Johan cuts in, Fritz bows slightly, says, "Thank you for the dance," and hands me over without a second glance.

A third girl has disappeared, and it's patently clear that Johan has placed all his bets on me. He pulls me to him and nuzzles my hair. When he groans, I feel why immediately. He's swollen and hard as he presses against my abdomen.

Oddly, even though he's attractive and big enough, I want nothing to do with it. Instead, I look over at Fritz for help. He arches his eyebrows and watches, taking it all in.

Johann catches the meaning of that look, however, and places his fingers against my chin, forcing my face back to his, his mouth covering mine, hard, probing, attacking me from two directions at once. I try to pull away, but he's leaning over me. One arm pulls my shoulders to his chest as his other hand cups my bottom, pushing my stomach firmly up against his throbbing erection.

"Please … I'm sorry … stop," I whisper as if ashamed to be saying the words.

He responds by squeezing my butt so tight it hurts and pushing his engorged member into my belly just above my pubic bone. He hisses in my ear, "You know you want it. I'm no sorry-ass Polish boy. This time it won't be a mercy fuck."

"No please." What is wrong with me? This is out of character. I'll blow my cover. I mentally prepare to suck his brains out if that's what it takes.

"Johann, stop." Fritz's voice demands compliance.

Johann turns his head, but doesn't let me go. "You know what she is. You heard what she did with that pissant Polack over in Caen." It's an accusation.

"Let her go." This order is softer but somehow more threatening.

"And you said you have no claim to her!" Johann's voice rises and he pulls me even closer.

Suddenly Fritz is looming, six inches taller and a foot wider at Johan's side. "I don't, Johann. But you are a member of the German Military. Behave like one!"

He's barking orders now, and Johann's grip starts to loosen.

"Soldiers of the Wehrmacht are allowed to consort with local women. We are even allowed to ply them with wine and try to convince them we are the second coming of the Archangel Gabriel. But we are under direct orders from the Fuehrer himself not to force Aryan women against their will. Not even if they are prostitutes!"

Johann holds his ground for only a moment longer before throwing me aside as if he's disgusted and stalking out of the parlor.

I flee through the kitchen, sobbing for some reason I don't understand and saying to whom I'm not sure, "I'm sorry. I'm so sorry."

By the time I reach Fritz's room, I'm angry enough with myself to kick my suitcase. It wasn't the wine. Alcohol never affects me like that. What was I thinking?

I stand just inside the door wondering how badly I've screwed things up and randomly scanning the room as if it could reveal some secret answer. All I see is sketches and the bed. The bed. Suddenly it's clear. It's his bed I want to spend the night in. His long, strong arms I want around me. I've got a fucking schoolgirl crush on a big fucking German. Shit. Not good. Not good at all.

On the other hand, being reminded about that big-mouthed Stanislaw has gotten my juices flowing, and just thinking about Fritz in that bed is making me twitch. There's lemonade still to be made out of this lemon. I strip off my clothes and search for my sleeping shift. I'll fluff my hair and dab on a little perfume. He won't be able to resist me.

An hour later, my hair's wilted and I'm still alone on the bed, warmed only by the blanket I've thrown over my shoulders, flipping through another of his sketch books, when I hear footsteps on the cobblestones. He fills the doorway, but stars are visible in the small bit of sky between his shoulders and the door frame. They glitter like fairy dust trailing him in the wind. Oh, yeah. He makes me wet between the legs. I can't help smiling.

"What was it about Johann you didn't like?" he asks closing the door behind him without looking at me and hanging his coat. "He's a pretty good sort."

I don't get the look of surprise and disappointment off my face before he turns back around.

Seeing it, Fritz chuckles, "For a spoiled Bavarian," and throws himself on the bed beside me, making my breasts bounce enticingly beneath my shift.

Which of course he ignores. Instead, he elbows my ribs and adds, "And a prick."

"Bavarian?" Anything to keep him smiling and interacting.

"Oh," he breathes out slowly giving me a look that wonders if I'm smart enough to comprehend what he's about to tell me. "I'm from the north. Old Prussia." Then he pauses, obviously giving up, "You'd have to be German to understand."

Nonplussed, I hold the sketch book against my chest with both arms as if I'm ashamed of my personal accoutrements now.

"What are you doing with that?" He takes the book from me.

"I didn't think you'd mind," I say pointing at the sketches posted miscellaneously around the room and getting flustered.

Ignoring my nipples even though they jut out at him pointedly, demanding attention, he turns the pad over to see the dates and idly flips through the pages, saying, "It's an early book. From back when this was all new and exciting." Then he returns it casually, as if both it and I are totally irrelevant.

We're so close. Smelling the scent of wine and kitchen that lingers in his hair, mixed with his masculine musk, I lean my head against his upper arm, and he doesn't move away. Instead, he says in a steady voice, "Really. What was that show all about?"

"What show?"

"That oh-don't-touch-me act you put on with Johann?"

"That wasn't an act," I answer, sliding my hand over his arm onto his chest where I rub little circles in the indentation in the middle in a way that clearly says, "If you take me it won't be against my will."

All that elicits is a sigh. His shoulders rise and fall once before he pushes my hand away and asks, "So, what am I going to do with you now?" Then he crosses the room in three strides and pulls the extra blankets he has stored away for the summer out of a chest. Within a minute, he constructs a pallet on the floor as far away from his bed as you can get in the room.

"You can sleep here," he sighs again as he throws the final blanket down in a heap and starts to undress as if I'm not there.

I make a show of ignoring him. Without moving, I pretend to study the sketch book while I follow his movements out of the corner of my eye. He hangs his shirt and pants precisely on wall hooks and returns to the bed in his underwear. There's no doubt now. There's no chance I'll be taken tonight.

As if to put that issue to rest for good, Fritz says, "I have to be up early. Johann set his expectations so high after hearing the Pole's obvious embellishments that I'll have to spend most of the morning cajoling him if we are to get any work done at all."

He leads me by the arm to my side of the room. As I settle to floor level, he finally notices how little I am wearing. "You might want to put on more clothing. It'll get colder down there."

After I've added a layer and pulled the covers up over my chin, he turns out the light as if he's done with me. Then he tells me "Sleep well," in French instead of German.

However, I'm not one to give up so easily. "How does a German soldier come to have such very good French?" I ask the dark.

His sigh is audible fifteen feet away, but he answers, "I went to university in Paris."

"You went to study art?" At least that makes some sense of the few facts I know.

"No." The bed squeaks. He's adjusting his position. "Business."

"But how—"

"Good night." His tone is decisive.

The lovesick schoolgirl is back. She's crushed on the floor, asking, "What did I do to make you hate me so much?"

"Hate you? I don't even *know* you."

"Then—"

He cuts me off. "I do not choose to consort with whores."

What can I say to that?

After a long silence, Fritz sighs and adjusts himself in bed again. "I didn't tell them … Johann and the others, you know. Stanislaw told Johann the story in vivid detail, and he recognized you as easily as I did." After a short silence, he chuckles. "Guess he learned you can't believe everything you hear, though."

After longer silence, Fritz sighs again. "And, now I've got to figure out what to do with you."

His bed frame squeaks and covers rustle. I imagine he's rolling over on his side. The schoolgirl whispers, "I'm sorry," into the infinite space between them, but I'm still not sure for what.

JOE – *Montreal, Canada, the Last Day, 1992*

"Ouch. That went well," Joe couldn't help rubbing it in a little.

Turning only part way to glare at him in response, Nanette joined his quiet chuckle and said, "And that's not the half of it."

"It gets worse?"

"Oh, yes. It gets worse."

She lit a cigarette. Somehow she didn't seem to need as many out there in the park. As the smoke leaked slowly out of her nose, she surveyed the greenery around them and said, "I really ought to get out more, you know."

"Yeah, it's beautiful," Joe agreed. After a few minutes, however, his curiosity got the best of him. "So what happened?" He'd known from the look on Nanette's face the day before that there was a lot to the story.

She was ready to continue. "Fritz, Johann, and the boys were gone the next day and night. My next meeting with the Queen was near there. So I spent the day chatting up Monsieur and Madame

Roget. Picked up some interesting military information, but mostly they raved about Fritz."

Nanette paused and gave Joe a look that made it clear she hadn't been able to understand why the French couple had adopted the German who had occupied their country and then their house at first either.

"They said they were fortunate Fritz had been staying with them since the Germans took control of the coast in 1940. Went on and on about him. A man of principle and discipline. In other houses, the younger Nazis who'd come and gone over the years had stolen or broken almost everything of value. But Fritz had always said Hitler was right to require respect for the occupied peoples and their belongings. Fritz had maintained order and decorum."

"Hunh?" Joe let out a little burst of air. "A regular upright German citizen?"

"Indeed." Nanette shrugged. Deciding at the last minute not to hurt her hand again, she passed the flask for Joe to open and then took a small sip.

Twenty-Seven

NANETTE – *Bayeux, France, May 1944*

The Queen's waiting for me at the designated time and location, but again I have so much to tell her that she has to improvise an unobtrusive place we can talk at length.

"And you say he's a sergeant involved in logistics for all of the coastal fortifications?" she asks. We're speaking French. Although that makes it more likely someone overhearing our conversation will understand it, speaking in English or German would instantly draw attention. It's a trade-off we've decided is prudent.

I've told her all the non-embarrassing, non-personal details, including very solid information about specific tank traps, and artillery sites and the tasks and chain of command involving the other seven soldiers staying at the manor.

"Good. That's very good." She's excited by the information we've collected. "Do you think you can find a way to stay there till our next meeting? I want to ask headquarters if it would be okay for you to stay even longer."

I have mixed emotions about that, but it's a good plan. I had picked up more intelligence in that one night of dining and drinking with the house boys than either of us could have hoped, and I'll be able to handle Johann and the other boys, now that I've got my wits about me again.

Plus, and I have to keep from grinning as I realize this, I haven't given up on Fritz. He didn't mention the fact that I slept on the floor at breakfast. And he didn't tell me to move out. In fact, he hardly said anything before leaving that morning.

So, as the Queen rides off into the countryside, I pedal back to join Madame Roget and one of last-night's girls, Julia, in the kitchen where we make girl talk while preparing dinner. The Madame is cool, but cordial. Apparently after four years, she's learned to put up with the idea of loose women wandering in and out of her kitchen.

Julia, a short dark, somewhat pretty girl, had gone upstairs with a slightly taller blond soldier named Karl at the end of last evening. But it turns out she's not a prostitute as I had assumed. She's a town girl who's been in love with Karl for over a year. They intend to marry as soon as the war is over, and she's already made the decision to forsake her homeland and move to Germany if he's not allowed to stay in France. She's so cute about it. You wouldn't think something that sweet could rise out of all this death and destruction.

Rather than take a chance one of the un-spoken-for housemates will try to start up where Johann left off, I help myself to Fritz's bed and sketch books as soon as Julia and I have cleaned up after dinner. I smell him in the sheets and imagine him next to me. That's a mistake because now I have a hard time getting to sleep.

The next day after making myself useful to the household, I pedal around Bayeux and the countryside picking flowers and taking in every detail. I even venture the five kilometers to the beach and sit in the shade watching the construction of metal structures Stanislaw had explained were something they called a gate that's supposed to stop tanks. It's apparent that the Nazis are seriously concerned about an invasion. The entire Normandy coast will be lined with them before long.

Fritz and Johann are not back in time for dinner and may not be home that night at all. So, I retire to Fritz's room early again, and decide to show him I can make myself useful. Once I've tidied, dusted, and straightened everything, I paw through his drawings trying to figure out what else I can do to get closer to him.

That's when I find a sketch book that's filled with images of young men. Or rather, I should say, the bodies of young men. Muscular, bending, pulling, resting, all lovingly rendered with Fritz's delicate, but sure touch. I'm reminded of sketches I've seen by Michelangelo and da Vinci.

Suddenly all the pieces come together. Fritz is a homosexual. Part of me wants to laugh with relief, while the other part wants to cry. Imagine how hard it must be for him. Homosexual in an army that deports homosexuals to concentration camps and makes them wear pink triangles on their prison garb to warn off the other inmates. Surrounded by attractive young boys you can only dream about but dare never touch. Given my own state of agitation, I particularly empathize with this second dilemma. This is a truly fucked up world.

But also what a waste! I'm sitting there mourning the fact that he prefers men to me so deeply that I don't hear him coming. When he opens the door, he's so damned attractive, stars trailing along behind him like they do. I just want to wrap him in my arms. But, I don't. Instead, I cover up the semi-nudity I'd intended to bait my trap with if he came home and bound off his bed, promising myself to behave as his new best friend and proving it by saying, "I saved you some dinner."

He's tired. He eats, strips as if I'm not there, and drops into bed. I'm so bold as to kiss his forehead, saying, "I'll get the light," and then falling to my mat of blankets on the floor.

But, he sighs and tosses about instead of falling right to sleep. Eventually his voice reaches out through the dark, "I don't know what's going to happen."

I know he's talking to me instead of himself, because he's speaking French. I wait to see if he'll go on before trying to answer.

"They can't agree."

"Who can't agree?" It seems okay to ask.

"Rommel and von Geyr."

My spy ears perk up instantly. I have no idea who von Geyr is, but Field Marshal Erwin Rommel is the Desert Fox, the German military genius who caused the Allies so much grief in North Africa. We were briefed that he'd been reassigned to France a few months ago.

"Who are they?" I play dumb on both counts.

"Generals." He snorts the word derisively. "Rommel must defend this part of the coast, but von Geyr refuses to send the Panzers."

"Panzers? Those are tanks, right?"

He grunts.

I continue, "Why won't he send what you need?"

Fritz sounds so weary. "There are rumors everywhere. Intelligence and spies all saying different things. Some say the Americans and British will attack within the month up north at Calais. Others say they'll attack here."

It sounds like he's doing flips on his bed. "Calais is closer to England and to Paris," he continues, "but Rommel's smart. He believes they will attack here because it will be a surprise. He says it does not matter to them how far they have to come, so long as they succeed once they get here."

He's breathing hard now. "In the middle is von Geyr. He wants to split the difference. To hold the Panzers in abeyance near Paris until he knows where the attack is. But if he does, they will get here too late!"

After a pause, Fritz's voice is now melancholy. "And it's not just the tanks. Rommel asked for ten million mines, and we have been allotted only ten thousand. The Americans will swat them off like flies. How are we supposed to hold out against them alone? With no mines? No training? Ditch diggers and foreign boys instead of German soldiers?"

I'm thinking about all this when he adds, "Rommel's going to meet with Hitler. I can only pray he can convince the Fuehrer to defend Normandy, because I feel in my bones that Rommel is right. They are coming here."

JOE – *Montreal, Canada, the Last Day, 1992*

"Wow," Joe couldn't believe what he was hearing. "Did Hitler listen to Rommel?"

Nanette held his eyes as she shook her head. "We might be living in a different world if he had."

"Why didn't he?"

"Perhaps because Baker Street, which is what operatives like the Queen and me called the S.O.E. headquarters, was tipped off about the split in the Nazi leadership and bolstered up leaks about the Calais threat as a decoy." Nanette's eyes glistened in the sunlight.

"Wow." Joe repeated himself, this time running the palm of his hand up his forehead and over the top of his head in disbelief. "*You* ... you and the Queen tipped them off?"

"I'm sure there were others, too." She shrugged then added before taking a long slow drag on her cigarette, "By then the Queen and I were very small cogs in a wheel that had grown very large."

Joe wasn't sure that was true. How many Allied spies could have found out such detailed inside information? Joe stared at Nanette, marveling and thinking he'd never look at any little old lady the same again.

Then, she flashed her salacious grin and handed him the flask with a wink. "Better take a swig … a big one. We're coming to the *good* part."

He tipped his head, holding the flask in front of his eyebrows in a toast and drank deep. Nope. He might never be able to look at little old ladies at all.

He raised the flask again. "Okay. I'm ready."

NANETTE – *Bayeux, France, May 1944*

The last thing Fritz says tonight is, "Oh, and thank you. The room looks nice."

He sees everything.

And he's pleased with me.

The next day, Fritz is up and out early, and I make myself indispensible to the mistress of the manor, cleaning, cooking, tending the garden, even milking the cows, because I have a feeling that Baker Street will want us to stay here a while. This way, even if Fritz decides to kick me out, I might be able to convince the mistress and master of the house to let me live upstairs with them.

And I'm right. The Queen reports back that Baker Street does want me to stay a bit longer. And that's before they've received all the new info I've wheedled out of everybody. I bring the Queen up to date, focusing on the debate between the generals over the intended target of the Allied invasion they expect within weeks.

"Damn," she says, walking in a tight little circle as she listens. "Damn, that's important." She looks at me in wonder.

When I ask how she's doing out there, she says, "Fine, but I have to stay away from the resisters. The Nazis have been here so long the people have gotten used to them. I'm afraid there may be more than a few collaborators."

I nod, thinking about Julia and Madame Roget. I don't ask her where she's staying or what cover story she tells people she meets. Remaining in one place for more than a few days is more dangerous for her than for me. Every time we meet we reiterate that if either of us doesn't show up for a meeting without leaving a coded message, the other's to immediately run as fast and far as she can.

"Especially you," she says, and I understand that's because she knows where to find me, and she won't even pretend she can't be made to talk. The Nazis have no compunction against using torture to get the information they want. I'm glad I don't know where to find her. It lets me rest easier.

Tonight, Fritz doesn't seem surprised to discover I'm still in his room. Or upset. He even smiles. It's been a hard few days, and all of the boys are tired. So, this is not a party night. After a quiet dinner, we read and discuss the events of the day like a long-married couple. Given the lack of physical chemistry between us, that's exactly what it feels like.

At bed time now, we've established a pattern of talking across the room in the dark like girlfriends at camp. He has no news to report. I'm bored and curious. Just to make conversation, I ask him, "So, what's an Old Prussian?"

"Huh?"

"You said you're an 'Old Prussian' and I don't know what that means."

His low laughter squeaks the bed frame. "I said I am from Old Prussia. My grandfather is the Old Prussian."

"Okay. I meant I don't know where Old Prussia is." I keep going, because he doesn't sound upset to be asked about his homeland.

"It's northeastern Germany. Actually, it was the first Germany." He's proud of that. "It's beautiful, really. Well-tended, fertile farms. Strong people."

"Is your family still there?" I'm thinking that the more I can get him to tell me about himself, the easier it will be for him to keep me here as a friend.

"Yes. Where else would they be? In truth, I miss them."

Aw. He's so cute. "What do they do there?"

He pauses and finally says, "Hunh," as if he's thought of something for the first time. Then he hesitates again before telling me, "My father is the eldest son of the eldest son of the eldest son of one of the last Prussian princes, one of those who helped Bismarck make peace with the Pope and unite our country back in the 1870's. I guess you could say they run the place."

I'm surprised. "Then, why would you ever leave?"

"I'm not the eldest son." His tone is unreadable. After a pause he continues, "And actually, that's a good thing. My brother Frederick is up to his neck in the family businesses. He never had a choice."

He's quiet again for a while, thinking. "I guess, I'm lucky not to be the second son either. Hans was destined for the military from the day he was born. Last I heard, he was in Russia. My mother is very worried."

"I can understand that." I don't tell him I've learned that the Russians are proving a lot stronger than Hitler expected. I can tell from his voice he's worried about his brother, too.

"So, what are third sons destined to do?" I ask.

"Third sons?"

Something about his tone tells me I've guessed correctly.

He confirms my suspicion almost wistfully. "In my family, third sons have always been destined for the priesthood." After a pause during which I don't say anything, he explains, "It's like a tithe the family promised to pay in the last century."

"But..." I start. He's clearly not a priest.

"But, this third son went to university in Paris instead," he answers my question.

"Did your family give you a hard time?" I'm guessing he took more than a little heat.

"No." He's obviously thinking. "I got them to understand that in those harsh economic times, it made sense for me to study business. I can become a priest later, once the world has settled down."

"So, you studied business."

"No."

I can't read his voice, but he sounds subdued.

"I went to Paris to study art. Business was a decoy," he explains.

"You simply enrolled in art school instead?"

"No. I went to university and studied business." He's dragging this out. "But only for a while ... a short while."

Then he turns plaintive, as if it's important I understand. "I have studied art all my life. I quit university thinking I would work with the great Parisian painters, learn from them. And I did. They were welcoming enough, but it turned out we weren't a good fit."

He's speaking in short bursts separated by contemplative silences. I hold my tongue.

"They are ... too disorderly. Their art has lost its structure, its discipline. They're vain, actually. They paint as if their inner feelings and thoughts are more important than the subjects they are painting. I believe that art exists to exalt the world God created, the world he has given us eyes to see."

Based on the sounds emanating from his side of the room, I envision him gesturing with his hands in the dark as he tells me this.

"So, I stopped working with the French painters, too. I guess you could say I rebelled against the rebels." He lets out one loud ironic breath. "I'm sure there are others like me, but I did not have time to find them before the war came to Paris. I had to join the army."

This makes me wonder how he, the son of the sons of Prussian princes, ended up stuck as a noncommissioned officer occupying a beach in Normandy. "Why did you enlist here instead of going home?"

This time it's not just the outflow of breath I hear, it's the long hard intake, too. "If I had gone home..." He ponders his next words. "If I had gone home, they ... my father and brothers ... would have seen to it that I was made an officer. As an officer, I would have to be responsible. Have to make decisions. It would have consumed not only my body but my mind as well. Here all I have to do is what I am told, and when I'm done, I am free. Free to cook and eat with friends, free to sketch and paint. Free to lie here at night talking nonsense with you. And when the war is over..." His voice drifts off, leaving the thought unfinished.

In my mind, he's walking a fine line here, trying to fulfill his obligation without committing to it. Maintaining his position in his family and world even though it's not the position he wants.

And one other thing bothers me. "But, you've been here in Normandy for four years," I say. "That means you joined up right away. Why'd you sign up so fast?"

He answers in a flat voice, "I'm German. My country was at war. What would you have had me do?"

Twenty-Eight

JOE – *Montreal, Canada, the Last Day, 1992*

"Sorry about that," Nanette giggled. "I forgot about that non-sexy part until I started telling it. I'll get to the good stuff now.

"That's okay. I wasn't in a rush to get to the bedroom scenes anyway." Joe widened his eyes raised his palms to Nanette as if to ward her off.

Nanette narrowed her eyes in contrast and glared back, but couldn't keep the corners of her mouth from twitching upward. She lifted her cigarette to her lips to cover them.

Joe was sure Nanette was gearing up to finally tell him something scandalous even if Fritz was gay. And he was sure some people might think he was a pervert for encouraging her to do so, what with their age difference and all.

But he kept coming back to what she had said the day before. She wasn't going into all those details just to shock him and titillate both of them. She was doing what she said he needed, getting him to feel, and therefore to understand, at least some small part of the emotional ups and downs his grandmother had gone through and how much she had lost. And Nanette was right. Everything he knew about his grandmother and what she did after the war was starting to make better sense.

Plus, this day was what it was. It was the only gift he could think of to give Nanette. The only thank you he thought she'd appreciate, a chance to tell her story to someone who cared and sincerely wanted to hear it. And if it took listening to the gory details to make her happy, so be it. He was a big boy. He'd heard most of it before.

"Fritz was complex, wasn't he?" Joe asked to let Nanette know he'd been paying attention.

"Very." She looked up at the sky as if she were counting the clouds that had gathered as the afternoon wore on and then blew a stream of smoke up to join them.

After Nanette watched it fade to nothing, she picked up the sketchbook again and handed it to Joe, saying, "Go to the back."

The last seven drawings were not military subjects or landscapes. They were sketches of Nanette. One of the pages had been carefully cut out of the book. Pointing to it, Joe asked, "The sketch on your wall?"

She nodded and smoked as she watched him scrutinize the others.

The rest of Fritz's drawings of Nanette were equally exquisite as the one she had framed and hung up for the world to see. Two of them showed her playing with a kitten. Surprised, Joe raised them up for her to see and asked, "You had a kitten?"

Sighing, she answered, "Yes. Fritz brought it home one night in his pocket."

The way she said home, surprised Joe. It sounded like she really thought of the room she had shared with Fritz as home.

"He found it lost on the road," she explained and turned away, emotion cracking her voice.

Four more sketches captured her doing various domestic tasks, working in the garden, reading in the shade, things like that. In every one, however, there was a hint of mystery, as if Fritz had captured a moment in time when something more was going on, if you could only see outside the picture frame. The guy had talent.

When Joe flipped to the last sketch, he quickly closed the book and turned to Nanette. She assiduously avoided his gaze by staring off into the distance, but she had a smug smile on her face and he could tell she'd been following his reaction out of the corner of her eye. He opened the book again and studied the drawing in detail.

It was a nude, a totally tasteful, yet overwhelmingly erotic night-time nude, full of curves and shadows and sensuality. Facing slightly to the artist's right, Nanette knelt on a flat surface, thighs pressed together, feet and heels tucked underneath her buttocks. She was upright, but her arms disappeared behind her as if she were handcuffed. That arched her back and thrust her left shoulder, left breast, and abdomen forward into a strong illuminating light that came from even farther to the lower right. Their edges formed a series of delicate, interconnected peaks and curves that stood out against the dark background.

Her face was hidden, turned down and away from the light, creating a tension that permeated the image. Deep, dark, voluptuous shadows revealed a soft three-dimensionality that begged to be touched and explored rather than admired from a distance. The image was at once demure and erotic, realistic and ethereal. Something monumental and eternal about it struck Joe with awe.

"It's beautiful."

"I know." Her voice was a whisper in the wind.

NANETTE – *Bayeux, France, May 1944*

The "friend" thing is working. Fritz never does ask me to leave, and I eventually tell him the story I've had time to concoct. I'm not really a prostitute. I'm just one of the lost girls. My parents are dead, and my fiancé fled to England without me when he got the chance. I've been doing the only thing I'm qualified to do to survive the war. I thank him for letting me stay in a place where I don't have to service every male who gets the inkling, and he seems to buy it.

And now that I've stopped trying to seduce him, we're getting along so famously that everyone else thinks we've become the fondest of lovers. As I cook and garden and clean my way into the hearts of all the other manor-house residents, even Johann eventually lightens up.

I think Fritz is glad to have me around for two reasons. He really enjoys having a friend, and it turns out I'm the perfect beard. Apparently, Stanislaw is now quite a hit with the ladies. I take some pride in that, and the fact that he keeps giving me all the credit, embellishing the mythology of our nights together more with every telling, has made me the most notorious whore in Normandy. As long as they think I'm in Fritz's bed at night, they'll never suspect he's homosexual.

Stanislaw's promoting my business, and his word-of-mouth, so to speak, advertizing seems to be working. German soldiers hoot and holler when I pedal by, but maintain a respectable distance, because they think I'm with Fritz now. They rush to talk with me when I smile and wave back, and I can get them to tell me anything I want to know. All I have to do is say something that's the least bit suggestive, and their tongues start wagging. That's one weakness in the male of the species I hope they never find a cure for. I so love wagging tongues.

It works especially well when Fritz takes me with him to Cherbourg on the back of a motor bike, and we stop at every camp and construction site along the way. In the last week, the Queen's given Baker Street the locations and fortifications of almost every Nazi installation on the coast.

But I'm starting to feel like Fritz. I can't wait for the free times, the times I bring him his lunch and watch him sketch in the shade, the times we sit outside in the courtyard at dusk and watch the stars switch on one by one until they fill the sky.

One night, a party night, we join the others in the parlor and dance. At first it's that animated Polka thing he enjoys so much, with him flinging me around the room, my feet off the ground. But, it ends up as all such nights do with couples pairing up and slow dancing their way to bed. We, too, fall into the magic of the slow dance, and the distance melts between us, leaving an intimacy that doesn't dissolve when the music ends. From that night on, we remind me of the Queen and Gen touching each other reassuringly and playfully, but not erotically.

That's not a bad thing. I like touching him. But being his beard rather than his lover is a challenge. I'm a sexual creature by nature, always have been, and now that I'm apparently happily involved with this seemingly perfect specimen of a man, I can't get any. Not from him and not from anybody else. Cheating on our non-relationship would destroy everything.

Plus, and this is the hardest part to rationalize, he's the only one I want. Except for this one thing, he really is the perfect man. He's smart and kind, thoughtful and God knows sensitive and talented. And now that I know him, really know him, he's attractive to me in ways I have never thought of before. I want him so badly all the time I can hardly see straight. Sometimes I can't even walk for the craving between my legs. Frustrated does not begin to describe how I feel.

The bottom line is I can't fall at sleep at night after all the good conversation and casual touching. I'm more alive and alert than I've ever been, and even touching myself doesn't satisfy my hunger. I'm starving to death only fifteen feet from the feast.

And something's bothering him, too. At times when I'm lying there my eyes open in the dark, I hear him moaning. Or, a groan will awaken me after I've finally drifted off. I've asked him about it, but he assures me I'm mistaken. He has nothing to groan about. Still, I know something's going on, because he always makes a fast getaway after telling me that lie.

And another thing has changed. He's started sketching me instead of the war. It started after he brought Babette the kitten home and drew her sleeping in my lap. Then he surprised me by capturing me toiling in the garden and reading.

When he showed those sketches to me, he revealed, "I've never worked with a female model before." Then, almost shyly, he asked, "Would you sit for me?"

Of course I did. He situated me in the shade next to the house so that the late afternoon sunlight bounced off the wall, illuminating my face with soft, diffused light. I could feel his eyes on me. They pierced through all my veils, identified every minute detail of who I am, distilling each one, telling his hand how to capture me forever on paper.

When he showed me the portrait, he was excited, and I was both humbled and brazenly proud. After this war is over and he's world-renowned, I'll go down in history as his muse. That at least will be a meaningful reward for all this longing and agony.

This morning Fritz told me he wants to try something new tonight. Artificial lighting. He's planning to draw me sitting by the work table and sets up the lights before dinner, which we eat quickly. Then we race to our room like giddy children escaping from the adults to have a grand adventure.

Once we get started, however, he can't find a pose that pleases him. When he finally complains that the folds of my skirt look too sharp in the shadow cast by the light bulb, I tease him, "Perhaps that's why so many artists paint nudes. Maybe they can't do folds either."

He pretends to be offended then gives me the oddest look. His eyes light up, but immediately fade back into shadow as he peers underneath the table looking for nothing.

"All the classical artists did nudes," I say, unbuttoning the top button of my blouse. In fact, now that the thought has wormed its way into my head, I won't have it any other way. I enjoy the befuddled expression on his face. Jaw slack, eyes wide, he looks like a frightened child, and the exhibitionist in me takes control. He's putting me through hell. No reason he shouldn't suffer a little, too.

Undoing the second button, I tell him, "Don't worry. I'll sit very still. And I promise not to bite." I try to act as matter-of-factly as I can, even taking the time to fold and put away my blouse and skirt.

I finally drop my bloomers revealing my buttocks and when I turn to face him without a stitch to cover an inch of me, he's not looking. Instead he's handing me a sheet to cover myself with. I accept his gift, but let it dangle to the floor. I have no intention of hiding anything.

Instead, I challenge his eyes to dig deeper, and once he starts, the artist takes over. It's as if he forgets me, the thinking feeling me, all together. I become one more intricate object he's never seen before.

He blatantly gauges the length and breadth of my lines, the highlights and depths of my contours, already starting to arrange them in his mind.

"Come, sit here." All business now, Fritz takes my hand and leads me to the table, and for the next several minutes I am a mannequin to be twisted and bent. He tests pose after pose, adjusting the lights for each one.

I sense it immediately when he's envisioned the pose he wants. After he folds the blanket from his bed and lays it on the table, he lifts me up as if I have no weight at all and has me kneel on the pad, pushing my weight backwards till I'm sitting on my heels. Then, he has me reach behind my back with both hands and grasp my toes for stability. This forces my breasts forward. My nipples stiffen ... fetchingly, if I say so myself.

"Can you hold that position for a while?" he asks. The solicitousness with which he treats me as an inanimate object is fascinating. I feel lucky to see the inner workings of a great artist's mind at the moment of creation.

"Yes." I can hardly get the word out. The breathlessness he's worked himself up into is contagious.

Fritz scrutinizes, then leans back and says, "Good," as if he's talking to himself. "Here, turn your head like this." His fingers coax my chin to rest on my right shoulder, away from the light. "Lean a little bit more this way." His hands play gently across my skin as he makes exact adjustments. I bite my tongue.

And then he steps away, tweaks his composition one more time, and begins to sketch. I can't see him, because my face is turned to the side and my eyes are closed. But I hear the intermittent "scratch, scratch" of charcoal on paper. When it stops, he also stops breathing.

Then after a moment, he must see what he needs to see, because he starts shuffling his feet, scratching on the paper, and inhales again.

It's a surreal experience. Time stops. I'm no longer there, but I can feel his eyes caress my body. He knows me now in ways no one else ever has or ever will. I want him so bad I think I may be consumed by the passion that's throbbing inside me.

"Damn!"

I hear the charcoal hit the table. His pacing feet thud on the floor. "What's wrong? Did I move? I'm sorry. I didn't mean..." I'm afraid my body has subconsciously responded to the tragic comedy playing out in my head.

"No, it's not you." His voice sounds frustrated. "I just can't get the line right." Without hesitation, and apparently without thought, he takes three giant steps to the table saying, "This line. From here..."

I almost scream as his finger brushes the little bone at the top of my left shoulder like a jolt of electricity. I know that shoulder is highlighted in sharp contrast against the darkness of the room behind me because I can feel the warmth emanating from the light bulb. But now it burns with his touch.

"All the way to here." Light as a feather but as hot as fire, his finger traces the convex curve of my shoulder down to the concave line where it meets my upper chest and transitions to breast. He follows that line all the way out again to the ultimate thrust of the nipple that's standing alone in defiance of the night, hardening and elongating in wanton anticipation as he makes his way to it.

I can't help myself. My whole body trembles as if I can no longer hold the pose. It's all I can do to keep from whimpering with need and effort, my eyes squeezed so tight I'm not sure I'll ever see again.

Then he's gone. No sound. Just my own labored breathing. No touch. I can't lift my eyelids, can't move. I'm desperate to remain in position.

And then, like a dreamed-of kiss, soft, warm lips brush the tip of that troublemaking libertine teat, and my whole body jerks, almost crying out. Before I can unravel my limbs, his hand is on my back as his mouth clamps on my breast. He sucks and pulls it one hard time before he groans, and his giant hands on my back and butt compel me up onto my knees.

There is a God! I have died and gone to heaven, but the rough stubble of his beard scratches the tops of my breasts and my focus is drawn directly back to earthly pleasures. He pulls away for an instant, and his eyes reveal a hunger that matches mine. Where has this been hiding?

Holding his gaze, I force my hands loose to unbutton his shirt as he frees the amazing bulge I thought I'd never see from his pants. I touch it. It stands alone, smooth like velvet and warm as fire. It's big, not so big that I'm afraid. But even if it were it wouldn't matter. I've wanted it too much and waited too long to shy away now.

He groans then kisses me deeply for the first time. At the same instant, he lifts me off the table and I wrap my legs around him where he stands. His chest is warm. He holds all of my weight with one hand, as our tongues play teasing probing games and his soft, silky chest hair stimulates my breasts.

He must have been desperate, too, because there's no foreplay. Now that he's made his move, he gets directly to the point. As we ravage each other's mouths, one finger of his free hand spread the folds between my legs and he positions the head of his cock between them.

We're no longer kissing. We're in a bizarre suspended animation, anticipating, building tension. He sucks in ragged breaths between his teeth, his cheek pressed against the top of my head. I bury my face in his neck, waiting, wanting. Ready for pain, if that's what it takes to reach the release I desperately desire.

But he doesn't take me. Almost as if he's afraid to enter the door he's opened, he supports me now with both hands as if he's keeping me from slipping any lower to my death. But I want to die. I want to be pierced. I move my hips ever so slowly, forcing them downward. So I do the taking. Relishing the sensation, I draw the first small part of him inside.

As he slides against my most sensitive skin, every nuance is magnified in slow motion. After all this waiting, I'm so close to climax already that my body is frenzied. It wants to devour him. The feel of him sliding into that tight little gap triggers a violence of lust I've never experienced before. My hips and stomach and breasts assail him, slapping, grinding, rising and falling over and again. He withstands my assault like a stoic, strong, straight and unmoving, as each spasm each contraction pulls a little more of him inside. When I finally come he's in so deep he's pressing against my heart.

Out of breath, covered in sweat, thinking I'm totally spent, I'm so close to crying for joy that I relax my grip and collapse like a rag doll. But, I'm still impaled on his engorged, still unsatisfied member. When it shifts inside me, I experience something I've heard about but never believed was real. An entirely different need starts to burn in a hidden new place like an ember I hadn't known was there. It lights a revelation, an entirely different fire.

But it takes work to fan this burning coal into a flame. I hover close but it seems like I'll never get there. If I stop it'll fade and disappear. If I move this way, I'm nearer. I'm so focused on this new sensation I forget he's still standing there holding me. Pushing, grinding, grunting and moaning again, I use him to get what I want. There's nothing to hold back. I'm so close. So close! So close!

And he comes. The hot wet of him shooting into me, the ferocious grip of his hands on my hips pulling me down onto him, and the guttural noises he makes as he thrusts upward in sudden jerks take me over the edge. We're falling, screaming, dying together and nothing else matters. Nothing else could ever be this good.

Some time after we're both finally done, he starts to lift me off of him, and I whisper an urgent, "No!" I'm not ready to lose him yet.

So he gives me what I want once again. Still inside, he slides us the few steps to his bed and stretches out on his back with me on top. I am so full, so complete and so afraid he'll slip out. That would leave me empty in ways I cannot endure. I never want us to be parted, not ever again. He strokes my hair. I'm the happiest I've ever been.

I don't know how many hours later, I awaken to the feel of large smooth hands treating me roughly. It's pitch outside, and he breathes in sharp, uneven gasps as he bites my neck and sucks my breast, stretching it up and away from my body. Then he kneads the nipple with his fingers, while digging the fingers of his other hand beneath my back to lift my butt into the air. Finally, I think, I'm to be taken.

And I'm right. No more holding back. This time Fritz is all over me like a carnivore, biting, sucking, squeezing. His body temperature is so high it's almost frightening, but I have waited so long to kindle this passion that it's contagious. I moan. The sound of it drives him to a higher frenzy.

He stands, lifts and turns me until I'm sideways on the bed, my head toward the wall. He leans over me, panting, holding his weight by his hands on either side of my head. I know this because I feel his hot breath on my forehead, the press of his belly on my knees. He's invisible in the dark.

Then his hands slide down my abdomen and, grabbing me by the waist, he pulls my hips to the edge. When I'm where he wants me, his fingers slip between my legs and push hard against my inner thighs, spreading them wide, and without warning his hard, hot cock forces its way into the gap he's created.

No waiting, no please or thank you. No time wasted on niceties at all. I've got him now! This is the animal Fritz I've been praying for, holding me down by the shoulders, pushing into me in one fierce thrust that lifts my lower body off the bed. Grunting and repeating the gesture, banging the bed frame against the wall so hard with his thighs, I'm afraid he may break it down.

My ankles locked around his back, I intend to ride this wild, bucking creature for all he's worth, but he gets the best of me by taking control of my hips. He moves them up and down, side to side. He's doing it for his own pleasure, but I'm the beneficiary as my clit and inner lips rub back and forth against the hair on his belly.

They react with a rage of desire, and I can't hold myself back. When I start to come, he grunts guttural German grunts and slaps my butt with the palm of his hand as if he's spanking me. Like an electric shock that small pain sharpens the pleasure, making me want it more!

He tenses and grunts again. His palm stings my skin a second time, and that's all it takes. I'm gone again, lost again, writhing in pleasure. At the same time, he strains, pushes, and jerks, not caring a whit about me, seeking his own release, pulling my hips to meet his thrusts so that he can bury his seed far inside.

One more stinging spank and he stops at the deepest point, holding me tight against him, growling, and shuddering. Without withdrawing, he thrusts again, slightly less violently, moans, and shudders again. He does this three more diminishing times.

As he stands next to the bed, heaving and sweating, I hold him tight against my body with my legs, loving the fact that I've finally made him lose control. No more solitary moaning in the night. Now he truly is the perfect man. A short time later, I drift back off to sleep, satisfied. I am the luckiest girl in the world.

Twenty-Nine

JOE – *Montreal, Canada, the Last Day, 1992*

Nanette's pause lasted long enough to let Joe know she needed a break as much as he did. Coming back to the present, he realized that despite his resolution to keep his eyes open, once again he'd been watching her story play out on his mental movie screen.

In that instant, it dawned on him that this was a rare opportunity to talk with a woman openly and honestly about things men and women don't usually talk about. Sex and ... well ... women. How they think. What they feel.

After peering out beneath stealthy eyelids to make sure Nanette's energetic and vivid descriptions hadn't attracted an audience of drooling voyeuristic eavesdroppers, he asked. "So, that's what women want then?"

When Nanette didn't answer immediately, he rotated his gaze in her direction to find her grinning broadly at him with that gleam in her eye again. Sitting up straighter, he opened his eyes completely, arched his eyebrows, and shrugged as if to say, "What?"

"It's nice to see you haven't been dozing through my confessional," Nanette chortled, looking down at the bulge in his pants.

Before he could respond, she continued, "And I guess we've determined that you have a definite preference for heterosexual content." She paused, screwing up her face as if contemplating some great mystery. "That surprises me, because I've always been led to believe that men particularly enjoy girl-on-girl action."

Joe blushed and then wondered why. If Nanette had been his age ... the girl she was at the time she was with Fritz, the girl holding the rifle in the photo with Georges and Pierre ... this kind of talk would not have embarrassed him in the least. To the contrary, he would have taken it as a come-on and followed her lead as far as she would take him. Why did hearing the same words from the same girl, only fifty years older, seem so improper or at least so strange?

Nanette had been quite a woman and had quite a tale to tell. If she wanted to tell it, and he wanted to hear it, what was wrong with that? So sex played a big part in it? Why should she be required to dance around the titillating parts, especially when they were so integral to who she was ... to her story?

And would he even be asking these questions if she was a little old man recounting his amorous conquests during the war? Probably not. Most likely, he'd slap the old guy a high five and they'd both revel in the fact that he'd been such a stud in his younger days.

Plus, underneath it all, Nanette's tales with all their passion and intensity made the war personal. He'd always thought of war, when he'd bothered to think of it at all, as larger-than-life, mythological characters immortalized in books and making grand historical gestures. But now he saw that war was fought by discrete individuals, each trying to hold onto a life, longing for love, and having to decide how much they were willing to sacrifice ... for the cause or just to live another day.

And another thing. He'd been a fool to ever assume people Nanette's age didn't have the same appetites and needs as they did when they were young. If they didn't they wouldn't be the same people any more.

Joe didn't know where all those random thoughts were taking him, but having second guessed his position to the point he was fairly sure he was on morally high ground, he relaxed a little. Nanette was one of those mythological heroes, but she was also a real person, his friend, and she was trying to one-up him again.

She loved the competition of it, and he wasn't about to disappoint her by going down without a fight. Blowing air through pursed lips in a slow whistle, he arched his eyebrows and waved the back of one hand up and down in front of his belly to let Nanette know the story she had just told was hot.

"Oh, girl-on-girl is usually fine." He grinned. "But..." He held his palm out at her to keep her from talking. "It's just not all that easy to fantasize about your own grandmother."

Nanette giggled. "Point well taken. But does that mean then that it's easy to fantasize about a different little old lady?" she asked coyly.

"Oh, I wasn't imagining a little old lady," Joe responded quickly, picking up the sketch book and flipping through it to the last sketch. "I was envisioning her." He held up the sketch of Nanette in the nude. "Now that's one hot chick."

Then, he pointed at her face, grinning broadly. "Look. I think she's blushing," he teased, pumping the air with his fist, loving the fact that he had the upper hand for a change.

Indeed, color had risen up Nanette's neck into her cheeks. Her eyes watered up a bit, and she pulled on her lower lip with her teeth. After a few seconds, though, she recovered and said with a sigh, "She was, wasn't she?"

Then she changed directions on a dime once again. "So, Joseph..." She patted her lap with the palms of both hands. "Is *what* what women want?"

It took Joe a moment to get back into his earlier mindset. "To be taken," he explained. "For us … for men … to lose control?"

"Hmmm," Nanette put her forefinger to her lips as she thought. Then she adopted a straighter posture, straightened her skirt across her knees, and clasped her hands together demurely before answering, "I wish it was that simple. And I can't claim to speak for all women, you understand."

She was playing this for all it was worth. He rolled his eyes to the heavens.

"But the answer to your question is … it depends."

Joe groaned, leaning back in his chair and throwing his hands up in the air as if exasperated.

"No, really," Nanette continued seriously. "It's complex. It depends on the woman, the man, and the situation. I wanted Fritz to take me, to lose control and take me hard, because my body had craved his for so long, and he had denied me."

She paused for a moment as if replaying what she had just said in her head, one eye closed and lips pulled up to that same side. "You know…" She blew out a little breath. "I wouldn't be surprised if *that* is what most women want, though." She looked at Joe openly, sharing her revelation.

"What?"

"For the man she wants to want her the same way she wants him."

Gen's words echoed in Joe's mind. "I want to make you love me the way I love you." That was certainly what he wanted from Carrie. Were they all the same? He shook his head. "Like Gen."

Nanette raised her eyebrows and pursed her lips as if surprised. Then she nodded.

Joe chewed on that thought for a while, then shook his head again and continued, "But what can a man do to make a woman want him in the first place?"

"You're not going to like the answer," Nanette responded with a sighing smile.

"It depends." It was Joe's turn to let out a little breath of mock derision.

"What it's all about, mon cher ... is chemistry." Nanette shook her head and reached for the flask. After taking a sip and passing it over to Joe, she continued, "And chemistry comes in many forms. The first, the easiest, is purely physical ... sexual attraction, like the way I was attracted to Fritz." She paused and closed her eyes to think. "It really can happen at first sight, you know." She met his eyes again. "Like they say in the songs ... when someone catches your eye from across a room. Stuff like that." Another pause. "Physical attraction can be very potent."

Joe nodded his understanding. Nothing new there. He'd been in the throes of such an attraction for weeks.

Nanette continued, "And it's easy to confuse physical attraction with the other kinds of chemistry, the intangibles we talked about before. Emotional. Spiritual. The whole soul-mate thing. But for those, you really do need to know some part of the person. Something about who they are."

She squinted at Joe to see if he was still following her reasoning. "That kind of attraction can grow slowly ... take time." Tilting her head, she scrutinized Joe. "But one thing the Queen's story taught me is that it can be just as intense."

Joe rubbed the tips of his fingertips back and forth over his lips as he listened and thought about what Nanette was saying. "And when you put the two together?"

"Ahhh, mon ami." Nanette nodded vigorously and clasped her hands under her chin. "That's the gold ring everyone is reaching for ... the stuff dreams and fairytales are made of."

Then she stopped herself and a sequence of emotions played over her face. Recognition followed surprise, then understanding on the heels of sadness. She turned back to him with red-rimmed eyes and said, "That's what I thought I had found with Fritz."

"Thought?"

She looked him hard in the eye. "It's complicated."

NANETTE – *Bayeux, France, May 1944*

When I wake up, Fritz is gone. He's so thoughtful, he didn't rouse me when he dressed and left for work. I brazenly stretch and loll in his bed, basking in the smell of us and fantasizing about the nights to come. A different kind of moaning in the dark. The thought makes me giggle.

When I do get up, I waltz around the room, tidying and straightening my nest and humming some dramatic, romantic nonsense. Life is good as I dress and cross the courtyard to the kitchen. The sun is shining. The sky is blue. The air still has the coolness of morning.

Madame Roget gives me a strange look. I guess noise carries farther in the courtyard than I thought. But so what? It couldn't have come as a surprise. Jealousy maybe? I drop my face to hide my grin. Then she says Fritz wants me to meet him at lunch time in the cathedral square, and I'm almost giddy with excitement. Maybe he'll be sketching and I can sneak up on him like I did the first time.

He's not sketching. He's sitting in the shade of the Liberty Tree on the stone bench that runs along the cathedral wall, his elbows on his knees and his head in his hands. Something's wrong. When I grasp his fingers and try to sit on his lap, he stands and fends me off.

On tiptoes, I reach up to touch his cheek, hoping he'll bend down to kiss me. But he doesn't.

Instead, he says, "I'm sorry for what happened. I've been to confession. It won't happen again."

"Oh, no." I cup his cheek in my hand. "You have nothing to be sorry for. It was wonderful ... what I wanted, what I've been dreaming of on my pallet for days."

He turns away. "It won't happen again."

It's him. He doesn't want it to happen again. I react backwards to that realization as if struck a physical blow. I can hardly stand. "What's wrong?" are the inane words that come out of my mouth. "I thought you wanted me?"

"I do ... did," he corrects his misstatement too quickly. "But I was wrong to act on my desires. Fornication is a sin."

I find myself sitting on the bench. From that position, he seems so far away. No one else nearby, he paces back and forth as he talks.

"In my youth. In Prussia, I was a libertine," he explains. "We all were. But I was not happy. There was a hollowness ... here." He taps the indentation in the middle of his chest with the knuckles of his right hand. "In my soul. And when I looked around, really took a good look, I realized that my culture, my people, we were being destroyed. But not by an outside enemy. We were rotting from within, because we had no self discipline, no morals. No dedication to structure, I guess you could say."

I sit silently, a prisoner listening to my sentence.

He stretches his neck, moving farther and farther away before he looks down. "I returned to the Church. Went to confession," he says, "to cleanse my soul. And then I took a vow that, even though I am not ready to commit my life to the service of God, I will not be part of the destruction of my culture, not a cause of it. I at least will live by a code of honor and righteousness."

As he says this I see a bulge in his pants. He's getting stiff again. These are mixed messages. But he reiterates my fate by asking, "It cannot happen again. Do you understand?"

What can I do but nod?

"Good." He sucks in air as if he's not been breathing for some time and sits next to me as if relieved our little talk went so well. Then he announces, "So, we have to figure out what to do with you. But I have to leave now because the generals are meeting about the panzers tomorrow. I won't be back until late after the meeting. We'll talk more then."

Trapped with no other option, another inanity slips out of my mouth. "Okay. Whatever you say."

What to do with me? It always comes back to the same question.

Later that day as I pedal off to meet the Queen, I do my best to push Fritz back into the corner of my mind. I'll figure someway to deal with him later. Now, I have to face my other problem. Guilt. I've been safe and self-satisfied, living the domestic life while the danger the Queen's in has been growing.

And then when I find her, she makes it worse by telling me, "Things are getting rough out here. I don't know how much longer I can last in this location."

"What happened?" I ask. She's always alert and edgy, but is even more so that day. Something had to have happened.

Holding her thumb and forefinger about an eighth of an inch apart, she explains, "I came this close to getting captured two nights ago." It had been a very close call.

"Thank goodness I packed up the radio and left the barn as soon as I finished transmitting," she continues. "Within seconds, I heard someone coming. It was the Gestapo. I was still near enough to overhear that someone had reported me. They're not sure who I am, but they know I'm transmitting from somewhere nearby, and it sounds like they've put an even bigger bounty on my head."

"So maybe it's time to get you out of here." I'm seriously concerned for her safety.

The Queen surveys my face for what feels like a long time before answering, "It might be smart to leave." She pauses and when I don't say anything, asks, "But you're thinking something. What is it?"

Am I that readable? I go ahead and ask the question she had seen on my face, "Can you hang on for a two more days?"

"If I have to. Why?"

I explain the official reason, "There's a big strategy meeting with the generals tomorrow. I should have the info about their plans by the next time we get together. In the meanwhile, you ask Baker Street what they want us to do."

Unofficially, it also buys me time. Time to work things out with Fritz.

The Queen nods.

"And tell them this, too," I make staying worth her while by giving her the only other bit of info I have. "Tell them that Rommel seems more certain than ever that the invasion will come here. He's doing everything he can to escalate the construction of fortifications along the beach. And he's even started fortifying the inland areas by planting upright logs in as many open fields as he can to destroy any gliders that try to land. Johann calls them Rommel Asparagus and says it's his job to plant them all over the countryside."

"Interesting," she responds, nodding. Then she gives me a bright, excited smile. "That could be meaningful."

It's a relief. Somehow I need her to verify that staying here will serve a greater purpose. And what's tomorrow's meeting about?" The Queen tries to maintain a strict agenda. It isn't safe to lollygag.

"The big topic will be Hitler's decision about where to station the Panzer divisions to defend against the invasion. You remember the generals have been arguing about it. They couldn't decide whether to protect here or Calais. So, they asked Hitler to make the call."

The Queen nods again, saying "Good," under her breath. Then she tells me where she'll meet me two afternoons from now and disappears back to wherever she's hiding that night.

I head straight back to the manor. With Fritz gone and the boys at work on the fortifications, I don't have to explain my comings and goings. But I always make it a point to be home in time to help Julia and Madame Roget prepare dinner. Often I'll come back with vegetables or fruit to add to the meal, but the Queen and I have talked longer than usual and I'm so lost in thought that I forget to stop at the market. Luckily, the other ladies have put together a decent meal without me and don't seem to notice.

The next day and evening seem to last forever, and not in a good way. Simultaneously bored and anxious, I can't sit still and can't think of anything to do. Fritz's meeting with the generals must run late, because he's not home in time for dinner. When he finally starts across the courtyard, I rush to meet him. But instead of sweeping me off my feet, as he does in my dreams, he gives me a weary, "Hello," and walks past.

"Come to the kitchen," I reach for his hand intending to pull him back, "I saved supper for you."

"I've already eaten." He resists and keeps moving toward the one-room out building that has transformed from purgatory to paradise and back again in a matter of forty-eight hours.

Inside, he undresses without looking at me and drops onto his bed so hard the legs bow and he bounces. When he sees me standing there watching him, waiting, he finally says, "I'm sorry. I'm just too tired to talk now. Can we wait until tomorrow?"

Can *we* wait? Actually, judging from his demeanor, it's probably a good thing. I see little hope of changing his mind about us when he's in such a distracted mood. "Okay," I say leaning over to kiss him. But he rolls away to face the wall before I get the chance.

"The pallet?" I ask the back of his head.

"Please," is its answer.

From my cold, familiar spot on the floor across the room, I can tell sleep is not coming easily to him. Covers rustle and the bed squeaks as he tosses and turns. And then suddenly, as if he decides we can still be friends even if we can't be lovers, his voice reaches out to me through the night.

"I'm worried."

"What are you worried about?"

"Everything." I hear him rolling onto his side to talk to me. "It doesn't sound right," he continues.

All ears now, I give him a chance to organize his thoughts before asking, "What doesn't sound right?"

"The intelligence. It's still mixed."

Good. It's not me he's upset about. It's what went on at that meeting.

"Most of it indicates that the Americans and British are going to attack within the month and that they'll come ashore at Calais. But those are mostly intercepted messages … could easily be decoys. And a spy, someone who's working in London, someone Rommel knows and trusts, says that's what they are, a trick, a diversion to pull forces away from here."

"Do you trust this spy?" The fact that there is a mole in an apparently high position in London's chain of command is disturbing. I hope to learn more.

"I don't know who he is," Fritz answers. "But, Rommel trusts him."

So, it's a man. "And he says they're coming here?" I whisper with mixed emotions I can't quite fathom. "What do you think?"

My stomach sinks as Fritz answers, "In my gut I have a feeling he's right. Rommel does too, but—"

"Was he able to convince the other generals?"

"No! Damn it! And it gets worse." Fritz's voice sounds sad and hollow. "What does the Fuehrer do? He cuts the baby in half. He's decided to hold the bulk of the Panzers in reserve away from the coast. Two divisions are being sent to Calais and only one here … to Caen."

The bed squeaking escalates. He's working himself up. "If the spy is right, we won't be able to stop them on the beach. Not with so few mines and so little training and only one Panzer division to defend a hundred kilometers of shore."

He's never sounded so forlorn, so at a loss.

"There's nothing I can do." He goes on, a sense of inadequacy flooding his voice. "I can't build fortifications without the proper materials. Rommel is correct. We won't be able to hold out long enough for the other Panzer divisions to get here."

In a raised voice he concludes, "If they take the beach, we won't be able to stop them. This will all have been for nothing!"

My mind races. He's a drowning man crying out for a life preserver, and I can't toss him the only one I have.

Thirty

JOE – *Montreal, Canada, the Last Day, 1992*

"Fritz was right, wasn't he?" Joe shook his head.

"Yes, he was." Nanette reached for her first cigarette in a while and lit it. Then she asked, "Will you please take the damned cap off the flask and leave it off."

Her gruff words and tone didn't match her face. It was almost apologetic, as if she were saying, "What's left for me to do but take a little comfort where I can find it."

But she smiled when he took a sip of the amber Canadian anesthetic before handing her the flask. Then he slipped the cap into his pocket, and she held his eye while she took a long slow draught.

"And how long before the Allied landing was this?" Joe was trying to get a firm grip on the significance of the story he was hearing.

"Two weeks and four days."

"Wow." He collapsed back into his chair, puffing up his cheeks to blow out air. "That was cutting it close." Then he added, "Did you know they were coming?"

"No. But Rommel's logic made sense. And wherever they landed ... the sooner the better as far as I was concerned."

She waved her cigarette hand in the air and took another gulp of whiskey. "You see, from what I'd seen I could tell that, if the landing was successful, the Nazis wouldn't be able to hold France. And once they lost France, it would be only a matter of time before they'd lose Germany. What with Russia taking up so much of their energy and resources on the Eastern Front."

She paused and closed her eyes as if she was thinking, before adding, "And, you need to understand. For the first time in my life, I dreamed a different future ... a future with Fritz. Grand gallery openings, a small garden, children's voices. It was as if an entirely new me had been born and I was ready to start living that new me's life."

She looked over to make sure Joe was following and ended flatly, "As we talked that night I still truly believed, or at least hoped, we'd be able to work it out somehow. But we had to get the war over and done with first."

She took another long, slow sip from the flask, making Joe fear that he hadn't brought enough whiskey to sustain her through this part of her tale.

NANETTE – *Bayeux, France, May 1944*

My whirling thoughts combined with Fritz's fretful tossing and turning keep me awake most of the night. By the time I finally drift off, the rooster's crowing, and Fritz is dragging his feet across the floor. I jump up and follow him wordlessly to breakfast. We're both so bedraggled the others look away. An odd reaction?

Back in our room, the Nazi coffee has brought me almost back to life. I touch his arm and say, "Fritz, we need to talk."

He faces me, blue eyes peering out over puffy dark circles and says, "I don't know what to say."

"Why not?" He's the one doing this. It's his decision. He at least ought to know why this is happening.

Then it hits me. "This is really about me, isn't it? What I am."

He shakes his head, but he's just trying to spare me. I can tell by the way he looks at his shoes, I'm right.

"No, Fritz. You can tell me the truth. I need to know." I realize I'm pleading, but can't help myself. To the contrary, I blurt out to my own surprise, "I can change. I'm in love with you." Now that's a fine kettle of fish.

His reaction is not what I hoped. Wide eyed, he looks panicked, searching the room for some place to rest his gaze on anything but me. "I'm sorry. I can't. I don't know..." He unconsciously shifts to German. Can't formulate his thoughts in French.

Then he grabs his uniform jacket from its peg on the wall and stuffs his right arm into the sleeve as he starts toward the door. But he pauses before exiting to insert the other arm and do his buttons.

After he's straightened his folds, he shoves the door open and steps through the opening. Fearing all is lost, I stand mute, prepared to watch him disappear across the courtyard without saying another word. After all I've fired the biggest cannon I possess, and it has had no apparent effect.

But he stops and turns to face me, framed once more by the door jamb like a hero in an epic painting. "I'm sorry," he says again. "I just don't know..." He stops and shakes his head. "I need time to think."

A crumb! There's hope! He's tossed me a crumb!

I nod, and he says, "I'm going to the fortifications. I'll be back for dinner," before walking away.

Yes. There's still a chance. But first, we both have to survive the invasion. And then the rest of the war.

At ease with that thought, I keep myself busy. After helping Julia and the Madame with household chores, I explore the countryside in search of wild flowers and miscellaneous intelligence to share with the Queen that afternoon. Not that I need more than the information Fritz gave me last night. That's a bonanza in itself. But I feel the need to keep moving. Anything to get this conflict over with so that I can get on with my life.

By the time I set out for the rendezvous point on my bicycle, I've pretty much worked it all out in my mind. It's clear that the Queen has to leave. For her own safety and mine. But, unless Baker Street specifically orders me to go somewhere else, I'm staying here. I've uncovered too much good intelligence to leave now, and I can find a new way to get information to JuJu or some other agent. It's likely the Queen's figured this out for herself, and I expect it's also what Baker Street will have told her.

Another reason is that the two of us have pretty much run out of places we can meet safely. That's why she's waiting for me in the ruins of an ancient chapel some distance off the road between the manor and the city. I approach it through a graveyard that's so old it's impossible to read the names on any of the worn, gray tombstones.

After I tell her the news that Hitler has decided to leave the beaches of Normandy with less protection than Rommel thinks they need, she replies, "I'll get that to them right away."

"And what did Baker Street say about us?" I ask.

She knows this is the pivotal moment and watches me closely as she gives me the answer. "We're to get out of here immediately."

"Both of us?" I'm surprised and not pleased with that news. I was counting on them wanting me to mine Fritz for all he was worth.

"Yes," she nods, "we're to get out right away."

"Did they say why?"

"No." She studies me through narrowed eyes.

"They're coming!" I leap to the conclusion. "Here! When?"

"They didn't say that." She's trying to keep us both calm. "It was more like an alert to a heightened possibility. But, this new information could be what they need to pull the trigger."

The Queen is so excited, she actually throws her arms around me and pulls me close for the second time since we crossed the Pyrenees. With my head pulled to her bosom, she's whispering into my hair. I think I hear tears in her voice. "We're finally going to make them pay. We're going to drive them all the way back to their poisonous Fatherland and make them pay ... for everything." She repeats it like a litany.

When she releases her grip on me and pushes my shoulders to arms' length so we can see each other's faces, I'm still ambivalent. Her smile is both sad and optimistic, and the edges of her eyes are definitely red. It's small consolation. There's no way to undo the damage the Nazis have done, but at least they'll have to pay.

Then the Queen looks over my shoulder and stiffens. Her smile disappears, and her eyes widen.

"What the hell is going on?" It's Fritz.

I turn. He's standing in the ruins of the doorway, breathing irregularly, his face red.

"Who the hell is she? And what—"

I stop him by rushing to his side, throwing my arms around his waist, and burying my face in his chest as if I'm happy to see him. He pushes me away, standing to face the Queen.

"You must be Fritz." The Queen smiles and takes a step toward us with her hand outstretched, as casually as if we were just normal people. It's a good move.

"Who the hell *are* you?" He demands again.

"I'm Nanette's friend, Regina," she tries to calm him. "She's told me so much about you."

I marvel at her coolness. But Fritz doesn't accept her friendly gesture. Instead, he steps back. The Queen stops walking toward him, but keeps smiling, waiting to see what his next move will be.

What Fritz does is turn so that he can see my face and ask, "Women? You service women too? Is this who you've been running away to see all along? Or is it someone different every time?"

I have no idea what he thinks he knows. But I'm optimistic. It appears he's jealous. Maybe that's why he pushed me away in the first place. Some fear I've been seeing other men or now women. If that's all it is, perhaps we can pull this off and everything will be okay.

But, I'm not entirely sure how to play this scene yet. I fake it trying to get more information before I commit to anything. "All along?"

"Madame Roget says you've been sneaking out in the afternoons."

"I have not been *sneaking* anything!" I'm actually indignant at the characterization and furious with Madame Roget. However, it does explain the coolness I've noticed in the compound lately.

But Fritz isn't really listening to me. He continues, "She says you're a whore and that you leave every day or so and stay out the right amount of time for an assignation." He spits the word out with disgust. "Then you come back trying too hard not to look guilty."

"She told you I've been meeting a lover?" I want to kill the woman.

"More likely meeting clients … conducting your *profession*." He nods harshly. Suspicious, his eyes are oddly hard and wild at the same time.

"Clients?" It comes out unexpectedly gentle. I'm touched by his jealousy, and want to reassure him that he's all the man I need and the only lover I will ever want. I reach over and take hold of his left wrist. "Fritz, my dear, my love. Madame Roget is wrong. I told you. I have no clients. *You* are my lover. My only lover."

The Queen's eyes widen at this news. I'm surprised. It was always understood I'd be sleeping with him. Perhaps it's the tone of my voice that catches her off guard. I don't have to act to make it sound convincing. It's the truth.

I relax a little when Fritz does not pull his arm away. It's the first time he hasn't winced when I've touched him since our talk at the cathedral. We can still work this out.

But he turns his attention back to the Queen. "So who is she, then, and why did you come all the way out here to meet her?"

"Like she said, we're friends." I've been putting together a story. "We met in Bayeux a few—"

"Wait a minute!" Fritz extends his arm across my chest and pushes me behind him, as if protecting me from a threat. His amazing, wonderful eyes have discerned something no one else would ever have noticed. In a flash, he unsnaps his holster and draws his pistol, aiming it at the Queen's mid section. "Come here, closer … into the light where I can see you," he orders.

The Queen complies. Fritz's eyes narrow as he scrutinizes her. I recognize the look. He's cataloguing the details of her appearance, comparing them with something.

He steps away from me as he says, "You match the description. A farmer near Caen told the Gestapo you were there."

Fragonard! Damn Fragonard!

"And what's that?" Fritz points at a small tan smudge on the Queen's collar, right next to the St. Christopher's medal she always wears.

With horror, I realize it's makeup. A small bit has rubbed off the Queen's neck revealing the darker skin below. Her cheek also looks mottled. That makeup's probably on my hair. There's a good reason not to hug people when you're in disguise.

Fritz tosses her his handkerchief, ordering, "Wipe your cheek."

The Queen does, revealing the richer natural tone of her skin. Fritz tilts his head, never shifting his gaze from the Queen's face.

"I know who you are." He sounds as amazed as I am. "You've lost weight and changed your hair, but you're the one they've been looking for. They sent out a bulletin a while back. The Mulatto."

He's still thinking, piecing the puzzle together. "And you're the one who's been sending the radio messages we've been trying to track down ... aren't you?"

But Fritz still hasn't put it all together. Having reached that conclusion, he takes my arm and pushes me towards the doorway, saying, "Come on. We've got to get her to the Gestapo right away. She's a spy. I'm supposed to kill her here and now, but I think it would be smarter for them to question her first." He looks at me hopefully. "Maybe we can get her to tell us something that will convince Hitler to send the panzers or at least help us catch whoever's helping her."

It's decision time. The Queen isn't looking at me, by which she's telling me to play along. To save myself. But, I know Fritz. I know I can win him over.

"That would be me, Fritz," I confess. This is a chance I feel comfortable taking. Fritz is not a true Nazi, not a murdering megalomaniac like Hitler and his henchmen. He only joined the army out of a sense of duty.

The Queen reacts by cutting her eyes toward me.

Fritz wavers, his gaze swinging like a pendulum from the Queen to me and back. He still doesn't get it. "Don't say foolish—"

"No, it's true, Fritz." Placing my hand on his forearm, pleading without words.

The Queen takes the opportunity created when he looks down at me to slide her hand into her pocket where she can reach her derringer. I shake my head. She's still too far away for the derringer to be effective. Plus, I can save us all.

Fritz is not good at shifting his focus back and forth. It stops on me when I continue, "But it's good it happened like this. You told me yourself. The Americans and British are coming soon, and there's nothing you can do to stop them. It's only a matter of time before the war will be over."

I throw my arms around him now, begging. "Come with us. We can hide in the hills. The Allies will treat you—"

"No!" He cuts me off. "She's a spy. I am under direct orders to kill her now or bring her in for interrogation after which she will immediately be executed." He's sweating visibly, ignoring my suggestion as if he hasn't heard it.

"But those are Nazi orders," I cry. "This is a Nazi war, and you are *not* a Nazi!"

His eyes flit wildly.

"You're a good man, a kind man." I keep pushing. "You know right from wrong and that what the Nazis are doing is wrong. You told me so yourself. And you know they can't possibly win this war."

"No!" He's suddenly firm and solid, his voice low."We must win."

We? He said "We?" I don't believe my ears.

"Win? Why must they win?" I demand.

"To save Germany. To protect the Fatherland."

"Even if that means you have to do everything the Nazis tell you to do?" I demand. "No matter how horrible? Torture and slaughter innocent people who have never done a thing to you? That's wrong Fritz, and you know it."

He takes a long time answering. Without lowering his gun, he closes his eyes, thinking. He's reconsidering. The Queen must be letting this play out for my sake. She doesn't take this opportunity to attack.

Eventually he turns to me with the greatest sorrow I have ever seen on his face. In a calm, soft voice, he explains the logic that's led him to his decision in slow formal sentences as if he's memorized the argument.

"I am German. It is to Germany I owe my allegiance. It is true that the Nazis are in control today. But it will not always be so. Once this war is over, more reasonable and rational men will come together to forge a new government and a better Germany."

"So to be German … is to be Nazi." I draw the conclusion for myself.

"For now."

With those two words, the bottom falls out of my world. Yet I try again, hoping the morality I know is in his soul will save us. "But what about all the women and children, the Jews and the Gypsies and everybody else in the detention camps? It's murder, Fritz! Murder. How can you justify aligning yourself with murderers?"

I'm angry now. Not at him, but at the Nazis who have placed us all in this position where we have to make these choices.

He pauses again then, having emptied his voice of all emotion, he finally and completely shatters my illusions. "Sometimes bad things are unavoidable." Sighing as if this is hard for him to say, he adds, "And … and maybe they're right. Perhaps the future will be better if we keep our race pure. Maybe that's the price we have to pay."

It takes a while for the awful reality of what he's just said to sink in. He used the word *we* again, but this time it was a false we. He's not offering to pay the price. He's the one exacting it.

"You actually mean that?" I still don't believe him. My voice is so weak it's almost inaudible.

He looks pained, but shrugs and says, "Maybe it's the only way."

"So, then..." Devastated, I stand before him, arms at my sides and play my final card. "What are you going to do about me?"

That never-ending, recurring question stops him once again. His mouth opens and closes, but no words come out.

Holding my wrists out as if surrendering to be handcuffed, I push my advantage. "I'm a spy. Will you turn *me* in to be executed, too?"

He almost panics. It's a small consolation to know he seems to care. His eyes search the room in confusion. Then they land heavily on the Queen, and the decision he makes hardens his face and tenses his body.

The Queen recognizes that look for what it is. Her body also tightens, her hand behind her back. I'm sure she's retrieved her little pistol while he's been focused on me, but I shake my head again. He'll shoot the instant he sees it.

I push my point. "I'll stay here with you. Go to confession. Be the woman you want me to be. We can move to Paris or even back to Germany after the war."

"You're right. I can't take her back," Fritz ignores my words, breathing harshly. His wild eyes find mine as he confirms my belief that he really cares about me. But his gun's still steady and still aimed at the Queen's abdomen. "If I turn her in, they'll get her to talk, and then you…"

I smile, letting him know I'm thankful he's willing to give up interrogating her to save me. Then he reveals how horribly I've miscalculated.

"I have to execute her now. That way they'll never get the chance."

"No, Fritz, please." If he's willing to break one rule to save me, I can get him to break another. I move closer again, pleading my case. "Just let her go. That'll accomplish the same thing. She can't stay here to do any more damage anyway." I caress his chest with my palm in small firm circles.

He shakes his head like a dog with water in his ears. "No."

"Please." I bury my face into his side and beg, "I want to be with you."

His left arm is holding me so close I can hear his heart pound as he considers the possibility. Then he lets me go and jerks away. "You told her about the Panzers, didn't you?"

I shake my head. "No. You got here too soon." I look from Fritz to the Queen then pull on his arm. "Don't say any more. She doesn't know anything."

"You're lying."

Damn those eyes! They see through me.

"If she tells them about the Panzers, they'll know this is the place to land." Now he's looking at me as if he can't believe what he sees. How could I betray him by betraying Germany?

"And if they come here, we won't be able to stop them!" He starts to sight his pistol at the Queen. "I can't let her tell them that!"

"I'm sorry," I moan, pulling my derringer through the hole in my skirt pocket.

"You couldn't have known."

That's a strange thing for him to say. It's as if he's not willing to face the full import of what he's learned about me. Well, at least his focus is divided again.

"And you don't need to be involved in it at all," he adds, smiling now as if something he's thought of excites him. "All I need to tell Rommel is that I caught the Mulatto here. That'll be enough to force Hitler to change his mind."

Fritz has figured out a way to turn my infidelity to the Nazis' advantage. "This is good. We'll have time to set a trap with the Panzers."

"You don't know how sorry I am," I lay my forehead on his chest and restate my heartfelt sorrow.

His arm drapes protectively over my shoulders again as he encourages me, "Don't worry. Everything's all right now. This is exactly what we needed!"

I press my little pistol into Fritz's back just below his left shoulder blade. He stiffens.

"It's a gun, Fritz. Let her go," I say calmly.

His arm is still around me, but with the muzzle pressed so firmly into his body, I can get the shot off if he tries anything. The problem is he doesn't take my threat seriously. He gives me a little squeeze and says in a husky voice, "You won't shoot me."

"Drop the gun, Fritz!" I try to sound firm, strong, committed, but my voice still rises.

"You're a woman. You don't understand. Once we destroy the Americans and British on the beach, the war will end quickly." His tone is cajoling. "My father will be proud. He will give us a fine house in Prussia, and..." He takes a quick look down at me but turns immediately back to the Queen. "And our children..."

While he's making plans for the children he and I will have together, Fritz is also sighting down the barrel at the Queen preparing to kill her in cold blood. It's the final inconsistency.

Yet, I have to try again. "Please, Fritz," I moan, nuzzling his chest one last time as I make sure the angle's right so I won't hit myself. "Don't make me do it."

"Don't worry," he still discounts the threat I pose. "It'll take time, but once we have defeated them, you'll see. Everything will be good. We'll—"

"Okay, then." I accept my fate with a whisper.

Misreading my intention, he's pulling me tightly to his side to seal the deal he thinks we've made when I squeeze the trigger. His body muffles the shot. It's not likely anybody outside of the chapel ruins could have heard it. At first, it seems like nothing's happened. Just a little jolt that's not big enough to knock him off his feet.

But I've done a better job of aiming than I did with Fragonard. Fritz starts to go slack. His gun hits the stone floor with a thud. He turns to me as his legs give out and he slowly drops to his knees. Those eyes, those eyes that are capable of seeing so much, hold mine, transitioning from surprise, to betrayal, to sadness as the light within them fades, and they close.

Thirty-One

JOE – *Montreal, Canada, the Last Day, 1992*

"No!" Joe had not been prepared for that ending to Nanette's love story.

Nanette stared off into the distance as if she had been telling it to the sky. Each emotion played unashamedly across her face. When tears finally ran down her cheeks, Joe slid from his seat, knelt beside her chair, and drew her into his arms, taking care not to squeeze too tight.

For a while she heaved and sobbed violently against his chest, and he wept into the red of her hair, saying, "I'm sorry. I'm so sorry," over and over, while two thoughts endlessly cycled through his brain. It's not fair! How can anyone survive something like that intact? It's not fair! How can anyone survive...

He had no idea how long he held Nanette like that, and he didn't care. Nor did he notice when she slipped her hands underneath his arms and started stroking and patting him on the back as if he were the one who needed comforting.

Eventually though, he let her go and sat back on his heels, as they both brushed the tears from their cheeks. "I'm so sorry," he said again.

She quieted him by laying her fingers lightly on his arm. "For what, Joseph?"

Taken aback, Joe clarified his meaning, "I just wish it hadn't turned out like that. It seems so unfair."

"Hunh." Nanette let out an ironic little breath. "Unfair?" She tilted her head closing one eye to think. After a bit, she shrugged and said, "Fairness was never one of the rules."

Joe couldn't fathom the depths of the woman. "But, how do you survive something like that?"

That question required even more consideration. Nanette pursed her lips, lowered her eyelids to half mast, and bobbed her head slightly up and down for some time before answering, "I don't know, Joseph." A few more contemplative bobs. "You go on. But, I'm not sure you actually survive."

Joe squinted down at her. After determining that she was thinking again, he decided to give her time. Rising from his knees, he sat back in his chair. Her gnarled hand slid off of her armrest and patted his knee, as if to tell him he'd done the right thing.

"Okay, so how do you go on then?"

"You do what you have to do."

NANETTE – *Bayeux, France, May 1944*

"Kiss him goodbye," the Queen whispers in my ear, her hand on my shoulder.

Kneeling on the hard, gray stone floor next to Fritz's body, I turn my head and look up at her as if I'm at the bottom of a well, not really comprehending.

"Kiss him goodbye," she repeats. A look of sorrow has replaced the sense of urgency that had been in her face.

My head clears enough to understand she's telling me this for my own good, something she knows from her own experience. I look down at the husk that had once been my love and place my hand on his cheek. It's still warm. He could just be sleeping. Please let him just be sleeping. Placing my other hand on the hard cold floor to lower my face to his, I kiss his lips lightly, then his eyes, and finally his forehead, brushing the sandy-colored hair back with my fingers. I don't need to voice the words.

Then the Queen drags me to my feet by my arm, saying, "We have to get out of here."

I'm not with her. Suddenly sleepwalking.

"I need my transmitter. Got to send Baker Street the Panzer information right away. Then we'll get as far away from this place as we can." She's more firm, trying to wake me, "Come on!"

I step listlessly in the direction she's pulling. Moving my body triggers at least part of my brain. I stop, whispering, "He made drawings." Only now do I realize how stupid I was to let him.

The Queen turns to face me, eyes narrowed, questioning the meaning of that statement. I explain, "You won't be safe with me. They'll recognize me from the drawings."

As the Queen chews on her thumb thinking about our dilemma, I come up with what seems to be the only solution. "You go ahead. I'll stay here." I'm prepared to face the consequences of my actions on my own.

"No! I'm not losing you, too."

At first I think she's going to slap me. But, instead, she chews her thumb again. After a minute she adds, "Okay. Here's what we're going to do."

I await her orders, not really giving a shit. My life is over any way you look at it.

"We have to split up." She lays out her plan. "But only for a little while. You will sneak back into your room at the manor. Pack your bags and take every sketch book with a drawing of you in it. Then you will write a note in French that says, 'Fritz. It's been fun, but I have gone with Henri. He owns a factory and can give me the things you will never be able to give me.' Sign it, and leave it on the bed. If anyone sees you on the way in, pretend everything is normal. If they see you on the way out with the suitcases, tell them you're leaving Fritz and running off with Henri."

It must look like I'm having trouble making sense of this through the dull roaring in my head, because she grasps my shoulders firmly and squeezes them together pulling my face up to hers. "Did you hear what I said?"

I repeat her instructions almost verbatim.

"Good." The Queen nods. "Now, do you think you can do it?"

I arch my eyebrows and give my head a slow-motion toss. Who really cares? But when she shakes me by the shoulders, I answer, "Yes."

"Okay, then," she tells me the rest of the steps I have to take and how to take them, apparently having decided that I might be capable of following instructions if they're detailed enough, even if I can't think for myself.

When she's finished, she turns me around and pushes me out the door. We both know that once I'm on my own, it'll be up to me whether I even try to survive this night. She'll monitor our next meeting place from a safe distance until the designated hour, and if I'm not there on time, she's out of my life whatever that's worth. Probably forever.

As I walk away, the Queen calls softly after me, "Don't forget, it'll be our turn soon. We're about to start paying the bastards back."

I so get it now. Making the Nazi bastards who did that to Fritz and the rest of us pay is the only thing in this world that motivates me in the least, the only reason I might choose to live.

As I right my bicycle, a muffled gunshot echoes from the chapel, and in my mind's eye, I see the Queen repositioning the body, placing Fritz's still warm fingers on the grip and through the trigger guard ... hiding the entry wound in the back by making it look like he shot himself in the chest with his own pistol. The thought doesn't upset me as much as it might. She was so right in the Pyrenees. He's not there anymore.

The Queen's plan is brilliant. It plays directly into both the image of the happy couple Fritz and I had created and Madame Roget's snooping gossip. It will look like Fritz couldn't stand living in the face of my infidelity and absence. Such a loss.

The odd thing is that the second new me of the day turns out to be better at following orders than the old me. I make it to the meeting place without incident and with fifteen minutes to spare. The Queen's been busy too. She's already informed Baker Street that Hitler has hung the Normandy coast out to dry.

The next two days are a weird reverse déjà vu. The Queen walks with her arm around me during the night and keeps me safe during the day. This time it's me talking, mindlessly, pointlessly, mourning both Fritz and the new Nanette I hardly got to know, both of whom made the ultimate sacrifice in Normandy. But mostly mourning what could have been.

That night, Baker Street lets us know how to find JuJu. He's a little farther inland and he's expecting us. Two nights later, JuJu fills us in on what he's been up to.

The Maquis have been harvesting Rommel's asparagus almost as fast as Johann can plant them. They've also been clearing new fields. The Queen and I know instantly it's for the gliders. The Allies are coming to Normandy and they're coming soon. Anticipating the taste of revenge wakes at least part of me, and I begin to function more effectively.

Things start pulling together. When the next S.O.E. airdrop contains really nice long-range rifles and ammunition, I silently thank my father and brothers for all those days we spent hunting squirrels and rabbits.

"JuJu," I say. "Did I tell you I got the highest score ever at the firing range during training?"

Not one to take anything for granted, JuJu arranges a test, and he's smiling when it's over. That makes me happy. I haven't given him much to smile about lately. The grin on my own face feels alien.

These new rifles break down quickly and are easy to hide, especially if you're wearing a skirt. No one will ever suspect that a woman, much less a cute little thing hardly as tall as her rifle, is the long-range sniper assassinating S.S., Gestapo, and Nazi officers of all ranks behind their own lines.

The next day, the Queen tells me she'll be leaving. "JuJu already has a radio operator," she explains. "I'm moving to a band of Maquis farther inland. A collaborator turned theirs in. They need a transmitter."

It's another loss. But I don't get much of a chance to dwell on it. The Queen is gone within the hour, tossing me a smile and calling out over her shoulder, "See you in Berlin."

JOE – *Montreal, Canada, the Last Day, 1992*

"So," Nanette sighed, picking up their earlier conversation where she had left it, "You asked how one goes on? First you will yourself to breathe. Then you put one foot in front of another and keep forcing the next foot forward until one day something distracts you and you forget to think about doing it." Shooting Joe a meaningful look, she added, "And it helps if you have a reason."

Joe shook his head. "Payback?"

Nanette nodded, her fingers playing idly along the sketch book's binding. "Revenge may be the most effective reason of all."

Then, she added, challenging Joe to judge her for it, "Like the Queen said, 'It feels good.'"

Joe stared at the little old lady sitting in the wheelchair next to him. It was hard to believe she and the grandmother it turns out he never really knew had lived this story, but it explained so much. And really, who was he to judge? He'd never been to war. Never watched a loved one die. Hell, never really loved anyone the way they had loved. Until now maybe.

Joe didn't say a word. He let Nanette keep going.

"I came close to making one mistake, though," she softened and let the air slip out of her lungs slowly. "Had my sights lined up on an unteroffizier about a month after the landing. Held my breath, started squeezing the trigger." She paused to make eye contact with Joe. "And then I realized something about him looked familiar. It was Karl, Julia's Karl."

Nanette pursed her lips and arched her eyebrows while shrugging, then added, "He must have received a field promotion." A sigh. "I hope they made it through the war."

"You didn't pull the trigger? Why not?" The question slipped out of Joe's mouth as he realized the import of her statement. She'd let Karl live. He was the only one.

The old woman, shrugged again, holding her palms up to the sky. "Love." She said wistfully with a sad smile and then turned a serious look on Joe. "What can I say? To this day I still believe in love." She waved a hand, indicating Joe should wait, while she recomposed herself.

"Karl was a good boy. Little more than a conscript like Stanislaw, just trying to stay alive. He and Julia had been together for a year, and she loved him so much she was willing to give up everything to be with him. She even planned to go with him to the prisoner of war camp if he was captured. I couldn't be the one who destroyed that dream."

"But you loved Fritz..." As the words slipped out, Joe remembered how shocked he'd been to learn that Nanette gone ahead and pulled the trigger. He regretted asking the question as soon as he started to ask it, afraid the answer would hurt Nanette too much.

But he was wrong again. Nanette waved a hand and replied calmly, "There was nothing to be done about that." She paused again, looking to see Joe's reaction.

He didn't know how to react.

"Later the Queen helped me put it into perspective." She paused, screwing up her face to think. "She asked me if I had loved the man Fritz was ... or the man he could have been."

Joe's eyes widened. He was paying close attention.

"It was a good question," Nanette continued. "Remember? I started fantasizing about Fritz the first minute I saw him. He was so damned physically attractive and the whole sensitive artist bit played right into my fantasy." She sighed and gazed unfocused at the sky for a moment. "He had so much potential."

Joe leaned back in his chair, trying to draw one coherent conclusion from all of the revelations Nanette had made that day.

"When the Queen asked me that, I couldn't answer at first. The Fritz in my mind was handsome, educated, charming, and talented, and he had been forced into the military by his culture and his overbearing family," she continued. "In my mind, he was different than the others ... a thoughtful man with a kind heart. He couldn't possibly be a true Nazi. When the time came, he'd do the right thing. He loved kittens for God's sake!"

Nanette was working herself up. Joe sat still and watched.

"What it boiled down to?" She looked over at him as if seeking validation.

He nodded, encouraging her to continue.

"The Queen was right. The Fritz I fell in love with existed only in my imagination. My hopes ... my dreams." Nanette wiped a tear from in her eye. "The real Fritz tuned out to be just one more German who decided it was expedient to be a Nazi."

Joe laid his hand on her arm, sure that she was shoring herself up, pretending to need no consolation. But, she shrugged him off, her voice turning to steel. "It was the way of the world. He had to die."

The irony of her word choice wasn't wasted on Joe. The Queen had tried to save the pig. Nanette would have saved Fritz if she could have. Joe couldn't imagine living in a world where he had to face such realities.

He wished he could make it better, but there was nothing he could do. He watched Nanette take another swig out of the flask, his heart ripping in half. She had to tilt the bottom high. He'd failed her there. If they weren't already out of Crown Royal, it wouldn't be long. Soon there'd be no consolation in the flask either.

"Don't look so sad."

Could she read his mind?

"Fritz was never half the man Stanislaw turned out to be."

"Stanislaw?" Joe couldn't believe his ears. "He made it through the invasion?"

Nanette nodded, glee lighting up her features. "Turned himself over to the Canadians the second day."

"How do you know this?"

"I went back to the chateau almost four months later. After we finally drove the Nazis out of Caen." Her smile was broad now. Good news is much easier to deliver.

"It survived too?'

Nod.

"And Madame Orly?"

"She was very happy to see me."

NANETTE – *Normandy, August 1944*

I replay the past few weeks in my mind as I steer my borrowed motor bike down roads that should look familiar but don't. Trees, buildings, and fences lie in piles of rubble. Artillery and mortar craters pock the fields. New roads weave around and through them, carved first by Nazis rushing to defend the coast and then retreating, followed by convoys of Canadian jeeps and trucks and tanks in hot pursuit.

It feels especially fitting that this section of the coast was liberated by my Canadian boys. I'm duly proud of the way they performed that first day and over the months that followed.

Word is that the chateau survived the onslaught as if it had been protected by a magic shield, but I don't believe it until I see it for myself, looming above the ragged horizon. Even the barn seems relatively unscathed, and a few of the Madame's cows are grazing in a small pasture enclosed by a newly-repaired fence.

I knock and hold my breath. Madame looks a little tired and frazzled when she opens the door, but her smile brightens the day. Over tea, she relives the invasion.

"The bombardment started a little up the coast. At the first explosion, Stanislaw came to get me. 'Hurry,' he said, 'to the trench!' We gathered food and water on the way. Before dawn, we could hear shells passing overhead."

Madame Orly catches my eye. "They make a whizzing sound. Did you know that?"

I did. "He stayed with you?"

"The whole time. Explosions all around us, but nothing struck the house. It was a miracle."

I nod my agreement. It *was* a miracle.

"And by that afternoon, the bombardment had stopped."

I smile. The bombardment had stopped because my Canadians had taken their part of the beach by noon and were already working their way inland.

"The next morning," Madame Orly continues, "I see trucks coming up the road from the beach. I go out to meet them, and to my surprise they speak French."

I laugh, wanting to tell her, "Of course they do. They're my boys." But the war's not over. It's still too early to give up my cover. Instead I ask the other question I came here to have answered. "And Stanislaw?"

"I tell the French-speaking soldiers that I have a Polish boy who was kidnapped by the Germans and wants to turn himself over to them. 'He's not the first,' they say. 'Bring him to us.' I do. They make sure he has no weapons and take him with them. He waves and wishes me good luck, saying he'll come back one day and to take care of the cows."

Madame Orly reaches out and places her hand on my arm. "That's what he'd been doing before they got here, you know, helping me round up the cows."

Thirty-Two

JOE – *Montreal, Canada, the Last Day, 1992*

"And how do you know what kind of man Stanislaw turned out to be?" Joe asked when Nanette paused in her story.

"I went to Poland to visit him and his wife."

Joe's jaw dropped open in an amazed smile. "How did you find—"

Nanette shook her head at him as if she still couldn't fathom the depth of his ignorance. "The Canadians kept excellent records of their prisoners of war. And don't forget I had a few connections in the intelligence agencies." She looked smug then admitted, "Plus he had told me a lot about his home. I knew he'd go back."

Joe was tempted to ask her when he had the time to tell her anything, but before he could decide whether to take the chance, she seemed to read his mind.

"Pillow talk." She shook her head again. "You'd be amazed at the topics it can cover."

"Did you go as soon as the war was over?"

"No. I was too busy. Even after the Germans surrendered, there was a lot of clean-up work left to do. And then the Queen asked if I wanted to help gather evidence for the war crime trials in Nuremberg."

"What?"

"You didn't think she stopped did you?"

Joe's ears were ringing again. He had been so caught up in Nanette's story that he hadn't given much thought to what his grandmother had done next. He knew from what Nanette had said earlier that she hadn't left the spy business behind once the Nazis were defeated. But he'd assumed… What had he assumed?

Nanette scrutinized his reaction and lit a cigarette. "You don't know about the Israelis, do you?"

He shook his head, mouth still open.

"Blue Eyes tried to get her to join the O.S.S., you know. By then, he was part of the plans your president Roosevelt and his friends in Washington were making to create a new central agency to gather intelligence and carry on secret operations after the war. She was a seasoned operative, and with all the questions out there about the Russians, she'd have been a real asset to the C.I.A. But, she wouldn't have any of it. She was interested in only one thing."

"Payback?" That word again. Joe dreaded it even as he said it.

Nanette nodded. Smoke drifted slowly out of both nostrils. "You could call it justice."

Joe still couldn't believe it. "So she joined the Israelis?"

"Not in the beginning." She shook her head. "You really should review your history. In the beginning, there was no Israel. But, she met a Jewish man named Wiesenthal while we were gathering information for the war crime trials. He'd survived the concentration camps just as she'd survived her own personal hell. They shared a common enemy."

The matter of fact way she said it was like a slap in the face. How much more was there that he didn't know, would never know?

"And neither one of them was satisfied with the way it all ended. Too many high-ranking Nazis and other evil men had simply walked away and disappeared. They started hunting them down."

Joe shook his head. "They had a list?"

"The Queen didn't need a list. She knew who she was looking for."

Joe's wide eyes waited for her to answer his unvoiced question.

"Renee Duphresne."

Elbows on knees, hands covering his face, Joe fought off the tears. All the pain. All the questions and mysteries. All the years. The puzzle pieces fell into place. Made sense. And it was all so sad, so God-damned sad.

Nanette rubbed between his shoulders. Waited.

Eventually Joe lifted his head, red rimmed eyes searching for hers. "Did she find him?"

"I don't know. I think she was getting close when Blue Eyes had his accident."

They were both quiet as Joe pushed Nanette's wheelchair back across the street and through the heavy glass door that once again defined the limits of her world. In the confines of her apartment, Joe accepted her offer of Crown Royal, but asked for ice this time. Then he sat heavily down at her small table as she placed a plate of bread, fruit, and cheese in front of him.

"Eat," she said. "We must never forget we are still alive." She bit into a strawberry and inhaled deeply savoring its taste the same way she had savored that first sip of hard liquor the day before. "And that the world is full of beauty and love … and good whiskey." She lifted her class of Canadian to him.

He raised his, toasting her back, then sipped and looked at her, shaking his head and wondering where the hell her reserves of positive energy came from.

As if reading his mind yet another time, Nanette rolled herself to the low boy, pulled out the second drawer and removed a scrapbook. Placing it on the table between them, she opened to the first page. Smiling faces shone out. A tall, ruddy-faced young man with his arm around a lovely, equally-young woman. Two tow-headed boys, stood in front of them, looking to be about three and two years old.

As Nanette turned the pages, the family grew and aged. By the end of the book, the man and woman were an older couple surrounded by what were probably grandchildren, and possibly great grandchildren.

Having paid attention to the backgrounds and clothing, Joe had a pretty good idea the family was European. "Stanislaw?" he asked, disbelieving even as he drew the conclusion.

Nanette beamed at him. "We keep in touch."

There it was. The family she had allowed herself to dream about having with Fritz. Joe almost broke down again, but fought it off. "How much does his wife know?" He couldn't help asking.

"He told her I was a spy and that I taught him tricks that helped him survive the war. Every time I see her she tells me how much she owes me." Nanette tapped the woman's smiling face with a crooked finger and giggled like a school girl. "If she only knew."

Joe studied a photo of the Polish woman beaming up at her man and smiled in spite of himself. "It looks like he's made her very happy."

"*Very*." She winked. "Some secrets are good to keep."

Joe raised his glass to the wanton young woman who sat across the table from him and tipped his head in acknowledgement.

"Here, try a strawberry." She slid the plate in his direction.

Thirty-Three

JOE – *On the way home, 1992*

Joe replayed his conversations with Nanette in his mind during the flight home. So he still didn't know who his grandfather was? He'd just have to keep looking.

But the more he thought about it, the more confident he was he'd find out it wasn't McPherson. The Queen, as he now thought of his grandmother, had proudly regaled the man's family with stories about her daughter while she worked for them. That meant McPherson knew about the baby, and everything Joe had learned about the man indicated he was not the kind to abandon his child.

On the other hand, according to Nanette, the Queen had loved him her whole life and when she finally got the chance to be with him she took it. There was more to that story.

So, how did Gen fit into it? Joe laughed and shook his head. Nanette. He wouldn't put it past the old spy to have invented Gen out of thin air ... to teach him something he *needed* to know. After all, she hadn't mentioned Gen until he'd made that slip of the tongue about Maya and Carrie.

Still, something about the story seemed right. It explained so much, especially why the Queen went back after she was shot and her mysterious disappearances after the war. He shook his head and stared out into the dark empty sky. As Nanette kept saying, love could be so damn complicated.

By the time the plane's wheels touched down, Joe had decided that it didn't matter whether the story was true or not. He got the point. Your body and your heart don't play by anyone's rules. They want who they want and love who they love, and there's nothing you can do about it.

The line of passengers heading into the terminal stalled as a couple with young children unfolded a baby carriage, and Joe was startled to see Maya and Carrie waiting for him at the gate. He studied them from a distance.

They looked changed somehow. No. Joe chuckled to himself again. It was more likely him who had changed. Or was it just that he could really see them now?

Maya, strong, independent, irreverent. There was a lot of Nanette in her. He could imagine the two of them, tiny sirens striding side-by-side across the Limousin like pint-sized Amazon warriors, wreaking havoc on the Germans by day and on the Maquis by night. He suppressed a smile. He'd have to get those two together one day. Then he laughed out loud. He wasn't sure how he'd survive that encounter.

And Carrie? As if he had called out her name, she turned, tilted her head, and brushed honey-blond strands out of her eyes with long, delicate fingers as she searched the faces of the deplaning passengers. Carrie was the perfect—

Whoa. He stopped himself. Nanette had thought Fritz was perfect. But when the Queen had asked the question…

He shook his head and rolled his eyes at his own stupidity. The old spy had probably made that story up too. Another object lesson for a poor love-struck idiot who obviously needed all the help understanding women he could get? "Hunh." He blew a little burst of air out of his nose.

But still, how well did he really know Carrie?

The truth? That didn't matter, either. It was this simple. He could hardly breathe just from looking at her, and there was nothing he could do about it.

As the line started to move again, Carrie leaned down so that Maya could say something into her ear and they both laughed broad, carefree laughs that made Joe's chest tighten even more. Whatever was going on between those two … and he still didn't believe that anything was … Carrie looked happy. And he'd give anything to make her happy.

Maya saw him and waved. Carrie stood on her tiptoes, searching again. When she finally made eye contact, her smile flashed above the heads of the crowd, lighting up the terminal. This time, she was smiling for him. Damn. His cock was already stiff. How was he going to survive this?

Remembering the bottles of Malbec he'd brought home as souvenirs, he smiled and waved back. At least he knew where he'd start. They'd all be sitting with his mother at her kitchen table in the old brownstone. He'd pour them each a glass as he described his first encounter with Nanette. Then he'd explain about the black wine of Cahors, and they'd raise their goblets in honor of the Queen, Nanette, and Eleanor of Aquitaine. And then again to all the other women before their time who lived the lives they wanted to live.

Then he'd explain that the Queen had chosen the name Angelique for her first mission. That was his mother's name. She needed to know that.

But how many other details of Nanette's stories should he share with them? Everything was so mixed together, so complex. And Nanette was right. Some secrets are good to keep. The question was which ones.

Time. That was what he needed. Time and more answers. But they would have to wait for another day.

Epilogue

NANETTE – *Montreal, Canada, a Month Later, 1992*

"Allo?"

"Nanette?"

"Joseph, how are you?"

"I'm good, Nanette. Really good."

"Your mother?"

"Good, too. Everyone's doing great."

"Even Carrie … and Maya?"

He was ready for the question. "For the moment, I'm at a safe distance. Maya's hard at work finishing her Master's Thesis, and Carrie's home in Florida. I'll be going back down soon to follow some new leads, but the reason I called was I had a thought."

"A thought, Joseph? Just one?"

"Hunh," he sniffed. Had he lost his edge that quickly? He parried, "Yeah, but sometimes one really good thought is all you need."

Nanette chuckled into the receiver. "You are right, mon cher. I stand corrected. What is your really good thought?"

"D-Day. The fiftieth anniversary's coming up. I just checked. They're planning a huge celebration. Sort of a reunion. In Normandy on the beaches."

A sharp intake of breath followed by silence on the line told Joe he'd caught her by surprise. He went on, "I think we should go. You and me."

More silence, followed by, "I don't know, Joseph," and another sound.

Was that a sob? "I'll make all the arrangements. There'll be lots of accommodations for wheelchairs."

A longer period of silence, then, "It has been so long. Perhaps we should just leave things—"

"Please Nanette," he coaxed. "I *need* to know what it feels like. Please show it all to me … the chateau, the manor house, and the Liberty Tree if it survived the invasion."

"They could all still be there." She barely squeezed the words out.

"My mother wants to come," Joe continued in a softer tone. "And maybe by then Carrie'll want to. And Maya of course. She wouldn't miss it." He waited then added, "Heck, we could even invite Sigrid."

A pause. Then, "But so many women, Joseph? Are you sure that you are *up* for that?"

Women Before Their Time Who Inspired This Tale

THE FOLLOWING LIST OF HEROINES who volunteered to spy on the Nazis in occupied France and help organize the Resistance doesn't begin to scratch the surface of women who played essential roles in the Allied Forces war effort.

From a variety of ethnic groups and countries and often armed only with their intelligence and feminine wiles, they accomplished things the men could never have done. Yet, most of their names, exploits, achievements, and sacrifices remain largely unknown and unheralded to this day.

Some remained anonymous for over fifty years because they had signed secrecy oaths, but others were simply being realistic. Publicizing that they had lived, loved, fought, and killed as freely as their male counterparts would have scandalized their families and the society they returned to at the war's end, which largely still considered women the weaker sex, suitable only for secondary support positions, such as housewife, secretary, and nurse.

In their later years, a few did tell their stories. Some described the war as the best years of their lives because of the freedom it allowed them. Others explained that they had initially gone to war for personal reasons, to save a family member or someone they loved. Those insights inspired this tale.

THE WHITE MOUSE—Nancy Wake, an Australian journalist who was living in Marseilles, joined the French Resistance at the beginning of World War II. When her network was uncovered by the Nazis, she fled to England and joined the British spy network, the Special Operations Executive.

Wake parachuted back into France and is noted for having killed a Nazi with her bare hands. By 1943, she was the Gestapo's most wanted person with a price on her head.

In 1944, Wake helped coordinate Resistance attacks with the D-Day landings, leading an armed raid against Gestapo headquarters and German gun factories. One of her Resistance members said, "She is the most feminine woman I know, until the fighting starts. Then she is like five men."

Wake was awarded the Croix de Guerre three times, the George Medal, the Médaille de la Résistance, and the American Medal of Freedom, making her one of the more decorated heroes of World War II.

PEGGY—Margaret Taylor grew up in France. When World War II broke out, her Canadian father evacuated the family to Britain, but her mother had to stay behind to care for Peggy's grandmother. In 1941, twenty-one-year-old Peggy learned that her mother had been sent to a concentration camp and joined the Free French Forces in an effort to save her.

A beautiful "temptress" described as "all legs and red lipstick," she parachuted into France twenty-two times with her high heels tied around her neck. In 1944, Peggy gathered information about the German tanks and other military structures that lined the beaches of Normandy by posing as a prostitute and bicycling along the coast, singing and blowing kisses to the Germans. The details she provided are said to have been crucial for planning the Allied invasion on D-Day. She was awarded the Croix de Guerre and the Médaille de la Résistance twice.

After the war Peggy worked for the Canadian government as a stenographer and died in anonymity in a nursing home in 2006.

THE LIMPING LADY—Virginia Hall, an adventuress from Baltimore, joined the British Special Operations Executive at the beginning of World War II and was sent to Vichy France to help coordinate the Resistance, despite the fact that she had lost the lower part of one leg in a hunting accident. In 1942, she escaped on foot over the Pyrenees Mountains into Spain.

She joined the American spy agency, the Office of Strategic Services, when it was created and in November 1943, she returned to France disguised as an elderly milk maid with her hair dyed gray and a shuffling walk that hid her limp.

In September 1945, she became the only woman in World War II to be awarded the American Distinguished Service Cross, but by then she had joined the C.I.A. and refused all publicity, saying she was "still operational and most anxious to get busy."

AIMEE AND JAGUAR—During the war in Berlin, Lilly Wust, the wife of a Nazi soldier and mother of four children, fell in love with Felice Schragenheim, a lesbian who was a member of the German Resistance. Schragenheim was ultimately sent to Auschwitz to be exterminated, not for being a lesbian or for fighting back against the

Nazis, but because the Nazis discovered she was Jewish. Despite Wust's effort to save her, she died.

Heartbroken, Wust left her husband and worked to protect other Jews for the remainder of the war. She published the story of her relationship with Schragenheim in 1995, and it was made into the German film *Aimee and Jaguar* in 1999.

JOSEPHINE BAKER—Born in St. Louis, Missouri, in 1906, Josephine Baker started her career as a vaudeville dancer. Barred from major venues in the United States because she was African American, Baker moved to France in the 1920's where she became the toast of Paris, dancing at the Folies Bergère and becoming the first African-American woman to star in a major motion picture in 1934.

She returned to New York in 1935 to headline the Ziegfeld Follies, but white audiences in America did not embrace her as enthusiastically as European audiences did. She was soon replaced by Gypsy Rose Lee.

In 1939, when Germany invaded Poland to start World War II, Baker was living in France with her husband who was Jewish. She immediately joined the Resistance, using her celebrity status to gather information and smuggle it across enemy lines, sometimes written in invisible ink on her sheet music and other times pinned to her petticoats.

This part of Baker's war effort ended when she was hospitalized in North Africa, after which she spent the rest of the war performing to raise the morale of Free French troops. For her work during the war, she was awarded the Croix de Guerre, the Médaille de la Resistance with rosette, and the Médaille de la France Libre and was made a Chevalier of the Légion d'honneur by General Charles de Gaulle.

After World War II, Baker became an activist for racial equality in the United States, refusing to perform before segregated audiences in Las Vegas and Miami. In 1963, she was the only woman invited to speak in front of the Lincoln Memorial the day Dr. Martin Luther King delivered his "I Have a Dream" speech.

She took the podium wearing her French Resistance uniform and medals and explained that she had fled to France, which she described as being "like a fairyland place," to avoid racism.

But Baker also hinted at the additional challenge female African-Americans faced in the United States: gender bias. She ended her speech by telling the 250,000 people in attendance that she had just been handed an invitation to visit the President of the United States in the White House. She said that she was greatly honored, but that she would not be going as a "colored" or "black" woman, but as "a woman."

When Baker died in 1975, traffic came to a halt in Paris. She became the only American-born woman to receive full French military honors at her funeral.

MADAME MARIE-LOUISE OSMONT—Marie-Louise Osmont embodied the spirit of the French people in both World War I and World War II. She served as a nurse in World War I, driving an ambulance and working in a field hospital, where she met the love of her life, a physician from Normandy.

They married and moved to a large Chateau in Periers near Caen, three miles inland from the beaches that were stormed by the Canadian forces on D-Day.

When the Germans invaded in 1940, they occupied northern France and all of the coastal regions, housing their soldiers in commandeered homes, including Madame Osmont's chateau. Although by then a widow, she refused to leave.

As a result, she lived side-by-side with her German occupiers for four years, during which time she kept a diary. It was published in 1994, as *The Normandy Diary of Marie-Louise Osmont: 1940-1944.*

A noncombatant at Ground Zero, she described the German, Polish, and other soldiers who stayed with her as polite and well-disciplined, but infuriating as they moved in, created a mess, and then moved on, only to be replaced by newcomers.

Observing that they became increasingly disheveled and depressed as the war wore on, she developed a maternal pity for some of the youngest, noting that they were "vibrant" and filled with "that terrible excitement of combat" on their way to be killed.

Madame Osmont's diary records both the hectic build-up of German forces before the invasion and the invasion itself, down to the tinkle of breaking glass, the staccato "acks" of gunfire, and the peculiar hissing sound missiles fired from distant naval ships made as they passed overhead.

But its greatest value is that it brings the manifest horrors of war to life in concrete personal terms: cherished plantings crushed by the treads of advancing armor, fine old trees lost to fortification builders, livestock slaughtered in the artillery duels that ravaged her lands, and her daily fears that friends or loved ones were being killed, wounded, or dispossessed by the fighting.

"Someone in some future time
Will think of us."
—SAPPHO—

Made in the USA
Middletown, DE
21 July 2020